The Infidel

The SS Occult Conspiracy

A Novel by
John Scott Gruner

Editor: Julee Schwarzburg

ISBN—13: 9781632695567
Library of Congress Control Number: 2021904535

Printed in the USA

Cover design and artwork by Reid Martin
2021—First Edition
30 29 28 27 26 25 24 23 22 21   10 9 8 7 6 5 4 3 2 1

The Infidel

The SS Occult Conspiracy

Acknowledgments

The Infidel: More than twenty-five years in the making . . .

The Creative Consultants

Julee Schwarzburg has been a creative force and an inspiring teacher in the art of fiction writing and editorial craft. During the journey, she guided my refinements in character and story dynamics. Robert Don Hughes modeled the art of weaving narrative scenes together. Les Stobbe believed in the story I strived to tell.

The Media and the Press

On many occasions, Dave Browne introduced me to publishing colleagues, conveyed key marketing insights, and consistently provided the gift of encouragement to finish the race. Film producer Jack Cowden was faithfully "on call" as a media advisor for over 20 years.

The Counselors

Throughout our friendship, Daniel Hoffheimer, Esq. has offered sound perspective and guidance for Holocaust research and editorial development. Over the years, Maria C. Miles, Esq. has championed the project through negotiations on my behalf with media and publishing professionals to bring this story (and the history behind it) to the public square.

The Scholars (1985–present)

This story began as a historical research project exploring causes of the Holocaust. Many scholars and Holocaust survivors gave generously of their time, knowledge, and experiences, which profoundly impacted my thoughts and feelings about this violent era. I would like to honor Rabbi R. Steckel (survivor) and Rabbi K. Freeman (survivor), who mentored me in their class so many years ago. A score of librarians guided my study of a vast array of books, articles, and photographs about the Holocaust era at the University of Judaism – LA; Yad Vashem – Jerusalem; American Jewish Archives/Hebrew Union College – Cincinnati; and the US Holocaust Museum – Washington, D.C. Through numerous introductions by Holocaust educator Ellen Fettner, I have been privileged to interview many survivors, scholars, and a Nuremberg trial journalist.

May I express my appreciation to Holocaust historian and author Michael Berenbaum, PhD, who consulted on selections for "Jewish Perspectives on the Holocaust," a brief bibliography which follows as an appendix to the novel.

The Publishing Consultants

David Lambert provided ongoing creative advice for editorial, publication, and marketing resources. Bill Carmichael placed the novel with Deep River Books, and Andy Carmichael managed all phases of the project. Tamara Barnet and Carl Simmons led in creative production development. A special thanks goes to graphic designer Reid Martin, a gifted artist who created the engaging book cover design and supporting elements.

The Ever Faithful

The prayers of many friends have stood the course of time in their support of my efforts during this long journey. I especially thank my daughter, Christen, who inspired the character of Eva Kleist and lobbied for essential romantic themes in the story. I am truly indebted to my wife, Laurie, for her presence, encouragement, and prayers, which have sustained me throughout a lifetime together.

My Inspiration

The Infidel is dedicated to the God of Abraham, Isaac, and Jacob, and to all who survived the Holocaust and lived to tell us their stories. It is presented in honor of the life, ministry, and death of Dr. Dietrich Bonhoeffer, who faithfully demonstrated the true "cost of discipleship." For it is in Christ I stand, to God be the glory!

Germany Circa 1938

Character Map

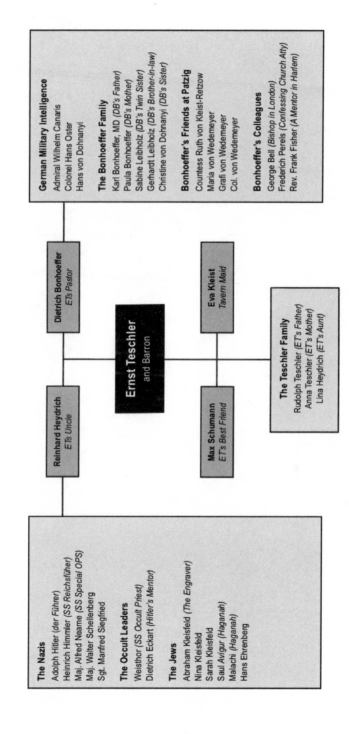

German Military Intelligence
Admiral Wilhelm Canaris
Colonel Hans Oster
Hans von Dohnanyi

The Bonhoeffer Family
Karl Bonhoeffer, MD *(DB's Father)*
Paula Bonhoeffer *(DB's Mother)*
Sabine Leibholz *(DB's Twin Sister)*
Gerhardt Leibholz *(DB's Brother-in-law)*
Christine von Dohnanyi *(DB's Sister)*

Bonhoeffer's Friends at Patzig
Countess Ruth von Kleist-Retzow
Maria von Wedemeyer
Grafi von Wedemeyer
Col. von Wedemeyer

Bonhoeffer's Colleagues
George Bell *(Bishop in London)*
Frederich Perels *(Confessing Church Atty)*
Rev. Frank Fisher *(A Mentor in Harlem)*

Dietrich Bonhoeffer
ET's Pastor

Eva Kleist
Tavern Maid

Ernst Teschler
and Barron

The Teschler Family
Rudolph Teschler *(ET's Father)*
Anna Teschler *(ET's Mother)*
Lina Heydrich *(ET's Aunt)*

Reinhard Heydrich
ET's Uncle

Max Schumann
ET's Best Friend

The Nazis
Adolph Hitler *(der Führer)*
Heinrich Himmler *(SS Reichsführer)*
Maj. Alfred Neame *(SS Special OPS)*
Maj. Walter Schellenberg
Sgt. Manfred Siegfried

The Occult Leaders
Weisthor *(SS Occult Priest)*
Dietrich Eckart *(Hitler's Mentor)*

The Jews
Abraham Kleisfeld *(The Engraver)*
Nina Kleisfeld
Sarah Kleisfeld
Saul Avigur *(Haganah)*
Malachi *(Haganah)*
Hans Ehrenberg

Chapter One

Berlin, Germany

E rnst Teschler accelerated his Mercedes toward the Flossenbürg concentration camp and smashed the vehicle through the barbed-wire gate. In the passenger seat, his aide tapped his watch. "It's too late. We will never make it."

Ernst glared at Max as he slammed the vehicle into high gear. "Bonhoeffer saved my life. I must save his!" After veering off the gravel road, Ernst sped across the grassy field toward the gallows in the distance.

Naked, the two male prisoners were prodded up the stairs onto the platform by drawn bayonets, the rising sun serving to backlight the macabre scene. Their limbs shivering, the two men gazed at each other in silent consolation. Their lives as German patriots would soon end.

An SS soldier grasped the trapdoor lever beside Dietrich. Ernst slammed on the brakes, jumped out of the automobile, and sprinted toward the gallows' timbers staked into the ground.

Three meters of empty space beneath the platform separated a human being from heaven or hell.

The camp commandant stared at the condemned men with black, lifeless eyes. His soldiers cinched the prisoners' hands behind them with worn leather straps and then tightened a loop of piano wire around their necks.

Strangely calm, Dietrich looked up at the sun with a childlike expression.

The commandant opened his orders. "'Reverend Dietrich Bonhoeffer, you have been found guilty of conspiracy against the Reich. You have been condemned by the People's Court in Berlin. By the authority of the Führer, I sentence you to death by hanging. May you linger and suffer for your treasonous crimes against the people of Germany.' Signed Reichsführer Heinrich Himmler."

Just yards away, Ernst reached out to Dietrich with both hands. Dietrich gazed fondly at his young protégé.

"Stop! I command you to stop!" Ernst shouted at the very moment the order was given and the trapdoor released. Terror distorted his face as he witnessed Bonhoeffer's body fall.

His friend's neck snapped like a twig. Dietrich's body twitched as it swung at the end of the taut wire.

Tears streamed as Ernst slumped upon his knees. Trembling, he reached out into space and bellowed a curdling scream. . . .

Ernst bolted upright in bed, his chest rising and falling with rapid breaths. All of his influence in the SS hadn't been enough to save his friend. Perspiration trailed down his cheeks, and a shaft of early morning light streamed over his pillow. He stared at the neatly pressed jacket of his SS uniform hanging by his dresser mirror. *A dream. . . . It was only a dream.*

He wiped his cheeks with his forearm, trying to rid himself of that haunting image of his friend's innocent eyes, and froze. Just beyond the foot of his bed stood a shadowy figure in silhouette.

The adrenaline coursing through his veins propelled him to his feet. He rushed to the door and flipped on the light switch. The glaring beams revealed the regal profile of his Doberman Pinscher.

The tension in his shoulders relaxed. "Barron, *kommen!*" Ernst snapped his fingers.

The tall, angular canine rose off his haunches and gracefully trotted across the wood floor. His muscular physique boasted a short-cropped blue-grey coat. On cue, the dog stepped past him, then circled back to lean affectionately into his master's leg. Ernst had become a knight errant for the *Schutzstaffel,* and next to him stood his canine squire.

"That's my boy, Barron."

A terse knock at the door revealed a middle-aged woman in a worn wool robe. "What is all that racket? Did I hear a scream?"

"It's alright, Mother. It was just another nightmare."

Anna Teschler's tired brown eyes betrayed her concern. "This is the third nightmare since you've returned home. What did they do to you at that school?"

"Bad Tölz is the most elite officers' training school in all of Germany."

"Just the same, you have changed."

Ernst gave her a hug. "I have grown up, Mother. As an officer in the German army, I am in charge of many soldiers." He stepped back. "Did I wake Papa?"

"*Nein.* He came back from the tavern after midnight and is still asleep in his easy chair." Lips pressed tight, she shook her head and moved for the door. "I will see you for breakfast in an hour."

Ernst nodded with a yawn as he closed the door behind his mother. Since the Depression, the Bismarck Tavern had laid bitter claim to his father's company.

Ernst retrieved his wire-framed spectacles from the nightstand and hooked them over his ears. He strode over to the dresser mirror, slipped on the tailored grey coat of his military uniform, and fastened the buttons. The silver braid came into sharp focus as he stroked the smooth, silken cord with his fingertips.

He snapped to attention and presented a regular army salute. "Lieutenant Ernst Teschler reporting as ordered, sir!" Before him was the fruition of his childhood dream—to become an army officer. Finally. In the wake of Germany's shocking defeat in the Great War, Ernst had answered the call to redeem the German people.

Papa, be proud. I have followed in your footsteps.

He snapped his braided hat upon his crown, and his silver officer's bars on his collar sparkled. His training at Bad Tölz had been grueling, but he had earned the right to be an officer before his twenty-sixth birthday.

"Heil Hitler!" he barked into the mirror. He stood perfectly rigid with his straight arm thrust out before him.

Ernst stared at Barron as he expanded his chest and flexed his biceps. With a hearty bark, the dog shied away and then yelped.

*   *   *

In the afternoon, Ernst and Barron wandered into the kitchen. Dressed in a flowered housedress and apron, his mother was basting a roast au jus. Ernst sat at the table. When she was not looking, Barron arched up, placing a singular paw on a place setting.

Not again. Ernst quickly removed Barron's paw and playfully grabbed the dog by his muzzle, clamping those great jaws tight. Barron swiped at Ernst's head with his huge paw, knocking the cap off his head. Ernst laughed and hugged his dog. "Good boy."

If only his parents would show him the same affection.

His mother turned from the oven with her fists propped on her hips. "*Ach*, what is that animal doing in my kitchen?"

Barron's ears reared back at her shrill tone.

"Careful, Mother. He is very sensitive." *And so am I.*

"Aunt Lina and Uncle Reinhard are expected in an hour, and here you are playing with that raucous *Hund*!" She walked over to the hall mirror and primped her light-brown hair bun. "Lina's blonde pageboy always looks perfectly coiffed."

He rose to his feet with a smile. "Mother, I do believe you are jealous."

She leaned close to the mirror and stroked the crow's feet stamped at the corners of her eyes. "It's hard to believe I'm almost forty-five years old." She glanced down at her plain dress. "I'm sure Lina will be wearing the latest Parisian fashion. She always does."

"Aunt Lina has style, but her beauty pales compared to yours." His words brought a generous smile to his mother's face. If only Papa would say something romantic to her so she'd smile more often.

"Honestly, Ernst, you can be so charming when you try. Why don't you ever spin such enchanting phrases around a young Fräulein? A gentleman your age should be married!"

"Of course, and Reichsführer Himmler tells me it is my duty to seed the Fatherland with golden-haired babies." He chuckled.

His mother frowned. "Seriously, there are lovely young ladies all around you."

He gently kissed the back of her hand. "None have ever measured up to you."

"Humph!" She broke his grip and started for the door. "See to it that you straighten your uniform before your uncle gets here. And as for your dog—I have never understood what you see in him."

Ernst stroked Barron's head. "Uncle Reinhard gave him to me when I began cadet training. At Bad Tölz, Barron trained with me and my unit every day. We depend upon each other." He stepped over to his mother. "Just like you can depend on me. And one day, I will reclaim the honor of the Teschler name."

Tears glistened in her eyes as she patted his cheek. "You are a good son. Your father won so many cases as a trial lawyer. Litigation was his specialty." Mother gazed out the kitchen window for a moment. "Rudolf was the toast of legal society. Those were the best days of our marriage." The sparkle in her eyes at her remembrance dimmed.

"By the way, where is Papa?"

"He's in the city . . . on *errands*." She lowered her head and turned back to the oven and basted the roast again.

Ernst sighed. So Papa was out on "errands" as usual. His parents used to be so happy. Why did his father continue to succumb to his demons?

*   *   *

The Bismarck Tavern in Potsdam Square stood three stories tall with its stucco and dark wood façade, crowned by seven ornate gables overlooking Berlin. Its brightly lit marquee hovered above three large sets of double doors. Given the dinner hour, only a few patrons sat at the bar.

Rudolf Teschler gazed at the near-empty glass before him as he savored the taste of his schnapps. Reaching for the tumbler, he was stymied by a slight tremor in his left hand. "Herr Braun, another glass if you please."

The burly bartender continued to polish the countertop in circular motions.

"Herr Braun!"

The barman bristled as he poured the amber-colored liquid into a glass and delivered it to Rudolf's table. "But you still have not finished your last glass."

"Sir, that is the point."

The barman scoffed. "Herr Teschler, this will be your last for the night. You don't want your brother-in-law to find you here. His office calls from time to time to check up on you."

"German civilization is under threat, and Reinhard finds time to spy on me here at the Bismarck. You must be duly impressed."

The patrons nearby paused at the banter, then looked the other way.

"Why, the exalted general has become the patriarch of my family." With a sneer, Rudolf swigged the schnapps down in one gulp.

Herr Braun corked the bottle. "Teschler, go home. Get some sleep."

Rudolf sighed as he stood, buttoned his wool topcoat, and wrapped his grey cashmere scarf snugly around his collar. Where could a gentleman and a scholar go to buy some respect?

As Rudolf stepped through the main tavern doors, he was greeted by a burst of crisp, cold wind. Snow flurries whipped about his face. The frigid air filled his lungs with the lingering aromas from an adjacent bakery.

He salivated as his eyes consumed the apple strudel still steaming in the window display. In the latticed window, his own reflection taunted him. He licked his fingers and slicked a misplaced grey lock of hair over his bald spot. He had been ravaged by the sands of time.

Just who are you staring at?

As a young man, he had fancied himself a silver-tongued attorney. The taste of victory in the courtroom was long remembered. But arrogance had blinded him. So he borrowed and lost large sums in speculative investments. So what? It was his money to lose.

With a shiver, he stuffed his scarf inside his coat and plowed through a new dusting of snow.

"The Fatherland shall prevail! The Fatherland shall prevail!" A chorus of young voices chanted in the distance. The rhythmic thud of soldiers' jackboots grew louder on the cobblestone street just south of Tiergarten Park. "The Fatherland shall prevail!" The shouting voices of virile young men grew louder like the cries of ravenous wolves lying in wait.

Rudolf slowed his steps to a cautious pace on the Volkstrasse. He rounded the blind corner of an alley and slammed squarely into a squad of Wehrmacht soldiers. His eyes widened as he stumbled back against a trash can.

The brute before him stood almost two meters tall—all muscle. "Didn't you see me?" The corporal flicked his cigarette butt away and shoved Rudolf with both hands.

Rudolf slammed into a brick wall. "*Ja*, I see you."

When the soldier clamped his hands onto Rudolf's shoulders, he squirmed like a fly caught in a spiderweb. "You, sir, have no respect for your elders!"

"Here, I'll give you respect." With a snide grin the young man cocked his fist.

A voice rang out from the shadows. "Siegfried, stand down!"

The soldier turned to Max Schumann and growled, "This man is *mine*."

"You fool! That is Rudolf Teschler—General Heydrich's brother-in-law."

The big ox of a man's face blanched. "Heydrich?"

Max nodded. "Now, apologize!"

Siegfried mumbled a few words and the group of soldiers backed away.

Max picked up Rudolf's scarf. "Herr Teschler. I'm sorry. They are young and stupid."

Rudolf steadied himself and removed his flask of schnapps from his worn overcoat. *Ah, justice prevails.* He held up his pewter flask. "To respect!"

*   *   *

When Ernst opened the front door, Aunt Lina and Uncle Reinhard swept into the foyer of the Teschler home.

"Ernst, my dashing young knight." Lina Heydrich kissed his cheek, leaving a bright-red imprint of lipstick. The gentle scent of her favorite Parisian perfume wafted around him. In her late thirties, she was the daughter of a German aristocrat. Her extravagant gestures still amused him. He'd had a crush on her since he was twelve, but it had subsided over time.

"Let me look at you." Her eyes aglow, she held him at arm's length. "Ach, you're so ruggedly handsome. I'm sure the women of Berlin are scheming to get their hooks into you." In one fluid motion, she slipped her arm around his.

"Lina, tell him it's time to find a wife," Anna said as she embraced her brother Reinhard.

His five-foot-eleven frame looked dashing dressed in his SS uniform, midnight black accented with medals and insignias. A wry smile creased his hawkish, oblong face. "Lina, you are embarrassing him."

"Nonsense." She batted her bright-blue eyes. "Tell him you are flattered, Ernst."

"Well . . ." he cleared his throat.

"See there, Reinhard. You have intimidated the poor boy."

As the women scurried down the hall, his uncle shook Ernst's hand. "You do look impressive with those officer's bars."

"Thank you, Uncle. I made rank ahead of my class."

"As well you should with top marks at Bad Tölz, beating out the fierce competition." Reinhard offered a handkerchief from his pocket as a hint to Ernst to remove the crimson evidence from his cheek. "Promotions will come easily from now on. Cream always rises to the top, you know."

Ernst swabbed his cheek. "Sir, I'll try to follow your example."

Heydrich glanced over his shoulder. "The women are already jabbering. We'll never get a word in all evening." He slipped an arm around Ernst's shoulders and led him down the hallway. "Listen closely, Ernst. The British and French have already handed us the Rhineland on a silver platter. When the Führer assembled the general staff a week ago, he informed us that there will be war, regardless of all the posturing of that English puff Chamberlain."

"Then I will have a field commission?"

"I did not sponsor you at Bad Tölz merely to have you shot by some crazy Czechoslovakian. Even Himmler knows of your splendid performance." Heydrich leaned closer. "It is time for you to move into the SS security service."

"But I have trained for the regular army." Ernst had waited a lifetime to receive his commission.

"My boy, Germany has many enemies—and some are inside the Wehrmacht."

"But I have no experience with espionage."

Heydrich stopped. "I have all the experience and contacts you will ever need. Let other men's sons roll lifeless under the tanks. You have much more to offer the Fatherland alive." He balled his fist and gave a mock blow to Ernst's shoulder. "Become a wolf—like me."

Ernst raised an eyebrow.

"What are you two talking about?" Lina called from the kitchen. "Wars, armies, guns—all the little boys' favorite toys? It's so *boring*." She turned back to her sister-in-law. "Anna, I'm starving. Where's Rudolf?"

A sharp rapping on the front door echoed across the foyer.

Ernst took the lead and opened the door. "Max?"

Rudolf stepped forward. "Greetings, everyone! Herr Schumann was kind enough to accompany me on the way home."

Anna grimaced. "Rudolf, our guests have been waiting." She skewered him with an unflinching look. "Well, don't just stand there. Get inside out of the cold."

"Hello, *liebling*, did you miss me?" Rudolf skirted around Anna into the foyer.

Heydrich didn't hide his disdain at Rudolf's brazen entrance.

"Uncle, you remember my good friend Max Schumann."

"Heil Hitler!" Max saluted.

Heydrich stepped forward. "Sergeant, we all thank you for your assistance and . . . your discretion."

"It is an honor, Herr Obergruppenführer!" Max clicked his heels together and departed.

Rudolf sauntered into the living room and removed a cigarette and a match from a tarnished silver tray. "You make yourself quite at home in my *Haus*, don't you, Reinhard?"

"I believe I was invited."

His father ignited the match. "Invited. But not by me!"

Ernst could feel the heat from the sparks shooting between the two men. "Uncle, why don't . . . ?"

"Anna, that roast in the oven smells heavenly." Heydrich walked past Rudolf and led the family into the dining room. "We all look forward to a sumptuous feast."

His father stood resolute in the hall as he exhaled the acrid smoke of his cigarette. "Ernst, why does Reinhard treat your mother and me like one of his black-suited lackeys?"

Please, don't make a scene! "Mother has slaved all day making your favorite meal."

Rudolf's smile transformed his haggard face. "That's right. Come on, son. I smell the delightful aroma of a standing rib roast."

After a delicious meal, his father excused himself for the evening. Heydrich and Ernst donned their overcoats and stepped out of the house into a brisk, wintry wind. Heydrich signaled the driver in his polished Mercedes to follow at a distance as they walked through the powdery snow.

"My boy, I knew you didn't want to listen to a pair of hens squawking all night." The Mercedes' headlamps enlarged their uniformed shadows as they appeared to float across the virgin-white dunes. "I wanted to talk to you alone, to share my plans for your career. Ernst, it will be an honor to serve with you in the SS. We are Germany's future, you and I!"

Ernst gazed up into the night sky as if to discover some celestial sign. "It's just that . . . Papa made his mark in the army. He has always spoken of traditions, ethics—honor."

"Your father was heroic in the Great War. Now, your time has come. You must forge your own path. Earn the respect of the German people."

"Papa often talks about the military code of honor."

"And what is honor to you, Ernst? What does it really mean?"

Ernst slowed his pace. "Fidelity to family, to justice, to truth. To act with honor and to honor God."

"Certainly, you know the Führer promotes all these things! You have high standards. That's exactly why I want you at my side. In the SS I will commission you to hunt down and eliminate our enemies inside Germany."

"But Papa says—"

"Your father lives in his past glory, not the new Germany. The SS means power, my boy, and power breeds both arrogance and laziness. You have the inner strength to avoid these weaknesses. I need people like you to help purify the SS. Will you help me?"

Conflict roiled in his gut over the challenge. "I will consider your generous offer."

"Think about it over the weekend. Then report to SS headquarters Monday 8:00 a.m. Major Alfred Neame will brief you further on opportunities available in the SS. It's a place where you can make a name for yourself."

"Sir, thank you for your vote of confidence."

"I am confident you will make the correct decision Monday." On cue Heydrich's driver drove the vehicle beside them, ushered his superior into the rear seat, and closed the door. Heydrich leaned back and saluted his nephew. Decorated with a brightly colored swastika flag, the ominous command car disappeared into the staggered streetlights of Berlin.

Looking into the night sky, Ernst sensed a storm brewing in the Teschler home.

Chapter Two

Berlin

Ernst stepped through the large baroque-carved front doors into the Bismarck Tavern. Ushered through the grand foyer, Ernst stepped into a pool of garish lights haloed by wafting smoke. Huge Nazi flags and the pungent smell of German beer prominently marked the arched entrance. Red, white, and black swastikas were embroidered on the uniformed sleeves of Wehrmacht grey and the sky-blue uniforms of Göring's Luftwaffe. The beer and schnapps flowed freely and fed the euphoric mood of the unruly patrons.

"Ernst, over here!" Max waved from a table in the corner.

Ernst edged his way through the crowd, dodging a few barmaids who scurried about with stein-laden trays.

Max stood and grasped Ernst's shoulders with a crooked smile. His breath announced that he'd already downed a few tankards. "So, did your father win the fight?"

"Everything is under control." Ernst glowered at him. *Not here, Max.*

"Listen, everyone!" Max shouted at the men surrounding them. "Behold, Lieutenant Ernst Teschler. He is General Heydrich's nephew!"

Scattered, almost mocking, applause followed the effusive announcement as Ernst circled the table and sat in the back corner of the alcove. "You talk too much, Max."

"Only to honor my best friend." Max clapped Ernst on the back and dropped onto the seat beside him. "Say, I must introduce you to the new mystery girl at the Bismarck."

"Another girl? Why would any girl find you handsome?"

"I don't see the humor in that remark." Max pointed toward the bar. "Look, there she is."

Ernst's gaze settled on one particular barmaid across the room. Carrying a tray of beer, she dodged multiple undesired hands on her way between tables. She slowly made her way to their corner. *Oh my, how lovely.*

Max moved unsteadily to his feet, grabbed two steins from her tray, and placed one in front of Ernst.

Ernst was awestruck by the radiant blue of her eyes. Her narrow, angular face was nicely framed by hair the color of corn silk.

Max raised his stein. "A toast!" The young woman glanced at Ernst, then Max elbowed him. "I said, 'Let's have a toast. To the Führer!'"

The men clinked their steins together. "Heil Hitler!" As Ernst tilted his stein to take a swig, his eyes met the barmaid's again. With a flirtatious smile, she disappeared back into the crowd.

Over Max's shoulder, Ernst caught a glimpse of the girl as she broke into laughter with a boisterous officer at the bar. Ernst took a stiff drink. "Who is she, Max?"

His friend's ice-blue eyes glistened. "Ah, the mystery girl. I tried my ways with her, but she was stone cold to me. Cold as a North Sea fish."

Ernst chuckled. "What did you expect? She seems like a decent girl."

"Ja, she . . . Was that an insult?"

Ernst tilted his head and cracked a grin.

"I'll have you know that I treat all women like—"

"Like dogs in heat."

Max burst out laughing. "Of course! When you're as handsome as I, these women can't help themselves." He tipped his empty stein upside down with a dazed look of disappointment. "Fräulein! Another round if you please." Max bellowed across the aisle at the mysterious blonde.

At the bar, she loaded another tray and made her way back to their table. She smiled as she replaced their empty steins with new ones.

Ernst drew in her scent, and her floral fragrance nudged his senses.

She leaned forward and placed their bill on the table. "I'll collect that now while the two of you are still sober."

Ernst shot a knowing glance at Max. "You heard the lady."

Max stood and listed slightly. "Time for me to go."

"Max, pay the lady!"

"Me? I'm just a poor Wehrmacht sergeant with a full bladder. You were just promoted. Fräulein, this man is very rich indeed."

Ernst shrugged. "My friend's a little drunk."

"He's not alone." The girl nodded toward the other patrons.

Ernst placed neatly folded Reichsmarks on her tray, including a generous gratuity.

When she counted the money, the young lady brushed her golden hair out of her face. "My, you must have appreciated my service."

"It was the beauty of your smile."

"Then you deserve another." She tucked the currency into her cleavage, and a smile curved her full lips.

Ernst leaned forward. "What's your name?"

"Ah, but I do not mingle with patrons."

"But I'm not a patron. I just come and watch my friend drink. By the way, my name is Teschler, Ernst Teschler."

"Well, thank you, Herr Teschler. It's been a pleasure serving you tonight." The rowdy soldier at the table behind her raised his voice. "Maybe I'll see you in here again."

"Wait! I didn't get your name," Ernst shouted as she turned away.

She tossed an amused smile over her shoulder. "I didn't say. Until the next time, Lieutenant."

Ernst traced her shapely figure with his eyes as she forged through the patrons' gauntlet of boisterous slaps and pinches. He scowled. That was no way to treat a lady.

Max returned from the bathroom and slid back into his seat. "Ah, that was a relief."

It had been too long since Ernst felt such attraction. When the spirited blonde walked, her hips and legs danced to a rhythm of their own.

"So, did you get her name?"

"Not yet." But he would.

"What did I tell you—a cold fish." Max gave his friend a knowing look. "Ernst, you're heart-struck." He lifted his newly filled stein. "To romance—and to our future when I join the SS!"

"Max."

"Your uncle can arrange it. We could have power then, even glory!"

"Is that all you want out of life—power and glory?"

"No. . . . I want power and glory *and* an endless supply of fräuleins. Of course, I would share all of those things with you."

Ernst shook his head.

"Then you'll do it? You'll ask your uncle to take me into the corps? Ernst and Max—Max and Ernst, we'll be part of the Thousand Year Reich!"

Ernst looked fondly at his friend from childhood. "To Ernst and Max—to the Fatherland!" They clinked their ceramic steins together with enthusiasm.

*   *   *

Berlin, SS Headquarters, October 25, 1938

Reinhard Heydrich's intercom buzzed. "Ja, Gertrude?"

"Alfred Neame, mein herr. Calling from Bernau."

He picked up the telephone. "What is our status, Neame?"

"We will have all equipment at Delbrückstrasse 6a moved from Berlin to the Bernau School facility by the end of the month. Our forged documents section will be operational two weeks later."

"And?"

"And we will begin work on the forged British currencies—just as you ordered. We have a crew of twenty already and have identified five more craftsmen to perfect the plates."

"I hear that early tests have revealed a number of flaws."

"Yes, sir. We have identified a Jewish engraver in Wittenberg who has the necessary skills. They say he is exceptionally talented."

"Abraham Kleisfeld."

"But how did you know his name, mein herr?"

"Göring knows of this man's talents. He was apprenticed by his father at the Giesecke & Devrient mint in Munich."

Neame paused. "If we succeed, these forged currencies would disrupt England's economy."

"A convenient prelude to war, don't you think?" Reinhard steepled his fingers, then tapped them against his lips.

"*Jawohl*, Herr Obergruppenführer!"

Heydrich leaned back in his chair. "Now listen carefully. I want you to accelerate your training schedule for Lieutenant Teschler. Teach my nephew the lethal arts. And be sure he qualifies on the new Walther P38."

"Jawohl, I have just machined a suppressor for the prototype pistol."

"Teach him well, Neame. I will make it worth your while." Heydrich placed the receiver on its cradle.

He picked up his violin, then played a hauntingly beautiful melody from Wagner's *Die Meistersinger*. Such virtuous music brought him to tears—tears of self-adoration. Gliding through the evocative notes, Heydrich fondly envisioned Ernst in his own image. He leaned forward and glided his bow across the treble strings with finesse.

On the other hand, Rudolf Teschler was a splinter in his eye. The searing pain—the irritation! Heydrich clenched his teeth as his bow danced across the violin strings to resume the frenetic melody. Underscored by staccato notes, he imagined Rudolf's ballet of death.

"Ah, when my brother-in-law disappears, Ernst will become a lethal weapon in my hand. Together, we shall assail Hitler's throne of power!"

*   *   *

Wittenberg, Germany, October 27, 1938

Abraham Kleisfeld peered through the thick magnifying glass, holding his hands steady as he etched the plate for a wedding announcement with his precision engraving tool. He leaned back and massaged his aching fingers. These ten-hour days were catching up with him. Occasional arthritis in his delicate fingers marked his thirty-year career as an engraver.

He picked up a black-and-white photo of the bride and groom and studied the rendering of the greyish tones of her skin. She would make a beautiful Jewish bride—just like his sweet Sarah. Perhaps one day soon. . . .

He remembered the fear, the emptiness the day his daughter left home—and she with no husband to protect her. It had been a year, but the image of Sarah's becoming smile lifted Abraham's spirits and his hands. He sang a prayer, *"Blessed are You, LORD our God, King of the universe, Who has sanctified us with Your commandments and sealed the Law upon our hearts."* In his heart, he could sense the presence of the living God.

The bell above the shop's entrance rang and the door creaked open. "Abraham?"

He recognized the deep baritone voice of Saul Avigur. Abraham turned from his workbench to see his tall, thin cousin dressed in a sailor's wool peacoat. Saul's high cheekbones were covered by gaunt flesh, and short-cropped black curls crowned his head. "You're late!"

"Abraham, I heard your prayer. You sing like a cantor. You speak like a rabbi. Your words are so—"

"Wise. 'By His holy words, I try to live by faith. Amen.' So, why are you late?"

The bell above the door signaled the entrance of another man with dark olive skin wearing a brown wool jacket. His face was devoid of expression.

Saul scoffed. "Malachi, you have kept Abraham waiting."

"I was checking the streets for Gestapo. You can't be too careful."

Saul dismissed his colleague with a wave of his hand. "Abraham, is my package ready? The Haganah needs the gold to purchase ships."

Abraham removed his wire-framed bifocals, wiped the lenses with his shirt, then put them back on, hooking the cable temples around his large ears. "We've collected forty-two ounces from five synagogues in the region. Our Jewish friends, the old and the young, dream of Palestine. Will the ships sail from Greece?"

"It's best that you don't know in case you're arrested."

"I never thought I would want to leave Germany. It is our home."

"Abraham, our people will need forged travel papers. If we give you authentic documents, can you duplicate them?"

"I will need the proper equipment, the best—and a quiet place to work, away from my shop."

Saul nodded. "Your family will have priority on the first boats to sail."

An unsettled feeling overcame Abraham. Would he be able to find Sarah in time?

Perspiration trickled down his cheek into his scraggly salt-and-pepper beard. "The Nazis breed like cockroaches. Each day, I think about Sarah, my son Aaron, and Nina. When I wake at night, I wonder if I can protect them for even another day."

"The gold you have collected will help our people escape these Nazi vermin. Malachi and my men will return later tonight to pick up the shipment."

Several hours later, the chime above Abraham's shop entrance rang again and the door creaked open.

"Herr Kleisfeld?" The cold voice of a short, square-faced stranger penetrated the pit of Abraham's stomach. When he turned from his workbench, he faced three German officers in black uniforms.

"Herr Kleisfeld, my name is Major Neame—SS. The Reich government requires your professional services."

Abraham stepped back. "What do you mean? I'm just a humble printer of stationery and wedding—"

"The SS maintains excellent records. Years ago, you were a skilled engraver in the currency department of Giesecke & Devrient." Neame slapped an envelope against Abraham's chest. "Here is your employment letter. If you cooperate, you will be moved near Berlin and be well paid."

Abraham fumbled with the seal and opened the letter. As he read its contents, he trembled. All of his plans to escape disintegrated! "No, no. This has to be a mistake." His cheeks flushed as he began to hyperventilate. "Please, I have a family . . . and friends."

"We could escort you today or . . . we could return in a few days. You could speak to your friends—Jews with money! Fifty ounces of gold would appease us. Talk to them, Kleisfeld, as fast as you can."

Neame stepped over to the front picture window. "Lieutenant Teschler, demonstrate for Herr Kleisfeld what will happen to him if he fails to produce our gold."

Teschler slipped his truncheon from his belt. Cocking his wrist, he plowed its wooden shaft into a glass display case. Abraham reared back as shattered glass cascaded upon the polished wood floor.

Another soldier leaned over the counter. "Fifty ounces of gold will keep you and your neighbors safe."

Neame signaled to his men to leave. "Herr Kleisfeld, we will be back. *Auf Wiedersehen.*"

The hair on Abraham's arm bristled as the cold wind blew in through the open shop door. Alone once more, he just stared at the shimmering pieces of glass scattered before him. What would the Gestapo do to him and his beloved family if he did not obey?

The telephone rang. The crackling sound of broken glass followed his steps to the telephone. On the third bell, he picked up the receiver. "Ja?"

"Sh'ma Yisra'el Adonai Eloheinu Adonai echad." Saul's Hebrew accent was distinctive.

Abraham instinctively repeated the words. "'Hear, O Israel, the Lord is our God, the Lord is One.' What can I do for you, Cousin?"

"Tell me what the SS wanted."

Abraham raked his fingers through his shock of grey hair. "But how did you know they were here?"

"We have a man watching your shop. Your service to the Haganah is very important."

"They want me to work near Berlin—on counterfeit documents."

"Berlin?"

"And they have demanded a ransom in gold for my family. Saul, how do they know about our gold?"

"Maybe they don't know. The Gestapo has been extorting jewelry and gems from our people for years."

"They will hurt my family—they mean business!"

Saul's voice became cold over the phone. "Pack your bags. By sunset, I want you, Aaron, and Nina on the back roads to Zossen. I know someone there who will hide you for a few weeks. In the meantime, my men will be waiting at your shop for your SS visitors. They will reap the whirlwind of Jehovah God!"

Abraham blinked and the telephone line went dead. The silence was deafening. He stepped upon broken glass and felt the icy cold breath of the SS around his neck.

*   *   *

Three days after they had vandalized the engraver's shop, Ernst and Max followed Major Neame and his driver, Schneider, back to Wittenberg. While Max drove, Ernst inspected his Walther P38 pistol. "Gold or no gold, we are to deliver Kleisfeld to Bernau center by Saturday."

As they crossed into the Jewish district, Ernst looked at the shop windows desecrated by painted Jewish symbols. The lettered strokes behind the colored scrawl were angry. A few pedestrians scattered as the two cars came to a stop in a sparsely populated courtyard in front of Kleisfeld's shop.

Neame cautiously emerged from the car in front. "Ready your weapons. Schneider, you and Schumann stay in the street to keep guard."

Neame and Ernst entered Kleisfeld's shop. Ernst surveyed the shattered glass still strewn upon the floor, untouched from their last visit.

"Herr Kleisfeld?" Neame edged slowly around the counter. "Herr Kleisfeld!" Ernst and Neame peeked into the back workroom and saw an empty workbench. Neame's eyes widened. "It's a trap!"

Priming his Walther, Ernst rushed through the glass to the front door.

Outside, Max pointed across the courtyard. "Look out!"

Across the street, cloaked behind a half-walled patio, a man stood armed with a German MP-38 submachine gun. In an explosive volley, bullets raked across the display window of Kleisfeld's shop, showering shards of glass onto the sidewalk.

Max reared back and dove behind the front end of their Mercedes. His hand clipped the fender, propelling his pistol out into the street. Unarmed and vulnerable, Max shouted a string of curses.

From inside the shop, Ernst spotted the smoking gun across the street as the assailant slammed a new magazine into his weapon. Stepping on shattered glass, Ernst crouched by the open front door. When the shooter loosed another spree of lead, Neame fired through the shattered window.

Bullets ricocheted to either side of the gunman when he bolted across the street. Unleashing his weapon, he pinned Max behind the car in a hail of bullets. The spray of hot metal punctured the polished enameled doors of the vehicle.

For a moment, the thundering echo of automatic gunfire subsided. Ernst heard the distinct click of a gun hammer behind him. He spun around and slipped on broken glass.

Just behind the counter stood a man with a revolver leveled at Neame's head. When Ernst raised his pistol, the intruder targeted Ernst. Neame pivoted and fired his gun. The bullet penetrated the man's cheek, pelting his molars into the wall beside him. Dazed, the man lifted his barrel again, but Neame finished him with one more shot. The intruder slid down the wall, his head slumped with eyes glued open.

For only a moment, Ernst froze. Then, in a flash, he rushed out onto the sidewalk. Neame provided cover fire, forcing the machine gunner to duck behind the Mercedes, street side. Max was still pinned to the front, down on the ground.

Pumped by pure adrenaline, Ernst darted out into the street. He dipped his shoulder, tucked and rolled in front of the Mercedes below the assailant's line of fire. Arms extended above the pavement, Ernst sighted the gunner and rapid-fired—three times. The bullets ripped through the man's arm and shoulder, pummeling him into the side of the car. His eyes gaped open as he slid down the polished door.

A cool calm settled his nerves. Ernst placed one final bullet just below his assailant's sternum, who then keeled over on the cobblestones basted in his own blood. *Better you than me.*

Neame rushed over to Max. "Where's Schneider?"

Max turned toward the car behind them.

Schneider slowly stood, surveying the scene just as a thunderclap echoed throughout the courtyard. Schneider's body lofted into the air, his arms and legs dancing in flight. With a thud, he landed on his back. Blood pooled at his shoulder, then began to pulse onto the cobblestones.

Ernst pivoted to see Neame fire at an open window of the building across the yard, second-floor balcony twenty meters out.

Ernst sprinted pell-mell across the street and charged into the apartment building. After rushing up three flights of steps, he broke out onto the rooftop just in time to see a dark-haired man with a rifle disappear over a ledge two buildings away. With no chance to catch up, Ernst ran back down to the street.

While Neame tended to Schneider's shoulder wound, Ernst and Max returned to Kleisfeld's shop. There was no sign of Abraham Kleisfeld or the gold.

Ernst searched the pockets of the corpse behind the counter. He pulled a leather folio from the man's trousers and thumbed through its contents. "This man is not German—he is a Czechoslovakian Jew."

Max shook his head. "Just who are these people?"

Ernst stooped and held a shard of glass in his gloved hand. "Kleisfeld must have fled days ago. The gold was the bait—and we walked right into their trap."

Chapter Three

Westphalia, Germany, October 31, 1938

The castle library boasted thirteen thousand volumes of occult lore. Only the select few were invited to see Himmler's private collection of arcane relics. "The spear that pierced the side of Christ," Heinrich Himmler crowed with glee. "Your work looks very much like the original."

"An exact replica." Karl Muenster puffed out his chest. "Of course, it matches the photographs I took in Vienna, the Habsburg Museum. Before the Führer—"

"Stole it from the Austrians." Heinrich's lips formed a twisted smile as he turned to his rotund SS associate. "Weisthor, I wonder if Herr Muenster knows too much concerning the Spear of Destiny." After all, they were planning high treason.

Standing silent, Weisthor raised his bushy salt-and-pepper eyebrows. They matched his full mustache. In his late fifties, crow's feet accented the corners of his hawkish grey eyes, which twinkled with devilish delight.

Muenster cleared his throat. "No one knows that the Führer 'confiscated' the relic—I meant no offense, Herr Reichsführer."

"Have you have told anyone about our little secrets?" Heinrich squinted through the bottle-thick lenses of his spectacles as he drew his finger down the spine of the spear's long, curved blade. He could smell the fear pooling in Muenster's eyes. It was like taunting a rat in a cage. Heinrich pressed the point of the weapon against Muenster's chest.

The man flinched as the sharpened tip penetrated the soft cotton fabric just beneath his ribs. "Herr Reichsführer, I meant no disrespect. Please, forgive me!" The craftsman bobbed his gaze between the two vultures circling him.

Heinrich abruptly withdrew the spear and examined the tip. "See this, Weisthor? Look how he's blackened the iron to age it."

"The tapered blade is split at its base and is clamped tightly onto the wooden shaft with this iron nail—exactly matched to the original."

"A superb forgery of the spearhead." Weisthor compressed a pinch of tobacco into his Tibetan pipe. When he struck a match, its flame illumined his stark hollow eyes. "Legend holds that this was one of the original nails that had tacked Christ to the cross."

"This spike proves our Dark Lord's victory over the Hebrew God, then and now," Heinrich said.

Weisthor puffed a billow of smoke. As it rose, the firelight penetrated its shadowy veil. Its bold aroma was pungent. "The Angel of Light has deceived our Führer. For the prophecy says the Spear must pass to another."

Heinrich's eyes widened with excitement. *I am the chosen one. Only I am worthy.*

"Whoever possesses the Spear of Destiny will control the world!" Weisthor spoke in his deep baritone.

As if cradling a baby, Heinrich carefully placed the replica back into its polished mahogany case. "Soon our armies will be marching through Poland. Certainly, the Führer believes that he will wield the true Spear in battle."

Muenster frowned. "So you plan to exchange the Führer's original for my copy?"

Weisthor expanded his barreled chest. "Why, Herr Muenster, that would be treasonous."

"Anyone associated with such a forgery would certainly be executed." Heinrich snapped the wooden lid closed and Muenster flinched. With his silken voice, he began to spin a web of fear across Muenster's face.

The heels of Weisthor's long black boots echoed across the marble floor. "Heinrich, Herr Muenster needs a drink to calm his nerves." He poured two fingers of brandy into a glass and offered it to his guest.

Muenster's fretful gaze darted from side to side with a nervous smile as Weisthor placed the snifter into his trembling hands. Heinrich could almost taste the beads of perspiration that speckled his prey's furrowed forehead. Then the middle-aged craftsman swallowed the strong liquor.

Heinrich scoffed. "You've done your job well. As promised, your gold is over there. Go ahead, count your money."

Muenster shuffled over to the table. He intently stroked the smooth bars stacked in a neat pyramid and then the small, gleaming ingots.

Heinrich moved closer. "You are like Wagner's Alberich the Dwarf, lusting after the Rhine gold. The dwarf stole the hoard of the gods and fashioned from it the Ring of Power. Likewise, with this replica, I shall obtain the power of the true Spear of Destiny. Go ahead, Herr Muenster, relish your treasure—before you fall."

Suddenly Muenster's face contorted. Gasping, he grabbed his throat as if he was in the grips of an unseen assailant.

Heinrich so enjoyed the first course. "Hemlock is a very effective poison. Weisthor poured twice the lethal dose into your brandy."

Muenster staggered into the table, and his body began to convulse.

"At first, the poison constricts the arms and legs," Heinrich said.

Unable to break his fall, Muenster crashed to the floor. His eyes pleaded for help as his hosts gathered around his quivering body.

"Weisthor, I find the scent of death so . . . intoxicating."

Sprawled across the cold marble floor, Muenster gasped for every breath. His eyelids frozen open, he stared at his two willing executioners towering over him.

Heinrich patiently watched as life drained from Muenster's petrified eyes. "It is a pity. The man was so talented."

"Indeed. But he died for a greater cause, Heinrich." Weisthor opened a second bottle of brandy and poured two glasses, then handed one to Heinrich. "Soon we will possess the true Spear of Destiny."

"And with its mystical powers, we shall become the master race!" With a dainty sip, Heinrich's lips tingled with demonic delight.

*   *   *

An SS guard stood at the door of Heinrich's suite. When he passed by, the guard saluted. "Heil Hitler!"

Heinrich barely glanced at the guard as he sauntered into his quarters. He fondled the mahogany case as others might caress a beloved pet. Adjusting his pince-nez spectacles, he imagined the spearhead penetrating the flayed olive skin of Christ upon the cross. He chuckled. It was an image he relished, mixing as he did both blood and blasphemy.

Inside his bedroom, the floor-length mirror cast a reddish aura around his reflection. Ecstasy awaited him in the "Well of Souls," deep below in the bowels of Wewelsburg Castle. Once again the sulfurous smoke of burning torches would signal the unholy pleasure and terror as demons would penetrate his nostrils and lips. They would torment him to their own delight—and to his.

He felt the exhilarating embrace of his Dark Master as he opened his eyes. There in the mirrored frame stood the "Prince of the SS," encased in a half suit of black armor. His attendant cinched the latticed cords to tighten the breastplate into place.

An hour later, Heinrich glided down the grand staircase of the castle with helmet in hand. He had designed the half suit of armor himself, patterned after the Renaissance armor of the Templar Knights. Steel plates, hand-enameled in glistening black, made it look like the shell of an enormous wasp. To that end an SS death's head emblem had been sculpted into the grill of the visor and upon each shoulder pauldron. On the breastplate, where the ancient Templar Knights had worn a silver cross, Heinrich had placed that most mystical symbol: the *hakenkreuz*— the swastika. It was stark black against a white circle, surrounded by a field of blood red.

At the bottom of the staircase, he joined eleven other SS chieftains, each armored from the waist up, drinking and smoking cigars. The room had the look and feel of an exclusive men's club. Each man present was a "führer," commanding thousands in his own right, but Heinrich commanded them all.

He swallowed his prideful smile at the sight of Reinhard Heydrich. His second-in-command was certainly dashing. Tall, built like a natural athlete, he carried his muscular frame like a dark, lean panther. His small black eyes were perched above his imperial Roman nose—a hawk-like beak invested with menace. Heydrich's gaunt, high cheeks and pointed chin were adorned by closely cropped blond hair. Heydrich was the ideal Aryan aristocrat—cool, controlled, and utterly self-assured. *If only I could trade places, then I would garner more respect.*

In the midst of their casual chatter, Heinrich scanned the faces of the power elite. No doubt the dark secrets of virtually everyone in the room had been recorded in the four-by-six card file in Heydrich's safe—including his own. Heydrich considered him weak and unintelligent, and for that Heinrich despised his executive officer.

"Heydrich, how is your lovely wife?" Heinrich feigned some interest but knew the woman to be insufferable.

"Lina has become a prominent socialite in Berlin, no doubt by her incessant chatter."

Heinrich smirked. Surely Lina Heydrich had some idea of her husband's free-spirited escapades with a bevy of young women, though it was Lina who actually bore the aristocratic blood and money in the family. "And your young nephew, the one you constantly boast about?"

Heydrich's dark eyes sparked. "Ernst Teschler. He graduated from Bad Tölz in '37—at the top of his class. In combat he has the disposition of a Doberman. If I may be so bold, one day he will be a candidate to sit at our table."

At our table? Heinrich glanced across the open archway at the beautifully crafted table that graced the center of the dining hall. It was his rendition of Arthur's Round Table at Camelot, and Heinrich was king. "Strong words for a mere pup, Doberman though he may be."

"In time, he will earn your favor. You will find him a perfectly honed blade in your hand, a weapon as devastating as any magical sword of your mythology."

Heinrich arched an eyebrow above the rim of his spectacles. *My mythology?* He doubted if Heydrich had even read the great occult scholar Rosenberg, much less Rahn's more arcane works. "I believe you mean *our* mythology."

"The Templar myths bind the Reich together and give us our passion, our racial purity, our strength. Ernst Teschler may be young, but he is all sinew and steel with a fierce loyalty to the Führer."

"Do you have a ritual name in mind for your loyal young pup?"

"He shall be known as The Infidel."

Heinrich chuckled. "How ironic. This ever-faithful lad called the 'Unbeliever!' You can be sure I'll keep an eye on him, Heydrich. If only to keep an eye on you."

Heinrich turned back to the group and shouted, *"Achtung!"*

All eyes turned to him.

"Gentlemen, it is time to begin!"

*   *   *

The Black Knights entered the cavernous dining hall and took their places. Their helmets encircled the center of the enormous table. Each high-backed chair was beautifully carved in rich mahogany and bore each man's coat of arms with his name engraved upon a silver plate.

Weisthor craved the souls of his disciples, the Overlords of the Order of New Templars.

Thirteen chairs circled this sacred table, but now one stood empty. An elder member of Weisthor's coven, Erich Strausser, had been discovered in a Munich hotel—poisoned. By their oath of blood, their fallen comrade in arms would be celebrated tonight. They would release his spirit borne away to Valhalla by the Valkyries to the "hall of the slain."

Weisthor raised a silver goblet filled with blood-red wine. "My honor is loyalty."

Himmler took the cup. "Our loyalty is to our Führer, Adolf Hitler."

"*Sieg heil!*" the group roared in response. "Sieg heil!" they shouted again, like a choir reciting a chorused "Amen." In a conscious parody of Christian communion, each man in turn stood and drank from the goblet of Baphomet.

Weisthor was the last to drink from the cup. "Through his unholy blood, our souls have been united with our Dark Lord, *Ha Satanos.*"

Weisthor lifted both hands across his chest as he led the processional. Himmler fell in step behind Weisthor, and they all filed solemnly past the great stone hearth, where massive red embers glowed upon the iron grate. The column of black-armored initiates stepped through a hidden archway behind the hearth and descended upon hewn stone steps into the darkness.

The Well of Souls had been built as a ritual cave inspired by the twelfth-century sacred grottos of the pagan Cathari sect. Fifteen meters in diameter, its carved stone walls arched upward to form a smooth cone. It was crowned by a sculptured swastika, embossed in smooth stone two meters across. Twelve stone pedestals, one for each knight, circled the cavern's perimeter, each lit by a flickering lamp. The pale-blue light of the moon streamed in through three large window shafts cut high upon the wall. Weisthor marveled at its macabre ambiance.

At the center of the floor loomed a darkened pit, two meters across. It was covered by an iron grate through which faint sounds of a mechanized drone could be heard. The darkened shaft gave the illusion of dropping straight down to hell itself. As Weisthor's disciples gathered in a circle, the priest invoked the dark powers from the abyss.

"*Ave Satana!*"

All could hear the demons chatter below at his sacred words.

Within the Dark Spirit, Weisthor could feel Himmler's pulse race, could see his skin slick with sweat.

The flickering lamps surrounding them mysteriously ignited. Tall, animated shadows danced upon the stone walls in the rhythm of the flames. After a breathless silence, Weisthor signaled an SS guard bearing a large silver tray covered in a black velvet cloth. The soldier placed the tray on the raised iron grill in front of Weisthor. He gestured again, and the medieval congregation took their seats upon three arched stone benches.

The acrid scent of the unholy permeated Weisthor's nostrils.

"The Order of New Templars assembles this night to bid farewell to the soul of our fallen comrade. Erich Strausser was a man hated and feared by the masses, yet to our illumined Order he was a blood brother and a devoted disciple. Herr Strausser's life ended as each of ours shall, in the realm of our Master, the Dark Lord of the Golden Light. Behold the crown that held his memories and his dreams!" Weisthor whisked off the velvet covering, revealing the neatly severed head of SS General Erich Strausser.

Given a perfect Aryan specimen, Weisthor reached out to stroke its soft blond hair. His very touch sparked a surge of power through his limbs as Weisthor arched upon the balls of his feet. A pungent aroma stung his nostrils, his eyes watered, his ears began to ring. "Our Master has come!" He yielded himself completely to this overwhelming seduction, and his eyes crossed as he received the vision. . . .

Suddenly Weisthor saw a flaming swastika rotating across Europe, thrashing down the hordes of mongrels who dared to defy their Master. With each victory, the vanquished morphed into twisted skeleton-like creatures. The tortured screams of thousands rose in their worship of the Dark Lord.

Then he saw the Führer seated upon a throne, holding the Spear of Destiny triumphantly over the masses bowing before him. In the distance a young, dashing SS knight upon a dark horse appeared. When he mounted the throne, Hitler embraced him and seated him by his right side. But when the Führer rose to prophesy to the crowds, the knight stole the talisman of power.

With the power of the Dark Lord in the knight's grasp, the Führer was cast into the throng, shredded by chattering fangs and consumed by screaming skulls. To the cheers of the masses, the gallant knight held up the Spear. Upon its hallowed blade was engraved his title—The Infidel.

Eyes wide and dazed, Weisthor staggered back to the edge of the stone bench. His disciples' eyes were rolled back in their sockets, transfixed upon the flames. The ghoulish whites of their eyes reflected the sinister presence of the Dark Lord.

Weisthor stepped behind Himmler, seated on the bench, and placed his hands on Heinrich's short-cropped dark hair. Weisthor witnessed the invading Spirit merge with the Reichsführer's mind.

Himmler reached out and cupped Strausser's severed head with both hands. His lips moved in an unfamiliar language. In his mind's eye, Weisthor saw a great battle. He could see The Infidel's challenge to Himmler's throne of power.

Himmler's face was streaked with sweat when he finally released the severed head.

Weisthor resumed his place before the altar. "Who now commits our brother to the eternal flame?"

Himmler stood. "The Order of New Templars commits our brother's soul to his eternal enlightenment!"

The pit beneath them exploded into a column of flame. The flame leapt up through the grill, engulfing the skull. The Knights recoiled as they were blinded by a bonfire of dazzling light and billowing smoke. As

the flesh melted from Strausser's skull, the stench of burnt hair permeated the now dank and dismal cavern.

Weisthor smiled. The intense pleasure of the Dark Lord was his.
The priest could taste the utter awe and fear branded upon his disciples' faces. Yet he could not help but wonder about the meaning of
his vision. He suspected that the unholy Spear of Destiny would pass
through many hands before its rightful heir would command its mystical power.

Chapter Four

Munich, November 8, 1938

Reinhard Heydrich took an elevator down to the ad hoc SS command center set up on the third floor of the Hotel Vier Jahreszeiten. There he met Major Neame in his private office. An attractive secretary served morning coffee with danishes as Reinhard sat at his desk and glanced at the morning headlines.

JEWISH ASSASSIN STRIKES IN PARIS

Member of German Embassy Critically Wounded by Gunshots

The Murdering Knave, a 17-Year-Old Zealot

Reinhard drew a wolfish grin. "So Grynszpan cooperated in the assassination."

"I can be most persuasive."

"Then Operation Black Angel can proceed!"

Neame stood by a map of Germany. "At your signal, a coded message will be sent to thirteen SS offices throughout Germany. Our storm troopers have targeted synagogues, stores, warehouses, factories, and homes of prominent Jews."

Reinhard's heart raced. Newspaper headlines would boast of beatings, murders, and mass destruction of Jewish property. "Then let Black Angel fly tomorrow night at midnight."

"With the fury of the SS, no one will help the Jews."

"Neame, paint their doorsills with the blood of their firstborn!"

"Jawohl, mein herr!" Neame clicked his heels together.

"One more thing. My nephew Ernst Teschler—make sure he participates in all of this. Let him stand in Jewish blood."

*   *   *

Wittenberg, November 9, 1938

At sunset, Abraham arrived home from Berlin, and Nina embraced him. "Oh, Abraham, I thought they had arrested you!"

He gently stroked her greying hair as he gazed into her gentle brown eyes. "Nothing could keep me from the love of my life."

"Such flattery will get you wine and some cheese."

Perhaps we have been married too long. "Well, dear, I was hoping for something a little more passionate."

"Let's pretend we are at a Parisian café, and a French waiter serves a cultured merlot and brie cheese. Now, that's romantic."

They sat together on the living room couch as he related the events of his trip. Eventually, they snuggled close. Nina kissed him passionately, then sat up. "Sixteen years ago you enjoyed the fruits of our love, and God gave us Aaron."

Abraham sighed. "Yes, our son is truly a blessing."

"Well, that blessing is due home any time now."

"Oh." *I guess there won't be any more* blessings *tonight.*

An hour later, the back door slammed shut, and their son, Aaron, tried to sneak through the hall unnoticed.

Abraham stood. "Aren't you going to greet your father?"

Aaron hesitated, then turned toward the living room. "Sir, I thought you were in Berlin. Mother has been so worried."

"I was searching for your sister."

"Sarah chose to leave!" Aaron pursed his lips. "If she wanted to be a part of this family, she would come home."

Abraham's heart ached. The memories of his children as playful toddlers were cherished—before the pain . . . before the anger.

"I'm going out!" With that, the boy stomped out the front door. The screen door slammed closed.

Nina joined Abraham at the front window. Together, they watched their son walk away. She frowned. "Where is he going?"

"Across the street to Samuel's house."

Nina moved to the staircase. "Dear, you look exhausted. Perhaps we should go to bed?"

He looked intently at his wife. "You know I love Aaron."

"We both do, but he is struggling to be a man. You should spend more time with him." Nina gently kissed him. "Come to bed, Abraham. You should spend more time with your wife."

After they ascended the stairs to the melodic chimes of their grandfather clock in the downstairs hallway, Abraham forgot all thoughts about fatigue.

*   *   *

Sometime during the night, Abraham stirred. Still groggy, he heard random shouts from the street below, or so it seemed. When he slipped on his spectacles, the grating sound of a collision outside penetrated their peaceful abode.

Abraham rushed to the front window. "Nina, wake up!"

Her puffy eyes stretched open. "What? What is it?"

"Come quickly! Nazis are in the street!" He pulled the curtains back to reveal a horrifying scene.

Two military trucks eased down the street. When they braked, twenty or thirty young men in brown uniforms and jackboots vaulted over the tailgate onto the pavement. Brandishing axes and picks, the soldiers ran down the street like a pack of jackals. They stormed the first row of houses, pummeling doors and smashing windows. The sound of shattering glass penetrated the crisp night air.

"Nina, they are coming for us!" Ice-cold fear gripped Abraham as he swung around the bedpost and snagged his bare toes. Wincing, he limped over to his wife at the side window. He embraced her, and she began to cry. *O Lord, extend Thy arm to protect us. Give me courage. . . .* "Nina, our God is with us."

He drew the curtain aside and cracked the window open. "No, no—this cannot be." Across the alley through lit windows, he saw SS soldiers ransacking Samuel's house. Reaching the third floor, the intruders threw open the balcony doors.

"Aaron's in that house!" Nina screamed.

They both watched in terror as three young Nazis pushed a large object out onto the balcony.

One of soldiers shouted below, "Here's a present for you, Franz!"

The three men lofted a small upright piano over the railing. It somersaulted through the air and smashed onto the sidewalk. The wood casing splintered into jagged beams that protruded upward, entangled in a mesh of piano wires. A soldier by the curb hurled a burning bottle of kerosene upon the debris, and it burst into flames.

Abraham and Nina's eyes remained riveted to the scene playing out on the balcony. Aaron and his friend Samuel stumbled out onto the platform. In a fury, Samuel attacked a soldier but was clubbed down. Aaron rushed to his aid, wildly swinging a fireplace poker at one soldier, then the next.

"Aaron!" Nina wailed from their bedroom window. But then she leaned back to catch her breath.

"Nina, don't look. It's too much to bear."

The soldiers easily deflected their son's youthful blows. Then one of them pinned Aaron's arms behind him while his colleague grabbed both his legs.

Abraham thrust his head out the window and shouted, "Don't you touch my son!"

Nina turned away and held her hands to her face.

Abraham stepped back from the window. In shock, he could feel the clock ticking, but there was not enough time to rescue his son. "Aaron, Papa is coming."

"Do something, Abraham!" Nina pounded his arm with her fist. "Save our son!"

Beyond Abraham's reach, Aaron squirmed for his life. For just a moment he ceased struggling and looked at his parents across the alley.

Abraham reached out into empty air to embrace his son one last time as tears erupted, and he cried out, "Aaron, I love you. We both love you so much!"

All time and motion appeared to stop.

With eyes frozen open, Nina turned to look at Aaron.

The two soldiers swung their struggling son between them like a skip rope—once, twice, then they casually tossed him over the railing.

His arms momentarily free, Aaron reached out across the chasm. "Papa!"

Nina shrieked as Aaron flailed his arms and legs in the air, trying to right himself like a cat. He seemed to fall in slow motion toward the shattered, burning debris.

Nina and Abraham heard their son's last wretched scream cut short as he was impaled upon the jagged splinter of a piano leg. The burning rosewood timbers quickly engulfed him in flames.

No. It cannot be true.

Nina buried her face in Abraham's barrel chest, sobbing out her grief. They both slumped to their knees, trembling. He cradled her head in his hands.

"Oh, my Lord—not my son!" Abraham's body shuddered as the fusion of his rage and sorrow swelled into one bloodcurdling scream.

*   *   *

For some time Abraham and Nina did not move. Their tears spent, he lifted his wife gently from the floor and helped her down the stairs into the hallway. There in darkness, they stood, numb. Despite the distant sounds of mayhem down the street, Abraham could still hear the subtle ticking of their grandfather clock.

The raucous voices of the soldiers returned. A large rock crashed through their front living room window. Nina shrieked and Abraham clutched her as more objects pelted the house. "O God of Israel, shield us with Your mighty arm!"

The soldiers cackled outside. *How can you sneer at us? My son is dead and you laugh!* When the soldiers mounted the front porch, Abraham and Nina cowered back into the hallway. It seemed as if the front door exploded.

Then—silence. Something stayed the soldiers' axes. Someone stilled their laughter. One of the soldiers shouted, "What is that?"

When he ran to the dining room window, Abraham saw it—a bluish-white flame in a brilliant, burning arc stood between the front door and the intruders. *The Shekinah Glory of God!*

Abraham whispered, "Nina, come over here."

When the pillar of fire stretched up over their heads, the soldiers reeled back from the luminous barrier. A moment later, the assailants fled back to the troop carrier and sped away.

After retreating to the living room sofa, Abraham cradled Nina's trembling body across his lap. Exhausting all tears, she finally dozed off. *O Lord, let me hear Your voice. God, why did You spare us but not our son?* Nina was sure to ask him. Abraham must have God's answer to give her. *O Lord, why is this happening to us?*

Nina stirred in his arms. "Abraham, you must bring Aaron back home—before the scavengers come in the morning."

Abraham imagined the sight of his son's charred remains still hanging upon his funeral pyre. He shuddered again. "The angel of death has passed over our house. Oh, Nina, if only our son had stayed within these walls—"

Nina stiffened and abruptly sat up with terror in her eyes. "Abraham, you must find our Sarah. Don't come back until you find her. Promise me you will protect her from these animals!"

*   *   *

Berlin, November 10, 1938

Major Neame and Ernst Teschler stood in the center aisle of the Rykestrasse Synagogue as their troops doused the wooden pews with kerosene. It was a significant temple located in the Pankow district. Ernst surveyed the ornate architecture and the tall stained-glass windows. The building was beautiful. He leafed through his orders one more time. There was no threat to the Reich here.

A few steps away, Max barked out orders to their scattered SS squad. His words echoed throughout the empty hall, three stories tall. "Snap to it, men."

The young men in black tunics swarmed the pews like locusts.

A trooper tossed an empty fuel can aside. "The Jewish swine will get our message tonight."

Ernst stepped outside into a chorus of angry shouts. Ordinary civilians armed with shovels and clubs protested in the street. Demons of hatred contorted their faces as they transformed into a vigilante mob. It was as if something alien penetrated their very souls. Then utter chaos broke out. In waves, young men and senior citizens alike cursed the Jews as they pelted rocks through shop windows and pummeled Jewish men and boys bloody.

Adrenaline surging through his body, Ernst watched the train wreck in slow motion. Stepping into a nearby alley, he looked up into the night sky. A bluish-white cloud hovered above the temple. It was eerie—and luminous. As if a thousand eyes were watching him. In the moment, Ernst sensed something intensely holy.

Neame marched out the massive wooden doors and shouted above the chaos, "Bring the firebombs!"

Constrained by his duty, Ernst took a deep breath and pushed through the crowd of angry faces. At the tailgate of their truck, young SS soldiers retrieved a handful of wine bottles filled with kerosene.

Neame handed Ernst a bottle. "Teschler, you have the honors."

Ernst walked up the stone steps to the entrance of the synagogue. A fellow soldier leaned in and ignited the wick. Mesmerized by the bobbing flame, again Ernst stared over his shoulder at the bluish cloud.

"Teschler, you have your orders!"

With a deep breath, Ernst marched into the sanctuary with the first torch lit. Under his breath, he recited his oath, "My honor is loyalty," over and over again. He cocked his right arm and launched the burning missile into the pews.

The sound of the shattering glass was jarring. The wood kindling burst into flames. Soon the volatile liquid ignited into a sea of angry flames. The other SS soldiers rushed out of the inferno for safety.

Inside, Ernst stared at the Hebrew symbols memorialized in the stained-glass windows. As the heat intensified, a sound like a mighty wind funneled a draft upward, igniting the rafters. Ernst looked out the window up into the sky a third time. The luminous cloud hovered over the sacred structure as flames and smoke billowed through the melting colored-glass panes.

"Ernst, let's go!" Max grabbed his arm and pushed him toward the exit.

Coughing and gasping for breath, Max and Ernst made it out to their truck.

A fire engine careened around the corner and lurched to a stop. A fire marshal leaned out of the cab and screamed, "You fools! That synagogue is right next to a munitions factory. Göring will skin you alive when he finds out."

Neame cursed as they watched a caravan of police and fire vehicles arrive at the scene to "save the building." Powerful streams of water from municipal fire hoses soon cascaded upon the flames that now had reached the parched shingles of the ancient roof.

Ernst gazed up to the heavens. The solitary cloud had morphed into what appeared to be a pillar of fire over God's temple. "Max, up there! Do you see that?"

With a blank stare, Max looked beyond Ernst's pointed finger, then back at the burning building. "All I see is the glory of the Third Reich."

*   *   *

Berlin, November 11, 1938

The November pogrom had raged through the night, assailing residents in several cities and towns. Where it began with the Nazi SS and Brown-shirts, local civilians joined the violent cause in earnest. Like a swarm of black wasps, SS units descended upon their next Jewish prey late the next day.

The Maarov Temple was an ornate three-story stone building constructed in the 1860s, located in Mitte. At sunset, Ernst's SS squad arrived in three trucks. Surrounded by Hebrew symbols embossed in stone, brass, and stained glass, Ernst walked around the street corner and entered a side door to the sanctuary.

The rabbi stood behind the podium with lifted hands. His silver beard matched the shocks of coarse hair curling underneath his ceremonial yarmulke. With his deep baritone voice, he chanted ancient Hebrew verses as if they were a spoken melody. Seeking refuge from the calamity of the streets, his congregation filled every pew.

"Let us remember the families who grieve this day, let us honor those who have died. God is present to us in all circumstances. Nothing happens apart from His providence—"

Ernst felt as if those words were spoken to him. He looked again at the families in the pews. Strangely, he sensed God's hand upon them.

The large wooden doors at the rear burst open. Max was in the lead as he fired his pistol twice into the ceiling. "No one moves! By order of the SS, we condemn this pagan shrine!"

The audience reared back into their seats as five SS troopers armed with submachine guns stormed up the aisle.

The rabbi stepped toward Max. "Please, we were just offering prayers—"

"Silence!"

The rabbi stepped closer. "Officer, we will do whatever—"

Max slapped the elderly rabbi with the back of his hand, and he sprawled to the floor. When a faithful member bolted to the rabbi's defense, Max aimed his pistol. "Choose your next words carefully."

In a sweat, the brave young man braced himself. "Only a coward would shoot a defenseless rabbi."

Max leveled his barrel between the young Jew's eyes. A woman's scream pierced the veil when a short burst of machine gun fire raked the altar wall above. Max pivoted to return fire when he spied smoke coming from Ernst's barrel.

"Sergeant," Ernst shouted. "We're here to destroy this building. Nothing more!"

"But these are only Jews." Max's eyes were callous.

"Take these people out of here, schnell!"

Scattered shouts and cries peppered the crowd as the SS soldiers shoved women, children, and men outside into the backs of waiting trucks, prodding them like cattle.

A young Jewish couple in their mid-twenties managed to slip through the cordon of guards and tried to walk away unnoticed. A trooper shouted, "Halt!" When the fugitives broke into a sprint, scattered gunshots rang out and chipped the cobblestones around their feet.

Another soldier snapped back the bolt on his submachine gun. As if shooting cans off a fence, the soldier's gun roared to life. The bullets' spray sprinted up the street behind the fleeing couple and hammered holes into the man's buttocks and back, then clipped the girl's shoulder. Their bodies appeared to fall in slow motion, landing on the pavement with graceful relief. Racked with pain, the young man reached out his quivering hand to touch his motionless bride.

Ernst ran up to his men. "Cease fire! Who gave that order?"

Inside the trucks, women and children cried out frantically.

"Corporal, contain these people. Now!" Ernst stomped back into the building and found Max's men planting sticks of dynamite.

"Max, let's get this over with. Remember, two packs of explosives to each pillar—no more."

"Ja, Ja, enough to blow this synagogue to hell!" Max and his men connected the charges and unreeled the detonation wires out the main doors and across the street in front of a bakery shop. The SS trucks drove down the street for safety, leaving the prisoners a ringside seat for the fireworks.

As Ernst paced behind his explosives team, he noticed a beautiful wedding cake, three tiers high, in the bakery window.

The last of the soldiers dashed out of the condemned building, unreeling the last string of wires across the cobblestone road. "Sir, the charges are set."

Twisting the last wire into place, Max grinned. "Would you like to do the honors?"

Ernst looked up in awe at the grandeur of the old stone sanctuary. He remembered the terrified expressions upon the Jewish faces.

"Ernst?"

Ernst shook his head. "No, you finish the job." He looked down the street. Like lambs crowded in a pen, the Jews watched helplessly from the rear of the SS trucks. "Now, Max, you did set two charges by each pillar?"

Max raised the plunger with a devilish smile. "I used three to make certain."

Ernst whirled around, his eyes wide. "What?"

When Max compressed the plunger, a series of three deafening explosions lit up the night sky in an expanding fireball. The compression wave generated from the excess dynamite blew out the front doors and windows of the synagogue. The blast catapulted Ernst up in the air and propelled Max sideways against the brick wall of the bakery.

Ernst's body crashed through the bakery window and smashed into the display case. For an instant, it felt as if a hornet's nest unleashed hundreds of wasp stingers across his face and body.

Unable to scream, Ernst's head plunged into a sea of blackness.

*   *   *

In a daze, Max stared across the street. The explosives had sheared off half the roof of the Maarov Temple. Bright-colored columns of flames and smoke towered above the rubble. Yet, as if by some miracle, the exterior walls still stood. Down the street, Max heard the Jewish prisoners cheer.

"Look what God has done, Rabbi. He's killed the Nazis with their own bombs!" The Jews broke out in thunderous applause.

Max's head throbbed. Smoldering pieces of wood and debris riddled the sidewalk, and the acrid smell of cordite permeated the air. When he probed the searing pain on his forehead, his hand came back bloody. With the help of his men, Max managed to stand.

Through the smoke, he could barely see. Then he saw the jagged shards of glass bordering the remains of the bakery window. "Ernst!" The darkness whispered only silence in return. Then came a sickening feeling.

I just killed my best friend!

Max climbed through the broken bakery window and stood inside the darkened shop. "Ernst? Ernst, where are you?"

Another soldier shouted through the broken window. "Sergeant, can you see him?"

"Find Teschler, schnell!" Max yelled.

Two other soldiers forced the front door open and scurried throughout the debris with flashlights. Max heard a faint sound as smoke clouded his vision. There it was again behind the upturned glass display case or what was left of it.

Max rummaged through the debris to discover Ernst sprawled across its twisted frame with his legs splayed wide. Max leaned down as a soldier shone a light at his best friend's face. Ernst's skin was pale and sopped with blood. Max tapped his cheeks. No response.

"Ernst, wake up!" Max held his breath as he frantically searched for a pulse.

Ernst's dull, listless eyes rolled open. "Max?"

Max leaned back on his haunches. "I thought you were—"

"You idiot! I told you, two packs of dynamite!"

*   *   *

Berchtesgaden, Southeast Bavaria, November 12, 1938

Perched atop Mount Kehlstein, the Eagle's Nest was nestled high above Salzburg, just across the Austrian border. Adolf Hitler stood alone in the observatory, gazing out on the majestic sunrise peeking over the rocky abyss. He rubbed his silver SS Honor ring on his right hand. Its embossed skull was bordered by two rubies.

He read the SS reports of Kristallnacht, the "night of shattered glass." He relished the tales of Jewish blood flowing in the streets of Berlin, Munich, and throughout his kingdom.

In his lap, he stroked the mystical relic—the two-thousand-year-old iron Spearhead of Longinus. The Roman executioner of Jesus had once wielded its long, tapered point, supported at its base with metal flanges depicting the wings of a dove. Within a central aperture in the blade, a hammerheaded nail was secured by a bronze cuff threaded with metal wire.

As Adolf fingered the dull edge of the nail, the ruby gems on his finger glowed. Satan transported him back in time to stand at the cross of Jesus. He reveled at the *Savior's* agony with each hammer blow into flesh. The legend of the Roman centurion and his Spear was legendary.

"He who controls the Spear will control the world." Adolf repeated the words his mentor, Dietrich Eckart, told him years ago.

Hitler lifted the relic to his lips. Drawing his tongue across its ancient blade, the salty taste of his own blood was sublime. He felt the surge of wicked delight as the Unholy Spirit embraced him once again.

Chapter Five

Berlin, November 12, 1938

As he ascended, Ernst climbed dangerously close to the edge of the precipice. Then a bright light blinded him. Flailing his arms, he slipped on the sheer rock face and was swallowed whole by the mouth of the dark abyss. Suddenly he was transported back inside the Maarov Temple at the moment the dynamite ignited and expanded into a huge fireball. The sound was deafening.

There was only silence as flames engulfed the bimah, the holy shrine of the Torah. A majestic being of light descended upon the altar before the burning scrolls of the Torah. "Saul, Saul, why do you persecute me?" the voice asked.

"Teschler, my name is Ernst Teschler."

"By any other name, it is you who persecutes My people!"

"Jews are enemies of the state."

"You persecute the people of God!"

The angel leaned over and placed his fingers on Ernst's eyes. A surge of energy traversed his whole body, and he was enveloped by the Light. He found himself floating again in the abyss.

"You have been chosen. But you alone must choose to follow Me."

Ernst tossed and turned. "But, but I can't. . . . My honor is loyalty to the Reich, to our Führer."

Then the temple walls crumbled. The scattered cries and shouts of their victims pounded Ernst's ears. The marble floor of God's temple caved in and swallowed Ernst whole. Again, he was falling, down, down, until he stood in the depths of hell. His body melded into darkness, and Ernst could no longer breathe.

"Guten Tag, Herr Teschler," a deep, raspy voice said.

Startled, Ernst leaned forward and saw a rotund man. His face was framed by a bushy grey mustache. His cheeks were pouched and ruddy. "My name is Weisthor. We are the master race! By the dark powers of hades, it has been prophesied. You will retrieve the unholy Spear of Longinus, the talisman of power, and you shall rule with the Aryan elite forever."

Ernst looked deeply into the man's shimmering silver eyes. Seductive and horrid, they were not of this world. Ernst could sense the presence of pure evil. He lashed out at the man's taunting face, but his wavering image dissipated into thin air.

Something pinched Ernst's right hand. It was as if his finger was thrust into a ring of fire. He fell back into his shattered body, where he was embraced by intense, indescribable pain.

∗   ∗   ∗

A young woman dressed in white tucked a white sheet up under Ernst's chin. As she leaned down, her angelic face came into sharp focus.

"Good morning, Lieutenant. I'm Christine Dohnanyi." The nurse's blonde hair was drawn up tightly into a bun and pinned under her nurse's cap. Her blue eyes sparkled. As she applied a damp cloth to Ernst's feverish forehead, he smelled the pungent odor of alcohol. The cool sensation was soothing. "You're in Augusta Hospital, Berlin. You survived a nasty explosion yesterday."

Ernst swallowed, his mouth dry as cotton. Then he remembered the synagogue—too much dynamite—and the searing pain. "Do I still have my leg?"

"At my last count, you have two. The surgeon removed multiple glass fragments from your buttocks. And you had a severe concussion." Christine handed Ernst his spectacles. "You're a very lucky man. You could have bled to death. I'm sure it was only by God's providence."

"God?" Ernst squinted through his circular lenses.

"That's right. Sergeant Schumann told me you became a human cannonball, blown five meters through a window. The surgeon gave you 139 stitches. One shard of glass was imbedded next to an artery. You could have died."

Ernst lifted one shoulder. "Guess it wasn't my time."

"God must have a plan for you."

"God, you say. In my dream . . . I saw something miraculous." Ernst reached up and felt a bandage swathing his head.

"Your headaches will come and go." Christine's eyes glistened as she gently held Ernst's hand. "Tell me your story, for I—"

A commotion erupted outside in the hallway. Loud voices and footsteps followed, then an attendant opened the door slightly.

"Is this Lieutenant Teschler's room?" A familiar voice sounded from the doorway as General Heydrich strutted into the room. "Tell him his commanding officer is here to see him."

The nurse's eyes narrowed.

Reinhard glared at the nurse. "The family would like its privacy now."

She circled around to the foot of the bed. "Lieutenant, I will pray for you later."

"Yes, much later. Do have God bless the Führer, the Reich, and my favorite nephew." Reinhard's thin lips formed an insincere smile.

Ernst flinched in pain. "You mean your only nephew."

The nurse departed without looking back and closed the door. Ernst paused. Now, what was her name?

The formidable general transformed into Uncle Reinhard. He removed his hat and offered a sympathetic grin. "So, you took wounds in the rump, did you?"

"Ach, does everyone in Berlin know?" Ernst winced as he shifted positions.

"You nearly died! Now tell me, who was responsible?"

"Responsible?" Ernst frowned.

"Schumann kept mumbling about the explosives. It was that dolt Schumann, wasn't it?"

Ernst hoisted his shoulders up from the bed but keeled back in a muffled groan.

"I told you, Ernst, I cannot afford to lose you."

"Please, it was our first mission. It was my command. I take full responsibility."

Reinhard stepped closer. "All things considered, you did accomplish your mission—if perhaps with too much mercy. You know, Lina and I have grown quite fond of you. And my boys look up to you."

Ernst blushed. "Sir, you have always been there for our family. Mother and I are grateful."

His uncle eased himself into a chair by the bed. "If you don't mind, I'll just sit here beside you for a while, ja?" They talked for a little while, and then Ernst calmly drifted back to sleep.

*   *   *

Berlin, November 12, 1938

The Abwehr, German military intelligence, was housed in a four-story brick building in Berlin's Tiergarten district. Admiral Wilhelm Canaris's office was sparsely furnished, accented by an old, worn, brown rug and bordered by large picture windows overlooking a stone courtyard two stories below. A portrait of Canaris's longtime friend Franco, the Spanish president, hung above the ornately carved mantel. A marble paperweight in the shape of three monkeys sat at the center edge of his desk over the chiseled slogan: Hear No Evil—See No Evil—Speak No Evil.

With a lit cigarette in hand, Colonel Hans Oster paced behind Canaris's formidable oak desk. He stopped, tapped his watch with his index finger, then drew down on the cigarette again. Where was the man? They needed the captain on the bridge!

Finally the phone rang, and Hans picked up the receiver. "That's correct, Admiral. Heydrich's people have assaulted Jews in every major city. Preliminary reports indicate over seven thousand retail stores, thirty factories, and over two hundred synagogues have been destroyed. I think we can assume that he did this under Himmler's orders. No, sir. No response from the police. None of our people thought it would go this far. . . . Without the military, what can we do? . . . Yes, I will track down Heydrich." As Hans hung up the phone, he crushed his burning cigarette into an ashtray.

The legal advisor to the Abwehr, Herr Dohnanyi, entered the room and placed his briefcase on the conference table. "Well, do you smell anything burning in Berlin lately? Unbelievable bedlam in the streets, full-scale riots!"

"Himmler authorized the attack, but it has Heydrich's fingerprints all over it. That is German efficiency for you—the SS initiates the riots, then German citizens finish the job. Arson, mayhem, murder." Hans ran his fingers across his short-cropped brown hair. *This is insanity!*

"And yet, all perfectly legal," Dohnanyi said.

"My next-door neighbor, Herr Meumann, is an attorney—a Jew. Last night, I called them to offer sanctuary in our apartment. They said they were grateful, but they were more concerned about what the Gestapo would do to us if they were caught." Hans shook his head. "I have never felt more indecent in all my life."

Dohnanyi removed a file from his briefcase. "What did the admiral have to say?"

Hans shrugged. "What matters is what we will do about it."

"If the police and the regular army will not intervene, the only way to stem the violence would be to address the people directly—to speak to the conscience of Germany."

"What about the churches?" Hans removed another cigarette from a silver tray on the desk.

"The Reich Church is peppered with political clergy. And the silent ones would not dare oppose a government initiative. It wouldn't surprise me if some of Hitler's men might be out on the streets inciting the flames."

"What about your brother-in-law? Would Dr. Bonhoeffer be willing to mobilize the Confessing Church pastors?"

Dohnanyi nodded. "Possibly. The Confessing Church is the faithful remnant in Hitler's Babylon. Anyway, Dietrich travels a circuit in Pomerania, teaching theology students—quite illegal, of course. He should be in Stettin today."

"Then send him a telegram. Ask him to come to Berlin, immediately."

"By orders of the Gestapo, he's forbidden to speak in Berlin."

Hans Oster clenched his jaw. "But he knows authentic pastors who can. And, someone has to say something!"

*   *   *

Pomerania, the Northern Coast of Germany

The city of Stettin was a large seaport nestled between the Elbe River and the Baltic Sea. Secluded, the town had avoided most of the SS violence during the nationwide pogrom on Kristallnacht. When Dietrich Bonhoeffer arrived at the train station, he received a telegram from his brother-in-law, Hans von Dohnanyi. It had just three words in simple code: *Dietrich, return home!*

The white-haired man behind the ticket counter was listening to a radio when Dietrich approached. *"We now bring you a live broadcast from the Reich Chancellery, where Dr. Joseph Goebbels is addressing members of the Reichstag during this time of national crisis."*

Dietrich pushed some Reichsmarks through the window slot. "One-way ticket to Berlin, please."

The clerk tore a ticket off a roll but hesitated as Goebbel's nasal voice droned on. *"Today, our citizens have risen against the tyranny of the Jews. The murder of Ernst von Rath has been avenged. People of Germany, take up arms and strike a blow for victory! Scour your neighborhoods, take to the streets and use whatever force is necessary. We must make the Third Reich Judenfrei!"*

A shrill whistle signaled his train's departure. Dietrich grabbed his ticket, then rushed to the platform to board just in time. As the train surged into motion, he found a seat in a half-empty compartment and retrieved a newspaper from his briefcase. The headline captured his attention:

GERMAN CITIZENS RETALIATE AGAINST JEWISH AGGRESSORS!

Dietrich was stunned by the black-and-white pictures depicting the violence. Graphic close-ups showing elderly Jewish men and women being shoved into trucks in their nightclothes. German citizens pelting rocks through store windows and clubbing young Jewish boys.

Good Lord! The captions beneath the images were infuriating. The bigoted, intolerant statements that had been widely traded on the streets, in universities, and in German homes for years were now here in bold print.

Dietrich sighed as he neatly folded the paper. Through the window, he pondered the quiet streets of this sleepy Pomeranian town. Restless, his thoughts drifted back to one of his recent classes a few days earlier. One student had raised his hand.

"Dr. Bonhoeffer, this fellow Grynszpan claimed that Germans have persecuted Jews for centuries, so he felt justified in murdering a rich German diplomat. Surely everyone must know that it was the Jews who have persecuted us."

"They've gotten what they deserved!" another student said.

Dietrich frowned. "Nein! We in Germany must never forget that Jesus Himself was a Hebrew. The Bible teaches that the sacrificial lamb was born to die for our sins, Jew or Gentile. Does the crucifixion justify Germans or anybody else persecuting Jews now? Not according to the Word of God."

"The Jews incurred God's wrath by rejecting the truth. God has cursed them!" a young man insisted.

"The same can be said for you, for me, the Pope, and every Christian who has ever lived. Gentlemen, God judges sin regardless of blood, color, or nationality. Like us, the Jews have fallen short of God's ways. Like us, they can be redeemed through the seed of the house of David. He who is without sin, cast the first stone."

Dietrich had been shaken by the students' belligerent expressions. Like so many in Germany, too many young people were convinced by Nazi myths and hatred.

Just as the train gathered speed, a gaunt little man in the aisle stumbled into Dietrich.

"Excuse me." His brown leather coat was worn and his black-tie shoes were scuffed. His face looked quite ordinary, and his dark hair was thinning. The man sat down across from Dietrich. "Are you finished with the front page, Herr Bonhoeffer?"

Dietrich instinctively reached for the newspaper on the seat before he realized that the man had called him by name.

"Don't be alarmed, Herr Bonhoeffer. The Gestapo is carefully watching you and your meddling colleagues in the Confessing Church—for your own safety."

Dietrich blinked. "Am I . . . under arrest?"

"My, my, no."

"Then what do you want?"

"Merely to read the good news." The Gestapo agent snatched the folded paper from Dietrich's limp hands. "It's been a glorious week for the Reich. Over thirty thousand Jews have left the country so far. All faithful members of the Reich Church should rejoice, don't you agree?"

Dietrich held his breath, waiting for the bear trap to snap shut.

The little man's plastic smile boasted his crooked teeth. He stood, politely tipped his hat, and retreated down the aisle.

Dietrich leaned back in his seat, his heart pounding. They must have been following him for days! He wiped his damp brow and looked again, but the little man had vanished.

*   *   *

Berlin, December 17, 1938

The Heydrich home in the Lakes district was furnished like a palace. Reinhard sat behind his desk in the study, meticulously sorting his four-by-six notecards. Each held a savory secret or two on his enemies within the Reich. With such evidence, blackmail was a thrill and a hobby he so enjoyed. With these nuggets of incrimination, Reinhard controlled the nerve centers of the SS.

He looked down at his stopwatch, then up at his visitor. He pondered the muscle fatigue of standing still for over ten minutes. "At ease, Schumann."

Max saluted again. "Jawohl, Herr Obergruppenführer!"

The study door opened behind Max, and an SS man appeared. Reinhard shuffled through some papers and held up a file. "Take these to Himmler."

His brow furrowed, Max stepped forward to take them.

"Not *you*." Reinhard dismissed Max with a glare as his adjutant retrieved the papers.

"Ja, mein herr." The adjutant tucked the papers in his leather pouch, saluted, and strode toward the door with an amused glance.

My, Schumann, you are a dolt. "Schumann—sit down."

"Ja, mein herr!"

"My people say you have a great deal of influence over my nephew." Max blinked.

"I have plans for Ernst, and you can participate in his success. The more I know about his activities, associations, even what he reads, will help me plot his career within the SS."

"I am at your command, mein herr!"

"From time to time we shall meet in private. You will report everything about Ernst to me in confidence. Schumann, my nephew must never know about these conversations."

"Jawohl, mein herr."

"These are violent times. To violate my trust would be lethal—to all whom you hold dear. Understood?"

Max squinted. "M-My honor is loyalty, Herr Obergruppenführer!"

Reinhard presented a sealed envelope. "I have an assignment for Major Neame. Our target is a Jew, Dr. Herbert Aronstein. His colleague at the medical school, Karl Bonhoeffer, has become quite vocal against our Führer. I wish to send a personal message to the faculty. Make sure Neame receives these orders right away."

"Jawohl, mein herr."

Reinhard leaned closer. "If you are to serve my nephew, you must demonstrate blind obedience to me, and me alone. I have Ernst's mind, but now I want his heart—his very soul. Schumann, if you succeed, soon you will wear SS officer's runes on your collar." Lies and seduction were Reinhard's addiction.

"Sir!" Max snapped to attention and clicked his heels together. Clutching the envelope in hand, Max departed.

Reinhard left his study and paused in the spacious foyer where his wife was struggling to put on an earring in front of a mirror.

"Wasn't that Ernst's friend?" Lina asked coolly as she dodged his hand that tried to stroke her hip. "You're using him to get to Ernst, aren't you?"

"It was SS business, my dear."

When she leaned toward the mirror to affix her earring, Reinhard crowded in behind her, his cold, calculating eyes morphed into pools of sly adoration.

"Ernst will never be like you, Reinhard." Lina's manner was aloof.

"My dear—first, I will mold Ernst into my image. And the day you celebrate my demise, he will secure the future of our sons."

"How so?"

"Klaus is only five years old and Heider a year younger. I will train Ernst to pass down the mantle of power to our sons when the boys are old enough."

A faint smile crested her voluptuous lips. "What a comforting thought."

Chapter Six

Dressed in his robe and slippers, Dr. Herbert Aronstein turned out the lamp in their living room. He kissed his wife, Rebecca. "Go on upstairs, dear. I will be up shortly."

As Rebecca rounded the midstair landing, muffled voices and shouts erupted outside on the street. She cracked open the blinds to a thicket of red-and-white swastikas swarming on their doorstep.

A soldier rapped his nightstick on the door. "Open up in the name of the Third Reich."

Herbert opened the front door until the door chain pulled taut. "My name is Corporal Siegfried. We have orders to search this house. Orders from the Gestapo."

"We are law-abiding citizens. Please, we want no trouble."

Rebecca frantically paced on the landing. "Herbert, get away from the door!" She peeked out the window to view their intruders.

The corporal slapped his oak nightstick in the palm of his hand. Clenching his teeth, the brute battered the door frame with his shoulder until the security chain gave way. His momentum propelled the corporal across the threshold and pushed Herbert against the back wall.

"What is it? What do you want?" Her husband demanded.

"Herr Doctor? We want a pure race!" Siegfried kicked him in the shins. Herbert keeled over holding his leg.

Rebecca emerged from the shadows. "Leave my husband alone! He is a respected physician."

The soldiers laughed, and Rebecca shot the short one a thorny glance. "Just how rude are you people?"

Undeterred, Siegfried slammed his jackboot down onto Herbert's knee. With a shriek, he wrenched his head back against the wall. "Please, please take what you will, but don't hurt my family. Rebecca, go back upstairs—now!"

They are going to kill us. Light-headed, she leaned against the stair railing. *If Herbert and I could just get to the back door, we—*

Siegfried smashed his nightstick across Herbert's forehead. With the sound of splintering bone, blood flowed from his nose and mouth as convulsions rippled through his thin torso.

This cannot be happening. . . . "Herbert!" Rebecca flew down the stairs. One soldier caught her and dangled her in midair. "Oh please God, Herbert!" She kicked and screamed and then the soldier slammed her head into the wall.

In a daze, she stumbled to the railing. She reached out to her husband. "Stop it! Stop hurting my husband."

From outside the open door, the shrill blast of a whistle penetrated the still night air. One of the soldiers shouted, "Two policemen are at the street corner." The two men laid Rebecca down by her husband's body as the sound of whistles grew louder.

From the doorstep, Corporal Siegfried looked up the street. "There's no more time. Let's go, double-time."

Rebecca heard the crunching thud of their jackboots' retreat. Shaking her head, she sobbed as she reached out to Herbert. Cradling his battered head gently in her arms, she swabbed the blood pulsing from his wounds with her white nightgown. "It's alright, dear. Those ruffians have left. I'm right here, darling."

Unconscious, he began to choke on blood pooling in his throat. His eyes opened and he reached out to touch her.

Rebecca brushed his cold cheek as his breath became irregular. *Herbert, you promised never to leave me.*

He struggled for air. Tremors consumed his limbs for just a moment, then he was gone.

She had a piercing headache, and tears flooded her cheeks. Rebecca gently rocked his head in her arms as she would an infant. "Oh, Herbert, you look so tired."

*   *   *

Chamber music and formal conversation permeated the large house of Dr. Karl and Paula Bonhoeffer. Their home was a gathering place for family and friends during the Christmas holidays. Tonight they were hosting several faculty members from the Berlin medical school where Karl was a professor.

Though he was the guest of honor, Dietrich had retreated from the dining room to the library. He stood by the roaring fireplace, listening to the casual banter of the guests.

Karl and a colleague strolled by, glasses in hand. In his late sixties, Dietrich's father was a distinguished neurologist who boasted thick, snow-white hair—perfectly coifed. He was immaculately dressed in a three-piece grey wool suit. His voice was enthusiastic as he spoke. "Dr. Knopf, you know my son's new book will be published next month."

His colleague was polite. "You must be proud of him."

"He is brilliant but stubborn. He could have been a physician, but who could have guessed he would become a famous German theologian."

Standing nearby, Dietrich twinged inside with embarrassment.

"Famous, perhaps, but too outspoken for his own good," Dr. Knopf said.

Dietrich stepped forward. "Excuse me, gentlemen. Indeed, I am stubborn but outspoken only when the cause is just, Dr. Knopf." Dietrich shook his hand, but the man's eyes were guarded.

Just then his mother gracefully arrived and presented a tray of glasses. "Talking about the university, I imagine," she scolded her guests with a smile. "Do have a glass of sherry. It's imported."

Dr. Knopf chuckled. "My dear, is there anything in your home that's not imported?"

His father retrieved a glass. "I was just bragging about our son."

Paula beamed. "Oh, Dietrich, Countess Ruth was asking about you."

Dietrich removed two glasses of sherry from the tray. "If you will excuse me, I'll see to our other guests."

His mother led the way over to the arching bay window facing the street. The countess stood looking at several Bonhoeffer family portraits. With a small photograph in hand, she fingered the polished silver frame. "Dietrich, I was just admiring some photos from your youth. Here, you looked like a blond Dutch boy."

Dietrich's cheeks flushed. "And I had hair back then."

"Ja, and next to him is Sabine, his twin sister," Paula said. "Both of you had beautiful blond locks. These other two were taken when Dietrich was sixteen. He has such a broad smile, and his brilliant blue eyes. Look, they are slightly magnified by his round spectacles."

"There, you see, ladies? My receding crown and thinning hair reflect my maturity, don't you think?" Dietrich's laughter was contagious.

"Countess, what an honor it is to have you for our Christmas party. Dietrich, we're about to unveil the cake."

"Did you get chocolate?"

"Would any other flavor do, my boy?" With that, his mother picked up her tray and disappeared among her guests.

The countess's eyes sparkled with anticipation. "When you're seventy-two years old, you can still enjoy buttercream icing." The grand matriarch sat down in the cherry rocker and swayed back and forth. Dietrich sat on the adjacent couch.

The countess placed her hand on Dietrich's arm and lowered her voice. "So, what will happen with the Confessing Church now? Tell me the latest news."

"Leadership in the Reich Church is turning away from sound doctrine. There are things Christian believers must do, actions they must take."

"But, dear boy, Hitler and the Nazis have demanded that the Protestant church march goose step in time with the 'New Germany.'"

Dietrich shook his head. "The Christian faith has been compromised. I've tried to persuade my colleagues, but they've been intimidated, and recently, imprisoned. As you know, just last year the Gestapo closed our seminary in Finkenwalde."

"And then there was your radio broadcast a few years ago."

"Yes, everything was acceptable until I stated that Jesus was a Jew, born in the royal bloodline of King David. The Nazi cowards cut me off. Now, it appears heroic, but then—" *I was frightened to death.*

"That took real courage, Professor." The countess leaned back in her chair as she fingered the flawless ruby necklace that accentuated her brocade evening gown. "I admire your rebellious nature, but I am afraid for you."

Just then his mother returned. "Dietrich, come with me. Karl is about to propose a toast!"

When the countess and Dietrich entered the spacious parlor, his father began. "Ladies, gentlemen, honored guests. It gives me great pleasure to present the Countess Ruth von Kleist-Retzow and my son, Dr. Dietrich Bonhoeffer. Dietrich's new book, *The Cost of Discipleship,* is controversial and will challenge many at the university." He proudly lifted his wineglass. "To Dietrich!"

"To Dietrich!" the assembled guests echoed.

Painfully shy, Dietrich lowered his head with a faint smile.

A frantic knock pounded at the front door. When a servant unlocked the door, it burst open. Startled by the sound, every head turned. A bedraggled woman limped through the foyer dressed in a dark wool overcoat draped over a nightgown drenched with blood.

"Ach, Rebecca, what's happened?" Karl rushed into the corridor. Wheezing and out of breath, Rebecca Aronstein collapsed into the physician's arms. "Karl! Karl, my Herbert has been attacked. He needs you!"

"Dietrich, quickly—help me get her to the couch."

As the trio stumbled into the living room, scattered guests cowered back. "Karl, Herbert needs you. Come quickly!" Rebecca gasped.

Dietrich could see patches of bruised purple painted across her bare shoulders. The woman's face was a pale-white tombstone perched atop a pool of red.

Karl eased her down upon a patterned couch. "Who did this to you?"

"Nazi thugs invaded our home. They attacked my Herbert!"

Dietrich kneeled by her side, and she grabbed his sleeve. Blood oozed from her nose and ear. "Father!"

"She has a concussion. Paula, blankets, some lukewarm water, please! Quickly, dear." It was as if the physician had suddenly transformed the parlor into his operating room and those nearest became his medical staff.

Dietrich draped a thick wool quilt over the shivering woman and took her by the hand. The metallic odor of blood wafted in his nostrils. He rubbed the moist stained gown between his sticky fingers. The smell of salty brine sickened him as he gazed at the open wound on her forehead and her bloody hands. Raw anger started to boil in his stomach.

Dr. Knopf leaned over Karl's shoulder. "She is a Jewess. That's why the Nazis did this."

Rebecca's eyelids fluttered open, and she glared at Knopf. "Nazis! They killed him!" Her eyes flashed again. "Karl, you are a doctor. Why did you not come? Those animals killed my Herbert!" Her head bobbed around as if her neck was on a spring.

Dietrich looked helplessly into his father's eyes. *O Lord, touch this woman.*

Stethoscope in hand, Karl listened to the woman's heart. "There's cranial bleeding and her brain is swelling. We've got to get her to the hospital."

"For heaven's sake, Karl, she's a Jew!" Dr. Knopf said. "We can't be seen taking this woman to a public hospital."

Rebecca shook uncontrollably. Grimacing, she arched back into her pillow. Evacuating her lungs of air, she collapsed. Her swollen vacant eyes appeared to follow Dietrich wherever he turned.

Karl took her pulse, then reached over and gently closed her eyelids.

Still holding Rebecca's moist hand, Dietrich noticed many of their guests slipping out the front door. It was a hollow feeling—like drowning in a swimming pool with guests standing idly by.

Like a proper hostess, his mother shared muted goodbyes with the shaken guests as they politely departed. Soon, only the family remained—with the countess. She was seated off to the side with her hands clasped across her lap, praying.

His father shook his head. "I warned Herbert to leave Germany a year ago, but he was too proud. Just a week ago, the Gestapo accosted him at the university. All of his colleagues—his friends—we said nothing."

We are the silence of the lambs. . . . Dietrich drifted his gaze down to the innocent woman, battered and marred. He lowered his head, whispered God's blessing upon her lifeless body—and wept.

Chapter Seven

Berlin, January 8, 1939

Sunday was a crisp, sunny day. Ernst's prized Doberman Pinscher bolted down the street with his master in tow. When both were exhausted, dog and master eased their way home.

The dog sat quietly panting by Ernst's bed, while he showered and donned his black SS uniform. As he brushed his light brown hair, he imagined the face of his mysterious barmaid at the Bismarck. She was feisty, elusive, and there was that twinkle in her blue eyes. She had beauty and charm, but she would not be an easy catch. *So, what is her name?*

His private moment was rudely interrupted by the sound of his father's muffled shouts from downstairs. "I am not going to church this morning. Not with your wretched brother!"

"Rudolf!" his mother said. "Respectable families go to church together."

With a sigh, Ernst's fantasy moment with the mystery blonde evaporated.

His door creaked open and Papa appeared. He leaned back against the door and rolled his eyes. *Why do you always come to me when you two bicker?*

"I suppose you heard us downstairs?"

"Ever since I graduated from Bad Tölz, you've given Mother nothing but grief about Uncle Reinhard."

"I'd give anything if I could keep you out of Hitler's private army. Soon they will send you off to war."

"I will fight for the Fatherland. It is my sworn duty."

"You will fight for Hitler."

Ernst closed his eyes. He expected another tirade about the Nazis, and his father didn't disappoint.

"He's a madman," Rudolf snarled. The guttural sound alerted Barron. He lurched up onto his front legs and barked.

With a shrill whistle and hand signal for Barron to stand down, Ernst stroked his short-haired blue-grey coat. "Papa, there are a few who share your opinions about the Führer, but be careful what you say in public."

"Ah, Nazi spies everywhere."

"Good Germans have simply disappeared for saying less."

Papa sat on the bed and pulled his prized pocket watch from his vest pocket. Dangling by its golden chain, the watch captured the sunlight shimmering across its fourteen-carat gold casing. "You know what this means to me?"

"Yes, it is your golden charm."

"This is a symbol of the best days of my career. Son, you are the future of Germany. Mark my words, when the Third Reich falls, Germany will need trained legal minds for the reconstruction." Papa popped open the watch's lid to reveal a picture of himself with a ten-year-old Ernst propped up on his knee.

With a grin, Ernst looked on. That was a happy time for their family.

"It's more than just a watch. It's a legacy that I will pass on to you. You must come back from this war alive and accomplish something noble with the Teschler name." Tears misted his father's weathered eyes.

Ernst slipped his arm around his father's shoulder.

His mother shouted from the foot of the stairs. "Reinhard and Lina are here!"

*   *   *

The slender spire of Zion Lutheran Church reached high into the city skyline. The sanctuary's arched ceiling stretched fifteen meters above a sea of polished wooden pews. Sunlight streamed through ornate stained-glass windows, casting patterns of blue, red, and amber on the worshipers as they shuffled into their seats. A massive pipe organ resonated throughout the cavernous hall as Anna Teschler led her family entourage down the aisle.

Lina Heydrich fixed her gaze upon the organist who played Bach's Toccata and Fugue in D Minor. "I so rarely come to church."

Reinhard followed her into the pew. "My dear, the music is German culture at its best."

When Ernst took a seat next to his uncle, he noticed a black-uniformed SS soldier at the end of the aisle. Beyond him stood a clergyman adorned in a black Geneva gown. Was that Pastor Bonhoeffer? All too familiar, memories of his youth cascaded through his mind. Pastor Bonhoeffer taught his confirmation classes thirteen years ago. He revealed aspects about God in the kindest ways.

He reached out to a very lonely boy. He touched Ernst's life.

When the organist transitioned into an energetic German march, Uncle Reinhard whispered to Ernst, "Between God and the devil, I'll take my stand on my own cunning. Now that's a religion I can believe in."

"Shush!" an elderly parishioner hissed from the seat behind them.

With one look into Reinhard's piercing black eyes, the man sank back into his pew. "Ernst, people's minds are small. Remember that, son."

Thunder rumbled again from the enormous pipes as the organ cued the processional to begin. Dr. Bonhoeffer and the pastor proceeded up the center aisle, washed in the light of stained-glass colors. After climbing the chancel steps, they took their seats on the platform.

Ernst's memory stretched back to the day Pastor Bonhoeffer came to the Teschler house to speak with his parents. "Next Sunday is Ernst's confirmation into the church. The boy is very bright, and he asks deep questions about God. Rudolf, Anna—you will be asked to confirm your support of Ernst in the church."

"You mean in public?" Papa had asked. He did not attend the ceremony. Afterward, he rarely mentioned God or the church.

But Pastor Bonhoeffer stayed in touch. He took Ernst for walks. He told him the most curious stories about God. He calmed the storms at home. He took the time and cared for Ernst.

The organist swept into the triumphant first eight bars of Luther's "A Mighty Fortress Is Our God." Ernst's heart swelled as he stood with the congregation to sing.

At its conclusion, Dietrich mounted the towering pulpit. He began slowly. "Despite what modern history books ponder or what politicians pander, there is nothing new about 'national religion.' A national religion, by any other name, is nothing more than a realm ruled by earthly kings. Deceived by the perverse spirit of this age, too many Germans have pledged their allegiance to such a national religion, and yet another human god. But I say that the heart of the Christian experience is not the prison of man-made religion, but a personal relationship with the living God!

"Let us listen to Matthew, the sixteenth chapter: 'Then Jesus said to His disciples, "If anyone wishes to come after Me, he must deny himself, and take up his cross and follow Me. For whoever wishes to save his life will lose it; but whoever loses his life for My sake will find it. For what will it profit a man if he gains the whole world and forfeits his soul? Or what will a man give in exchange for his soul?"' The heart and soul of the church is the risen Christ! And though the Reich may reign a thousand years, only God's kingdom will last forever!"

Ernst lowered his head. The meaning of deeds past became clear. That luminous bluish vapor above the synagogue was a cloud of witnesses. God was watching him as he brandished the weapons of the Reich against God's people.

Ernst sat stunned, his heart hammering. Something ancient, something utterly holy and alive moved through Zion Lutheran Church. The heat of the sunlight bore down upon Ernst's cheek and neck. Looking up, he blinked. A rainbow of colors cascaded through the towering stained-glass portals. Though no one stirred, Ernst saw a halo of light suspended above Pastor Bonhoeffer. *Surely he must have the answers I seek.*

Dr. Bonhoeffer bowed his head as the quiet tones of the church organ underscored his mellow baritone voice. "Gracious Lord . . . as we find ourselves caught in the mounting waves of fear and uncertainty, fill us with Your presence, Your power, and Your peace. Help us to love—even those who seek to work evil against us. Let us not be molded into the image of this world. Let us instead be transformed by the Holy Spirit. We present our bodies, our minds, and our very souls to You in the name of Christ Jesus. Amen."

When the organist launched into a livelier tempo, the two clergymen proceeded down the aisle. The bells in the spire chimed as the congregation streamed back to the narthex.

Pastor Bonhoeffer greeted each parishioner warmly at the church doors.

Boasting a bright smile, Mother shook hands. "Pastor Bonhoeffer, it's good to see you here at Zion Church again."

"Hello, Anna. I didn't see Rudolf. How is he?"

"Perhaps he'll come next Sunday. May I present my sister-in-law, Lina Heydrich."

Dietrich extended his hand to greet Aunt Lina. She raised her pointed chin. "Dr. Bonhoeffer, that sermon certainly was an experience." She glanced down at his proffered hand and skirted past him.

Mother blushed, then quickly followed Lina outside.

When Ernst stepped forward, Dietrich stared for a moment. A broad grin greeted Ernst as they warmly shook hands.

"Ernst, my boy, how many years has it been?"

"Too many, sir. Pastor, may I present my uncle, Herr Reinhard Heydrich."

"General Heydrich, SS." Heydrich donned a subtle smile. "I must say, Dr. Bonhoeffer, to preach so boldly against the Reich in my presence takes courage."

"To remain silent before God would take even more."

Dietrich reached out a tentative hand. Reinhard countered by snapping out his right arm in salute. "Heil Hitler!" The SS chieftain curtly headed out the door.

Ernst stood in awe, his boots glued to the marble floor. "Pastor, you do realize my uncle is second-in-command of the SS?" *My uncle kills men for less.*

Dietrich held Ernst's hand and looked deeply into his hazel eyes. "It really is good to see you, my boy. Let's get together soon."

Uncle Reinhard called out from the church steps, "Ernst! We should *not* keep the ladies waiting."

*   *   *

Westphalia, Germany, February 1939

The full moon illuminated the cloudless night sky. Its cold light washed the stark ramparts above, silhouetting the black-uniformed sentries. Only their faces glowed, like ghosts floating above the walls. They stood rigid and watchful, eyes scanning the fields below for any threatening movement. Their tripod-mounted machine guns followed the intense beams of roving searchlights, strategically perched atop three corner towers. Ever alert, they marched with precision between shadow and light. They were Schutzstaffel—the SS. With a fierce arrogance, they secured the grounds of Wewelsburg Castle, the secluded occult lair of the Third Reich.

Weisthor gazed out the latticed window, taken with the beauty of the moonlight. The sacred fortress had been built by his Templar ancestors many centuries before, during the Dark Ages. Now it remained for Weisthor and his disciples to accomplish their ancient mission.

Reichsführer Himmler strode into the wood-paneled conference room located on the second floor of the north tower. He carefully locked the door behind him. "I just returned from the Eagle's Nest."

"You let Hitler manipulate our future." In the mystical realm, this little man was like a child. "You failed to secure the Spear of Destiny."

Himmler's gaze darted about. "But how did you know?"

"We both know your dream to become Führer will never come true unless we possess the original Talisman of Power."

"Hitler has the relic secured in a special vault—there were too many guards."

Such incompetence. Weisthor dismissed the lies with a wave of his pudgy hand. "Come, Heinrich, we must return to the Seeker's Portal."

Weisthor led his disciple to a chamber perched atop the north tower. At its center stood a black onyx table edged by silver Druid symbols. He opened an ornate wooden box and removed three silver rings, each the size of a human fist.

"These rings were passed down to our great predecessor Adam Weishaupt, when he convened the Illuminati to provoke the French Revolution. Let us meditate upon our Dark Lord, that he may illumine us with his esoteric mysteries!" Weisthor sensed Himmler's fear.

Taking a seat, Himmler lifted both of his hands palms-up and bowed his head. Weisthor spun the first ring on the polished onyx surface, then the next. By the time he turned the third, the first two had begun to wobble. Then, as if miraculously energized, the three rings each accelerated, spinning against gravity until a triangle of silver rings twirled in perfect symmetry.

With each ring feeding off the energy of the others, Weisthor knew his Master would soon speak.

Himmler's gaze followed the motion of the twirling rings upon the black polished surface. For several moments, the only sound was the whirling whine of silver upon stone. Then came the "voice," a melodic timbre emanating from the rings. Suddenly, Himmler arched back in his chair, his eyes frozen as he slipped deep into a trance.

Weisthor stood, extending his hands over his willful minion. "Heinrich, I can see you standing before thousands of Germans at the Nuremberg stadium. Hundreds of thousands of German citizens are wildly cheering for the new Führer. Yes, they are cheering for you!"

In the presence of the unholy, Weisthor stepped behind Himmler. He cupped his hands around the bureaucrat's crown. Together the Dark Lord embraced them with a bloodlust never seen before in history. The blood of the innocent would be spewed across a whole continent. Soldiers of the Reich would rise to conquer God's people. Through these victories, the master race would rise to take the throne and rule the masses for a thousand years.

The passage of time was lost when, suddenly, the three rings dropped with a synchronous clank upon the tabletop. Himmler awoke out of his trance, out of breath.

Weisthor returned to his seat and slumped back into his chair utterly spent. With perspiration beaded upon his brow, he too had been totally captivated by the demonic presence. "There is a young black knight who approaches your domain on a dark horse. You will meet him soon, Heinrich. His heart is prim and proper, a virgin no doubt."

"Is he friend or foe?"

"A foe. It has been prophesied—he alone will claim the Spear from Hitler."

"But it cannot be. I have the right to the throne. I will be the next Führer!"

Think again, you fool. "Once this knight has the Spear, you must take it from him."

"Tell me this man's name!"

Weisthor touched one of the fallen silver rings. "I see the Spear. And upon its hollowed blade are engraved the words—The Infidel."

*   *   *

Berlin

Eva Kleist's fellow barmaids at the Bismarck looked weary—late nights and hangovers having taken their toll. Below the harsh lights of their dressing room, these young women painted and powdered their faces to attract tips from soldiers on leave. Feeling no less worn, Eva batted her way through the swinging doors. Closing her eyes, she leaned back against the wall.

She remembered the night that Ernst Teschler walked into her life. His eyes were the brilliant color of river sand under a thin gloss of water, expressive and gentle, and his square jaw and dimpled chin exuded strength. Perhaps he was too handsome. But then the rowdy sounds of soldiers' voices interrupted her private moment. To think she had three more hours to go.

"Long shift already?" Her friend Liesel took a draw from her cigarette.

"The nights in this place are endless." Eva pulled several Reichsmarks from her blouse and counted. "I thought you were going home early tonight."

"Ja, with whom?" Liesel exhaled into a halo of smoke.

"What about that blond captain at table thirteen?"

"I wouldn't have a chance." With a wrinkle of her nose, Liesel stabbed her cigarette several times into an ashtray.

Gretel pushed through the swinging doors, shaking her head. "Did you see that loudmouth at my corner table?" With a grimace, she lifted her short skirt, exposing her thigh. "My bottom is going to be black and blue from all his meaty pats and pinches!"

Herr von Haupstang, the Bismarck's owner, leaned his bald head out the office door. "Gretel, telephone!"

"An older gentleman, no doubt," Liesel mocked with a smile.

The other girls all laughed.

"Schnell, Gretel! I am not your social secretary." Haupstang held the door open.

"Ja, I'm coming." She stepped deftly past her boss to disappear into his office.

Eva wiggled her hips and trudged back through the swinging doors. "It's showtime!"

*   *   *

The impressive marquee lights of the Bismarck again greeted Ernst and Max when they arrived. Once inside the massive wooden doors, Ernst's eyes adjusted to the bright lights. The familiar aroma of dank cigarette smoke and schnapps surrounded him.

Max led the way to an empty table in the corner. "Say, isn't that your mystery lady over there?"

Ernst looked up and there she was. The diminutive young Rhine maiden was clearing empty steins from the table across the aisle. Her spun-gold hair draped around her alluring face.

Ernst was blind to every other woman in the room.

She turned and their eyes met.

"Good evening, Fräulein." Ernst tapped his friend on the shoulder. "Max, would you excuse us—please?"

With a knowing grin, Max tipped his hat. "Fräulein."

Eva casually strolled toward Ernst's table. "Fancy seeing you again."

"So, you do remember me."

"Such a handsome officer, how could I forget?"

He casually glanced at the puffed collar of her chiffon blouse and caught the faint scent of her perfume. "Now, what did you say your name was?"

"I didn't say. But my name is Eva, Eva Kleist."

"But, Fräulein, you told me you don't mingle with patrons."

"Those are house rules, but I do break a rule now and then."

"My friends call me Ernst."

She fingered the silver bars on his collar. "Lieutenant SS."

Ernst snatched her hand and held it in midair. "Eva . . . what a pretty name." With a gentle twist, he guided her onto the chair beside him.

Eva leaned forward and raised an eyebrow. "Names have stories, mein herr. Tell me yours."

Ernst glanced at the crowd. "In a raucous beer hall?"

She glanced up at the clock on the wall. "I get off early tonight, in a few hours."

"Then we will go have dinner at a very special place."

Eva reached out and caressed his hand. "I would like that very much."

*　　　*　　　*

The cabaret at the Rhineland Inn attracted sparse crowds after eleven o'clock. The inn was located a few blocks from the Bismarck, and Ernst appreciated the quaint and quiet establishment. He was in the mood for a private conversation. Its orchestra played popular dance music and an occasional jazz tune from America.

In step with the romantic melody, Eva melded into Ernst's arms as they glided across the dance floor. He led—she followed. He was taken captive by her alluring expressions as the rhythm of the beat moved her bosom and hips. His wire-framed spectacles were partially fogged by the heat of the moment.

"Where did you learn to dance, Herr Teschler?"

Ernst hesitated. "My mother trained me as a boy, then I took formal lessons."

Eva gently laid her head upon Ernst's shoulder. "My, not only are you handsome but well cultured, too."

When the music subsided, the couple drifted off the wooden dance floor to their table in a dark corner. As Ernst held out her chair, he impulsively leaned over and kissed Eva full upon the lips.

She stroked her fingers across the nape of his neck, and her eyes held him spellbound.

Their waiter arrived. "Excuse me, sir, your champagne."

Ernst nodded.

"A Kessler vintage." The waiter popped the cork, poured the bubbly wine, and then disappeared.

With glasses in hand, Ernst and Eva tickled each other's ears with sweet nothings—into the early hours of the morning.

Chapter Eight

In the twilight of his dream, Ernst embraced Eva again at the cabaret. He buried his fingers in the silky tendrils of her blonde hair as their lips touched and touched again. The taste of her ruby lip gloss lingered as his endearing fantasy faded.

When he eased his eyes open, Barron sat panting by the side of his bed. For a few minutes, he lay there trying to recapture the romantic moment.

Ernst turned over and could sense Barron's eyes trained on the bedroom door. The door opened gingerly as Papa appeared.

"Good morning, son. You must have been out late last night."

Ernst stretched open his bleary eyes. "It's only nine o'clock."

"Come, I have made fresh coffee." His father's expression indicated something serious was on his mind.

Ernst braced himself. Would his father be lucid or condescending?

Ernst joined his father downstairs as he poured coffee for two. "Your mother is out on errands."

Ernst sipped the dark java. Like a breath of fresh air, the caffeine surged in his veins.

"Your uncle constantly carps about your future with the black coats. He tells your mother how he will manage your career." His father's coffee cup trembled ever so slightly.

"I serve the Fatherland!"

"Ernst, the SS and the Gestapo—they are not like the military. They kill Germans. Many of our people are poor with little education. Most do not come from pure Aryan bloodlines, but we are still Germans."

"Uncle Reinhard says—"

"This is *not* about Uncle Reinhard. It's about you, Ernst! You have honor, integrity. You have ethics. You bear the Teschler name. You must take a stand sometime. If they win you and your compatriots over, all is lost!"

"Papa, you place me in an impossible position."

His father clasped Ernst's arm. "I do *not* believe in Heydrich's sordid cause. But without question, I do believe in you. When the truth behind the SS is revealed, I know you will do the right thing."

Ernst stood. "I will be a good German. I will do my duty."

Papa rose from his chair. "Nobility comes at a price. Forge your own path!" He tenderly embraced Ernst.

*   *   *

SS headquarters was centrally located at 8 Prinz-Albrechtstrasse. The imposing five-story stone building was crowned by gabled windows. Walking past a line of parked Mercedes sedans, Ernst went in the main entrance and walked up two flights of marble stairs. Ushered into his uncle's office, he was welcomed by the sounds of a Wagnerian sonata.

A master violinist, Reinhard's fingertips danced elegantly upon the strings as his bow resonated each note with precision. Following a dramatic crescendo, he brushed a subtle tear from his cheek.

Ernst was touched by his uncle's sentimentality. His uncle could play the strings of the human heart with one stroke of his bow and pierce it with his rapier the next.

"Wagner was a genius. Only a true German could have produced such a perfect melody." Reinhard gingerly placed his violin in a polished wooden case.

"It's good to see you, Uncle."

"Do have a seat, Ernst." Reinhard opened a file on his desk. "By the end of the month, you and Sergeant Schumann will report to Bernau about a half hour north of Berlin. The technical school there is a front for SS foreign document production and covert operations. Major Alfred Neame will supervise your training in espionage, hand-to-hand combat, and sabotage. At all times, you will observe the strictest of SS discipline."

"I shall do my best."

"So you should. The SS is preparing the Aryan aristocracy to lead the masses in new Germany. Everyone will be watching your progress closely, including this man." Reinhard passed a photograph to Ernst.

Ernst widened his eyes. "Heinrich Himmler. Reichsführer SS!"

"You will meet with him personally this Friday. Everything I'm about to tell you must never leave this room."

Ernst nodded. State secrets would be a feather in his cap.

"The Führer has enemies inside the Wehrmacht. I have been ordered to expose these army officers, and you are my chosen instrument."

"Yes, sir."

"This new security unit will hunt down enemies of the state. You will be introduced to the upper echelons of power. Eventually, with the SS and Gestapo, you will lead *the* elite counterespionage force inside Germany."

"But, sir, why me?" There had to be an ulterior motive.

"If anything should happen to me, my two boys are too young to take my place. Until then, you are my chosen heir."

Ernst cocked his head to the side. So he was to be a glorified place-holder for his uncle's sons.

*   *   *

Westphalia, April 1939

Having been inducted into the SS counterespionage division, Ernst, Max, and Barron headed west toward Hannover by rail. The military transport carried a full platoon up into the Harz Mountains. As the caravan of rustic steel thrust into a dark cavernous tunnel hewn from solid limestone, Ernst felt the crush of the young Wehrmacht soldiers around him. Thrilled to be traveling under sealed orders, he was confident that the Teschler trio would prove their brave mettle in the cut-throat ranks of the SS.

When the train emerged from the rocky cavern, Ernst squinted at the bright sun as the majestic mountain range stretched out into the distance. With each hour, the steady rhythm of the metal wheels beneath them slowed as the angle of their ascent grew steeper. Brilliant spring foliage speckled the scattered mountainous peaks.

Later that day, an SS car awaited their arrival at the Bielefeld train station. Barron pressed his snout through the open window as they sped through the rolling hills toward the town of Paderborn. Ernst could sense his dog's pleasure as the brisk air rustled across the short hairs of his face. Across a small valley, a medieval fortress emerged, its silhouette cast against the late-afternoon sky. A relic of the past, its stone profile grew larger as they drew near.

From the rear seat, Ernst eyed the driver's face through the rearview mirror. "Sir, they call it Wewelsburg Castle. Its location—even its existence—is a state secret."

"So I have been told."

Ernst and Max exchanged knowing glances.

The sedan rounded the last bend, crossed a stone bridge, and passed through the imposing stone-arched gates of the castle. An SS officer saluted the entourage, then opened the rear door. "Herr Teschler, the Reichsführer is expecting you. Sergeant Schumann will stay in the south tower until summoned."

Ernst and Max stood by the car. Ernst's gaze scaled the weathered stone walls, three stories tall. The courtyard was bordered by stark medieval statues painting a gothic portrait laced with shadows.

"Heil Hitler! This way, mein herr." Two guards escorted Ernst and Max through massive oak doors into an enormous foyer, five meters high. They continued beyond, and at every point, a mere glance at a guard solicited an immediate salute. He could sense their respect—or was it fear?

At a certain point, Max and his escort were led down a different hall. The echo of their footsteps faded as they disappeared.

Ernst's guide cued him to follow as they climbed a maze of wooden stairs leading to the third floor. They were greeted by the sound of a muffled phonograph recording of a familiar Haydn sonata. At the end of the hall, the adjutant opened the door. "The Reichsführer will see you now, Lieutenant Teschler."

A surge in the music's volume welcomed Ernst into a well-furnished office. Ernst surveyed the spacious chamber lined with tall oak book-shelves along the inner stone wall and three tall, arched, latticed windows facing west toward the setting sun. When the music stopped abruptly, the phonograph's tone arm skipped repeatedly across the record's core paper label. Ernst hurried across the room and moved the tone arm onto its bracket.

"Lieutenant Teschler, I presume," a soft monotone voice interrupted from behind a tall silk screen distinguished by a stalking oriental dragon.

Like a boy whose hand was caught in the cookie jar, Ernst pivoted and snapped to attention. "Heil Hitler!"

Heinrich Himmler lifted his hand in response as he gingerly replaced the record in its paper jacket. Himmler's beady eyes stared at him through pince-nez spectacles.

"It is an honor to be here, Herr Reichsführer."

"Indeed." The sound of his boot heels echoed across the wood floor as he made his way to an ornate bay window.

The remaining sunlight filtered through colored glass, painting the panes very much like the windows of a sacred chapel. Himmler was dressed in a precisely tailored black SS uniform, and his dark hair was almost shaved on the sides with a tuft of long hair layered on top.

"So, Heydrich speaks highly of his young nephew. And that's quite a compliment, coming from a legend."

"A legend, sir?"

"Yes, Heydrich is a legend, according to half of the SS Corps." With a fleeting smile, Himmler peered out the window. "Teschler, come—look at this magnificent view. In 1934, I selected this ninth-century castle to become the temple of the SS. This ancient fortress was renovated at a cost of millions of Reichsmarks. Today the three-story complex includes a twelve-thousand-volume library of Aryan lore, meeting rooms, an array of offices and guest quarters."

"Most impressive, mein herr." Ernst looked out through the lattice-paned glass. "The sun has painted a palette of beautiful colors today."

Himmler nodded. "Perhaps you are not just a warrior, but a poet? I consider Wewelsburg the spiritual center of the SS. We administer all SS units from our offices in Berlin, but it is here that the inner circle comes and meditates upon the supernatural—the power of life and death."

Ernst felt uneasy. "I don't understand."

"This complex is known by very few men even in the SS ranks. At the core of the SS is the Religion of the Blood, and we study the arcane secrets of our spiritual ancestors—those who've mastered the Black Arts."

"Secrets?"

"With knowledge comes power." Himmler narrowed his paper-thin eyelids. "Teschler, are you true to the Reich?"

Ernst lifted his head and thrust his shoulders back. "Sir, my honor is loyalty!"

The thick chamber door rotated open. "Good afternoon, Herr Teschler," a deep, raspy voice sounded. Startled, Ernst turned to face a rotund man with a bushy grey mustache. His face was puffy and ruddy. Looking near the age of sixty, he appeared quite out of place in his black SS uniform. "My name is Karl Wiligut, but you may address me as Weisthor."

The man's eyes were riveting. His irises were black rims bordering bluish-silver pools of light shimmering from within.

"Teschler, you will accompany Weisthor now," Himmler said. "He has something very special to discuss with you up in the north tower."

Ernst snapped a salute. "Heil Hitler!"

Himmler limply raised his hand.

*   *   *

A few hours later, Weisthor returned to Heinrich's office. "Tell me what the rings revealed about Teschler."

"He knows nothing of the Spear yet."

"But you said that he—"

"Yes, he is the Black Knight!"

Heinrich looked out the bay window. "That means that Heydrich's involved." *That man is a thorn in my flesh.*

"No, Teschler alone will take the Spear of Destiny from Hitler. But he is a young man with noble ideals."

Just what we need. "Then we must break him down, remold him into a cold, callused Aryan."

"Heinrich, Teschler must taste blood."

"Major Neame will see to that. But somehow, we must position young Teschler closer to Hitler."

"I am confident that when the signs align, Ernst Teschler will exchange the counterfeit spear for the original."

And then the Talisman of Power shall be mine.

*   *   *

Long past midnight, Ernst and Max were asleep in the south tower of Wewelsburg Castle. Max's soft snoring had lulled Ernst into a deep slumber. Then his dream began. . . .

At dawn, four SS soldiers marched through the corridor of Flossenbürg prison until they faced the clergyman's cell. One of the men seized the prisoner, shaking him awake.

The commanding officer checked his clipboard. "Dietrich Bonhoeffer, you have been sentenced to death. It is time to meet your God." The camp commandant stared at the condemned man with black, lifeless eyes. His SS soldiers cinched the prisoner's hands behind him with worn leather straps and dragged Dietrich barefoot out of the cell and across the concrete hallway and out to the stone courtyard.

Joining a parade of six naked prisoners, Dietrich and the other condemned men mounted the wooden scaffolding. They stood upon the gallows guilty as charged. Dietrich looked at his comrades. Trembling from fear and the frigid morning air, they looked to him for solace and a ray of hope.

The commandant watched as the executioner tightened a loop of piano wire around Dietrich's neck. Strangely calm, Dietrich looked up at the rising sun with a childlike expression.

The commandant read his orders. "Reverend Dietrich Bonhoeffer, you have been found guilty of conspiracy against the Reich. You have been condemned by the People's Court in Berlin. By the authority of the Führer, I sentence you to death by hanging for your treasonous crimes against the people of Germany.' Do you have any last words?"

Dietrich's eyes were confident. "God has been with me in this life, so shall He welcome me into heaven this very hour. Sir, for all the lives you have taken, only God can forgive you."

The commandant shouted to the executioner, "Stop!"

As if he did not hear, the executioner grasped the wooden lever. The trapdoor sprung and Dietrich's body plummeted into space, pulled taut, and swayed back and forth.

The commander's screams thundered through time. . . .

Ernst twisted back and forth in bed. Half asleep, he cried out, "Were you there? Did you see my friend? His eyes! Did you see my friend's eyes?"

Max roused slowly, then rushed over to him. "Wake up! Ernst, it's just a nightmare."

"It happened too quickly. His neck snapped and his dead body swayed back and forth. But it was his eyes. . . . They never stopped staring at me." Ernst swung his legs over the edge of the bed in a silent haze, then he extended both of his hands and rubbed them with a frenzy. He took his bedsheet and wiped off his hands several times.

Max blinked. "What are you doing?"

"I went under the gallows and tried to lift his body. His blood dripped all over my hands. Can't you see?"

"What did they do to you today?"

"Weisthor told me that I will have to prove my loyalty. He wants me to steal the Spear of Longinus."

"Longinus has a spear?" Wide-eyed, Max just stared at him.

Ernst took a breath. His dream about the gallows was not real.

"Weisthor took me to one of the towers. There was a black stone table and three large silver rings. . . . Then I heard a strange voice—and everything became a haze."

Max leaned closer. "Look at your ring."

Ernst stared at his right hand. His silver Death Head's ring had been modified with two rubies bordering the skull-and-crossbones insignia. He had seen those stones before.

Max slipped back into bed. "You've had a bad nightmare and you are upset."

"Both Himmler and Weisthor have the same Death's Head ring encrusted with rubies."

Max shook his head as he dove under the covers. "Friend, we need to leave this place—and soon."

Palms down, Ernst stared at his hands and the ruby-red SS ring. Then a chill gripped his spine as a red substance dripped upon his sheet. He rotated his hands.

Blood had coated his palms.

Chapter Nine

Berlin

Ernst and Max dozed most of the way through Hannover and on to Berlin. The sound of the train whistle signaled their arrival at the station. Anticipating his master's move, Barron flexed his powerful legs, which made their way down onto the platform amidst a sea of faces surging off the train. Fellow passengers scurried out of the Doberman's way as they walked through the bustling terminal. At the baggage entrance, they found a black Mercedes parked.

Ernst recognized Major Neame. He was square-faced with black hair greased back over his ears. Despite his crooked nose, he might have been a pleasant-looking person if he smiled. He and his companion were both dressed in black trench coats and fedoras.

"Reporting as ordered, sir," Max saluted.

"Gentlemen, this is Sergeant Biedermann."

With a nod, Biedermann fetched their luggage. An icy silence prevailed as their sedan sped thirty-five kilometers northeast of Berlin. Eventually, they arrived at the suburban campus of the Bernau Technical School.

Neame led them to the administration building. "Welcome to Bernau. It appears to be a respectable engineering school, but inside, the SS operates one of the most sophisticated counterespionage programs in Europe. In the mornings, you will attend classes in cryptography, documents, and communications. In the afternoons, Sergeant Biedermann and I will supervise you in hand-to-hand combat, small arms, and explosives."

"How long will we train here?" Ernst asked.

"Six months, maybe less. General Heydrich tells me you learn quickly. You will bunk here during the week and return to Berlin over weekends."

"The women at the Bismarck know us well," Max smiled.

Biedermann laughed. "They may not think you're so handsome after we get through with you."

Ernst narrowed his eye. *And where will you be when Barron gets through with you?*

In the ensuing weeks, Ernst and Max explored the methods of espionage, studied cryptanalysis, and were certified in radio communications. They memorized multiple cipher systems and transmission protocols. Neame lectured them daily in the art of deception in the war of intelligence.

Ernst and Max wore a different uniform in the afternoons—black-and-blue fatigues. Military instructors punched, kicked, and drilled both men across the athletic fields. Then came knife combat with limited padding. The school doctors kept busy patching the trainees with stitches and ice. Max's favorite evening reprieve was soaking in an ice bath. Quickly, Ernst and Max built strength, stamina, and a keen eye on the pistol and rifle ranges.

A month into training, Neame called the men to the gymnasium. "Gentlemen, I wear the standard SS uniform. Biedermann has hand-cuffed my hands behind me. With your boxing gloves, I want you to beat me bloody."

Ernst bit into his mouth guard. He had a very bad feeling about this.

Max slapped his gloves together. "Major, I will treat you to an ice bath tonight—sir!"

Neame donned an insidious grin. "Schumann, you dance in the ring like a schoolboy. Are you a pansy?"

Max shuffled in for a jab but never saw Neame's foot sweep striking his knee from the side. With a yelp, Max landed on his side in agony.

Ernst gauged the distance and stepped into the fray. If he could narrow the strike zone. . . . Then he shuffled toward his opponent sideways. "That was not fair play."

"Pitch your ethics out with the garbage. Come on, Teschler, I will show you who is the master race!"

Ernst used his arms to block three kicks, but then Neame leaped into the air and swiped the ball of his foot across Ernst's jaw. Ernst felt a snap and his whole body spun, launching headlong onto the mat. Blood filled his battered mouth.

Ernst raged inside at his superior. The man simply was not to be trusted.

"That, gentlemen, is Savate. A little-known style of French kickboxing. I will teach you the forms, and you will master the techniques. Schumann, get some ice for your friend, then it's your turn."

A week later, Biedermann revealed a typewriter-like device encased in a wooden box. "The Enigma cipher was developed in 1923. The device encodes messages one letter at a time for later transmission by telegraph or radio. Each time an operator presses a key, an electrical impulse signals an encrypted letter and turns a mechanical rotor. With thousands of encoded combinations, it is impossible to understand the message unless the receiver possesses a similar device and the same code book."

In the operations center, Ernst stood by an SS operative who was translating an encoded message. The man ripped a page from his tablet. "Sir, by these coordinates, it looks like U-237 has confirmed a kill in the North Sea. A supply ship an hour out of port."

Neame stepped in and opened the code book. "Our wolf packs prowl the sea lanes of England unfettered. This unit requires two operatives—one keys in the code while the other records incoming messages.

Gentlemen, you have four weeks to memorize this process. Whoever fails the test will face me in the ring."

*　　*　　*

Ernst and Max battled in the boxing ring. Ernst feinted with his shoulder, then jabbed with his left fist. Max practically swallowed Ernst's leather glove. Pure adrenaline hammered each punch home. Max lifted his left glove to block a roundhouse punch, then pivoted 270 degrees and thrust a back kick into Ernst's exposed chest.

Ernst felt like his lungs had imploded as he caved to his knees. He wheezed to catch his breath as Max smacked his gloves together, egging him on.

"Come on, Ernst. Don't be a wimp. Get up!"

"Good move, Schumann," Neame shouted from the corner of the ring, "but why did you stop? When your opponent is down, always finish him off."

Max took his cue. As Ernst lifted a knee to stand, Max delivered a fluid roundhouse kick. Ernst twisted into the air and crashed to the floor. With his head glued to the mat, Ernst glared at Neame, cursing under his breath. His side aching, Ernst could taste the blood streaming from his battered lips.

"Savor the moment, Teschler. It will sweeten your aggression when you fight me next week."

"Come on, Ernst." Max offered his hand.

Neame picked up a towel. "Teschler, how did you ever graduate from Bad Tölz?"

With labored breath, Ernst climbed to his knees. "By fighting by the rules, Major."

"There is only one rule in the SS—kill or be killed. Understood?" Neame shouted the last word as he threw the towel to Max and turned to leave. "School is out early today. Clean up for the ladies."

Ernst watched Neame walk away. "Max, one day I'm going to beat him to a pulp."

Max handed him the blood-streaked towel. "You'd better kill him before he kills you."

*   *   *

Berlin

One Friday afternoon, Ernst stood in the Zion Lutheran Church. Adjacent to the main sanctuary stood the chapel. The room was encircled by twelve stained-glass windows. They displayed historical scenes from creation to the crucifixion, along with biblical citations. Pleased with himself, Ernst was able to quote some of the biblical phrases by memory. Pastor Bonhoeffer had been an ardent taskmaster during his confirmation classes in his youth. Echoing footsteps down the hall announced Reverend Bonhoeffer.

"Hello, Ernst, I'm sorry for the delay."

"Herr Bonhoeffer, thank you for seeing me on short notice."

"You are no longer a boy. Please call me Dietrich."

"I must confess that I attend services rarely."

"Your SS activities must keep you occupied. Your call sounded urgent. What brings you to Zion Church?"

"The newspapers called it the 'night of broken glass.' The SS was involved."

"'For all have sinned and fall short of the glory of God.' God knows our hearts, Ernst."

"Sir, the images of the burning synagogues and screaming victims are vivid memories for me. I still can hear their pleas for mercy."

"Tell me what happened that night."

"We attacked the Jews. I looked for residents to intervene, but they retreated into their warm, safe homes. Ordinary citizens rioted and beat innocent human beings, then came my turn. There I was, a soldier under orders. My superior lit the fuse of the firebomb, then he gave me the order. 'My honor is loyalty' rolled off my lips. It sounds so hollow when I say it now."

Ernst looked down and slowly shook his head. "It was a beautiful synagogue with gorgeous stained-glass windows just like this church. But when the order came . . . in the name of the Third Reich, I burned it down."

"God's people were harmed or killed that night. Have you come to confess your sins? For only God can forgive you."

"It was a house of God, Pastor. Forgiveness? I can imagine forgiveness for that one night, but we are about to begin a war. How many times shall I be forgiven for what I am about to do?"

Dietrich furrowed his eyebrows. "What are you saying?"

"I read reports all day long. Orders come down from SS Command. And there are rumors." His hands began to tremble.

Whatever dark thoughts he had choked him. With the force of will, he pushed them out of his mind.

Tears welled up in Ernst's eyes. He reached out and embraced his childhood pastor. Over Dietrich's shoulder, Ernst gazed up at the chapel's last stained-glass window that depicted the crucifixion. His eyes were strangely drawn to the face of Jesus on the cross. Etched in glass, the Hebrew's features morphed into a gallery of soulful Hebrew faces.

"Saul, Saul, why do you persecute me?"

*   *   *

General Heydrich's office was secluded upon the third floor of SS headquarters in Berlin. Ernst sat patiently as his uncle flicked an index card he was holding with his finger. "Now then, tell me about Fräulein Kleist."

A gnawing concern captured the moment. Uncle Reinhard had spies stationed everywhere. Ernst shifted in his seat and displayed a calm expression. "Eva is a barmaid at the Bismarck. I've seen her a few times over the last few months."

"You've met the young woman ten times to be precise." Reinhard paused. "Ernst, you work for the foremost intelligence service in the world. It is my job to know about your associations. Now, who are her parents?"

"She has never mentioned them."

"And you've never inquired?"

"Her papers state her home to be Vienna—and that she moved to Berlin in '37."

Reinhard glided out of his chair and around his desk. He flicked the index card again. "The Reich is based upon the concept of pure blood. We routinely check family lineage back at least—"

"Three generations." Ernst recited from memory. "Yes, sir."

"You will be expected to marry eventually, Ernst. Fräulein Kleist is a beautiful woman. If she was a mere dalliance, her parentage would not matter. But I know you, son. You rarely look at a woman's thighs but gaze into her eyes and heart. If Fräulein Kleist becomes a matter of your heart, then it is imperative that she be of pure blood." He presented the card to his nephew. "You will continue our investigation into this woman."

"Yes, sir."

"Remember, Ernst. Your honor—"

"My honor is loyalty!"

Reinhard placed his arm around Ernst's shoulder. "Come, we will join Himmler and the others downstairs."

In the SS banquet hall, a dozen of Himmler's highest-ranking SS officers laughed and joked over drinks. Ernst overheard Himmler's comment about the "Jewish problem," followed by a few chuckles.

"Reinhard, I see you brought your young protégé," Himmler said.

Ernst could feel all eyes upon him as they shook hands. He experienced a measure of nobility. Here stood legendary figures of the Reich. He had a thousand questions but not enough courage to ask.

As the liquor gradually relaxed him, he laughed with more vigor at their insensitive jokes. And through it all, Ernst felt the eyes of Heinrich Himmler watching him, ever vigilantly. Himmler circulated among his colleagues and then departed.

Reinhard leaned closer to Ernst. "Well, are you impressed?"

"Sir, I am overwhelmed."

"You belong here, Ernst. Soon, I will make you an SS aristocrat."

Ernst was extremely pleased with himself. *If only Eva could see me now.*

*   *   *

Bernau Technical School

With a darting feint, Ernst bounced off the boxing ring ropes. He squeezed down on his mouthpiece just as Neame's leather-gloved hand hammered his jaw. The impact spun him up on his toes, but he broke the fall with quick footwork. Sweat and blood seasoned his tongue.

Neame pitched a wry grin. "Nice catch, Teschler." Like a stork, the Savate master craned his leg and thrust the ball of his foot toward his opponent's stomach. Ernst pivoted as Neame's foot ricocheted off of flesh.

Ernst hooked his left arm under his opponent's leg and flipped him up into the air. Neame's shoulder blades slammed onto the mat.

Dazed but for a moment, Neame caught his breath. "Excellent move."

With a nod, Ernst offered to assist Neame off the mat. When in range, Neame hooked his right foot behind Ernst's ankle and compressed Ernst's kneecap with the other, knocking him down on his back. Rolling up to his knees, then with the side of his glove, Neame popped Ernst in the groin.

Ernst's whole body convulsed as the pain radiated through his paralyzed limbs. His eyes bulged in tears as he spied a wicked gleam in Neame's eyes.

"As I've told you many times, now you will remember. When your opponent is down, always finish him off. Show no mercy!"

Ernst rolled into a fetal position as the pain surged through his body. *The next time we meet, I will be sure never to forget!* Then he slipped into blackness.

Chapter Ten

Zössen, Germany, May 1939

Anxious to discover the fate of her family during Kristallnacht, Sarah Kleisfeld had taken a train to the town of Zössen, twenty-eight kilometers south of Berlin. Given the fickle spring weather, she wore a high-collar grey wool sweater beneath a brown canvas raincoat. Her blonde hair was swept back into a loosely braided chignon. Tussled by the wind, she entered the house of Dr. Hans Ehrenberg. Her stomach rumbled at the sweet aroma of something baking in the kitchen. Below her black-rimmed spectacles, Sarah posted a pleasant smile.

Elsa Ehrenberg was a pleasant, plump woman in her floral housedress. "Fräulein Kleisfeld, how good of you to come. Your cousin has been our guest this week." The matron of the house led Sarah into the living room. "I will leave you two alone to visit."

Saul Avigur gave Sarah a warm embrace. "You were a hard woman to locate. When I sent word, I wasn't sure you would come."

"How did you find me?" Sarah's words were tentative. Her efforts to hide her new life had obviously failed.

"The Haganah has friends everywhere. And your father asked me for help. It's too dangerous for Jews to stay in Germany. Anyway, I'm afraid I have bad news."

Sarah sat on the edge of the sofa. "Is it Mama? She has a bad heart and never sees a doctor."

"Your mother is fine. It's your brother, Aaron. I'm sorry to tell you . . . he is dead."

Saul's mouth moved, but she could not hear his next words. When she swallowed, her stomach threatened to rebel. Sarah leaned back on the sofa. "Of course, you're joking. Aren't you?"

Saul's somber eyes said it all. "He was killed by Brownshirts on Kristallnacht."

Sarah curled both legs up on the couch as she embraced herself. "Papa would have protected him. Papa will tell you where to find Aaron."

"Your father is a fugitive of the SS. Before he fled, he asked me to bring you home, Sarah. It's a long story, but we have to get you and the whole family out of Germany."

"Why? Because my family are Jews? Germans hate Jews! And now they kill Jews. Well, I have a life in Berlin. A respectable job. And a German man who cares about me. I'm safe, because I am not a—"

"But, Sarah, you are a Jewess."

Her rage simmered. It was as if her cousin were a complete stranger. "How dare you say such a thing."

Saul reached out to her, but Sarah slapped him in the face. Then she cradled her head in her hands. "I didn't say goodbye to Aaron before I left home. I told him I would see him over the holidays." She shook her head. All of it was a lie. "I lied to my little brother."

"I'll take you back home to your parents. You are all they have left in this world."

"How dare you call me a Jewess!" Stone-faced, Sarah rushed out of the house in a huff. She ran down the street when her tears overtook her.

It was a lie. Papa would never let anything happen to his favorite child.

*   *   *

Berlin

Dedicated to St. Anne, the Dahlem village church had been built of stone with its late Gothic chancel dating back to the fifteenth century. Within the Dahlem Synod, fear and tempers had embroiled the Confessing Church. To take a stand against Adolf Hitler had its perils.

Dietrich Bonhoeffer stood before thirty pastors gathered in the parish hall. Some stood silently, while others fidgeted nervously in their seats. He stood at the podium with his hand held high, signaling the crowd to take their seats.

"Dietrich, it is such a bold move to meet here. The Gestapo is everywhere."

"Will the Confessing Church protect our congregations and our families against madness?" another pastor asked.

Dietrich stepped beside the podium. "We must take a stand against the Nazi persecution. I am convinced that God will strengthen us to endure."

"It was Himmler's order that disbanded your seminary at Finkenwalde a few years ago," another cleric said.

Dietrich cringed inside at the terror of that raid by the Gestapo. The Nazis had released everyone with a collar of constant fear. "Indeed, we have placed our calling and our very lives at risk. And yet here we stand in this church resolute to our convictions."

A young man stood. "Where is Koenig?"

"The army drafted him last month," someone in the back replied.

"The Reich military has already drafted seven of our colleagues, and they have shipped them into harm's way," another voice interjected.

The momentary silence was broken when the door at the back of the hall burst open. Like tightly wound springs, every head whirled around. Dietrich held his breath until he recognized Dr. Friedrich Perels.

The thin, balding legal adviser to the Confessing Church made his way down the aisle, tossed his overcoat over a chair, and opened his briefcase. His green eyes flashed as he waved the Lutheran *Gazette*. "Gentlemen, the Reich Church has gone too far!"

Contagious banter crossed the room.

"Bishop Werner has demanded that all pastors in Germany take a loyalty oath. This is what it says:

"I swear that I will be faithful and obedient to Adolf Hitler, the Führer of the German Reich, that I will conscientiously observe the laws and carry out the duties of my office, so help me God.

"Anyone who refuses to take the oath of allegiance is to be dismissed from the Reich Church."

"They will take our salaries?"

"That's not all, gentlemen. This advance copy goes to press tomorrow morning." Dr. Perels read aloud. "'Mein Führer, in a great historic hour I have instructed all the pastors of the German Evangelical Church, obeying an inward command and experiencing joyful hearts, to take the oath of loyalty to our Führer and Reich. One God—one obedience in the faith. Heil Hitler!' It is signed, the Reich Bishop."

A flash of anger burned across Dietrich's face.

A colleague in front stood. "This is a mockery. And to think that Hitler appointed a Nazi attorney as bishop of Christ's church!"

Reverend Albertz approached the podium. "Dr. Bonhoeffer, we cannot go against these people. They are arresting Christian dissidents by the hundreds."

"What are you suggesting?" Pastor Bohm's face was beet red. "That we sign this oath—and join the Nazi church?"

Dr. Perels held his hand up. "Listen to me. This document is a line drawn in the sand. Individually, you must pray and make a decision. They will use your signature to mislead others and use them against you. But if you do not sign, you will pay the price."

Dietrich shook his head. "How in good conscience can we support Hitler's regime when it declares war on God?"

"I would agree, Herr Bonhoeffer," a loud, harsh voice bellowed from the back of the hall. Everyone turned to take a look. There stood a tall, lean man dressed in a black leather coat. "Our Führer has declared war on your petty Confessing Church."

A squad of seven Gestapo agents quietly made their way down the side aisles of the lecture hall, fanning out to secure the room. The clergymen froze at the sight of the invaders all dressed in black.

The Gestapo leader marched to the lectern. "You are aware that any meeting of the Confessing Church is strictly forbidden without proper authorization. We now take you into custody for questioning. But since you are clergy, we will treat you with Christian charity."

A deadly silence followed each man as they were herded through the church's back door and onto a darkened bus parked in the alley. The Nazis had used these kinds of buses to take Jews to the concentration camps. When an elderly pastor in front of Dietrich stumbled, a Gestapo man dragged him into the bus by his collar and shoved him into a bench seat.

Dietrich intervened. "Sir, we are complying with your orders."

"Silence!" As if removing a gnat, the Gestapo man slapped Dietrich with the back of his hand. "Speak only when spoken to!"

With blood seeping from his lip, Dietrich witnessed terror sweeping the faces of the detainees. Regret plagued Dietrich's heart. Despite all warnings, he had organized the meeting.

We are like lambs to the slaughter.

He wiped the perspiration from his brow. Dietrich could only imagine the insidious torture awaiting them at Gestapo headquarters.

*   *   *

Later that evening in the Bonhoeffer parlor, the ornate cherry grandfather clock chimed the nine o'clock hour. Dietrich's sister, Sabine Leibholz, played a sonata upon their grand piano as her mother and her husband, Gerhard, sat and listened.

Her mother followed the melody as she properly sipped her tea. "Sabine, you play with such sensitivity. Just like Dietrich."

Sabine ended the piece with a few final chords and looked at the clock, then her mother. "Dietrich did say he was coming home for dinner?"

Gerhard lit a cigarette. "But that was two hours ago."

"He is always late." *That's my brother for you.*

Mother placed her saucer on the table. "When Dietrich and you were born, neither your father nor I expected twins, but there you were."

As birth twins, they were two peas in a pod. "And I have followed his lead ever since."

The front door chimes rang, and one of the servants went into the foyer.

Sabine stood. "That's probably him now. You'll see. He will have his tail between his legs with some lame excuse for being late, Mother."

Dietrich appeared at the entrance to the parlor. His three-piece suit was disheveled, and perspiration and blood stained his open collar. He flinched as he slowly removed his overcoat and walked toward the sofa. When he turned, the bright lights revealed a fresh bruise across his cheekbone.

Mother gasped. "Good night! Son, what happened?"

Dietrich collapsed onto the plush sofa with Sabine close at hand. She probed just below the black-and-blue contusion. "It looks as if you got into a cat fight, and the cat won!"

Dietrich laughed and then gasped in pain.

Trained as an attorney, Gerhard stood nearby and asked questions as if Dietrich were on the witness stand. "What was the name of the person who did this to you?"

"The Gestapo arrested all of us—at the church. I don't recall names. Over thirty pastors were hauled to a police station. For six hours they interrogated us. No food, no water, and worse—no bathrooms."

Gerhard retrieved a small notebook from this coat. "Did they press charges?"

Sabine opened a decanter and poured some red wine into a glass. "Here, drink some of this. You look like you need it."

"No formal charges. We were detained for a few hours, when a Gestapo man discovered that Pastor Ehrenberg had Jewish blood. He whipped the poor man with his pistol. When I tried to stop the thug, he turned on me." Dietrich touched his swollen cheek.

Gerhard's eyes widened. "Did they ask about me?"

"Nothing about your Jewish ancestry. They must already know that you married into our family."

Sabine stood by her husband. Their blended marriage had stood the test of time. "Dear, we may have to leave Germany."

Dietrich emptied his wineglass and winced. "Let's not jump to hasty conclusions. There were too many witnesses at the station. With a stern warning, they released us. Unfortunately, I have been ordered to leave Berlin."

Her face reddening, their mother stood and stomped her foot. "Berlin is your home!"

"Don't worry, Mother. I will call the countess. I have a standing invitation to stay at her estate in Pomerania."

"But the northern coast is so far away. How could you get yourself in such trouble with the Gestapo?"

"By taking a stand, Mother. Don't worry. In Pomerania I can take the spotlight off of our family."

Sabine couldn't resist the urge for a little sibling needling. "Brother, I must say—I hope that Nazi's face looks worse than yours."

*   *   *

Zössen, Germany, Midnight

A black Mercedes sedan circled the town square and screeched to a halt in front of the local police station. Two Gestapo agents dragged Reverend Hans Ehrenberg out of the car, up the stone steps, and into the building. Facing the two policemen on duty, Hans recognized one of his parishioners. The middle-aged policeman behind the counter stood red with embarrassment. The Gestapo agents shoved Hans down a narrow staircase and into a small, dimly lit room in the basement.

There was a pleasant-looking bald man seated at the end of a long table. He presented the most polite smile.

"My name is Franz Schmidt—Gestapo."

Hans squirmed in the hands of his Nazi captors. What the Gestapo did to Jews was common knowledge. "But your people released me in Berlin just yesterday. I have done nothing."

"Herr Ehrenberg, it is only one o'clock in the morning. I promise that I will deliver either you or your remains to your wife by sunrise."

Hans shuddered. Would these thugs go to his home and terrorize his wife?

"Your papers say you have been pastor of the Lutheran church in Zössen for six years, and yet we know you were born a Jew."

The very word stuck in Hans's throat. He darted his gaze from side to side. "I was converted to Christianity twenty years ago, in Munich."

"So you say. The blood of your race convicts you. Religious beliefs are of no consequence. We understand other Jews have infiltrated the Reich Church. Tell us their names and addresses."

Just the sound of the officer's sinister voice sent shivers down Hans's spine. His fear told him that any person he revealed would be sent to a detention camp or simply disappear into the night. It wasn't fear but his faith in God that compressed his lips in silence.

"Now, Herr Ehrenberg, I am a very talented man. I have invented a device that will help your memory. Guards, take off his handcuffs."

Released from the cold steel manacles, Hans's hands tingled as he felt the blood flow back into his fingers. One of the agents lifted the lid off the heavy wooden box on the table. Hans froze when he saw the blood-stained sections cut out for a man's hands and fingers.

His jaw dropped. "O Lord, have mercy!"

"Yes, I'm sure God will help you remember the names of your Jewish colleagues—and so will my 'memory box.'"

The agents forced Hans into a chair and his fingers through the brackets. They secured his hands with leather straps with all ten fingers exposed. Herr Schmidt opened his satchel and slowly revealed a series of surgical instruments, one at a time.

The sight of Herr Schmidt's metal pincers with serrated teeth tore through Hans's last vestige of courage. In a panic, he jerked his arms and hands against his restraints but to no avail.

"Now, Herr Ehrenberg, I will ask you questions and you will provide me names."

Hans's head began to swim.

"For silent responses, I will insert this thin rod beneath your fingernails. If you lie to me, then I will sever your fingers, one knuckle at a time." Herr Schmidt slowly waved the pincers before Hans's cowering eyes, then snapped them shut, grunting cruelly for effect. "Shall we begin the game?"

*　　*　　*

Northern Germany, A Week Later

The train chugged northeast to Stettin less than half full. Dietrich was busily writing upon his worn leather briefcase in his lap. He paused to look out the window at the passing beauty of the German countryside. There he sat, exiled from Berlin, and yet the promise of spring in Pomerania brought him some solace. In between regular vibrations of the train wheels below, he furiously scribbled his words.

Across from him sat his colleague Friedrich Perels. "What are you writing?"

"I am drafting a circular letter to my students and colleagues."

The church lawyer retrieved a file from his briefcase. "By last count, the Gestapo has arrested twenty-seven of our pastors."

"Since the state suspended their salaries, their families will starve. I'm asking for a collection from Confessing Church members. Listen to this letter written by Bernard Riemer's mother."

I haven't yet come round to "Father, forgive them." You said not to worry. Your wife is brave and not one to be sorry for herself. On Sunday, Reverend Heider, too, was arrested and taken away right after services. Now there will be no more services in Völpke. Heider knew the Gestapo was in the audience, but in his last sermon he said clearly what needed to be said. His last instruction to the congregation was that if no minister was available, the bell should not be rung nor services held.

"Hans Ehrenberg called a few days ago. Soon after the church raid at Dahlem, the Gestapo arrested and tortured him. They wanted the names of other Jewish pastors."

"What happened?" Perels asked.

Dietrich shook his head. "They mangled his hand. He needs our help, Friedrich. He has been approached by other Jews for assistance to leave the country."

"My colleagues in Berlin say the Nazis are allowing some to leave, but they'll need the proper documents—and money for bribes."

Dietrich's nostrils flared. He could not muzzle his anger. But then, an idea sparked. "Can we smuggle endangered colleagues out of Germany?"

"No, my friend. Illegal Jewish emigration, and the Office of Church Affairs will shut us down."

"Well, I have friends in high places." Dietrich squinted again at his letter. "Listen to this."

It is often difficult for us to grasp God's way with his Church. The Lord confers great honor on his servants when he brings them suffering. We must stand firm upon the truth of the Gospel. We must stand upon the rock of our faith in the midst of increasing adversity, even when we experience the unrelenting attacks by the forces of the Antichrist.

Perels's mouth gaped open. "Dietrich, you're not going to circulate that letter, are you?"

Chapter Eleven

Northern German Coast

As the grounds foreman drove their sedan across the rural roads, the shadow of the Gestapo grew small, then ceased to exist in Dietrich's mind. As they passed through the gates of Patzig, his colleague Dr. Friedrich Perels was visibly impressed by the beauty and the grandeur of the two Pomeranian estates owned by the Countess Ruth von Kleist-Retzow and her family.

Four kilometers inland, Dietrich spied the main manor house nestled in an orchard of trees fed by two flowing creeks. He had met the countess and the von Wedemeyers back in 1935 at the illegal Finkenwalde Seminary nearby. It had been a shock for all when the Gestapo closed the school in '37.

As the servants carried their bags upstairs, a maid escorted Dietrich and Friedrich through the two-story entrance hall into the spacious parlor. There the countess's daughter Grafi and her husband, Colonel von Wedemeyer, were playing cards. Dietrich was duly impressed that the retired colonel had been thrice decorated during the Great War. He knew more generals by first name than Hitler. His rugged face boasted a bristly handlebar mustache, and ever the outdoorsman, he was deeply tanned.

"Herr Doctor, come in!" The colonel stood to greet his guests.

Ruth von Wedemeyer was a tall, slim woman elegantly attired in an afternoon dress with a blue check print. Her brown hair hinted undercurrents of grey, and it twisted up into a bun reminiscent of the fashion of an earlier decade. She was called by her childhood nickname, Grafi.

Dietrich shook the colonel's hand. "I'm sorry we're late. We had delays at the train station." Dietrich kissed the back of Grafi's hand. "May I present my friend and colleague Dr. Friedrich Perels."

Just then Grafi's mother, the countess, swept into the room. "Dietrich, so wonderful to see you! Everyone has been reading your new book."

One look at the feisty matriarch made Dietrich smile. "Countess, you are too kind. The Gestapo man at the station said he read it too, but I don't think he is a fan."

Grafi crossed her arms. "The Gestapo?"

"Dr. Perels is the legal advisor to our Confessing Church committee."

Friedrich shook the colonel's hand. "Thank you for the kind invitation to your home. Dietrich speaks of you like family."

The countess approached a cushioned chair. "He is my adopted son, and—"

"She was my best student at the seminary," Dietrich said. "By the way, where are the children? They usually are the first to greet me."

The countess carefully spread her skirt as she sat down. "Maria took them to Neubrandenburg for the day. They will be back late tonight."

"I look forward to spending time with them. Especially Maria."

The colonel pulled the servant's cord. Grafi sat on the edge of the sofa like a seasoned hawk. "Dietrich, rumors say that you have stirred up a hornet's nest with the Gestapo in Berlin."

"Well, let's just say that I can no longer preach or teach in Berlin. Your invitation came at a very welcomed moment."

The countess chimed in with an adventurous grin. "Can you imagine our Dietrich standing up to the Gestapo? How exciting."

Grafi bit her lip. "I call it dangerous—and you endanger anyone with whom you associate."

"Dr. Bonhoeffer's duty is to God and the church," the colonel said. "As a soldier in the Great War, I can appreciate such a stand."

The maid interrupted to serve lemonade with biscuits.

"I am just saying Dr. Bonhoeffer's presence here will create questions, and by the wrong people." Only Grafi would bat Dietrich's faults to and fro like a cat with a ball of yarn.

Dietrich sat up uncomfortably in his chair. "Please, I care a great deal about your family. I certainly would do nothing to cause you harm."

The countess opened a book by her chair and read. "'Costly grace is the gospel grace which must be *sought* again and again and again, the gift which must be *asked* for, the door at which a man must *knock*. Such grace is *costly* because it calls us to follow, and it is *grace* because it calls us to follow *Jesus Christ*. It is costly, because it *costs* a man his life, and it is *grace* because it gives a man the only true life.'"

The countess lifted her glass of lemonade in toast. "Cheers to our author in residence, Dr. Dietrich Bonhoeffer."

Such devotion touched Dietrich, who had been embraced by the family for some years. For him, Patzig had become a little slice of heaven away from the chaos of Berlin.

*   *   *

Dietrich nursed a cup of coffee on the expansive stone porch at the rear of the Patzig manor house. The song of the nestled birds in concert with the wind chimes lifted his soul for morning prayers.

As if caught up by the wind, Maria von Wedemeyer whisked through the rear door across the stone porch and almost floated down the rear staircase to the garden path. Startled, Dietrich watched the vibrant young woman disappear into a thicket of tall, dense arborvitae without once glancing back.

With curiosity, Dietrich followed the lady of intrigue. Down the garden path he went until he reached an elaborate flower garden. He discovered Maria standing off to the side by a white-coated equestrian fence.

The sunlight painted two white horses a light pink as they grazed in the meadow. Walking along the border of the carefully manicured garden, she picked some tulips.

In the distance, Dietrich could hear the mares whinny. "*Guten Morgen*, Maria."

She looked up with a startled expression of delight. "Herr Bonhoeffer—Dietrich! It is wonderful to see you."

Her contagious smile radiated across her rosy cheeks. With her blonde hair in a bun, she looked at the world through bright blue eyes. Her spring-colored sundress flowed with the gentle breeze. Dietrich basked in her countenance.

"Grandmama told me I would find you here." Smelling the fragrance of the flowers in hand, she presented them as they both sat on a wooden bench.

His broad smile emerged. "They are wonderful. Your gift is so thoughtful."

"You know, when I was young, I used to play hide-and-seek here in the garden. My sisters and I would run down these hedgerows and kneel on the ground. Whoever was 'it' would search for what seemed like hours before they found us. I always looked forward to being caught."

Dietrich gazed into her eyes. "I remember a precocious teenage girl who once lived here at the manor house. Now I see a beautiful young woman."

Maria placed her fingers on his hand. "Dietrich, you flatter me."

His heart skipped a beat.

"Perhaps you've traveled all the way from Berlin to sample my delicious apple strudel?"

"Fräulein, you tempt me." He squeezed her hand. Upon the bench, it was almost as if she were raised upon a pedestal—to look, yes, but not to touch.

"There are times when we all need a secret place. A place to hide, and when it is time, a place to be found."

Dietrich stood and once more pressed the tulips to his face. "Patzig has become my secret place, a sanctuary away from the storms of life. And you, Maria—you are my fair lady of the manor."

Maria stood and offered Dietrich her hand. He gently kissed the back of it. "Shall we go back to the house and make some of your famous strudel?"

*   *   *

Berlin, the Rhineland Inn, May 1939

Colonel Hans Oster sat smoking a cigarette and nursing a half-empty glass at the bar. After twenty years in the military, he still maintained a chiseled physique—or so he imagined, taking another swig of beer. He waited until an unenthusiastic musician finished playing a melancholy tune, then departed.

Walking down the hall, he checked his watch. He waited two minutes, then entered a private room right on time. Stout logs blazed in the stone hearth. The flickering flames profiled two men seated at a table. "Good evening, gentlemen."

Hans von Dohnanyi stood. He was tall but quite thin, his face framed by wire-rimmed spectacles, and the chief counsel for German military intelligence. "Colonel Oster, may I present my brother-in-law, Dr. Dietrich Bonhoeffer."

Dietrich arose and extended his hand. "Hans has told me many good things about you, sir."

"Not too many, I hope. The Abwehr is a very private organization."

"Dietrich is well aware of the risk in meeting with you," Dohnanyi said.

Taking their seats, Hans sensed Bonhoeffer's eyes scrutinizing his every feature. "Dr. Bonhoeffer, we understand that you have many contacts abroad within church circles?"

"I have traveled throughout Europe for the last fifteen years. I held pastorates in both Barcelona and London before Hitler took control."

Dohnanyi lit a cigarette. "Dietrich knows leaders in both Catholic and Protestant churches."

Hans leaned closer. "I am the son of a Lutheran minister." Bonhoeffer reminded him so much of his father and the discipline of his misspent youth. "Herr Bonhoeffer, there are influential leaders in the military who do not agree with the Führer and his politicians."

Dietrich fingered the edge of his glass. "I understand that you want me to travel to England on your behalf?"

Hans leaned back in his chair. "I have read your writings and studied your police file. It is remarkable you are not already in prison."

"Many of my colleagues rot inside Nazi camps at Sachsenhausen and Dachau. But for the grace of God, I stand free—for the moment."

Hans dabbed his lips with a napkin. "If the Wehrmacht should depose the Führer, we must install a new government. This will require the direct support of England and France. Your friend the Bishop of Chichester can get word to Sir Anthony Eden of the English government. You have the perfect entrée and reason to make the necessary trips for church missions."

Dietrich raised his eyebrow. "But I've been formally banned from church contacts in Berlin. What makes you think I can travel outside the country?"

"We would employ you as an Abwehr agent," Dohnanyi said.

"We will even pay you a salary, Herr Bonhoeffer."

Dietrich looked at Hans. "You can do all of this?"

Hans looked at the crackling fire for a moment, then back at Dietrich. "Many civilians work as couriers and spies for our networks. The Gestapo has limited access to our records. But make no mistake, Doctor. What we are planning is clearly treason in the eyes of the Reich."

Dietrich's eyes widened. "This—is astonishing. You want me to be a spy." He turned to his brother-in-law. "But if I participate, then everyone in our family will be in danger."

Dohnanyi lowered his eyes. "Because of my involvement with the Abwehr, our family is already at risk."

Dietrich looked intently at Hans Oster. "There is one person I need to consult before I give you my answer."

"Oh?"

"Don't worry. I'm certain God won't tell the Nazis."

Hans sensed a playful edge to Dietrich's smile. "Well then, I hope we can do business together, Herr Bonhoeffer."

All three men stood and shook hands. Hans pondered the extraordinary clergyman as Bonhoeffer and Dohnanyi departed.

The Abwehr officer took his seat and stared at the flames flickering in the hearth. A gentle knock at the door introduced an older gentleman with two glasses in hand. Admiral Wilhelm Canaris was a short man with high cheekbones, giving him a noble look. He was dressed in a crème-colored wool sweater and blazer. Who would imagine this small, quiet man was the shrewd head of the Abwehr, one of the most effective intelligence agencies in Europe? His smooth facial features and thick silver hair were benign features that deceived both friend and foe alike.

Canaris placed both steins of beer on the table, then stepped over to the hearth, holding both hands to its radiant heat.

"These are strange times, Admiral."

Canaris turned his head. "How so?"

"Dohnanyi was right. Herr Bonhoeffer is suitable for our needs."

Canaris hesitated. "But can he be trusted?"

"The real question is: Can Bonhoeffer trust us?" The smoldering log crackled and discharged a burst of colors up the stone chimney. "He is a man of spirit and conscience. He won't join our effort until he perceives God's approval."

Canaris returned to take his seat. "How refreshing. Somebody in Germany actually still believes in God."

Hans glanced at his superior over the rim of his ceramic stein. His face reminded him of a kindly old grandfather.

Canaris shivered again and grimaced. "This beer is sour. Come, let's go back to my office and open one of my prized Spanish vintages."

*   *   *

Berlin, Bismarck Tavern

As Eva waited for the barman to fill her order, she brushed some lint off her favorite green Bavarian peasant dress with a laced front. The wide neckline and a low-cut blouse with short puffy sleeves would be sure to garner additional gratuities from rowdy patrons.

At eight o'clock Eva noticed three Wehrmacht soldiers sauntering through the tall double doors. The tall, gruff one in a grey uniform commandeered a table at the center of the hall by pushing two sailors out of their chairs. With an exchange of obscenities, the navy men retreated grudgingly to a table in the rear.

With a deep breath, Eva approached the ill-mannered trio. "Well, gentlemen, what's your pleasure?"

The leader eyed her from head to foot. "Steins for all my friends—your best beer." He ran his fingers across her hip. "Wait. My name is Siegfried. I'm looking for Ernst Teschler. Have you seen him tonight?"

Eva slapped his hand away. "Nein!" She slipped out of his reach and edged through the standing crowd to the far side of the bar where Max Schumann was joking with another barmaid.

She arrived in a huff. "Max, do you see those soldiers over there? With the big one in the middle?"

He squinted. "Oh, you mean Manfred Siegfried. He used to be in my squad."

"Well, he's looking for Ernst, and he doesn't sound friendly."

Max leaned aside for a better view. "Ernst won't be here for at least an hour. Why don't you deliver double steins? Make sure Siegfried and his men are well lubricated. I'll pay for it."

"What good will that—?" In a beat Eva caught on. "But you can't take them on alone."

Max wiped the testosterone off his brow. "It will be all over before Ernst arrives."

With that, Eva carried six steins filled to the brim over to the table. "Gents, I've brought extras, compliments of the house."

Siegfried's eyes were like clammy hands, waiting for the right moment. His boys began to drink enthusiastically. Thirty minutes later, Eva brought a third round. The men were just a little tipsy when Max arrived.

Siegfried wore a thin foam mustache. "Well, well. Max Schumann—SS black and a master sergeant to boot."

"Siegfried the Ox, who let you in here?"

"Now that wasn't friendly." With a scowl, Siegfried lifted his empty stein. "Fräulein, bring me another, schnell!"

Max grabbed a full stein from the next table and summarily dumped it on Siegfried's head. Incredulous, the soldier slumped back his chair, his face turning beet red. His eyes raged.

Siegfried stood ever so slowly, then slammed his fist into his palm. "Tonight I rearrange your face—for fun and sport."

As the Ox cocked his fist, Max pivoted 270 degrees and delivered a sweeping back kick to his opponent's chest. The momentum toppled Siegfried into his chair, causing both to crash to the ground. To the cheers of the gathering crowd, Siegfried's two drunk friends charged into the fray but were easily dispatched by the sober Schumann.

Siegfried propped himself up on an elbow. "*Fahr zur Hölle*. Schumann, I'll get you for this!"

Max grabbed another full stein from a waitress's tray. He plopped it on the floor by Siegfried's head with a devilish smile. "This one is on me, Ox." A bevy of tavern patrons slapped Max on the back as he swaggered back over to Eva by the bar. "Ernst won't have a problem with them now."

Eva glanced over her bare shoulder with a shiver. Siegfried was now on his knees, glaring at both of them. Everyone around laughed at the loser.

"Max, watch your back. I don't think this is over."

Chapter Twelve

SS Headquarters, Berlin, May 1939

Distracted by street sounds below, Reinhard Heydrich looked out his office window as he cradled the telephone upon his shoulder. The voice of his sister droned on about her husband.

"Anna, Rudolf is a liability, both to you and Ernst. Himmler is very impressed with Ernst's performance, but he knows about Rudolf's disdain for the Party."

"Rudolf will never join the Nazi Party."

Heydrich sighed as he sat behind his desk. "He is an embarrassment to us all."

Anna began to cry. "Rudolf was once so respectable, successful. That's the man I married."

His sister was always the perennial victim. "You must remember, my dear, if those Jews hadn't offered Rudolf worthless stocks instead of cash for his legal fees, you would have money now."

"You were so generous last month. I hate to ask, but—"

"I will make another deposit at the first of the month. I only wish I could do more."

"Reinhard, I don't know how to—"

"—thank me. Don't worry, my dear, I'll find a way. Auf wiedersehen." Reinhard switched on the phonograph. He leaned back in his leather chair and picked up Rudolf's intercepted letter to Ernst. Nodding to the rhythm of the concerto softly playing, he began to read.

My dearest Ernst,

This is the third letter I've written you, but you've made no answer to any of my questions. While your mother and I are pleased to hear of your good progress at Bernau, I fear their indoctrination has further distanced you from me. Your words seem cold and remote— at least the ones not blacked out with heavy ink. Do you know your letters come opened, censored, and resealed? Your Nazi friends do not trust you.

In fact, I wonder if you'll ever read these words at all. I've tried to telephone you. "Too busy," they tell me. I've tried to get your mother to call for me, but she refuses. Things are difficult between us. We are now living separately in this house. I fear I shall never see you again. Oh, Ernst, Reinhard has taken you from me!

Please be assured that despite our differences, your mother and I both love you.

With deepest affection,
Papa

Reinhard glared at the words. The man was a proverbial tick under his collar!

*   *   *

SS Headquarters, Berlin

Heinrich Himmler sat erect behind his formidable oak desk awaiting Heydrich's return call. He took a deep breath to inhale some confidence.

The intercom sounded. "Herr Reichsführer, General Heydrich is on line two."

Heinrich slowly raised the telephone receiver to his ear. "Reinhard, I have chosen Werner Best to fill the open seat in the Wewelsburg circle." Heydrich's silence was a pleasure indeed. "Best is a banker from Darmstadt with a keen legal mind."

"Heinrich, the Circle consists of men of war. Why would you choose a banker?"

"Just as the Templars of old extorted funds from the crowns of Europe, we need such minds to legally drain the coffers of the Jews in countries outside of Germany—to finance further conquests. The Führer has confirmed this selection."

"But, mein herr, my nephew—"

"Did you really believe that I would seat a mere boy in the company of men? His father is an alcoholic!" Heinrich savored each word with a smug contempt. "Rudolf Teschler is not even a member of the Party."

Heydrich paused on the line. "Sir, I'm aware of the situation."

"Then perhaps you should take care of the problem." Heinrich calmly replaced the receiver on its cradle as his secretary escorted Captain Walter Schellenberg into his office.

Schellenberg was handsome, square-jawed with a swordsman's scar on his left cheek. Heinrich was guarded, as this twenty-nine-year-old lawyer was a woman's man whose words were silken and carefully measured.

Heinrich motioned his subordinate to take a seat. "You are early as usual."

"How did Heydrich take the news about Herr Best?"

"Rather poorly, I suspect. Schellenberg, I called you in to discuss the matter of Heydrich's confidential files." Heinrich cringed inside at what nightmare secrets Heydrich's collection must contain against him.

"I would consider it a creative challenge."

A terse knock at the door announced the arrival of Alfred Neame.

Heinrich provided a limp half salute. "Major Neame, what is your status on Teschler's tactical trials?"

"The men should be ready in the next few weeks. I am selecting the sites and his opponents myself. It must be a complete surprise."

Schellenberg slowly exhaled a wisp of cigarette smoke.

"I want Teschler to taste blood in this." With a wave of his hand, Heinrich dismissed Neame. When the door was shut, he poured two glasses of wine and offered one to Schellenberg. "Heydrich may be skimming our gold shipments from the Reichsbank to Switzerland. We don't have proof, but there are rumors."

Schellenberg removed another cigarette from his silver case and sparked his lighter. "Since we are moving metric tons every month, I will look into the accounting records. It will take some time."

"As a lawyer, you can help me against Heydrich. You will stand to gain immense wealth."

"And what about Ernst Teschler?"

"If properly manipulated, he could be useful in neutralizing Reinhard Heydrich."

"Then the unwitting Teschler becomes our double agent."

Heinrich raised his glass in a toast. "To the fine art of deception." He salivated as he added the shrewd young Schellenberg to his web of intrigue.

*   *   *

An SS Mercedes sedan waited at the entrance of Bernau Center as Major Neame approached. With Ernst and Barron seated in the rear, Neame handed Max a secure briefcase up front. "Teschler, your orders are to take these confidential files to Braumann & Company at Wandlitz. Be on your guard, these are orders signed by Himmler."

The SS driver was silent as he navigated the back roads. With the rear window cracked open, Barron delighted himself by pressing the short hairs of his blue-grey snout into the rushing wind. The Doberman's wind-blown jowls were charming.

As Ernst reviewed his mission log, he checked the loaded magazine of his Walther P38 silenced pistol. He engaged the safety and slipped the weapon back into its holster. The polished feel of gun metal gave him an extra measure of confidence. With that, he patted Barron's flank.

Max pivoted in the front passenger seat. "Neame said once you deliver the case, we will be given further orders."

"What do you think Himmler is up to?"

Max shook his head. "That is for us to find out."

On the outskirts of Wandlitz, the driver came to a halt at the entrance of Hotel Seeterrassen. It was an aging resort nestled lakeside with a private beach. With no luggage save the locked leather case, the trio entered the hotel and approached the front desk. The middle-aged clerk took uneasy notice of Barron as the Doberman lifted his snout.

"Reservation for three. Under the name of Teschler," Max said.

The clerk pressed his lips. "Sir, we do not allow pets in this hotel."

"Oh, he's no pet," Ernst stated wryly. "He's a weapon." He tapped the hotel register with his finger. "He will stay with me."

The clerk cleared his throat. "Of course, I assume all three of you are on official SS business." With signatures, the clerk offered two keys as he stared at the panting canine.

Once in their hotel suite, the telephone rang. Max spoke a few words, jotted down some notes, and replaced the receiver. "Ernst, you are to meet Herr Braumann at 236 Karl-Marx-Strasse—8:00 p.m. sharp. That's twelve blocks from here."

Ernst glanced at his wristwatch. "That gives us only forty minutes."

Max unfolded the map and handed it to Ernst. "Our orders are specific. You are to meet Braumann alone. I am to stay here to await Braumann's next call."

"They're splitting us up. That's not standard protocol."

"Shall we break the rules?" Max countered with a glint in his eye.

Ernst traced his proposed route on the map with his finger. "No, wait for the call, Max. Those are our orders." At his master's snap of the fingers, Barron sprung into position by his master's side. "Come on, boy. We're going hunting."

*   *   *

"Teschler—show no mercy!" were Neame's last words to his men before they departed Bernau Center. Briefcase in hand, Ernst noted the storefronts as he walked down the street. With the streetlamps illuminated, he and his Doberman bobbed in between light and shadow. He casually flexed his steel-tipped shoes to stretch his legs. Off and on, he fondled the handle of his Walther seated in his speed-draw holster at his waist.

Turning the corner, Barron panted lightly. At the intersection, the two streets were empty. With a deep breath, Ernst forged ahead. "Come on, boy!"

Barely ten meters down the sidewalk, a stranger emerged from an alley. Ernst could almost feel the adrenaline surge through his Doberman's veins. He removed his pistol's safety. It an instant, Ernst lowered his center of gravity. Dressed in a dark coat and denim trousers, the stranger veered toward Ernst. With a guttural growl, Barron lunged at the young man five meters away.

With the metal lid from a garbage can, the man shielded himself and pushed Barron through an open shop door and trapped him inside. Barking at a fevered pitch, the door shuddered as Barron repeatedly lunged at the thick glass with his front paws.

Incensed, Ernst rushed into the fray only to face a seven-inch stiletto blade waving before his face. His brain geared into slow motion as he released his wooden truncheon from his belt.

As the stiletto blade sliced through the air just grazing his chin, Ernst blocked the man's arm with his briefcase and applied a sweep kick to the back of his knee. With a groan, both feet arced into the air as the assailant landed on his back in front of the store window. Trapped inside the store, a frantic Barron continued to yelp and slam into the large windowpane.

The assailant rolled to a kneeling position, and with his hands vaulted to his feet. The maneuver was clearly military. He must be SS! Adrenaline pumping, Ernst faced the persistent stiletto. Several meters behind his opponent, Barron reared back to pummel the glass again. With his opponent stepping closer, Ernst cocked his truncheon and countered. In his peripheral vision, Ernst saw Barron burst through the windowpane in an explosion of shattering glass.

Startled, the adversary turned to see snapping jaws clamping down on his knife hand. In a butterfly-sweeping motion of his club, Ernst swung his truncheon across the man's kneecap. With a muffled scream, the target dropped to the pavement.

Barron's fangs went rabid as he shredded the man's arm, blood spurting. With a ghastly scream, the man slipped on the pavement trying to escape. Pasty white, the assailant's eyes begged for mercy.

"I should let Barron tear you apart." Ernst snapped his fingers twice. "Barron, retreat!" In an instant, the Doberman heeled as Ernst smacked his truncheon across his opponent's head. This time, the man was out for the count.

Ernst grabbed the briefcase and rushed into an adjacent alley. Barron trotted triumphantly behind. Breathing heavily in a shadowed alcove, Ernst brushed Barron's flank to calm the animal. *Max could have taken that man down in half the time, if we had stayed together. So much for obeying orders.* "Come on, Barron. We've got to keep moving. Only twenty minutes left on the clock."

Suddenly Ernst felt cold. He looked across the cobblestone street at the bloody carnage. Unconscious, his opponent labored for breath. Ernst stared up at the clear night sky. It was as if he could hear the man's voice—but there was only silence.

Hyperventilating, Ernst backed farther into the alleyway and cut through a twisted maze of stone corridors behind the shops. Surely the man needed medical attention. But there was no time to stop. At his side, Barron kept nudging his master forward. "Come on, boy, let's keep moving."

Somewhere in the darkness Ernst could sense another threat. After jogging twenty-five meters down the alley, the two companions emerged from the darkness. According to his map, Ernst had to risk crossing the street, then walk several blocks to make his delivery. He slipped behind a brick column with his pistol primed. Ernst ducked his head out and back a few times to draw fire, but there was only silence. He could feel the pulse of someone out there.

Ernst snapped his fingers, and Barron followed his master down the sidewalk. In his peripheral vision, he saw a flash twenty meters up the street, then the store window beside him shattered, followed by silence. Barron reared back on his haunches, growling. Ernst clamped his jaws closed, and a swooning high-pitched whistle quieted the dog. A large caliber pistol with a suppressor to be sure. Straining to see through the shadows, Ernst spotted the shooter crouched beside a pillar.

Ernst and Barron retreated behind the building and quietly jogged a full block in parallel. He inched out to the sidewalk, then stopped. Ernst removed his officer's hat and leaned out around the corner, just enough to see the man across the street crouched behind a railing. The man leveled his pistol and took aim at Ernst's prior position down the street. *Now I have you . . .*

Ernst and Barron hugged the storefront wall, edging closer. Just ten meters away, the shooter stepped out into the open. Barron darted around Ernst into the street. Startled, the man whipped his semiautomatic toward Barron. With the shooter in his sights, Ernst squeezed his Walther's trigger. The silenced bullet tore into the man's shoulder, spinning him into a light post. Barron vaulted into the air and clamped down on the assailant's gun hand with razor-like teeth.

Ernst dashed toward his target. With dead-calm eyes, he raised his pistol again and fired. The bullet struck the man's sternum. Thrust into a wall, the shooter hooked his arm over a railing to buffer his fall. Ernst closed in upon his target with a hair-trigger on the next bullet.

As he approached, the man's expression was like a ghost, his eyes glazed, dying as he gargled upon his own blood. Ernst stared at the grotesque figure suspended in air. With each labored breath, the man slid down farther. Ernst could sense utter disbelief in the man's eyes.

Neame's voice taunted him again. *"Kill or be killed."*

An ice-cold calm enveloped Ernst. He raised his weapon and placed a bullet neatly into the man's forehead. The popping sound was like stepping on a peanut shell.

Ernst cued Barron to heel, then both stepped back into the shadows as Barron followed, panting with a limp. Still clutching the courier's case in his hand, Ernst scanned the empty street behind him. The faces of the dead littered the cobblestones. As the bitter taste of bile swathed his tongue, Ernst resumed his path.

If his thoughts were razor blades, he would make quick work of Neame's smug face. *I am the last man standing!*

Up the way and across the street stood the darkened offices of Braumann & Company. Ernst and Barron made their way to the entrance and opened the door. Down a hallway, a light glowed. With his Walther primed, Ernst nudged the door open.

Seated around a conference table were Max and a tall SS captain with a swordsman's scar down his left cheek. They were playing cards.

Max held up a half-empty glass. "The call came, and I was ordered here." He tapped his watch. "You're five minutes late."

Ernst stared at his friend. "Herr Braumann, Lieutenant Teschler reporting as ordered."

"Lieutenant, my name is Walter Schellenberg, Captain SS."

With a halfhearted military salute, Ernst placed the leather briefcase on the table. Barron nestled to his side.

"Congratulations, you have passed your field exam." He held up his field binoculars. "We saw everything from the second-floor balcony."

"Sir, what about the bodies in the street?"

"Those were clean kills. Himmler will be pleased."

Ernst frowned. "Clean kills? Those two soldiers were German."

"Foot soldiers are expendable. Officers are not." Schellenberg shifted in his seat to view Barron. "Your dog is quite savage. I don't approve of pets in the field."

"Sir, he's no pet. He's a lethal weapon."

*   *   *

Berlin, SS Headquarters, Three Days Later

Ernst followed Major Neame up the massive marble stairs at 8 Prinz-Albrechtstrasse. Neame stopped at the landing. "Teschler, stop grumbling about those two agents. They were careless—and now they're dead. A skilled assassin cannot be lenient."

The word *assassin* sent a chill through Ernst.

They passed through a maze of uniformed guards to enter the third-floor suite of Reichsführer Himmler. Schellenberg sat next to him as the new arrivals saluted.

With a peevish smile, Himmler folded his hands upon the table. "Lieutenant Teschler, Captain Schellenberg gave you high marks on skill and cunning at your Wandlitz trials. I congratulate you."

Ernst clicked his heels together. "Thank you, sir."

"Captain Schellenberg has a new assignment for you." Himmler cued his staff to take their seats.

Schellenberg stood before a wall-sized map of Germany, Switzerland, and Austria. "We have chosen Bern to be a secondary repository for gold shipments in addition to our main depository accounts in Zurich. The Reichsbank has two smelting facilities near Berlin. When we invade countries to the east, we will raid their treasuries and recast their gold into bars stamped with German insignias. Teschler, you and I will go to

Bern next week to finalize arrangements to commence banking operations by August 1."

Himmler walked over to the map. "This is first-phase funding for the
war effort." He turned to Ernst. "Teschler, you must be pleased at our
confidence in you."

"Jawohl, Herr Reichsführer!" Ernst's mind raced to absorb all of the
operational details. Just who was Walter Schellenberg?

Neame passed a folder around the table. "These appear to be British
one-pound and five-pound notes. They are counterfeit."

Himmler clasped his hands together. "Your progress report?"

"Sir, I have already begun to identify forgers, engravers, and paper-
manufacturing specialists. Since the forgeries must be perfect, it will take
some time. If we could flood the British Isles with five-pound notes, their
economy would be reduced to havoc!"

Himmler paced between the window and the map. "So with the
stolen gold and the counterfeit currencies, the Allies could cofund SS
operations in Europe—even our new labor camps. Think of the irony,
gentlemen."

Ernst was stunned. He now sat in Himmler's inner circle with a
front-row seat to the crimes of the century—yet to be committed.

*   *   *

The next afternoon, Ernst walked into his uncle's office. "Sir, you've
heard the news."

"So Himmler moved your trials to Wandlitz?"

Ernst nodded. "With no prior warning."

"They deliberately kept me away from your tactical trials." In a huff,
Reinhard quickened his pace. "What is Himmler's game?"

Ernst remained silent. Anything he said would send his uncle into a
tirade.

"In a week you will travel to the International Bank of Switzerland. After Schellenberg completes the registrations for the Reichsbank

accounts, make an excuse to talk to my banker, Herr Richardt, alone. Your assignment is code-named 'Rogue.'" The tall, lean spymaster placed a sealed envelope in Ernst's lap. "You will open three additional accounts. Only you and I will have access. Study the file, and we'll talk again before you leave Germany."

Ernst slipped the envelope in his briefcase. His head was spinning. What was his uncle really up to?

"It sounds so mysterious."

"Himmler and I are old rivals. When Germany declares war on Europe, the Reich territories are to be divided into two administrative districts. The administrative leaders will be determined solely by Hitler. Himmler is jealous and a weakling, so he will strike first."

"Sir, what is my role in all of this?"

"He is likely to use you to spy on me. So you will quarterback my grand counteroffensive." Two wine glasses were already poured, seated on a silver tray. Reinhard picked them up and offered one to his nephew. "No one—absolutely no one—is to know about these gold accounts."

Reinhard clinked his wine glass against Ernst's. "Cheers, son. You are about to become the master counterespionage agent in Nazi Germany. Your code name: 'Infidel.'"

Chapter Thirteen

Berlin, May 1939

Up most of the night, Ernst had desperately searched for courage. He stepped onto the back porch of the Bonhoeffer home just before sunrise. Seeing a light in the kitchen window, he tapped on the door. He tried again, then the porch light flashed on. His former pastor peered through the curtain and cracked open the door.

"Ernst? Are you alright?"

"Sir, I must talk to you right away!"

Dietrich ushered him into the kitchen. "Would you like some coffee?" Ernst paced while Dietrich poured two cups. "Please, sit down. What brings you out so early?"

Ernst sipped his coffee. "I have been assigned to Internal Security duties with the SS. I will be a liaison with officials in government, industry, and the like."

"I see. Would you like sugar?" Dietrich offered the jar.

Ernst's hand trembled as he measured sugar into his cup, then stirred. "It was during my certification trials at Wandlitz. Our assignment was to deliver confidential documents for the Reich. It should have been simple." He tasted the coffee, but it was still bitter.

"Go on."

"One of the soldiers attacked us. Barron rushed in to protect me just as the man aimed his weapon. I've never felt so calm in my life. My eyes locked on target, and I squeezed the trigger twice. I still can see his face—his eyes!" Ernst stirred in another spoonful of sugar.

"Did you know him?"

Ernst shook his head. "The man had a wedding ring. Pastor, I dream about his wife and children. Can you imagine if they ever were to meet me—what they would say, what they would do?"

Dietrich placed his hand on Ernst's arm. "Ernst, are you seeking forgiveness?"

He looked vacantly into his pastor's eyes. "Of course, not. My honor is loyalty! I obeyed orders."

"What?"

Ernst sat erect in his chair. "I had another dream last night. There I was . . . on a rocky precipice in Palestine with a spear in hand, standing in the shadow of three crosses. The two thieves were dead, but not the man in the middle. As ordered, I rammed my spear into his flesh. Blood and water gushed out. The man stared down on me in silence. His eyes did not hate. Perhaps pity, but . . . no, they were filled with compassion for a killer." Lost in his dream, Ernst emerged ever aware of Dietrich's kind, searching eyes.

"Confess your sins, Ernst. Turn to God, and He will forgive you."

"My friend, I did not come for absolution. I came to warn you. The Führer possesses the ancient Spear of Destiny. Hitler's legions are about to open the gates of hell!"

Dietrich stood and grasped Ernst's shoulders. "My boy, tell me what you know. I can help you."

"Don't you understand? My honor and loyalty have already been pledged to—" Ernst turned away in shame. Lifting his palms up, he still could feel the blood of the two dead men drip off his fingers. Ernst stood and backed away toward the door. "This is just the beginning of the nightmare."

Dietrich took a few steps closer to him. "Let me help you, *please*."

Then without another word, Ernst walked out the back door into the early morning twilight.

*   *   *

Bern, Switzerland, May 10, 1939

Having taken a commercial flight, Schellenberg and Ernst arrived in the city dressed in business suits, fedoras, and canvas trench coats. The scenic taxi ride over the Aare River welcomed them to the Breitenrain financial district. The International Bank of Switzerland maintained an institutional office in the Dressler Building on Viktoriastrasse.

Having cleared security, the private banking department was on the second floor. Schellenberg turned to Ernst. "Remember, they will address us by our code names. Officially, the SS was never here."

Schellenberg was greeted by Herr Richardt. "Ah, Herr *Mauser*, it is good to see you again. Do come into my office. I have the papers ready for your review."

Schellenberg pointed to Ernst. "This is my associate Herr Löeb." Ernst shook hands and quietly followed the men into a spacious office.

Herr Richardt opened a file on his desk. "As per your request, there will be thirteen corporate accounts initially. When gold shipments are deposited, they will be assigned to only these account numbers successively. Statements to the Reichsbank will be consolidated under one omnibus account name: Melmer."

Schellenberg retrieved a file from his briefcase. "Here are the names, signatures, and passwords for those authorized for access. The second page has secure telephone numbers listed should you need to contact us."

Herr Richardt offered a sterling silver fountain pen to Schellenberg. "Now, if you will sign these documents, we will take care of the rest."

Schellenberg scribed his alias several times, then returned the file. "Is there a private telephone available?"

"You may use this office. I will wait for you in the reception area."

"Herr Richardt, thank you." When the banker left, Schellenberg dialed a number. Ernst could hear only an occasional word of the brief conversation. "Teschler, I'm going to the German embassy and will meet you later at the hotel." He walked out in haste.

Ernst was suspicious. Things appeared too ordinary—too easy. His guess was that this bank held many secrets.

When the bank executive returned, Ernst remained in his chair. He retrieved an envelope from his satchel. "Herr Richardt, I have an important letter for you."

The banker eyed his guest as he read its contents:

"General Heydrich sends his regards and requests that three additional accounts be opened in the registrations listed. You are to assign 5 percent of all Reichsbank deposits to these three additional accounts. These will be 'private transactions' requiring absolute confidentiality."

"I assume Herr Mauser is not to know of these accounts?"

Ernst nodded as he handed the executive a thick envelope.

Richardt smiled as he thumbed through a wad of cash. "We insure everyone's privacy at this bank. Who are the authorized parties?"

Ernst handed the list to Richardt. At that moment, he felt a rush—a gold rush. His uncle was a genius. The man would steal millions from the SS incrementally and then hide it at the same bank. And Ernst would possess a key.

"To confirm, we will place 5 percent of each Melmer deposit into these private accounts, divided equally. I assume our normal commission is satisfactory, Herr Löeb?"

"That is correct. The general wants official statements for only the first thirteen accounts to be sent to the Reichsbank under the single name: Melmer."

Richardt paused. "And only General Heydrich and you will have access to the private accounts?"

Ernst closed his briefcase. "That is correct. Sir, one more request. I wish to rent a large safety-deposit box under the name Rudolf."

"As you wish, Herr Löeb."

"General Heydrich asked me to remind you what happened to your competitor last year, when he failed to maintain complete secrecy."

Herr Richardt stood with a nervous smile. "Secrecy is our stock and trade, I assure you. My secretary will give the box keys to you in a few minutes. Guten Tag, Herr Löeb!" Herr Richardt curtly walked out of the room.

Ernst's footsteps echoed down the marble steps as he was escorted to a large stainless-steel vault. It was bordered by a series of ornate cherrywood cubicles. Secured inside, Ernst stood alone in front of the large metal box. He removed a false bottom from inside his briefcase and produced a thin container. After snapping open the catch, he beheld 30 two-carat diamonds seated in six neat rows. *"They are investment grade—the highest quality,"* his uncle had told him. *"You will make several deliveries, Ernst. Only you and I will know of their existence."*

Ernst had already done the math before he put the diamonds into the safe-deposit box and closed the lid. Soon he would be the first Teschler worth over a million in history.

After a while, a bank attendant returned to seal the metal box. Ernst secured the box keys and soon arrived at their hotel by taxi. Did Schellenberg suspect any of his uncle's private arrangements? Ernst donned a prideful smile. Espionage was certainly a very profitable game of deception.

*   *   *

Berlin, A Week Later

Eva Kleist stood on a balcony of the historic Adlon Hotel, gazing toward the center of Berlin. The setting sun painted a mystical palette of intermittent light and shadow across the city's skyline. Enormous swastika banners hung from buildings down the street as far as the eye could see. The bright-red, black, and white colors flapped gently in the spring breeze.

Tonight in Berlin, SS elite would toast the corps and bandy their women upon the dance floor at the annual SS Cotillion Ball. The gentle breeze sparked Eva's imagination. After emerging from a warm bubble bath, she would artfully craft her makeup to accentuate her beauty and finish with an alluring hairstyle for her silky blonde hair. Ernst's admiring eyes would devour her in the elegant dress purchased just for this event. She would be a sight to behold at the gala.

*   *   *

Ceiling-high mirrors bordered the steps all the way down the grand staircase. Eva's azure chiffon gown flowed over her hips like a spring fountain. Its color complemented her brilliant blue eyes. She wrapped her arm securely around Ernst's as they slowly descended the banquet hall steps.

Midway down, Eva sensed the envy and desire of nearby SS officers gazing at her with Ernst.

He took notice. "Eva, I hope that you have eyes only for me this evening. I can't stop thinking about you."

On the marble floor below, Reinhard Heydrich awaited. As the young couple approached, his eyes feasted upon her exposed shoulders and décolletage. He was a rogue who knew no shame.

Ernst lifted Eva's hand. "Uncle, may I introduce you to Fräulein Eva Kleist."

Heydrich gracefully pressed his lips to her delicate fingers. "Fräulein, what a pleasure. Ernst has boasted of your beauty, but I see now that he understated the case!"

Eva pasted on a smile. "Thank you, Herr Obergruppenführer. My, this is a grand party. It's almost like being in the presence of royalty."

"Ernst has joined me in Germany's new aristocracy. Come!" Heydrich folded Eva's arm around his and led the way. "My dear, tonight I will introduce you to Reichsführer Himmler. Ernst made quite an impression on him recently." With his most charming smile, Heydrich seated Eva and Ernst at his table. With a wave of his hand, Heydrich caught the attention of a nearby waiter. "Your best champagne. Schnell!"

After dinner, Ernst finally reclaimed Eva from his uncle's chatter and led her to the dance floor. Her plumage of azure contrasted with the black, white, and silver adorning the other women as couples twirled across the polished parquet floor. After several vibrant numbers, the orchestra settled into a slow, romantic ballad.

Ernst held Eva close, her body moving with the ebb and flow of the music. She closed her eyes and savored the fragrance of his French cologne. When she kissed him on his lips, Ernst smiled.

"What was that?" he said.

"A token of my appreciation."

"Appreciation for what?"

"For introducing me to all of this."

Ernst wiggled his eyebrows. "You can appreciate me some more, if you like."

"Perhaps I will appreciate you much more, later on this evening."

Eventually, the music came to an end. As the dancers retreated from the dance floor, Eva and Ernst followed with reluctance. Eva's delight faded as they approached their table.

Heydrich was engaged in an animated conversation with another SS officer. Then he looked at Ernst with business in his eyes. "Excuse me, Fräulein. Ernst, I have been called away to a meeting at the Chancellery. I want you to attend. There is urgency in this."

Ernst frowned. "Tonight?"

Ernst, just one more dance and a magical kiss! Eva pleaded with her eyes. "But Ernst!"

"I'm afraid duty calls, Fräulein," Heydrich said.

Ernst lowered his head. "I'm sorry, Eva." Into her hand he placed a fine white Egyptian handkerchief embroidered with party symbols. "A memento of tonight's fantasy with you."

She leaned back in her chair. "But what about me? Am I to be stranded here with all these other men?"

Heydrich was polite. "Of course not, my dear. Schumann can entertain you."

"Eva, I will call you tomorrow." Ernst gently kissed her lips.

With Ernst's handkerchief in Eva's hand, his fragrance lingered, as did the sweet memory of their last dance at the Cotillion Ball.

*   *   *

Berlin, May 20, 1939

For hours, Abraham Kleisfeld stood in an alley across from a side entrance of the The Bismarck Tavern. Ambient street sounds echoed off the damp brick walls as a rat scampered across a nearby ledge. A solitary apple fed Abraham's growing fears with each bite.

In his pocket was a letter from Cousin Saul. He had discovered where Abraham's daughter, Sarah, worked in Berlin. For three days, Nina had begged him to find their daughter. With a Berlin address in hand, Abraham now paced in the alley, constantly glancing over his shoulder for the Gestapo. A father's fears were fueled by the gaudy façade of the Bismarck Tavern. So there he stood, praying—eyes wide open.

Now and then, through the tavern's side door, young women painted in cheap makeup and tawdry dresses would come and go. Exhausted, Abraham pried his eyelids open to keep alert. Eventually, two barmaids emerged into the alley, giggling. He squinted through his spectacles, then frowned at one girl in particular. Her hair was bleached blonde and her lips were painted red. *It can't be!*

As Abraham stepped out of the shadows, the light revealed more of her features. They were all too familiar. "Sarah!" His voice filled with emotion. "Sarah! It's Papa."

Startled, the young blonde hesitated and turned. Her eyes widened. Without a word, she picked up her pace and turned onto Bergenstrasse with her friend in tow.

"Sarah! Please wait!" Abraham tried to keep up with the two women, when he saw a policeman across the street. He abruptly stopped behind a fruit stand. In desperation, he waited until the officer departed, then he followed the women at a distance. Sarah and her friend eventually parted ways up the street.

A few blocks from the tavern, Abraham watched Sarah enter an old brick apartment building. He waited a few minutes, then followed her into the lobby. He slowly mounted three flights of wooden steps, breathing heavy. He tried to catch his breath on the top landing.

After a few minutes, he found the apartment number and knocked at the door. Again he knocked. Then he heard footsteps before a young woman cracked open the door secured by a chain.

"Sarah, it is Papa."

The young woman opened the door, checked the hallway, and ushered him inside.

"Your mother and I have missed you. Why did you run from me just now?"

"Papa, you should never have come to Berlin. It's not safe. The Gestapo is everywhere!"

Abraham stared at his daughter's brazen appearance. "Why are you dressed like that? And your beautiful brown hair—it's ruined!"

"It is fashionably blonde—a new look. It's cosmopolitan for the city."

Abraham's eyes widened. Her clothing and makeup revealed her trade.

"You are a waitress at the tavern? I saw German soldiers go in there. They do unspeakable things to Jewish girls, Sarah."

"My friends at the tavern—they don't know I'm Jewish."

"What! You are ashamed of your people? Your own family? What will I tell your mother?"

"You should have told me you were coming. My friend Gretel could tell the Gestapo."

Abraham slumped into a chair. "You are ashamed of your papa?"

"Jews are not welcome in Germany anymore. Here I have a new identity and the freedom to—"

"To prance around in a lewd dress and a painted face?" *O Lord, the mongrels have stolen my daughter's heart!*

"I dyed my hair, Papa. I have a job, some money. I blend into the crowd."

"Have you also denied your faith in God?"

"I've met a young man, Papa. He's a soldier and knows many powerful people. Soon, I will ask him for papers for you and Mama. It may take a few months, but you two must leave this country before it's too late."

Abraham crumpled his wool cap with both fists as tears pooled in his eyes. "That night, your mother and I watched as Nazis murdered your brother. We stood just meters away, but I could not reach him in time. They threw him off the balcony like a piece of garbage—my only son."

Tears streamed as Abraham leaned forward in his chair. "You cannot stay in Berlin. Something terrible will happen to you. You must come home. I promised your mother!"

Sarah's eyes were hollow with a few tears feathered across her cheek. Sarah knelt before him and placed her hands on his knees. "Cousin Saul told me about Aaron. I am so sorry, but Papa, I asked you—I pleaded with you and Mama—to leave Wittenberg. You refused. You said that God would protect us!"

Abraham lowered his head. "I know God is with us. I believe. Cousin Saul has plans for passage out of Germany—perhaps in a few months they will be ready. My child, we must have faith in God."

With a frown, Sarah stepped over to the hearth. She was silent but only for a moment. "Papa, both you and Mama must leave Nazi Germany before something happens."

"But what will become of you, Sarah?"

*   *   *

The next day, Abraham walked into the Berlin train station and stood in line to purchase a ticket back to Wittenberg. Alone and frightened, Nina would rejoice at the good news that he had found their daughter. He imagined her joy at Sarah's return home. Exhausted, he craved something to eat when he felt a tap on his shoulder.

"It is a very hot day for this time of year, don't you think, Herr Kleisfeld?"

Icy fear gripped Abraham as he slowly turned around.

"Your picture doesn't do you justice. You seem much older." With a black-and-white photo in hand, the Gestapo agent smiled. His breath smelled foul. "The SS has been looking for you. You will come quietly, ja?"

Chapter Fourteen

Northwest of Berlin

The truck bounced through the rugged rural terrain somewhere near Oranienburg. Abraham sat silently as his fellow Jews were packed in the rear compartment like cattle. With final destination unknown, fearful imaginings nipped at Abraham's shackled heels.

He dabbed his face with Nina's handkerchief. She had warned him before he departed for Berlin. "Abraham, how could I have been so foolish? You must get Sarah out of Berlin. Bring her back home to be safe with us."

From his pocket, he retrieved a crumpled black-and-white photograph of his daughter. Her abrupt departure had deeply hurt him, but he still loved her. He yearned to hear her sweet, young voice again.

Now on the road, Abraham was descending into the lion's den. Through the scattered cloud of dust spewed behind the truck, Abraham remembered the miraculous shekinah glory of God during Kristallnacht. *O Lord, it was You who saved us that night. If ever I am to see my family again, I need a miracle!*

The SS troop carriers lurched over a rain-rutted road, then began to slow. One of the prisoners peeked through the canvas flaps. "The sign says Sachsenhausen."

"That's a Nazi concentration camp." Word spread rapidly from man to man.

"Better just to call it hell," said another.

Abraham's fear became contagious. Some Jews were old, a few in their teens, but most were young men in their prime. Everyone could hear the sound of hinges grinding as the barbed-wire gates opened. The trucks rumbled into the camp, sloshed through the mud, and squealed to a stop. With the rear canvas flaps opened, armed SS guards rushed the tailgate. Angry, barking German shepherds promised to secure the perimeter of the barbed-wire fence.

Tailgates slammed open. *"Aus!"* the soldiers' voices raged. "Get out of the trucks, schnell!"

Abraham sat deep in the cargo bay as the prisoners jumped down into the sloppy mud. With fire in their eyes, the guards beat the Jews into a line, screamed into their faces, and sprayed them with spit. Feeling numb, Abraham almost lost his balance as he jumped off the tailgate.

When they were all counted, a young Nazi officer stepped carefully around the puddles, protecting his calf-high leather boots. "Welcome to Sachsenhausen camp. Here we will take away your name and give you a number. Here, you will work, and if you fail to work hard—you will die." The officer looked down the line of scraggly men. "Now, which one of you is the Jew Kleisfeld?"

Abraham held his breath. *If I keep perfectly still . . .*

From behind, the Nazi officer's voice thundered. "Kleisfeld, get out of line! Aus!" With the butt of his rifle, another guard prodded Abraham away from the others.

The officer drew his luger and chambered a bullet. "Now, let us show the rest of you proper German hospitality."

The SS troops evoked the image of his young son's terror back on their neighbor's balcony. Kristallnacht was only the beginning, and it was about to repeat itself. Aaron Kleisfeld's tortured screams devoured Abraham's courage.

On the officer's cue, the SS troops formed two lines about two meters apart, facing each other, and taunted their cowering prey with long clubs, spades, whips, and rifles. When the soldiers began to chant, the SS officer fired his pistol into the air, spooking the prisoners into the "gauntlet."

Abraham blinked as the herd of human flesh stumbled toward the pack of wolves. Sixty-two Jews entered the human meat grinder, but only thirty-seven survived the orgy of violence. With bones shattered and bodies bruised, the prisoners had been stomped and bludgeoned. Oblivious to their victims' cries, the guards walked away laughing and cracking jokes.

Abraham was left standing to one side as his guard detail dispersed. Compassion drove him toward the bloody scene. Scattered upon the ground lay corpses amidst the groans of the injured—cracked ribs, broken arms and fingers, flesh ripped open by knives and shovels.

He staggered through the mud and recognized a face from the truck. The man's eyes were lifeless, staring up at the grey sky. In a beat, the reality of death descended upon his heart. Deeply ashamed, Abraham touched the corpse's face and broke down in tears. "I cannot remember his name. O Lord, tell me his name?"

"In this place, they let the dead lie on the ground until sunset," a voice said beside him.

Abraham stumbled back, expecting a blow. Instead, a hand reached down and closed the dead man's eyes. The man's frayed sleeve was striped blue and white, and his head was crudely shaved.

"Come. Follow me if you want to live." The stranger grasped Abraham's arm and guided him away from the carnage. "I am Hans Ehrenberg. The Nazis brought me here some months ago." A dull, hollow look and frail limbs betrayed his endless days of work. He cradled his gloved hand underneath Abraham's arm. "Here, let me help you to the induction center."

"My name is Kleisfeld." Abraham's breathing was still labored.

Ehrenberg brought him to a large clapboard building. "Go inside. They'll strip you, shave your head, force you into a cold shower, then give you a uniform—and a number."

Abraham limped along. "You seem to be very calm for a place like this."

"God is my keeper. Despite what these Nazis do in this place, the Holy Spirit has a purpose for us."

"My friends call me Abraham." He searched his pockets and pressed a few papers and pictures into Ehrenberg's hand. "Please keep these for me."

Ehrenberg glanced at the guards. "I'll be waiting for you on the other side, Abraham."

An hour later, Abraham emerged from the induction center deloused, uniformed, and looking just like every other Jew in Sachsenhausen. He kept stroking his clean-shaven jaw. Without his beard, he felt naked before God. Without his braided kippot, his bald head would be his shame at the appointed hours of prayer. Most depressing of all was the identification number sewn upon the breast of his soiled striped uniform. Its numerals erased the name of Abraham Kleisfeld from among the living.

Ehrenberg furrowed his eyebrows and chuckled. "No one will recognize you now." They made their way to the dormitory huts. "This camp is so crowded, the guards are too busy to supervise."

Abraham limped along. "Jehovah God, spare us from more of such 'supervision.'"

A subtle smile appeared upon Ehrenberg's face. "A sense of humor? A gift from God, no doubt."

The two men trudged through a wire fence gate and approached a series of four barracks.

"You must be special, Abraham Kleisfeld. The SS reserves this compound for special projects."

Abraham passed through the north entrance of the sprawling barracks. They were greeted by a maze of wooden bunk beds, stacked four high. The forlorn eyes of thirty or forty Jewish ghosts adorned the strewn timbers. Abraham stopped in midstride.

Ehrenberg gave the assignment card to a prisoner seated near the front. "I have a new one for you, Jacob."

The young man had intelligent eyes. Stripped to the waist, the prisoner stood and circled Abraham. "He looks well fed."

"Major Neame signed his papers."

"Ah yes, special treatment for this Jew." The block attendant gingerly turned into the light. Abraham winced at the fresh, swollen welts that striped the prisoner's back. "We buried Bernard this morning. Come, you can use his bunk. Where are you from, Herr Kleisfeld?"

"Wittenberg. Before that, my grandfather and father were all craftsmen born and trained in Munich for three generations."

"I'm Jacob Weisen, from Berlin."

"May the peace of God rest upon you and your house."

"And upon yours, Herr Kleisfeld."

*   *   *

The next day Abraham was summoned to Blockhouse 13. He waited an hour in the administrative office when finally an oily haired SS major sauntered into the room.

"You remember me, Kleisfeld. My name is Major Neame." He opened his briefcase and placed currency samples on the desk. "Your job here at Sachsenhausen will be to duplicate these original British passports and currencies. Our crews are having problems matching colors to the originals. Fix these problems! Perhaps you will see your family again."

"Sir, I am just an engraver."

Neame's eyes narrowed, black as night. "Your wife has faith in you, Herr Kleisfeld. She's wagering her life against your success for the Reich. Our man Hinkle will get you started." Neame turned on his heel and departed.

A small man with thick spectacles and a thick Polish accent appeared at the door. "Welcome to the SS center for counterfeit documents. I am Herr Hinkle, prisoner in charge."

"Excuse me. Did you say counterfeit?"

"Yes, we forge currencies—British pound notes, American dollars, and French francs."

"But that sounds illegal."

Hinkle snorted with laughter. "It certainly is. And you have been recruited by the SS to help us. We are having a devil of a time obtaining original papers to match inks."

"Herr Hinkle, do you have any idea what my father, a master engraver at the Giesecke & Devrient mint, would say about this crime?"

"With all due respect, Abraham, your father is probably dead. If we are to live, this operation has to succeed."

Abraham blinked.

In the next room, Hinkle introduced Abraham to his staff, then moved on to the postproduction display. "Kleisfeld, you will compare these original documents to our new production certificates. Something is missing, but we have not found a solution."

Abraham held up a document frame. "I will need a Leitz Wetzlar microscope 10, 45, and 100 power—and additional solvents."

"Kleisfeld, make a list. Neame says to get what you need, but his superiors will expect results."

"Who is the press foreman?"

"The Nazis removed him just last week. Rumor is they shot him—he talked too much to the other prisoners. Just work hard and do what these people tell you. Hopefully, we will both survive!"

*   *   *

The weeks passed by quickly. One day, Abraham, Ehrenberg, and Jacob collapsed in the barracks after a ten-hour shift.

Jacob lowered his voice. "The Haganah is planning major transports across the Mediterranean—ships bound for Zion. I'm going to be on that ship, whatever it takes!"

Ehrenberg adjusted his straw pillow. "So, you're just going to walk out of this camp, board a train to the Balkans, and sail away?"

Crowding closer, Jacob whispered, "Some say you can buy your freedom from Sachsenhausen by signing your business or bank accounts over to the SS. Do you have money, Abraham?"

"I own my family's engraving shop in Wittenberg."

Ehrenberg scoffed. "Why would a man give his livelihood away?"

"To survive!" Jacob's eyes grew large. "The Nazis are buying businesses at 15, maybe 20 percent of their value. They pay with a note at interest."

"But that's—"

"Robbery, of course," Jacob said coldly.

Abraham stared at his shop-worn hands. "Months ago, the SS confiscated my shop. They even took my gold wedding ring. There is no money left."

Jacob leaned on an elbow. "When I get out of this hellhole, I'm going to purchase passage to Palestine. They have boats in Istanbul. If I can get there, I'll have a chance."

Abraham squeezed in between his straw mat and the upper bunk bed. Staring at the wooden slats, he pictured his wife hiding in his Gentile neighbor's basement. Though their friends had protected her, certainly she must think that Abraham had abandoned her. *O Lord, let my Nina know that I'm alive.*

"What about you, Ehrenberg?" Jacob asked. "Do you own anything?"

"On a clergyman's salary?"

Jacob stared at him. "But you are a Jew."

"I am, by blood."

Abraham frowned. "But how can a Jew be a Christian?"

Ehrenberg pressed his palms together. "My Lord is One, the God of Abraham, Isaac, and Jacob. I have committed my life to Messiah Yeshua. Jesus is the Messiah."

"But are you one of us?" Jacob asked.

Ehrenberg stood. "I am a Jew by birth, and it was no secret among those in the church. But I must tell you, the Nazis hate true Christians almost as much as they do the sons of Israel." He removed his glove and held up the stumps of his missing fingers. "This is what the Nazis did to a Jewish pastor of the church!"

Jacob was appalled. "But why?"

Ehrenberg shrugged. "They wanted the names of other Jewish pastors within the church. After they took my second finger, the Gestapo man clamped the pincers around my third and smiled. Then, as he began to compress the blades, suddenly the Shekinah Glory of God illuminated the entire chamber and, for no earthly reason, the Nazi stopped. They bound my wounds with a rag and let me go."

Abraham's heart lifted. "I, too, have seen the Shekinah! The night the Nazis raided our neighborhood. The thugs rushed our house. Then a pillar of fire appeared, just like Moses described in Exodus. The hand of God blocked their path. I'm sure of it! For no earthly reason, the Nazis left my house unharmed."

Jacob cursed, his eyes full of bitterness. "But to what has God saved us?"

Ehrenberg placed his good hand on the young man's shoulder. "My friend, Messiah Yeshua lives—even here at Sachsenhausen."

Abraham lifted his palms. "The God of Abraham, Jacob, and Isaac—may He provide a way for my friend, Jacob, to board that boat to Zion!"

*   *   *

Berlin, Abwehr HQ, May 25, 1939

Dietrich Bonhoeffer rushed into the lobby of German military intelligence to meet his brother-in-law. The two men found a conference room nearby. "I came directly from the train station. Is the family alright?"

Dohnanyi's expression was tentative. "Your sister was frantic when you didn't come home last night."

"Christine fawns over me like a mother hen."

"Dietrich, the Gestapo may soon take the Confessing Church to court."

"Their agents accosted me on the train in Pomerania."

"Come, I want you to tell Colonel Oster all the details."

Up two flights of stairs, the two men passed through security and waited in Oster's office.

Minutes later, Oster marched through the door, his face beet red. "We've been three steps behind Heydrich all the way. It's been six months since the pogrom. According to our reports, the SS have incarcerated almost twenty thousand Jews. The newspapers are promoting it as Kristallnacht, the 'Night of Broken Glass.'"

Dietrich retrieved a blue hair clip stained red from his pocket. "Hans, you remember Father's friends, Herbert and Rebecca Aronstein. They were Jewish physicians savagely attacked in their home. Rebecca wore this ribbon in her hair the night she bled to death in my arms." *If only we had taken a stand years ago.*

Touched by the moment, Colonel Oster stared at the satin ribbon. "Why do you carry that?"

"To remember a solitary Jewish life taken needlessly by tyrants. As I witnessed her death, this ribbon reminds me of the reason for the cross, the victory of our Savior, and the power of the living God."

The silence in the room was poignant.

Dohnanyi retrieved a document from his briefcase. "Colonel, perhaps you would share the news about Reverend Ehrenberg?"

"Yes, of course. Herr Bonhoeffer, they shipped your colleague to Sachsenhausen Camp, twenty-seven kilometers north of Berlin. We have made inquiries. Our SS contact can release him if he has valid employment outside of Germany."

"Why, that would be wonderful!"

"Perhaps Bishop Bell could arrange for Ehrenberg's employment in London. And then you could present our case to the bishop."

Dohnanyi gave Dietrich the file. "In the world of intelligence, everyone has potential value. I have summarized key points you will need to memorize before your travels."

Oster stood and fastened the top buttons of his tunic. "Herr Bon-hoeffer, I think it's time for you to meet the head of military intelligence, Admiral Wilhelm Canaris."

Their footsteps echoed across the marble floor as Colonel Oster led the way down the hall. Entering a large secretarial bay, Dietrich noticed an array of documents: maps, dispatches, and memos. Multicolored stick pins riddled a large wall map of Europe, Britain, Africa, South America, and the United States.

A dour secretary escorted them through a set of huge mahogany doors into a cavernous office. At the far end stood a short man talking on the telephone.

Dietrich could barely hear his words. In his mid-fifties, his thick sil-ver hair was a stark contrast to his wrinkled blue naval uniform. The ruggedly handsome gentleman looked more like a grandfather than a spy.

Scowling, Canaris leaned on his desk. "Reinhard, do you really expect me to believe you did not approve these actions? Good Lord, man! You began with two hundred Jews murdered in the streets and twenty thou-sand jailed in the camps. Now Germans disappear at night, never to be seen again." He rolled his eyes. "So you say, but we both know differ-ently." Canaris paused. "Göring said what? Alright, but I shall expect you to keep me informed." His face was flushed with anger as he replaced the receiver.

Colonel Oster cleared his throat. "Admiral?"

"Heydrich denies everything!" Oblivious to his guests, Canaris walked over to the hearth, where his pet dachshunds lay quietly beside the blazing fire. "Seppel! Sabine!" The two brown-haired dogs sprang to life and scrambled across the slick floor to their master. The admiral cuddled one as Oster ushered his guests toward the two couches border-ing the hearth.

Dohnanyi took the lead. "Admiral, may I present my brother-in-law, Dr. Dietrich Bonhoeffer. Dietrich, this is Wilhelm Canaris."

Dietrich could sense the admiral's mood shift. His placid blue eyes were warm as he shook Dietrich's hand with a firm grip.

"I've heard good things about you, Herr Bonhoeffer."

"From reputable people, I hope." Dietrich noticed something familiar about the admiral's face.

The admiral took a seat opposite Dietrich as he gently placed Sabine on his lap. "Herr Bonhoeffer, we have made you a serious proposal. What is your decision?"

Dietrich was on the cusp. He had already crossed the ethical line but did not know it until that moment. "Sir, I am a Christian theologian without a church, *and* I am a loyal citizen of a Germany that no longer exists."

Canaris pursed his lips. "You are a man of courage to say such things to me. You have contacts in England, Sweden, and Norway. As one of our agents, you would travel to Switzerland, Italy, Sweden, and England to meet with your church-related colleagues."

His brother-in-law tapped his briar pipe in an ashtray. "Dietrich's friend Bishop Bell knows Sir Anthony Eden of the British government. Dietrich could state our case."

Oster clasped his hands together. "The Führer intends to go to war in a matter of months. If we remove him from power, we will need military support to replace the government."

"With Hitler ranting in public, England will naturally be suspicious of any German resistance," Canaris said.

"But, sir, I'm a theologian, not a diplomat."

"Which is precisely why I want you involved. If I send any of our regular agents, the Allies will certainly not trust them. Your clergy friends, however, will trust you and may help persuade their government to our cause."

Oster glanced at his boss. "As a gesture of good faith, we have already ordered the release of your colleague from Sachsenhausen Camp. Herr Ehrenberg and his wife will have travel documents and safe passage to London."

"You can do this?" Dietrich was amazed. "You know they are Jews?"

Oster nodded. "Of course, you will need to contact Bishop Bell to make final arrangements."

Canaris's kind blue eyes sharpened. "You will be thoroughly briefed about our agendas with the good bishop. I have every confidence for your success."

Dietrich crossed his legs as he nervously brushed lint from his trousers. Could anyone truly depend on a novice spy?

Dohnanyi tamped down the tobacco in his pipe and lit a match.

"As an 'employee' of the Abwehr, your passport will allow you to exit and reenter Germany at will. The Gestapo may monitor your movements, but they won't be able to stop you."

Dietrich leaned forward. "Admiral, I accept your offer. How can I ever thank you?"

"By being a loyal German. Herr Bonhoeffer, as a military man, I do not believe in coincidence. Forces beyond all of us have brought us here to this hour." Canaris's eyes softened as he cuddled Sabine in his arms. "There comes a time when a man must ask himself, in what do I really believe?"

Dietrich gazed at the fire blazing in the stone fireplace. Two logs had fallen against one another at right angles. The flames licked the crossed beams. He pondered Canaris's question. *In what do I really believe?* "Gentlemen, I will take your message to Bishop Bell. And for the sake of Germany—I pray that he will listen."

*   *   *

Sachsenhausen Camp

The long workdays drifted into night, and the sun arose all too soon to expose the columns of bedraggled prisoners shuffling to their next work detail. Foul odors, undernourished bellies, and countless faces devoid of hope surrounded Abraham. The guards' cruelty to the other prisoners depleted his vitality of faith. "Abraham is special," the guards would mock. Neame had ordered special treatment to keep him and his fellow prisoners in Block 13 healthy.

Starving prisoners occasionally rushed the food carts and supplies wheelbarrowed into Block 13. Prisoner turnover was rampant. Jewish inmates either died of starvation, were murdered, or bartered their way to freedom.

Outside the barracks, Abraham offered a can of beans to Jacob. "For you, my friend. Go ahead, enjoy!"

At first, Jacob proudly refused. "And yet for my family, I must survive." He quietly slipped the can in his coat as he glanced in all directions.

One day Abraham and Jacob were surprised to see Ehrenberg dressed in civilian clothes.

Jacob grimaced. "So, Herr Ehrenberg, you had some money after all."

"No, I was summoned to the commandant's office and told that my release papers had been sent from Berlin."

Jacob's eyes narrowed. "I guess Nazis kill Jews, not Christians. Shalom, *Reverend* Ehrenberg."

Ehrenberg extended his good hand. "Jacob, perhaps I can help you with your dream to reach Palestine." The clergyman placed a small book into his hands.

Jacob scoffed. "No one can help the Jews."

"Read the book. They are the words of Messiah Yeshua in Hebrew. He speaks of those written in the Book of Life."

Jacob stepped back, his eyes widened. He opened the pages and disappeared into a mass of huddled prisoners.

Abraham tapped Ehrenberg on the shoulder. "Please, I want you to take this. It's a photograph of my only daughter."

"What do you want me to do?"

"That friend you have in Berlin—?"

"Dr. Bonhoeffer."

"You trust him?"

"With my very life!"

Abraham pointed at the photograph. "My daughter is working as a barmaid in Berlin. Ask your friend to check on her? The address is on the back."

Ehrenberg clasped Abraham's hand. "Perhaps, we shall meet again. Goodbye, Abraham."

Abraham watched as Ehrenberg walked through the barbed-wire gates as a free man. He pictured the day that he, too, would leave this godforsaken place. *O Lord, grant me a miracle.* In the comfort of home, he would once again feel the precious embrace of Nina and Sarah.

*   *   *

Berlin

Dietrich poured some red wine in honor of their guests the Ehrenbergs. "Hans von Dohnanyi is the one to thank. Soon both of you will be on your way to London—with the required legal documents."

Ehrenberg held his wife's hand. "It's like a dream. A few days ago, I was imprisoned. Now, I'm enjoying the company of good friends." He retrieved the photograph from his pocket. "I met a man at Sachsenhausen—a Jew by the name Abraham Kleisfeld. A few years back his daughter Sarah came to Berlin." Hans slid the photograph across the table. "He risked a great deal for me to give this to you. If you can, find this girl and see if you can help her."

Dietrich held the black-and-white photograph up to the light and noted the address on the back.

"Kleisfeld said she works as a barmaid."

Dietrich tucked the photo into his wallet. "I will look into it."

Early the next morning, Dietrich and the Ehrenbergs boarded the train to Stettin on the northern coast. They planned to visit the countess and her family at the Patzig estate for a few days en route to London. The passenger car was less than half full and unusually quiet as the train forged a path through northeast Germany.

Exhausted by their harried schedule, his guests dozed off. Dietrich glanced out the window as the train passed by familiar landmarks—and yet, everything in Germany was different now. Hitler's hand no longer held a veiled threat. His minions held sway over the leaders of the Reich Church.

Dietrich turned to Psalm 74. *"O God, why are You so fiercely angry with the sheep of your pasture? . . . They burn all the houses of God in the land. How long shall the adversary reproach, and the enemy blaspheme Your name?"*

The gentle hum of the train wheels droned on. Again, the innocent eyes of Sarah Kleisfeld stared back at Dietrich from the glossy black-and-white photograph. Then he looked across the aisle at the Ehrenbergs. He remembered Kristallnacht—when the Reich Church abandoned the Jews!

He took a pen and wrote the date November 9, 1938 in his Bible by Psalm 74. Dietrich lifted his eyes and gazed out on Germany. *If the synagogues burn today, the churches will be on fire tomorrow.*

Chapter Fifteen

Near Berlin, May 1939

E va lay upon the grassy shore of Müggelsee Lake, the perfect place at the perfect time. A row of sailboats moored to a wooden dock bobbed back and forth in the gentle waves. She adjusted the rose-colored ruffles on her vest just so. Through the spring months, she had painstakingly made the floral dress for just such an occasion. When Ernst looked at her, she felt secure and special. Sometime during their stolen moments together, he had touched her heart.

Ernst poured her another glass of Cabernet Sauvignon and raised his. "To the most pleasant-looking woman at the park."

She scoffed. "Pleasant! Why Ernst Teschler—"

"Excuse me. To the most gorgeous woman in Berlin." His mouth curled in a boyish grin.

"And in all of Germany!"

"I will ask my uncle to commission Max and me to conduct a formal SS inspection of the most beautiful women in all of Germany. I'm sure you will place favorably."

Eva pressed her lips together, grabbed his shirt collar, and pulled him close. "I suppose I will have to lobby for the prize." She locked her ruby-red lips upon his, and they eased into each other's arms.

"Well, with all this lobbying going on, I guess I won't have time to conduct the inspection after all."

Eva tilted her head, his eyes holding her captive. "Ernst, I'm falling in love with you."

"Fräulein, you have bewitched me." He nibbled her ear and stroked her blonde hair as his lips skimmed the nape of her neck. "Eva, I do have feelings for you, more so than any other girl I've known. But soon, Germany will be at war, and—"

"You must never leave me. You are the only man who can protect me."

"From what?"

She sat up and looked across the ripples in the water. That was the question she so desperately wanted to avoid. "Have you ever dreamed of escaping to an enchanted island? A safe place populated with gorgeous flora, furry animals, and people who embrace others from all walks of life?"

A gentle smile appeared as he stroked her blonde tendrils with his fingers.

"Ernst, you know so little about me and my past."

"Then we must spend more time together so you can spin tales of your youth in the magic kingdom: princesses, castles, and all." With the sun drifting lower in the sky, their lips touched again, and they melded into one.

*   *   *

Berlin

One Saturday morning, Reinhard came to the Teschler home to see his sister for breakfast. "My dear, your Bavarian apple strudel was delicious. The second serving bested the first."

With coffee urn in hand, she filled his cup to the brim as she cleared the dishes. "It was a rough winter this year. With Rudolf, I feel like I'm sinking in quicksand."

"Anna, you used to be the life of the party. You wore fancy dresses with your hair styled in the latest fashion." The shrill sound of a table saw filtering through the basement door was distracting. "That man is always making a racket!"

She hardly seemed to notice the commotion. "After we were married, my husband was so dashing, so brilliant in the courtroom."

Reinhard gently held her hand. "In '29, his mind was sharp, his legal record was the envy of Berlin. Everyone toasted his success, until Rudolf was betrayed. Now his blade is dulled by the alcohol."

The basement door creaked open. Rudolf emerged from the dark stairwell. His simmering looks confirmed that he had heard everything.

Reinhard emptied his cup. He braced himself for what was sure to be another of Rudolf's "when I was young" speeches.

Anna moved quickly to the stove. "Rudolf, Reinhard and I just finished breakfast. We were just . . . having some coffee."

Rudolf's eyelids narrowed. "Yes, dear, I'll take a cup."

Reinhard sensed something volatile in Rudolf's eyes. He was too calm, too focused. Perhaps the lawyer's tongue had been sharpened for the kill?

Anna poured her husband a fresh cup and set the steaming porcelain kettle on a trivet near the edge of the table.

Rudolf sauntered around the kitchen table and posed as if he were about to address the court. "Anna is a decent woman, Reinhard. Unlike you, she has dignity. Unlike you, she has loyalty to her family."

Reinhard leaned back in his chair. "If only you stood up to life like that, then I would respect you." And Himmler would get off his back.

Indignant, Rudolf picked up the steaming pot and doused its scorching contents onto Reinhard's left hand. He shrieked as the scalding-hot liquid and seared coffee grounds encrusted his fingers.

Anna screamed as she stood back in horror. Blisters bubbled instantly upon his quivering hand. Anna marched him over to the sink and plunged his seared fingers under cold running water. "Rudolf, how could you!"

She rotated Reinhard's fingers through the soothing stream of cool liquid. He clenched his teeth. If looks could kill!

Rudolf held up the kettle with a glint in his eye. "Reinhard, would you like another cup of coffee before you leave?"

*   *   *

Berlin, SS Headquarters, June 2, 1939

Reinhard winced as he probed his bandaged left hand. On his desk lay the remains of his prized SS Death's Head ring. Because of the swelling, the ring had to be sawed off his finger. With utter disdain, Reinhard pictured his brother-in-law's gloating smirk. Who would have the last laugh? Reinhard swigged the rest of the schnapps in his glass, then poured another.

His pain somewhat dulled, he turned his attention toward the beautiful silver-plated fountain pen beside his letter.

Dear Ernst,

I was present with the Führer at his signing of new political powers for the SS. Later at dinner when I bragged about you, he gave me the enclosed pen. I have every confidence in you. I look forward to your graduation from Bernau and your joining me in service to the Reich.

Affectionately,
Uncle Reinhard

A few hours later, Major Neame and a balding SS bureaucrat joined Heydrich in his office.

"Krüger, you're late!"

"Yes, General. There is a problem in the Balkans. Our people in Turkey have confiscated a number of forged German travel documents. They were taken by Jewish emigrants headed toward Istanbul."

Neame frowned. "General, you remember the incident at Kleisfeld's shop in Wittenberg? Teschler and Schumann were almost gunned down. The two snipers killed at the scene had Czech papers but were armed with German weapons. From the evidence, we think they may have been Jews—from Palestine."

"Jews, you say?" Reinhard perused the samples from Turkey. "If we're not careful, the Jews will soon counterfeit our Reichsmarks."

"—which could ruin our economy," Krüger said.

Neame lit a cigarette. "We need approval to forge the British five-pound note."

"Yes, accelerate all schedules for the operation." Reinhard cradled his hand. "Krüger, if Jews are behind this, we must sniff them out."

Krüger's gaze darted between his colleagues. "Sir, I will investigate these bogus documents and report back to you." With a half salute, the bureaucrat departed.

"Sir, is there anything else?" Neame asked.

Reinhard crushed his burning cigarette stub into a ceramic tray with his good hand. "Ernst's father has crossed the line. It's time to remove this embarrassment to my family."

"How do you wish me to handle it?"

"It should appear that Rudolf fell victim to Jewish thieves. All the evidence must be convincing. I want my nephew to rage rabid against the Jews to avenge his father's brutal murder."

"You have any particular method in mind?"

Reinhard paused as he caressed his bandaged hand. "I most certainly do. And Neame, make sure Rudolf's face can be clearly identified." Reinhard's eyes narrowed, his grin smug. "Vengeance is mine saith the Lord!"

*   *   *

Ernst searched through a kitchen cabinet. "Where's Mother?"

Newspaper in hand, Papa sipped his coffee. "At Frau Brunner's house, sewing. There's some cheese in the refrigerator."

"I can get something later at the Bismarck."

His father lowered his newspaper. "Ernst, the Gestapo has been tampering with our mail. The postman warned me again this afternoon."

"Are you certain?"

"Take a look around you. Ordinary citizens are being dragged from their homes at night. You can't say anything against Hitler for fear of prison."

"Papa, you must tread very carefully. What you say is treason."

"Be prepared to face the consequences of your actions, son. The SS is guilty of extortion, theft, and murder. Thousands of Germans will die, and you have become a part of it!"

"Stop it! Please. If you say these things on the street, I won't be able to protect you."

"Look in the mirror, Ernst. You're beginning to talk like Heydrich."

"I remember many years ago. You were a war hero from the Great War and a celebrated lawyer. Mother and I were so proud of you then."

Papa lowered his eyes. "My time on the political stage is over. But for you and your friend Max—your time has now come. Don't destroy the Germany we once knew. Help rebuild it into something worthy."

The clock in the hall chimed the six o'clock hour. Exasperated, Ernst stood and wrapped his arm around his father's shoulder. "Papa, please. If you can't bridle your thoughts, do curb your tongue." *I can't always be there to help you.*

Ernst snapped his black officer's hat smartly upon his head and opened the door. Looking back, he saw his father's saddened eyes. Something kind inside led him back to his father's side. Ernst leaned down and kissed him on his head.

"I love you, son. Remember that."

"I love you too, Papa. I will see you in the morning."

*   *   *

Bismarck Tavern, June 4, 1939

Ernst and Max walked into the Bismarck with a spring in their step. Tall and muscular, Ernst had a commanding presence. There was something menacing yet graceful about his stride—like a jungle cat. One look at Max, and Ernst could only smile. Always looking for a party, his friend usually assumed someone else would buy the beer, and he would provide the fun.

When they approached their customary table, they found it already occupied. Even with his back to Ernst, the broad, beefy outlines of Manfred Siegfried and his friends were clear. The "Ox" raised his stein and shouted to a barmaid for more beer. Ernst motioned Max off to the side.

"You're not going to let him—"

"I'm not in the mood to deal with that ill-mannered brute. We'll sit elsewhere tonight." Ernst threaded through tables and claimed an unoccupied spot across the aisle.

"But, Ernst, you're allowing Siegfried to have our table."

"I came here to see Eva, Max, not to get into another fight. We plan to have dinner after her shift."

A barmaid appeared and placed two steins on the table. Max struck a wolfish pose. "Fräulein, I find you quite attractive." He was rewarded by a flirtatious wiggle of her hips as she departed.

"Women are mere conquests to you."

Max's lips quirked in a wry grin. "A skilled fisherman catches as many fish as he can."

"I want something more for Eva." He lifted his stein. "To love!" They clinked their steins together.

Max chugged down most of his brew. When the barmaid placed a full pitcher of beer on the table, the perky Fräulein gave Max a clear invitation.

Ernst countered with a raised eyebrow.

Max stood and craned his neck to keep the short-haired blonde in sight. "I must go relieve myself." Like a loyal puppy, the brash young soldier followed his barmaid across the room.

Ernst casually looked across the smoke-filled haze above the crowd when he realized Max had walked right into Siegfried's enclave.

As the huge lummox stood, the waves of patrons around him parted. "Sergeant Schumann!" His voice boomed. "I could smell you from across the room!" The overgrown peasant in uniform picked up a pitcher of beer and gleefully poured it over Max's head. "Perhaps this will make you smell better, ja?"

Surrounded by laughter, Max wiped his face with the back of his hand.

Patrons stood and blocked Ernst's view, so he climbed up on his chair to see.

Red in the face, Max licked his fingers. "Look what the butcher brought in. Siegfried, you look like a pig on a stick." Max cocked his arm, but the beer had slowed his reflexes.

Siegfried caught Max's fist in midair, slammed his own into Max's belly, and Max doubled over. Two of Siegfried's friends jumped in and pinned Max's arms. Siegfried's knuckles pummeled Max's face twice.

Max struggled to fight back but was outnumbered and slow-moving. His battered body slumped to his knees as blood gushed from his nose and lips.

Ernst jumped off the chair onto the floor. It took several moments to push through the crowd to his friend.

As fellow soldiers applauded, Siegfried lifted both hands in victory, then poured the last contents of his stein over Max's head. Dazed, Max fell to the floor.

If looks could kill? Ernst's nostrils flared as he entered the fray. Siegfried's companions stepped back, carefully sizing up their new opponent. Ernst squatted over Max's limp body and lightly slapped him on the cheek.

When Max turned his head, his face looked like a bloody rump roast. Ernst narrowed his eyes, one hand on his truncheon as he tactically scanned the scene to position his opponents. One soldier edged behind him, while the other stepped over to his side.

From behind, a young Wehrmacht officer swung an opened wine bottle at Ernst's head. Ernst ducked, and his truncheon sprang alive in his hand. It smashed through the bottle into the man's hand. As its wood shaft crunched through the glass, he could hear multiple bones snap.

The man's jaw gaped. Ernst swung the club backhanded and slammed it into the man's lower leg. The force of the impact flipped the man into the air and flat on his back. Siegfried looked down at his friend with utter disbelief stamped on his face. Tapping the tip of the truncheon into his palm, Ernst's glare sent all of Siegfried's other companions scampering into the crowd.

In the calm before the storm, Ernst slipped his truncheon into his leather belt. Slowly, he circled Siegfried and backed him into a corner, blocking the only way out. "Ox, you will not walk away this time."

Siegfried shuffled backward. "Schumann asked for this."

"You are a disgrace to the German uniform." Ernst could sense the man's fear as he edged closer.

His eyes wide, Siegfried fumbled for his dagger. Its silver blade glistened as he waved the weapon from side to side. The crowd pulled back as Ernst dropped his focus to Siegfried's chest. Neame had taught him that the pectoral muscles would telegraph his opponent's intentions just before he struck.

Siegfried growled and thrust his knife at Ernst's face. Ernst rotated and applied a wristlock. Having trapped the knife, he forced the Ox to his knees. He plowed his knee into the man's face twice in rapid succession. Dazed, Siegfried crumpled to the ground. The watching crowd cheered.

Max propped himself up on one knee. "Ernst."

Ernst backed away slowly and stood by his injured friend while two SS soldiers nearby offered to carry Max out.

On his knees, Siegfried cradled his broken nose with his hand as blood gushed through his fingers. Their eyes met once more before Ernst turned to follow his friend being assisted toward the main entrance.

Ernst heard a gasp from the crowd. The familiar click of a pistol safety being released positioned his opponent behind him. Ernst could feel the barrel's line of fire between his shoulder blades a split second before he moved.

As the bullet whizzed by his ear, Ernst dropped to one knee, spun around, and fired his silenced Walther P38 from the hip. Two shots drilled into Siegfried's upper arm and throat. His eyes bulged as he toppled into a table, overturning it as he hit the floor.

As smoke and the acrid smell of cordite wafted from his barrel, Ernst stood and walked over to his opponent. Blood spurted from the severed artery in his arm in rhythm with his dying heartbeats. Ernst was fascinated by the crimson patterns painted by its flow.

The lummox attempted to speak but choked on his own blood. Then Siegfried's eyes glazed over as his body trembled in shock. Ernst calmly watched as the big Ox took his last breath.

No one would miss the likes of Manfred Siegfried.

From the crowd, cheers and applause erupted as if, for a moment, they had all been ancient Romans in the Colosseum. Ernst frowned. Without inspecting the corpse, Ernst holstered his weapon and strode toward the door, the sea of patrons parting around him.

Moments later, Ernst and Max reclined in the back seat of an SS staff car. In the front passenger seat was Captain Walter Schellenberg.

"David once again conquers Goliath. Teschler, your technique was spectacular."

Ernst was puzzled. Why was Schellenberg watching him? Did his uncle order him to surveil his movements or was it Himmler? Ernst was in the dark, and that was a bad place to be.

"Heydrich's right. You are a force to be reckoned with." Schellenberg mustered a wry smile. "Let's give Schumann a few days to recover. Report to my office next week. Then you two will see some real action."

Chapter Sixteen

Southeast Bavaria

That night Hitler slept restlessly in the Eagle's Nest high atop Mount Kehlstein. He twisted his head from side to side in the clutches of a recurring dream.

At the Lambach Abbey in Austria, a Cistercian monk led ten-year-old Adolf by the hand as they toured the ancient edifice. The monk's protruding hood shrouded all but his bony nose and pointed chin. The monk's swollen lips moved as if he spoke, but Adolf heard no sound.

In an instant, the monk transported him to a mass rally in the Nuremberg arena, where thousands chanted Adolf's name. Then mighty armies were unleashed under his command. In a mystical constellation of the stars, he saw the swastika branded upon huge banners of red, white, and black. He realized that the crooked cross was the key to the conquest of Europe. A spiraling swastika was both symbol and strategy for the great war to come.

The monk ripped off his cowl, revealing the golden hair of the sun itself and the chiseled face of Lucifer. The creature's black lips flexed, pronouncing the judgment against the Hebrews. Then, in an instant, the face of Satan morphed into a thousand demonic eyes with fangs chattering from the darkness.

Hitler screamed into his pillow. A hot, foul breath blanketed his face as something ominous stooped over him with taloned claws gripping his throat. Gasping for life, he threw himself out of bed. Kneeling on the floor, perspiration drenched his pajamas.

The Führer's attendant rushed into his chamber. Adolf was stretched across the floor, jerking convulsively—shouting a string of profanities. Suddenly he was still, his jaw stretched wide as if uttering a silent scream.

"Linge, look there!" he shrieked. "Over there! Can you see them? Do something—they're consuming me alive!"

Herr Linge scoured the room. "Mein Führer, no one is here. It was a dream, just a bad—"

"Silence!" The Führer held his breath to listen for the intruders. "You are a liar!" He dismissed his servant with a wave of his hand.

When Adolf was alone, he darted his gaze around the room. He turned on another lamp, nervously awaiting another glimpse of the specter. Something compelled him closer to his window. Black as night beyond, he observed his distorted image reflected on dark glass. His eyes stretched open—they shimmered like two transparent silver saucers striated with grey. They appeared almost lifeless, but then an eerie crimson light emerged beneath the languid pools.

His whole body stiffened as *something* inhabited his frail body. He could hear the gnashing of teeth as they revealed the future. The famished demons of the abyss were now ready to consume God's people—the Jews!

*   *   *

Wewelsburg Castle, June 5, 1939

High atop the north tower of the ancient castle, Weisthor faced Himmler, seated across the black onyx table. They had entered the Seeker's Portal once again to seek the voice of the sacred rings. The first ring was spun, then the second. When they wobbled, something beyond gravity energized their path. Weisthor sensed the manifestation of power, when suddenly, as if someone had snuffed out a lit candle, it disappeared.

Despite further incantations, the two SS chieftains encountered only the sound of the wind bellowing outside. In a fit, Himmler stormed out of the chamber. Weisthor waited. He repositioned the silver rings on the onyx stone table. In succession, he spun the glistening circles with renewed determination. Then, as each began to falter, a surge of supernatural energy spurred the spinning triad to open the portal. It was as if Weisthor was lifted above the astral plane. The harmonic lyrics of demons revealed the truth to the occult priest.

An hour later Weisthor entered Himmler's apartment. Looking utterly dejected, the head of the SS sat by the hearth, staring at the burning embers.

"Heinrich, we should have known. It was Hitler. He was exercising the power of the Spear at the Eagle's Nest!"

Red-faced, Himmler scooped the imitation spearhead off his desk. "Hitler keeps the original mounted on the wall of his subterranean 'sanctuary.' He held the talisman before me and told me its history, as if I were a mere schoolboy. This man treats this sacred object of occult mystery—this talisman of such incredible power—as a mere trinket!"

"The rings have confirmed the prophecy. The Infidel has tasted blood and more than once. Soon, Teschler will do our bidding."

Himmler looked at his mentor. "He stands too close to Heydrich. How can we trust Teschler?"

"The rings have spoken. Within days, a crisis will befall young Teschler. The stars will shift to a new cycle, and our young Black Knight will play into our hands. This very night in the Well of Souls, we shall commune with dark angels and celebrate our most Unholy Eucharist!"

*   *   *

Berlin, June 6, 1939

The sun touched the horizon, casting a heavenly purple hue upon the clouds. Soon it would be dark, but Rudolf Teschler felt secure with a streetlamp illuminating his park bench. He looked at the aged photo in his gold pocket watch, smiling at his ten-year-old son upon his lap. For all the late nights at work, how many school games with his son did he miss? For all the weekend political events, how many more fish could a father and son have caught at the lake together? Then there were all the misspent hours drinking with strangers at the Bismarck.

Ernst, how many more photographs of you could I have taken if I had just spent more time with you?

Snapping the watch shut, he walked toward the Bismarck. From inside the beer hall, boisterous music and muted voices could be heard. He sniffed the warm night air and could almost taste the brew. They must be having a grand time.

He looked again at his pocket watch. The regrets he had in life could be measured by the second hand. His wife would be angry. He could hear her shrill voice. "You're late again for dinner, Rudolf." *I am always late for something. . . .*

As he approached Temple Adath Adonai, two SS soldiers accosted a middle-aged Jew on the sidewalk. There were shouts and then a scuffle. With the butt of his rifle, one soldier jabbed the shopkeeper in the stomach, and he doubled over.

Rudolf rushed to the victim's aid, but in a flash, the two SS goons turned on Rudolf. They dragged him into a nearby alley. One pinned Rudolf's arms behind his back as the other drove his fist into his face. Blood gushed from his nostrils across his lips.

Rudolf struggled. "You can't touch me! I'm a German citizen."

"That is a matter of opinion, Herr Teschler." A deep, calm voice echoed from the shadows.

Rudolf blinked, straining to see the stranger. He could taste the salty brine of his own blood. A short, muscular man dressed in a black leather trench coat emerged from the shadows. The streetlight reflected off his greased black hair.

The serrated jaws of a steel bear trap snapped shut any hopes of escape.

"Herr Teschler, my name is Alfred Neame."

The sinister look in the man's eyes unnerved him. Rudolf tried to twist free, but they pinned him to the ground on his back. The soldiers ripped his shirt open as Neame pulled a vial from his coat. Straddling his victim's chest, the SS assassin twisted off the cap and waved the glass vial beneath Rudolf's nose. The pungent odor burned his nostrils.

"What are you doing?" Rudolf shouted.

"Smell the aroma, Herr Teschler. Sulfuric acid is like a cup of steaming-hot coffee from your brother-in-law, Reinhard Heydrich."

Rudolf's eyes stretched wide as Neame dripped the caustic liquid upon his exposed skin. Amidst his strangled screams, Rudolf reared back as his assailant burned a Star of David across his chest. Rudolf howled in agony, his whole body shuddering as the acid seared through layers of his bare skin. An acrid odor of burning flesh permeated the twilight mist as Rudolf's helpless tears streaked down his flushed cheeks.

Neame drew an eight-inch knife from his inside coat pocket. Hebrew symbols adorned its ivory handle. Neame waved the blade before Rudolf's face. "Should I gut your belly like a pig?" Then a flicker of reflected light danced across Neame's monstrous face. He reached down and ripped Rudolf's pocket watch and chain from his belt. Neame clicked the lid open. "My, my . . . a photo of the loving Teschler family. I will be sure to show this to your son on the day of his death. Auf Weidersehen!"

A wicked grin crossed Neame's lips. With a flick of his killer's wrist, the blade slashed across Rudolf's throat. His life blood spurted a vigorous stream over his limp body.

Then Rudolf felt himself floating in the air—above his body.

He looked down at the carcass lying on the cobblestones. *What a gruesome sight.* The gaping wounds, the pool of blood, and the contorted face all were strewn together in vivid colors. The corpse's eyes were frozen with terror.

Then it dawned on him—*the dead body is me!*

He would have shrieked if he had a mouth, if he had lungs. When he stared down, an icy fear propelled him away from the diabolical creature in rapid pursuit. There was one chance for survival. Rudolf swam feverishly upward toward the luminous whirling cloud like a fish caught in a wild current. Above, there was light at the pinnacle—a blessed light!

The light intensified. The radiant being was so bright, he could only sense His purity. Rudolf knew who it was. The glorious eyes of the Holy reflected an inexpressible sadness. He heard a simple, damning question. "Do I know you?"

Then the light disappeared. Rejected, all became blackness and despair. And the creature from the abyss ripped Rudolf's being from eternity. He was dead but still conscious. Rudolf knew it was so, as frenzied demons tore their razor-sharp teeth into the dark nothing that was his soul.

*   *   *

A warm summer breeze rippled the sheer curtains through the open balcony door of Eva's apartment. A solitary lamp illuminated her blue eyes as they danced. A slow romantic ballad resonated through the old phonograph as Ernst swayed Eva slowly back and forth. His uniform jacket lay over a chair, and his brown shirt was open at the collar. Her perfume from Paris was intoxicating. Her barmaid dress was adorned with puffed sleeves and a scooped bodice. Her skirt flowed gracefully over her thighs. With such alluring details, Ernst was unseasonably hot this evening. "Where are we?"

Eva looked intently into his eyes. "We're lost in a dream."

"Ah, a very pleasant dream, my darling."

"Ernst, I feel so secure in your arms."

He eased into a gentle smile. "We shall see." Their lips gently touched as the music merged their hearts together.

Then, uninvited, a terse knock sounded at the door. The couple blinked. Then someone pounded at the door. So rudely drawn back to reality, Ernst marched to answer it, steaming. He was always at someone's beck and call.

Ernst held the door open. "Max, I told you I wanted to be alone!"

"Something terrible has happened."

"What?"

"It's your father. He was attacked on the streets."

Eva entered the foyer with Ernst's uniform coat. "Darling, let me come with you."

The trio rushed down three flights of stairs and jumped into the parked SS sedan.

"How badly was he injured?"

Max braked for a light. "I don't know."

"Come on, Max. Run the light."

The automobile lurched forward at top speed past the bright lights of the Bismarck Tavern, turned the corner, and screeched to a halt in front of a police barricade. Ernst and Eva jumped out and faced a tall police officer.

"Halt, identify yourselves!"

"I am Lieutenant Teschler. I understand you have reported a crime."

"Ernst!" a familiar voice called out as Reinhard emerged from the alley.

"Sir, why are you here?"

Sadness filled Reinhard's eyes. "I'm afraid I have bad news."

Eva squeezed Ernst's arm as their eyes met.

"What is it?" His stomach twisted as he tasted his worst fears.

Reinhard paused. "Fräulein, it would be best if you stayed in the car."

Her eyes pleading with Ernst, Eva did not budge.

"Follow me then." Reinhard turned on his heel and led the group down the darkened alley. "Witnesses say your father was attacked by Jews."

Eva's fingers dug into Ernst's arm as Max brought up the rear. In the distance, they heard sirens arriving on the scene. Ernst's breath quickened as his imagination went wild.

Reinhard edged farther down the darkened alley into a battery of bright portable lamps. Three SS sentries guarded the crime scene as a physician probed the body for evidence.

Ernst smelled the stench of burnt flesh. The doctor's fingers were coated with blood as they approached. He wiped off his hands with a towel, shaking his head.

"I'm so sorry, Lieutenant. They must have tortured him to death—slowly."

Ernst's eyes were fixed on the bloody towel as the doctor stepped to the side. Like a curtain drawn, the physician unveiled the scene of his father's slaughter.

Eva swayed at the gruesome sight and stepped back. Max took her arm as Ernst ventured closer.

With the starry innocence of a little boy, Ernst looked down at the lifeless face of his father. It looked like his head had been placed atop a butchered pig. When Ernst slumped to his knees, his father's pooled blood soaked through his uniform pants.

Ernst reached out and touched his father's blood-splattered face. *That can't be—*

"Papa? Is that really you?" *Speak to me!*

His father's eyes protruded from their sockets and glistened in the moonlight. As he inhaled the sulfuric fumes, Ernst felt sick and tears clouded his vision. "Oh Papa, no!" *I warned you not to speak in public. . . .*

As Reinhard clasped his shoulders from behind, Ernst folded himself over his father's mutilated chest. "It can't be—Papa!"

Reinhard leaned closer with his face twisted. "The Jews did this! They branded your father like a steer. Butchers, that's what they are!"

Quivering, Ernst opened his father's shirt and spied the Star of David seared into his father's chest. He reeled back livid with rage.

"Look at your father's eyes! Remember them, Ernst. Together, you and I will avenge your father's death."

Burying his face into his bloody hands, Ernst shook his head. He arched his back and uttered a blistering, primeval scream into the blackness of the night.

Chapter Seventeen

Berlin, June 1939

Two SS staff cars were parked on the street in front of the Teschler house. From his open bedroom window, Ernst looked down upon the black uniformed troopers lingering on the sidewalk as Pastor Bonhoeffer arrived. In deference to his clerical collar, the guards parted to let Dietrich pass, but Ernst heard a derogatory jest as he stepped by.

Ernst sat back down on his bedroom floor cross-legged to massage Barron's flank with a brush. His Doberman sat on his haunches, panting. "You're smiling for me, aren't you, boy?" *Yes, I love you more than anyone in the world.*

Barron gave his master a loving lick on the hand. Ernst leaned his head against his short-haired coat. His faithful companion's heart thumped in a soothing rhythm.

There was a knock at the door, and Pastor Bonhoeffer entered, then closed the door behind him. "Hello, Ernst. I came as soon as I heard the news. I am so sorry about your father."

Ernst's eyes remained on Barron as they talked. "Jews did this. Jews with knives and a bottle of acid. No one knows why Papa went to that alley. No one knows why they were so cruel. Was it by chance? Or did God ordain it?" He shook his head. "No, I suppose Jews just hate Germans. That's what Uncle Reinhard says."

Dietrich sat on the bed. "Your father was precious to you and your mother. The crime was heinous. The violence—senseless."

"When Uncle Reinhard finds the savages, I will meet them in the ring." His last few brushstrokes across Barron were vigorous. *I will send them to hell with my bare hands.*

Dietrich sat next to Ernst on the rug. "Ernst, revenge and hatred can only consume you. After the crucifixion, there was a man named Saul who hated Jewish Christians. He hunted them down and participated in their imprisonment and death. God appeared to Saul and appointed him as a witness to the *Jewish* people and the Gentiles. Over the years, Saul experienced the Holy Spirit opening their eyes so that they could turn from darkness to light and from the dominion of Satan to God. On the road to Damascus, Saul encountered Christ Jesus and received forgiveness of his sins by faith. The Holy Spirit transformed the Jewish Rabbi Saul into the mighty Apostle Paul."

Dietrich placed a hand upon Ernst's shoulder. "Seek the face of God in your time of grief. Bring your anger to Him, that He might console you. I will stand with you in prayer."

Ernst looked up at his friend, his eyes too swollen to cry. "And what about the Jews? Who will judge them?"

"As a Hebrew, Jesus the Messiah died upon the cross for the forgiveness of your sins. As a people, the Jews did not kill your father—certain men did. As for those who murdered your father, trust in the judgment of God. 'Vengeance is mine; I will repay, saith the Lord.'"

*   *   *

Berlin, Zion Lutheran Church, June 9, 1939

A few days later, the brilliant midafternoon sunlight streamed through the stained-glass windows and down upon a sea of empty church pews. Through bloodshot eyes, Ernst looked up at Pastor Bonhoeffer seated in the chancel chair. The minister appeared regal in his black Geneva gown, crowned with a white collar. The huge sanctuary appeared almost deserted with only thirty-five or forty people in attendance at his father's funeral. At one time, his father had commanded crowds during his political speeches—back in the day.

To one side sat Uncle Reinhard and Lina, to the other—his mother. Ernst wrapped his arm around her. Through the dark veil shrouding her face, faint whimpers could be heard. He was helpless to take away her pain. For days through an icy mask of pleasantries, Ernst had bottled up both his grief and his rage.

Consoled by the ebb and flow of the organ music, Ernst pondered his father's virtues—his love of family, his brilliant legal career, and his bravery for social justice. Then he remembered the picture taken together when Ernst was a child—the one his father treasured in his favorite gold pocket watch. Ernst could still feel his father's strong hands steadying his ten-year-old son upon his knee.

The last tones of the organ died away, and Pastor Bonhoeffer stood behind the towering pulpit. Looking down upon the bereaved, his voice filled the sanctuary. "Let us now bow our heads and lift our hearts to the throne of God's grace."

As Pastor Bonhoeffer led the tiny congregation in the Lord's Prayer, Ernst found his eyes drawn to one particular stained-glass window. The intricate mosaic illustrated Christ's crucifixion. The afternoon sun highlighted one of the criminals hanging next to the Messiah. He remembered the thief's words. "Are You not the Christ? Save Yourself and us! . . . for we are receiving what we deserve for our deeds, but this man has done nothing wrong. Jesus, remember me when You come in Your kingdom."

Then, in an extraordinary moment, the cut-glass tapestry morphed. The face of the mocking criminal transformed into Ernst's own dark image as an older man, full of rage. Ernst looked away in an attempt to flee the haunting vision that lingered in his mind.

"For Thine is the kingdom, and the power, and the glory forever. Amen."

His mother's hand trembled as she reached for his hand and cradled it with her fingers. Ernst so wanted to be strong for his mother. But now, he alone would carry the family name into the future—alone, except for Eva, Max, and Barron. "What is the true measure of a man's life?" Dietrich asked. "As a lawyer, Rudolf fought and won many court battles. As a German, he upheld the traditional values cherished by all who love Germany. As a husband and father, Rudolf wanted to love his family, but he was ill and very much a tortured soul. And yet God was always waiting close by. Rudolf was a victim of violence, and yet we are reminded that it was Christ who was crucified for all of us. It was only by the blood sacrifice of the Messiah that any of us can be redeemed."

Dietrich gazed directly at Ernst. "God gives us many chances to welcome Him into our lives. God loves and wants to comfort you, Anna. Ernst, wherever you may go, whatever you may do, Christ will be with you. Christ is with us now, embracing us in our loss and sorrow."

It was as if Ernst swallowed the words whole, and they embraced the little boy inside who wept.

The service concluded, and Ernst took his place with the pallbearers. As the men surrounded the heavy casket, Ernst lifted the weight of his father for the last time. But he dared not cry, not in public.

The pallbearers proceeded out the main door and down the stone steps to the hearse. Ernst held his head up high. After the men slid the casket into the hearse, Ernst closed the door on his childhood memories. He stared back at the gothic church building and heard the bright-red Nazi banners snapping in the wind.

Oh, Papa, I will try to make you proud.

*   *   *

Later that afternoon, dark clouds overshadowed the interment of Rudolf Teschler. With compassion, Dietrich read God's Word and pronounced parting words for those gathered. With guarded eyes, Reinhard Heydrich stood stoically beside Ernst through the ceremony. The SS general gave new meaning to crocodile tears. Dietrich was afraid for young Ernst, given his future in the SS.

Afterward, Dietrich watched the Teschler family and friends depart through the cemetery gates. Bible in hand, he was heading back to his car when a black sedan coasted to a stop beside him.

With motor idling, a man got out of the car and held up his ID card. "You know who we are, Herr Bonhoeffer. If you don't mind, I will have a look at that." The Nazi agent snatched the Bible from Dietrich's hand and flipped through the pages. "You are Aryan, ja? You could be a leader in the Reich Church, but instead you pander these stories."

Dietrich stood speechless.

The man took a cigarette lighter from his pocket and struck the flint. "Hundreds of years to write—and in a flash, your precious holy words could be burnt to a cinder."

Closing the lid to the lighter, he slapped the leather-bound Bible against Dietrich's chest. "Just remember, Herr Bonhoeffer, these are dangerous times for you and your family." The rude little man strutted back to his car, and it disappeared down the cemetery road.

Shaken, Dietrich sat in his car for some time, clutching the steering wheel. He imagined the look of horror upon his parents' faces should the Gestapo raid their home—all because of their beloved son.

*   *   *

Stuttgart, Germany

A week later, Dietrich sat in a telephone booth on the station platform while his sister, Sabine, and her husband purchased train tickets inside. With a clear view of the foothills to the Alps, Dietrich listened to Hans Dohnanyi's somber voice on the telephone.

"The Gestapo has issued an order against you, Dietrich. It is now illegal for you to enter any church in Berlin."

"They are tightening the noose. What can we do?"

"I have filed a petition in court. You can live in Berlin, but officially, you can't attend church meetings of any kind."

"And my colleagues are shuttled to labor camps!"

"Dietrich, our Abwehr friends can protect you."

"So they say. Look, I've got to go, Hans. Goodbye." With a click, Dietrich replaced the receiver.

Sabine and Gerhard were inspecting their passports on a platform bench when Dietrich sat down.

He retrieved an old family photograph from his wallet. He held it up for Sabine to see. "With short blond hair and striking blue eyes, you will agree that you and I were handsome young twins."

Sabine placed her hand upon his. "We always will be. You know, Dietrich, you did not have to come this far to see us off."

"I wanted to make sure the border guards let Gerhard into Switzerland with a tainted passport."

Gerhard pointed to the prominent red circle on the first page. "*J* for *Jew*—not such a subtle stamp on our lives, is it?"

"The two of you are in love. You have a wonderful marriage to show for it." Dietrich removed an envelope from his coat pocket and placed it in Gerhard's hand. "This is an introduction to Bishop George Bell in London. Once you arrive and get settled, contact him. He's a good friend."

"You have friends in high places."

"He has many political contacts, Gerhard. I am hoping he can arrange a teaching post for you at Oxford."

"Just think—England. This could be a grand opportunity for us!" Sabine said.

Gerhard firmly grasped Dietrich's hand. "I have been part of your family for thirteen years. Dietrich, in you I have seen and experienced the love of God."

Just then, a shrill whistle heralded the train's arrival at the platform.

Sabine gave her brother a big hug. "Thank you for everything."

The two reluctant refugees made their way through the gathering throng to the steaming train. When Sabine looked back, in his memories Dietrich saw his six-year-old twin sister, waving like a little schoolgirl. He waved back over and over until, climbing up the steps, the couple entered the passenger car.

Through the compartment window, Dietrich could see his sister's lips form the words *I love you.*

"I love you too," Dietrich said. The train lurched forward, picking up speed as Sabine and Gerhard waved. With their future uncertain, the couple's silhouette shrank into the distance.

*   *   *

The Patzig Estate, June 12, 1939

Dietrich sat in his room in the east wing of the Patzig manor house, desperate for the right words to write. With each tick of the mantel clock, his open notebook beckoned, but the blank page just stared back at him.

His thoughts drifted back to the day before. Dietrich had discovered Maria in the gardens. She stood radiant in a bright floral-print dress. Her smile and laughter were infectious.

"Herr Bonhoeffer, I—"

"Please, call me Dietrich. We've known each other for so many years."

"Yes, and now that I'm a mature young woman, I look at you differently. Perhaps you've noticed?"

Dietrich was a deer caught in the headlights. "Maria, you have blossomed into an attractive young woman. You are like the swans on the lake, graceful yet shy."

"I, too, notice the swans every morning. I feel God's love in their songs. But I hear God's voice when you speak." Maria blushed. "Dietrich Bonhoeffer, have you noticed me?"

Her enchanting eyes petrified every romantic word on this tongue.

When the hallway clock chimed, his cherished memory lingered. *Good heavens, this young woman has bewitched me!* He shook his head, once, twice—but it was useless. Her spell had been cast.

With a sigh, he closed his notebook and turned to a letter from the Union Seminary in New York. It was another invitation to teach in America. It would be a safe place, and it would reduce the spotlight on his family. He could travel to London, meet with Bishop Bell, and then visit Sabine. Then in that moment, the Spirit of God spoke to Dietrich's heart. The distance from New York City to Maria von Wedemeyer might just be great enough to break her spell.

He retrieved a sheet of stationery and dipped his pen in the inkwell. Just like that, his mind was made up. How odd. One could stew over a decision for weeks and months, then suddenly discover that it had been made. He began to write. . . .

Dr. George Bell
Bishop of Chichester
London, England

Dear George,

I am thinking of leaving Germany soon. The Reich will soon be calling clergymen my age for military service. It would be impossible for me to join in a war under such a government. If I protest, great harm would come to my colleagues by my refusal to bear arms.

They've ordered all pastors to take an oath to Hitler. To refuse would be to resign from the Church. I need to talk to you about many issues and decisions facing me. I shall arrive in London by the 20th. It will be good to see you again.

Ever yours,
Dietrich Bonhoeffer

Dietrich sealed the letter in an envelope and tucked it into his suit coat pocket. There he felt something else. He pulled out a crumpled photograph of Sarah Kleisfeld. Holding her glossy image, he shuddered at the thought of Ernst and Heydrich discovering the truth about this young woman.

*   *   *

Berlin

At the core of SS headquarters was the communications room where personnel supported a network of more than twenty thousand field agents deployed throughout Germany and Europe. Captain Walter Schellenberg stood beside one of the Enigma cipher machines reading a decoded message.

Walter had been playing cat and mouse with a pair of British MI6 agents in Venlo, Holland, for months. His SS operatives baited the mousetrap with false information and a twist of truth to allow an occasional Nazi agent to be captured. Such sacrifices provided credibility for his grand deception.

Walter flipped to the last page of the message and scowled. "More documents—they want still more proof!"

"Have patience, my friend."

Walter whirled around to face Reinhard Heydrich.

"Your false stories have thrown them off track—made them careless. Come, follow me."

Snaking through the maze of hallways, they walked past the interrogation chambers. "Today Himmler is grilling General von Fritsch, the Wehrmacht's chief of staff."

Walter raised his eyebrows. "What did he do?"

Heydrich drew a mocking grin. "He is a traitor. With our methods, he won't last long. Come, I want to show you something." After climbing the stairs, the two men entered Heydrich's private office. "Here is a draft letter to Himmler."

21 June 1939

Reichsführer Himmler:

I look forward to joining your SS circle at the Quedlinburg Cathedral on 2 July to honor King Heinrich the First. We all shall gain from this spiritual exercise.

The Catholic Church is the stalwart enemy of the Reich. As long as the Pope lives, loyal Germans in the Church will never fully recognize the divine nature of the Führer.

First, we must secure administrative control of the German bishops. Second, we should stage morality trials against resistant priests to demonstrate to the public the spiritual bankruptcy of this perverse organization. Third, we should eliminate all Catholic lay organizations that demonstrate undue political influence upon the German people.

Heil Hitler!
Reinhard Heydrich

Walter returned the letter to Heydrich. "Why pursue the Church?"

"Himmler hates the Catholic Church, almost as much as I do. And we won't stop there. Racial cleansing of the German soul is essential. I have already initiated Operation Witches' Cauldron. Each year, we will eliminate one hundred thousand to two hundred and fifty thousand of the racially unfit in hospitals: the mentally ill, the handicapped, and all Jewish patients. Beginning with Christian hospitals, we shall move on to state institutions. Over time, I can envision our Nordic race growing more pure with each generation."

Walter paused. "Did you say racial cleansing of the German soul?"

*   *   *

The Patzig Estate, June 16, 1939

As the servants gathered his luggage in the foyer, Countess Ruth scrutinized Dietrich with her steely blue eyes. "When will you return to Germany?"

Dietrich hesitated. "It could be some time." As Maria came down the steps, he looked into her longing eyes. They were reason enough to flee to America—and quickly.

"Maria, I shall miss you and the family, very much. Give my best to your mother."

To the chagrin of the countess, Maria threw her arms around him.

Clasping her shoulders, Dietrich kissed her fondly upon her forehead. As their car pulled away from the manor house, Dietrich looked back, longing to touch Maria's heart and to embrace her infectious smile.

*   *   *

From Bremerhaven, Dietrich traveled across the Channel to England by ship. There was not one day where he failed to record his tender thoughts and feelings about Maria. Just before they made port, Dietrich realized the truth.

No longer able to fight the forces of nature, Dietrich Bonhoeffer had fallen in love with Maria von Wedemeyer.

In London, Dietrich met Bishop Bell on the platform of the Soho train station. Bell was a short, distinguished-looking gentleman—clean shaven with wavy snow-white hair. Unpretentious, he wore a black suit with a white clerical collar. Soon their car plowed through a thick morning fog toward Chichester Abbey.

Within the hour, they sat comfortably in Bell's study as the rectory maid served tea and crumpets. The wood-paneled room was luxurious by German standards, and the latticed windows brandished rich woolen curtains in muted country-themed prints.

Dietrich sipped the warm tea with milk, English style. "George, thank you for securing my brother-in-law a position at Oxford. Gerhard is a fine legal scholar. Jews have not been welcomed in Germany for some time."

"Anyone you recommend, my friend, comes with the highest credentials."

"I understand that apart from her work at the hospital, Sabine is helping you host various events in Sussex." To have his sister and her husband in a safe place was God's answer to Dietrich's prayers.

George handed a formal invitation to Dietrich. "I've arranged for a reception for you and German pastors at Amesbury House on Thursday. The Ehrenbergs will also be there."

"You know, the Nazis almost killed that man. They are hunting down members of the Reich Church with the slightest hint of Jewish blood."

George nodded. "To free Reverend Ehrenberg from a concentration camp was quite a feat. One might say it was a miracle."

"Indeed it was, but if I am not careful, I could end up in prison. Hitler has appointed a Nazi lawyer as Reich Bishop, and the Confessing Church in Germany is under siege."

"In these frightful times, tell me, how can I help you?"

Dietrich placed his saucer on the table. "My brother-in-law, Hans von Dohnanyi, has friends in German military intelligence. They have plans to depose Hitler."

George raised an eyebrow. "Oh, really?"

"Admiral Canaris and Colonel Oster of the Abwehr want to set up an orderly transitional government in Germany, but they need England's help."

George stood and walked over to the latticed window behind his desk. "What do they want of me?"

"You may know people in the British government who could help—important people."

"My friend, these men ask a great deal of you."

"The SS would execute me if they knew of my mission. The Hitler regime considers ministers in the Confessing Church movement political conspirators. Many traditional army officers deeply resent the Nazis. They serve at the highest levels of the armed forces. George, I believe their intentions are genuine."

"I know a few people in government circles, but an inquiry of this nature would be suspect." Attracted by the patter of gentle droplets upon the windowpanes, George methodically filled his artisan pipe with a dark tobacco. "Dietrich, you are at a crossroads. You hear many voices. I shall pray that God reveals His will for your journey."

"The Gestapo has outlawed my preaching and publications in Berlin. But I have received an invitation to teach at Union Seminary in New York. At least in America, I could preach and teach again, unhindered."

"You have become a man for all seasons. A man like you can render a significant ministry wherever you are. But you must seek God's will." George ignited a match and sparked his pipe's tobacco with a puff or two. "Suppose Jesus was faced with the same choice. What would He do?"

Dietrich was about to answer when there was a knock on the door. A maid entered. "Excuse me, gentlemen. It's the radio—the BBC says that Hitler and Mussolini have just signed an agreement. They say we are one step closer to war."

Dietrich joined George at the window. "I fear that it is going to be a very cold winter in Germany."

George pressed his lips together. "I can feel a great storm moving our way."

Chapter Eighteen

New York City, June 1939

A few days later, Dietrich sat upon a weathered oak bench in the central quadrangle of Union Seminary. Cigarette in hand, he exhaled a cloud of smoke that dissipated over a patch of brilliant sunflowers.

Surrounded by a cluster of stone and brick buildings stretching five stories tall, the gardens boasted a circular hub of mature cherry trees. Outside the arched entrance, taxis sped by, whisking New Yorkers to their favorite park or Sunday afternoon dinner.

Dietrich pictured Sunday afternoons at the Bonhoeffer home. Flavorful aromas from the kitchen permeated the first floor as family members lounged in anticipation. Sunday dinner—his mother's roasted sauerbraten, served piping hot out of the oven, was his favorite. Savoring the moment, his mouth watered.

That morning, Dietrich had attended morning services at a large church on Riverside Drive near the Hudson River. "The Horizons of God" had been a perfectly respectable, self-indulgent religious sermon. That worship service was more of a civic gathering than true worship.

The sacrifices of his pastoral colleagues in Germany humbled him as he sat in the parklike setting. He glanced at a note he had written in the margins of the church bulletin. "The American 'pride in freedom' is institutionalized in its churches. Rather, freedom arises from the Word of God in its hearing! Where freedom of preaching is compromised, the church remains in chains!"

Everyone loosed upon the streets of New York appeared to rush from here to there. Then reality settled in. He could walk anywhere in New York City but not in his beloved Berlin.

The news of Hitler and his threat of war sounded no better on this side of the Atlantic—only more distant. When his cigarette was spent, he stood and walked out into the harsh sounds of the city. New York City was a zoo. People were crammed together onto streets, subways, and trains. So close together, yet each soul living separately in their private world. A cab jammed on its brakes and whisked Dietrich way up north toward West 138th Street. Just north along Broadway—not more than ten blocks—he entered Harlem. In 1930, it had been his spiritual home.

In those days, snide German slurs were often spoken behind his back during his tenure at Union Seminary. As a foreigner, he was grateful when a black student named Frank Fisher befriended him and took him to the Abyssinian Baptist Church in Harlem. Most Sunday mornings and Wednesday evening suppers were spent in the company of faithful black members.

When his taxi pulled up in front of the church, Dietrich imagined the rich, booming voice of Adam Clayton Powell, Sr. thundering his sermons to a packed sanctuary. They were rousing, emotional services. Their "soulful" black spirituals were sung with sincere abandonment of their misery.

One day in 1931, Frank Fisher and Dietrich departed after exams. Over the semester break, the two traveled down South to visit Frank's relatives. With some irritation, Dietrich noticed that they "always" rode in the back seat of the buses all the way to Georgia. Dietrich remembered one painful episode at a country diner.

"Well, looky here, Harry," a man in a worn grey suit said so everyone could hear. "We have a white man with his 'boy' in our restaurant."

Dietrich kept his gaze to the aisle as Frank and he shuffled to an obscure booth in the rear.

The owner leaned over the counter. "Mister, you are welcome here, but your 'boy' will have to eat outside."

In a thick German accent, Dietrich said, "Perhaps, we can order sandwiches to take with us."

"Lordy me, Harry. We've got us a *Heinie* here. Mister, go back to Ger-ma-ny—and take your *boy* with ya'!"

Dietrich could still feel the searing barb and see the pain in his friend's eyes. He stepped out of the cab near Central Park. With nowhere in particular to go, he was compelled to walk the New York streets.

Kristallnacht had marked the end of civil constraint in Germany. Anti-Jewish poster art littered shop windows. One such cartoon depicted a filthy Jewish merchant standing above shoppers with an exaggerated hooked nose and beard. Hoarding coins stolen from innocent German citizens in one hand, he proudly cradled the Communist hammer and sickle in the other. The Nazis had no shame.

A decade earlier, during their travels down south, Frank told Dietrich about black houses being burned, beatings, and occasional lynchings. How ironic it was that nearly nine years later, Dietrich found himself trying to escape the hatred of Nazi Germany in the prejudiced streets of America.

Dietrich wandered the streets by himself for several hours. Finally, he returned to his guest room at the seminary, aptly named the "prophet's chamber." He sat near the open window with the sounds of the traffic below unabated. Eventually, when he had sensed God's presence, he knew what do. With some embarrassment but with great certainty, he wrote to his American colleague.

22 June 1939
Dr. Reinhold Niebuhr
Union Theological Seminary

Dear Reinhold,

I have made a mistake in coming to America. I must live through this difficult period of our national history alongside the Christian people of Germany. I will have no right to participate in the reconstruction of Christian life in Germany after the war if I do not share the trials of this time with my people. Christians in Germany will face the terrible alternative of either willing the defeat of their nation in order that Christian civilization may survive, or willing the victory of their nation and thereby destroying our civilization. I know which of these alternatives I must choose. I cannot make that choice in security.

Yours in Christ,
Dietrich Bonhoeffer

After Dietrich completed his lectures at Union, with great emotion, Dietrich said goodbye to his American friends. It was only by God's strength that he boarded an ocean liner bound for Europe and an uncertain future.

*   *   *

Berlin, August 1939

The weeks after the brutal murder of his father wore on. Ernst eventually emerged from his shell. Late one Saturday afternoon, he dressed in his standard uniform and arrived at the Bismarck Tavern. With a few scattered patrons around, Ernst stepped over to the bar. "When does Fräulein Kleist come on duty?"

"Four o'clock. Would you like a drink?" the barman asked.

Ernst looked at his watch. "Coffee, please."

After retreating to his customary table in the corner, he passed the time listening to a few droll conversations at nearby tables.

Quietly, Eva slipped into the chair next to him. Her subtle smile was touching. Her azure eyes sparkled. "How is my favorite customer?"

Ernst cleared his throat, trying to find his voice. "I take it one day at a time."

She caressed his hand between her fingers. "I've missed you, Ernst. Max too. Where is he?"

"He's on special assignment with Major Neame."

"The police—do they have any news about your father?"

Ernst shook his head. "So far, no witnesses. Robbery was probably the motive. They took Papa's gold pocket watch. . . . Eva, my father believed in me—and my future. There was a photograph in the watch. When I was ten, I posed on Papa's knee. That picture defined us and the times we had together. Now those memories have been thrown into a gutter. I'm still angry!"

Eva gently stroked the inside of his forearm.

He eased back into his chair. "If this is a ploy just to change the subject . . ."

"Sssh, don't talk. Just listen." Eva's eyes reflected devilish mischief.

He leaned closer. "I didn't realize that you were so . . . talented."

She moved her fingers toward his open palm. "You have very strong hands, Lieutenant."

"A soldier has to stay in shape."

"You wouldn't take advantage of a sweet young woman, would you?" Her expression feigned innocence.

Ernst chuckled. It had been so long since he had laughed.

Eva carefully peeled his spectacles off, folded them beside the hat, and ran her fingers through his silky light-brown hair.

"You are so beautiful." His words were lost in a dream.

"Dance with me, Herr Teschler?"

He furrowed his eyebrows. "But there's no music. . . . "

"Machts nichts." She shrugged.

Eva stood and Ernst's eyes followed. She moved her body to the slow rhythm of music she heard only in her head. She pulled him to his feet, wrapped her arms around his neck, and moved her hips to that same silent beat. Laying her head softly upon his shoulder, she gazed up into his eyes.

He could feel the warmth of her breath blowing across his face, and her alluring fragrance permeated the air.

They both moved to their own rhythm. "Just hold me."

When Ernst closed his arms around her, something inside broke loose. Emotions he had held captive for weeks sprang into tears that coursed down his face. Closing his eyes, Ernst drifted deeper into Eva's nurturing embrace.

*   *   *

Berlin, August 8, 1939

Eva Kleist was dressed in a brown skirt and a brightly beaded Bavarian vest, covering a white blouse with puffy sleeves. The sound of her patent leather shoes clapping upon the pavement quickened as she crossed the street toward the café. In her purse was an urgent message from Dr. Bonhoeffer. Out of breath, she entered the restaurant and spied him in the corner booth.

Dietrich stood with a warm smile. "Good afternoon, Fräulein. Thank you for coming."

"Coffee would be fine," Eva said to the waiter as she scooted into the alcove. She searched the pastor's eyes for a clue as to the purpose of the meeting. The waiter took their orders as she fished a cigarette from her purse. "Herr Bonhoeffer, you said you had news concerning Ernst?"

"I have known Ernst since he was thirteen years old." Dietrich flicked his lighter and lit her cigarette. Eva drew down, then exhaled slowly, sending smoke wafting into the air. "You care a great deal about Ernst, don't you?"

"Yes, perhaps too much."

"It must have been terrible, being in the alley that night when Ernst discovered his father's body." He let the sentence dangle between them as the waiter served their drinks.

"The Gestapo said a Jew killed his father. It seems as if Jews are responsible for everything wrong in Germany these days."

"That is what the Nazis tell us."

Eva felt herself in the wings of a stage, about to walk on. "They deserve whatever they get! Their odd looks, their mumbled accents, their ridiculous religious practices. Everyone scorns them. I know. I have seen it all my life."

Dietrich was taken aback.

"Do I intimidate you, Herr Bonhoeffer? Is my attitude too harsh for your Christian sensibilities? I merely reflect our times. Germany is changing—and so am I. I am proud to be a German. I am proud to be with Ernst. He is a very important man in the Reich."

"And you intend to marry him?"

Her heart skipped a beat. "Maybe you think a mere barmaid is not worthy of such a man?"

"I want to know if you truly love him."

If only she could turn and walk away, but there was something about this clergyman—his kindness, honesty perhaps? "Do I love Ernst?" She shrugged. "When he looks at me, I feel special. When he touches me, I feel safe. When he dances with me, I want to twirl off the floor into some fairy tale."

From his pocket, Dietrich retrieved a photograph. "Perhaps the dreams of a Jewish princess." He held up the picture for Eva to see. "Does Ernst know Sarah Kleisfeld?"

Eva was stricken. She threw anguished glances in every direction to see who might have overheard. Her heart pounded through her chest. "What do you want from me, Herr Bonhoeffer?"

"Your father gave this picture to a colleague of mine. They were imprisoned together in a concentration camp just north of Berlin."

She felt faint. "Is he . . . ?"

Dietrich replaced the photograph in his pocket. "Your father is alive, but worse for the wear."

Eva narrowed her eyes as she stabbed her burning cigarette into the ashtray. "Who else knows of this?"

"No one, not even Ernst. But please be realistic. Your relationship with him has put you near very dangerous people. If you hope to marry him, the Gestapo will investigate your background. You are in jeopardy, Fräulein."

"What do you want me to do?"

"At the very least, tell Ernst the truth."

"You want me to tell Ernst I'm a—" Eva choked on the very word. "Better I should just disappear."

"I'm afraid that is exactly what will happen if you do *not* tell him. Eva, I have seen the way Ernst looks at you. He cares for you. He will want to help you."

She leaned back in her chair. The back of her neck turned cold, bristling with fear. Every German at that restaurant had to be staring at the *Jewess*. When Ernst discovered her dirty little secret, he would never look at her again.

Clutching her purse, she spoke as to be heard. "So good to see you again, Herr Bonhoeffer. Perhaps I will see you at church on Sunday." She pivoted and walked toward the café entrance.

As she stepped out onto the sidewalk, Eva looked nervously up and down the street for the Gestapo. Her fears ran wild. *Who else knows my secret?*

*   *   *

The Eagle's Nest, August 22, 1939

Seventy meters below the cap of Mount Kehlstein, a German soldier ushered Weisthor into the elegant elevator. Its shaft was etched in solid granite. Diesel engines powered the room-sized cab with barely a tremor as it ascended slowly to Hitler's private sanctuary.

The complex had been built at the cost of thirty million Reichsmarks, three years of concentration camp labor, and many lost lives. At the top, the beveled glass doors opened, and Weisthor was greeted by Hitler's private attendant. "Good evening, sir. The Führer is expecting you."

The servant led Weisthor through the dining room and into an impressive crystal observatory. Hitler stood gazing out across a series of mountain peaks stretching up into the brilliant blue sky.

With a salute, Weisthor extended his hand. "A fitting shrine for the new Holy Roman Emperor."

"Or unholy, as the case may be." Hitler twitched the edge of his knobbed mustache. His eyes were a grey-blue so intense they would change hue with his moods. "Welcome to my private world in the clouds, Weisthor."

The two sat in oversized brown leather chairs before a giant window facing Salzburg to the north. The snow-capped peak of Mount Watzmann glistened across the gorge. The low-angled afternoon sunlight flooded the expansive crystal panes with a rainbow of colors.

Hitler opened a tattered ancient book before Weisthor. "As a young artist back in Vienna, I discovered Zoroaster's prophecies." He flipped through its pages. "For almost twenty years, I have collected divine insights, private symbols, and encrypted notes in the margins. These are the words spoken to me: 'You are the new Messiah of the Templar kingdom. You are summoned to conquer the new pagan world. The Third Reich will be invincible, lasting one thousand years!'"

Weisthor stroked his bushy grey mustache. "Ever since you acquired the Spear of Destiny, it simply was a matter of time. You are the promised Messiah. Soon the world will know of your ultimate destiny."

Perspiration beaded Hitler's face. "Only pure Aryan blood will flow in the veins of our people. And once again, the master race will dominate the world!"

"Sir, it is time for the ceremony."

Hitler led Weisthor down a case of stairs into the stone foundation of the fortress. The walls were made of polished granite. At the end of the hall, Hitler opened a one-inch thick steel door and flicked on a switch. The chamber was illuminated by a singular translucent sphere protruding from the center of the floor. Its diffused beam revealed an inverted cross shaped from rough-hewn timbers hanging upon the west wall. Where the beams crossed there was a short mantel from which hung the bronze blade of the Spear of Destiny.

Weisthor held his SS dagger encrusted with two rubies that matched his silver SS Honor ring. "Hail Lucifer, Lord of Light and Darkness, now empower your chosen heir to the throne of the unholy Templar Empire. I now invoke Satan's angels to infuse his earthly body with the power of Thor's Hammer. Bear your wrist, mein Führer." Weisthor made a light incision. With his other hand, he rotated Hitler's arm, allowing the blood to drip freely upon the ancient Talisman of Power.

Hitler stood erect, almost in tears. "May we glorify our Dark Lord with every soul we condemn to the abyss."

The SS Honor rings nestled upon their fingers glowed ruby red as the Unholy Spirit descended and in a flash of crimson flame consumed his blood sacrifice.

Hitler opened his eyes. "Soon, the winds of war shall rage! Weisthor, I see the swastika whirling across Europe like a sharp scythe across a field of wheat."

"Sir, the rise of the thousand-year Reich lies within your grasp. Sieg heil, mein Führer!"

*   *   *

Southeast Bavaria, August 1939

Seven kilometers below the Eagle's Nest, a small, picturesque inn had been transformed into an elaborate fifteen-acre resort complex called the Berghof. The two-story entrance hall captured the midafternoon sunlight cascading across an exotic display of cactus plants nestled on a Spanish tile floor. The dining room was paneled with costly cembra, and the great hall was exquisitely furnished, highlighting an enormous red marble fireplace.

The Führer had convened the greatest military leaders of the Third Reich. There stood Hermann Göring, Hitler's current favorite and head of the Luftwaffe; Reichsführer Himmler; Field Marshal Walther Brauchitsch of the Wehrmacht; Admiral Erich Raeder of the Kreigsmarine; as well as key members of the cabinet. The officers and their entourages had been nibbling hors d'oeuvres and trading rumors for over an hour, restlessly awaiting the Führer.

From an unobtrusive corner, Admiral Canaris quietly observed the guests in the hall. Military intelligence had files on virtually everyone there. Wilhelm reflected upon familiar faces—and their secrets—as fawning politicians greeted him with shallow chitchat.

Just then, Heydrich and a young SS officer arrived. In the early twenties, Heydrich had once been his subordinate in the navy. But ever since 1936, Heydrich's meteoric rise within the SS was legendary—as if engineered by some unseen power. Wilhelm stepped closer to the two SS men, unseen but within earshot.

"You're moving up in our ranks quickly, Ernst. Himmler invited you specifically to this briefing."

"The guest list is impressive, Uncle."

"My people tell me Himmler has taken quite an interest in you. Your new SS ring, for instance."

"It was a gift. I told you I don't know how I—" Teschler stopped in midsentence.

Weisthor approached in his dress uniform, sword, and epaulets. "General Heydrich, Teschler. This should be a glorious day for the Reich."

Heydrich's face remained stoic as Weisthor moved into the crowd. "I despise that man. He holds Himmler in the palm of his hand with voodoo magic."

Suddenly, the sprawling four-meter-tall picture window on the north wall was slowly lowered into the massive sill below to expose an open-air, sweeping view of the mountain peaks. When Hitler's entourage entered the hall, a hush fell across the gathering. The Führer stepped to the podium, and all present snapped to attention, shouting in a chorus, "Heil Hitler!"

The Führer smiled triumphantly. Canaris loathed him. Hitler was not a tall or imposing man, but his consummate command of an audience was admirable.

"Gentlemen." Hitler tilted his head, and an oily lock of unruly dark hair slipped down his forehead. "My vision has been confirmed. Our intelligence has told us that Poland has been moving troops to our border for some time. It is now time for us to launch a preemptive attack and lead our troops to victory!"

A shiver surged down Canaris's spine. Their intelligence sources said nothing of the kind! His stomach churned as the Führer outlined in detail the imminent military operation. Through the massive open window, Canaris could see a major storm brewing over his beloved Germany.

Chapter Nineteen

Berlin, August 25, 1939

O rders encrypted by the Enigma cipher arrived at Abwehr headquarters. The SS requested 150 Polish uniforms of various ranks.
Given his spies planted deep within the SS, Admiral Wilhelm
Canaris already knew their purpose. "Well, Oster, there you are. We are
to throw down the gauntlet for Hitler's war."

"Dressed in Polish uniforms, Heydrich's men will launch a fake attack
upon a German radio station at the border, then tell the world Poland
has invaded Germany."

Wilhelm's greatest fears of the SS were knocking at his door. "Despite
the foolishness of the British prime minister, England and France will
not ignore the conquest of Poland as they had winked at Austria and
Czechoslovakia."

"With Heydrich's scheme, Hitler will have his excuse for war."

"Have no illusions, Hitler's cronies are relentless." With a shrug, Wilhelm sank onto his couch and lifted his hands toward the smoldering
fire. On the coffee table were a photograph and the file on SS Lieutenant Ernst Teschler. "Heydrich is sending his nephew over to retrieve the
uniforms tomorrow."

"Sir, given Heydrich's blatant nepotism, Teschler should be considered a suspect and dangerous," Oster said.

Wilhelm read further. "This says that Teschler has been personally trained by Major Alfred Neame in hand-to-hand combat, Savate, firearms, sabotage, and assassination. Why, he's the perfect guest for your next dinner party." He flipped a few more pages. "He's Heydrich's nephew—by blood. As often as my wife and I see the Heydrichs socially, Reinhard has mentioned the Teschlers only in passing."

Oster looked out the window. "This young man was confirmed in the church by Dr. Bonhoeffer. Maybe he can tell us more."

Wilhelm flipped the file closed. "Disciplined, loyal, savage—yet devout. This young man is an enigma. He will be a worthy adversary."

*   *   *

The next afternoon Colonel Oster escorted Ernst, Barron, and Max through the anteroom and into Admiral Canaris's office. The two SS operatives and Ernst's regal Doberman stepped in military fashion and saluted.

Oster gestured toward their visitors. "Admiral, may I present Lieutenant Teschler and Master Sergeant Schumann."

Canaris gently placed Sabine upon the rug next to Seppel. Canaris's eyes were drawn like a magnet to the Doberman. One look at Barron with his snout raised high, and Seppel and Sabine cowered behind their master. "Welcome to Abwehr headquarters. I take it this is your first visit." Wilhelm shook their hands.

"Sir, this is an honor. Your record is legendary at Bad Tölz," Ernst said. Barron could easily eat the two "wieners" for a snack. His silken blue-gray coat reflected the brilliant sunlight streaming through the tall windows. He leaned into Ernst's thigh as was customary of the Doberman breed.

"At ease, gentlemen."

"Herr Admiral, General Heydrich sends you his regards."

Canaris's gaze never left Barron. "My, what a splendid Doberman you have, son."

"His name is Barron, mein herr."

Barron barked and, in turn, the stubby dachshunds yelped excitedly by the desk. The Doberman cocked his head to the side, his ears forward. Canaris knelt beside the animal and stroked Barron's head and neck. Slowly, the timid dachshunds waddled closer to explore their towering guest.

"Please sit down." Canaris gestured as he took a seat behind his large desk. "Your reputation precedes you, Herr Teschler. And you are highly regarded by a mutual friend."

"Friend?" Ernst raised an eyebrow and signaled his *Hund* to sit at his side.

"Dr. Dietrich Bonhoeffer."

Ernst narrowed his eyes. What business did this man have with the churchman? "And how do you know Pastor Bonhoeffer?"

"He's a friend of a friend. Colonel Oster, take Sergeant Schumann to the quartermaster. He can inspect the Polish uniforms and coordinate transport."

"Certainly, Herr Admiral." Oster led Max through the door.

Canaris placed Seppel in his lap and brushed his flank with his carefully manicured fingernails. "You've risen swiftly in the ranks, Herr Teschler."

Ernst shifted in his seat. "Sir, my honor is loyalty."

"And you have friends in high places. Your uncle Reinhard and Bonhoeffer, for instance?"

"Dr. Bonhoeffer was my pastor some years ago. When my father died . . . he provided great comfort to my family."

"I am sorry for your loss. As I said, Dr. Bonhoeffer speaks highly of you." Canaris patted Seppel's side. "One thing I've learned about dogs— they can sense everything about character. They know when a human being is genuine, ja?"

Ernst nodded. "My uncle says that you are both a friend and a worthy adversary."

The Admiral drew a knowing smile. "The uniforms are being loaded into your vehicles. The Führer wants a war with Poland, and the counterfeit 'Poles' are conveniently about to start one."

Ernst stood. "Again, General Heydrich sends his regards. Thank you for your assistance."

"Tread carefully in the SS, Herr Teschler." Canaris posed a wry frown. "Deception can be a dangerous business. But remember this, son—a man is most vulnerable when he is deceived by love." The admiral let his words hang pointedly between them as he stood, rounded the desk, and rubbed Barron's muscular shoulders. "What a beautiful animal! Now here is someone we can both trust."

Ernst was in the gentle hands of a master manipulator. He rolled Canaris's words over in his mind. *"Deceived by love…"*

*   *   *

That night, Eva waited for Ernst on the balcony alcove of the Bismarck. She walked out to the railing, taking in all the ambient chatter and music of the tavern below. She pictured herself again at the top of the grand staircase of the Adlon Hotel, displaying the azure chiffon gown he had given her. That would forever be a cherished moment between them. Her feelings for Ernst were now resolute.

After a time, Ernst swept through the velvet curtains and rushed into her arms. She searched his eyes. "Darling, I've missed you so much."

Their lips met and they kissed passionately. Her skin flushed warm and her knees weakened. Then as they gazed into each other's eyes, Ernst held her at arm's length. "We have to talk."

"Ernst, what's wrong?" She squeezed his forearms, a faint scent of dread wafting in the air.

"Your name has come up in several conversations. Some people very close to me have cast doubts on our relationship."

Eva's heart began to thump. *Bonhoeffer! Had the man told Ernst her secret?*

Her breathing became shallow. Then for fear that her tears would tell all, she clasped Ernst around the neck and kissed him long and hard.

He half tried to break free, but she clung to him. Eventually she would have to confess the truth. *I am a Jew! A despised, rejected leper of society.*

"Ernst!" shouted a familiar voice from beyond the curtain.

It was Max. *They must all know about me!* Eva trembled in Ernst's arms.

Max thrust his angular face through the veil. "Ernst, the car is waiting downstairs."

"Give us a moment, Max."

"We have our orders." Max tapped his wristwatch. "I'll be downstairs."

Ernst turned back to Eva, his eyes taut and anxious. "I was going to tell you—"

"That you're leaving me tonight!" Eva feigned disgust. "When did you find out?"

He stroked her cheek tenderly. "It's a military operation. It will be dangerous and—"

Crushed between truth and consequences, Eva needed more time. She wanted to tell Ernst the truth, but she simply wasn't ready to confess her dark secret.

He looked longingly into her eyes. "I love you, darling. I wanted you to know in case, I don't—"

She trembled in earnest now. She wanted to cry, but she was afraid.

Ernst pulled her toward him, cradling her forehead against his shoulder. "Eva, do you love me?"

She lifted her head and gazed into his eyes. "If only you knew how much!" She dove back into his arms and kissed him with all the passion inside her. "Ernst, you have to come back to me. That is an order!"

She opened her eyes at the soft timbre of his voice. "Eva, you are my life."

She felt the warm glow of his lips once more—then he was gone.

*   *   *

Berlin Train Station, August 27, 1939

Eva stood on the busy platform, an overnight bag slung over her shoulder and a ticket to Wittenberg in hand. With the carefully woven strands of her picture-perfect life unraveling, Eva yearned to see her mother, to hear her reassuring voice, to feel her loving strokes on her face.

Eva's long, auburn-colored wig riffled in the hot summer breeze, and she nudged her borrowed black-rimmed spectacles up on her nose with her forefinger.

"Fräulein Kleist," a calm voice said behind her.

Eva dared not move.

"Fräulein, come with me."

She turned around and stared into the indifferent eyes of an SS officer. She fumbled with her bag for a moment. "But my train leaves in—"

"That is not my concern." The man gripped Eva's arm and forced her through the crowd. Walking off the main platform, the two strode through the main terminal and emerged onto a side platform beside a sleek black train. It consisted of a massive diesel engine and five cars. The carriage cars were armor plated, followed by the caboose with gun slits in place of windows.

With mounting fear, Eva felt the furtive glances of two other SS soldiers as they carried her luggage onto the train. Chastely dressed in a dark-green blouse and muted plaid skirt, she was escorted through one car and greeted by an aide.

"General Heydrich is expecting you."

Eva's eyes widened. This could only mean one thing!

The steward ushered her back into the SS command carriage. It was opulently furnished with wood-paneled walls, green velvet curtains, and tan leather armchairs. Toward the rear, General Heydrich sat behind a large desk. He was deep in a telephone conversation while two assistants bustled in and out, bearing written messages. Without a break in the conversation, Heydrich gestured for her to take a seat.

Eva sat gingerly on a couch. She felt its cool leather under her manicured fingers. Crimson swastika banners hung on either wall. She remembered her father telling her the story of Jonah. Now, it was she who was in the belly of the great fish.

Heydrich spoke into the receiver. "You say Sachsenhausen is full? Well then, ship the Jews south. We have four other camps with capacity."

Eva sank deeper into the couch as she thought of her father.

A steward interrupted. "Fräulein, coffee or tea?"

She nodded. "Coffee, *danke*."

He reappeared shortly and placed a silver tray with fine china on a side table, then poured her a cup from a sterling silver decanter.

Eva felt like she was going to explode as she thumbed nervously through a magazine.

At last Heydrich hung up the phone, stood, and strolled forward, his polished boots sinking deep into the plush carpet. When he sat across from her, Eva forced herself to meet his gaze.

With a grand gesture he presented the richly appointed coach. "It's impressive, ja?"

"It's lovely, mein herr." She smiled.

Heydrich's appraisal began at her shoes, then traveled up the length of her shapely figure—slowly, as to be noticed.

"It's practical, of course, but it's a symbol as well—a symbol of power and authority. The Reich requires such symbols. It assures the people that we have the power to protect them. Power enough to rule them."

Silent, Eva affected a blank expression, as to be unnoticed.

Heydrich crossed his high-booted legs and grasped the leather arms of his chair. "Well, you look quite different today. Reddish hair, glasses, a bit dowdyish?"

"My job at the Bismarck is to entertain soldiers every night. When I travel, I like to be left alone."

"Most understandable."

Maybe he will just have me shot. Eva imagined her bloody body tossed onto the train tracks beneath them.

"We must protect Germans from the Jews, don't you agree, Fräulein?"

His high-pitched voice sent a shiver down her back.

"The bloodlines of those in the SS must be kept pure. Because of your relationship with Ernst, your background was thoroughly investigated."

"Ernst already mentioned—"

"What a lovely young woman you are. So beautiful, so perfectly . . . Aryan." His gaze darted about. It was like he played with her, cat and mouse.

"Thank you." She cringed at her polished red fingernails. Suddenly, they appeared quite garish.

"Ernst is like a son to me. He must not be distracted from my purposes. So, I trust you will be intimate but keep your relationship, shall we say, casual."

Eva pursed her lips. "Whatever you say, mein herr."

"Good! We understand each other. So then, my dear, where are you going today?"

Eva calmly looked into Heydrich's eyes and lied. "Leipzig . . . to visit friends." She took a deep breath and told a fanciful tale about her school years. On the canvas of her details, Eva painted a fanciful picture of a woman worthy of Ernst Teschler.

When Eva walked off the train unscathed, even she began to believe the lie.

*   *   *

Gleiwitz, Germany, August 31, 1939

Increasingly conflicted, Ernst disembarked after the two Luftwaffe transport planes landed twenty kilometers away from Gleiwitz, a small country town near the Polish border. In a few days, the eastern division of the German army would declare war against Poland, and the Gleiwitz operation would be the trigger. The lives of thirty-three Polish prisoners were now in the hands of SS Lieutenant Ernst Teschler, and Berlin was watching.

In gray German army uniforms, Neame, Ernst, and Max led the SS squad in the first of two troop carriers. In the second truck sat Jewish prisoners from Dachau who were dressed in Polish army uniforms. The SS soldiers in Ernst's truck joked about the stink of "Polish sausage" as they rumbled down the country road.

As per plan, the personnel of the German radio station had been evacuated from the building by the time they arrived. There would be no German civilians within three kilometers. The caravan screeched to a halt, and some soldiers stormed the station. Ernst's heart raced as his men rushed from room to room. They had only thirty minutes to prep the 8:00 p.m. broadcast. The "Polish" speech would be sent from Gleiwitz to Breslau and then rebroadcast throughout Germany.

With the scheduled program tape recording nearing its end, in a panic Ernst's men searched for the microphone routing switch. With the clock mercilessly ticking, Ernst cursed the dolt who had evacuated the German radio technicians they now needed. While his men stumbled over each other, Ernst threw open the door of a small closet, then stopped. It wasn't a closet but a broadcast booth. Ernst shouted for the SS linguist, and the radio drama soon began.

The announcer spoke in Polish. "The nation of Poland has been threatened by Adolf Hitler." Ernst signaled his men to shout, creating audible chaos as the linguist droned on. "The army of Poland must rise up and strike the German snake. It will be crushed! Danzig is Polish and must forever remain so!"

Just as the announcer's voice crescendoed, Ernst fired his pistol three times, transmitting thunderous reports to every radio receiver within sixty kilometers. The fake announcer feigned taking a bullet and slumped loudly to the floor, knocking over the microphone.

Ernst looked out a window to see Neame's men herding the Jews dressed in Polish uniforms from both trucks. With unloaded rifles placed in the prisoners' hands, Max and his men prodded them with their rifle stocks. As Ernst headed outside, the captives were deployed in military formation surrounding the station.

Neame's squad primed syringes and jabbed the needles into their victims' necks. The prisoners soon staggered, then slumped to their deaths.

Max brought another ten prisoners and spread them out in the front yard of the station. He signaled the squad to form a gauntlet surrounding the helpless Jews. The SS soldiers primed their rifles and submachine guns.

Max slung his MP38 Schmeisser from his shoulder and raised his arm.

"Halt! Max! Only on my command." The soldiers froze as Ernst primed his Walther P38 pistol and walked to the center of the meadow, blocking their targets. The Jewish prisoners were draped in ill-fitting Polish army uniforms. Ernst looked into the frantic eyes of those about to die. Drenched in perspiration, their oily hair framed their sunken, malnourished jowls, and their wet hands shook in the summer breeze.

In Ernst's mind, the image of Papa slumped across the gutter in the darkened alley loomed large. A monstrous rage boiled inside but was overshadowed by his father's voice. *Ernst, I do not believe in the Nazis' sordid cause, but without question, I do believe in you. When the truth behind the SS is revealed, I know you will do the right thing.*

Ernst reached out to touch his father's face, but it morphed into the face of an emaciated Jewish soldier. The man's expression was resolute. "Lieutenant, we are prepared to die!"

Max lifted his arm again. "Ready—"

Another prisoner stepped forward. "Sir, Jehovah God knows your name. He will remember this day."

Max shouted in the background, "Aim!"

The last prisoner dropped his empty rifle. "Only God can forgive you for what you are about to do."

Ernst's eyes were transfixed. Stepping back from the prisoners, he looked to Max.

Neame arrived on the scene. "Teschler, you have your orders. Do it now!"

Ernst wanted to shoot his superior, but stepped out of the field of fire instead. Imagining the carnage to come, he lifted his arm. It felt like an iron anvil.

"Squadron, ready—fire!" With each shot Ernst's body reeled as if he were struck by the bullets himself. Pieces of flesh and bone splattered upon the brick wall of the station. The cries and moans from the prisoners on the ground ripped into his soul. Terror was branded upon the victims' faces as Ernst gazed into their frozen, lifeless eyes. Staring up at him, they would haunt him all his life.

To add fuel to the flame, Neame emptied his clip, plowing more hot lead into flesh. Checking his wristwatch, Neame was satisfied. "We are on schedule!"

Ernst stood still, his gaze darting from one body to the next, his limbs numb. In the blink of an eye, he was transported back to the alley where his father was slaughtered. He could not save those whom he loved. With a scowl, his rage erupted into a silent scream.

Max walked through the maze of twisted, bloodied bodies strewn across the station yard. Of the original thirty-three Polish prisoners, only three were still alive, groaning in agony.

With his smoldering machine gun slung from his shoulder, Neame primed his pistol and finished the deed. He stepped over to Ernst. "Show no mercy! Those are our orders, Teschler. Remember, when you kill someone, leave no witnesses."

The SS troops randomly lobbed Polish grenades into the building, and the explosions shattered windows and blew the exterior doors off their hinges. From a distance, Ernst stared listlessly at the flames. It was surreal. It was a massacre—and all to the glory of the Third Reich.

*   *   *

Berlin, September 1, 1939

It was almost noon before Eva awoke after an endless shift at the Bismarck. Through a haze of cigarette smoke and three cups of black coffee, she eventually turned on the radio. When the announcer mentioned Poland, she recalled Ernst's parting words. A cold sweat beaded on her forehead, flattening her dyed-blonde curls. Ernst and Max were in the thick of it, and she was afraid.

At her secretary, she retrieved some stationery and a pen. With determination, she wrote, "Dear Ernst." To bare her soul, she wrote a full confession—her family history, her deceptions at the Bismarck, and her intimate affection for her beau. On her desk was a photograph of Ernst framed in shades of gray. She yearned to gaze into his hazel eyes once more.

Someone rapped upon her door. Startled, Eva jumped up. Could it be Heydrich? She dare not answer the door. She could not face his cold, steely smirk. There was another door knock—louder this time. Maybe it was the Gestapo? She stepped closer, taming wild imaginings outside the door.

She looked down at her robe with a frown. *I'm not dressed to go to prison.*

She drew in a stuttered breath, then opened the door to a tall, thin man with a mustache. "Fräulein, your rent is due." With a sigh of relief, she retrieved an envelope of cash and gave it to her landlord.

Eva returned to her desk and touched the edge of the picture frame. For the first time she imagined what her life would be like without Ernst, and she wept. "Oh, my darling, I have betrayed you. What will you do with me when you find out what I am?"

She picked up the letter and ripped it in half.

*   *   *

Leipzig, Germany, September 1939

It was the third day of the Polish campaign. Having transmitted intelligence reports all day long, Ernst and Max arrived at Auerbach's Keller, the second-oldest restaurant in Leipzig. The famous tavern was located on Grimmaische Strasse near the main market. Above the Large Cellar, they sat at a table in a secluded corner of the bar.

Max pushed a half-empty bottle of schnapps strategically across the center line of their table. "Checkmate."

"There's no chessboard, Max."

With eyes glazed, Max stared at the table. "What does that matter? You are playing the master, Herr Teschler."

"There are no chess pieces either."

"Face it, Ernst. You've lost to a superior intelligence. You see, like Faust, I made a pact with the devil." Max's confidence came with a swig of liquor.

Ernst raised an eyebrow. "You have been talking with the devil?"

"Sssh! Don't tell anyone. It's a secret." Max's mouth eased into a subtle grin.

Ernst poured another glass and pushed the bottle back across the imaginary line. "Here we sit in the infamous Mephisto Bar. Did you know that Mephistopheles is another name for Satan? Legend has it that Dr. Faust, in his quest for knowledge, conjured the devil and struck a deal. He pledged his soul for twenty-four years of demonic service. He rode out of this very cellar on a wine barrel, met the Pope in Rome, even dined with the kaiser in Innsbruck. After sixteen years, despite his fame and wealth, he finally realized his eternal doom and regretted the past. And the devil came to him again."

Max leaned closer. "What happened then?"

"Satan conjures up Helen of Troy and Faust sires a son. Eight years later at midnight, through a thunderous storm, Satan brutally batters Faust to death and takes his prized soul to hell."

Max's eyes loomed large as saucers. "So sorry I asked."

Ernst lowered his gaze as he downed the liquor. He winced as the liquid burned his throat. "By our hands, thirty-three men were murdered at Gleiwitz in a charade to fool the world."

"They were not human, Ernst. Just Jews. Besides, you didn't pull the trigger; the whole squad did."

Ernst leaned forward. "But I gave the order!"

Max tapped his empty glass. "We'll probably both be promoted."

"Thirty-three innocent souls—and thousands more will die in a trumped-up war."

"The Jews murdered your father, Ernst. At Gleiwitz, we just followed orders."

Fatigued, Ernst leaned back in his chair. "Just following orders? Well, Max, last night I had another nightmare. I saw the faces of those Jews. Their lifeless eyes followed me wherever I went."

"If you had refused to give the order, Neame would have shot every prisoner and then turned his guns on us."

Ernst swigged the last of his drink. "It was my command—my responsibility. One day, we will meet the devil, and he will collect his due."

Chapter Twenty

Berlin, October 1939

"**S**alon Kitty" was a swank bordello located in a posh suburb of Berlin. Operated by an endearing "madam," her ladies were consummate professionals, extracting not only money but diplomatic secrets from politicians, military officers, as well as foreign diplomats. The bedrooms at Salon Kitty were equipped with hidden microphones where SS staff recorded endless private conversations.

In the basement, Alfred Neame sat across from a bank of reel-to-reel tape recorders as he dialed the telephone. "Hello, Schellenberg. Our contact with the Brits, Franz Fischer, was here again last night."

"Did Major Stevens and Captain Best take the bait?"

"They actually believe you are a Wehrmacht colonel named Hauptmann Schammel. Your next meeting with them will be at the Continental Trading Company in Venlo, Holland."

"These British agents can be so gullible," Schellenberg said. "I have prepared a short list of ranking army officers to feed them. With luck, they will be convinced we're conspirators against Hitler. Give the list to Fischer. Let's see how far Stevens and Best swallow the hook."

Alfred hung up the phone and lit a cigarette, when General Heydrich stepped through the tunnel door behind him. Sergeant Donz and a secretary all snapped to attention as Alfred presented an informal salute.

Heydrich mumbled a halfhearted "Heil Hitler" as he plucked the current log off the duty desk. "Anything to report, Major?"

"Ordinary customers except for a diplomat from Stockholm."

When Heydrich lightly brushed his hand through the secretary's long blonde hair, she curled her head up like a kitten. His narrow-set black eyes devoured her. "My dear, where is Helga assigned tonight?"

The secretary's naive smile faded. "Room 7, Herr Obergruppenführer."

"Very well. Room 7. I shall be less than a half hour, Neame. My wife is hosting a dinner party at nine."

Donz turned off recorder #7. Heydrich whistled as he marched up the stairs. The staff exchanged knowing glances.

Alfred pointed at the blonde. "You need a break. Come back in an hour."

"Danke schön!" With coat in hand, she departed through the tunnel door.

Donz smiled. "Helga is a satin dream."

Alfred reached over to recorder #7 and flipped the switch back on. He sat down, lit another cigarette, and reached out casually for the headphones. He toggled a few switches to record every word of Heydrich's tryst with Helga.

After about twenty minutes, Alfred turned off the machine, rewound the audiotape, and placed the reel into his satchel. Almost as an afterthought, he swung Donz's swivel chair toward him. In one smooth motion, he flicked open his stiletto blade and stuck the tip under the soldier's chin, forcing him back into his chair.

"If you ever betray my confidence in you, your wife will be roasting your 'chestnuts' over an open fire. Understand?" Alfred pressed the tip into his flesh, then he wiped the blood on Donz's tunic.

Nonchalantly, Alfred walked out through the tunnel. He wrapped his black leather coat around him against the cool of the October night. In his satchel, he held his trump card against Heydrich. The very thought presented infinite possibilities.

*   *   *

Munich, November 1939

November 8 was the day before the sixteenth anniversary of the Nazi Beer Hall Putsch of 1923, Hitler's first attempt to seize power in Germany. The Bavarian government had easily crushed the uprising, landing Hitler and his cronies in prison. Tonight, Hitler would return to Munich in triumph over Poland and speak to the "Old Fighters" convention. With over three thousand alumni in attendance at the Bürgerbräukeller Hall, the "blood flag" from the '23 street brawl would lead the processional.

With Neame and Max on assignment in Holland, Heydrich had ordered Ernst to Munich on a special security detail. Ernst and Barron stood on the balcony of the cavernous hall watching workers drape large red-and-black swastika banners over the railings. He remembered his uncle's parting words in Berlin. *"Hitler wants to negotiate a peace with the British, but they are stubborn. There is a plan underway—something very hush-hush that will implicate England. Ernst, you will have a front-row seat in Munich. Protect the Führer at all costs!"*

Barron's bark alerted Ernst to a commotion on the main floor. Dr. Joseph Goebbels and his entourage swept through the hall. The chief propaganda officer of the Reich had come to inspect the lighting and sound systems for the press corp. Given Goebbels's invitation list of VIPs, plain-clothed SS agents would be scattered throughout the hall.

Eventually, Ernst's eyes were drawn to the empty stage. An image of the Führer pounding his fists and reciting his speech to war heroes and the elite of Germany would be enthralling. He imagined all the war heroes from decades past who passed through that hall. For a moment, he remembered his papa in his old Weimar uniform from the Great War. Rudolf Teschler had earned three military medals for courage and bravery in the field of battle. With a patriotic surge of pride, Ernst snapped to attention and with a Wehrmacht salute honored his father's memory.

Ernst then noticed the podium, their next stop. "Barron—downstairs!" The dog accompanied Ernst down the staircase, and they forged their way through an army of waiters and cooks. The aroma of roasted beef streamed from the kitchens as they mounted the podium steps.

Barron sniffed all around the platform and then moved to the columns that bordered the rear of the stage. When the dog's nostrils flared, Ernst could tell he caught another scent. Arching his snout, the Doberman beelined to the center pillar behind the podium. Sniffing the eighteen-inch square column, the Doberman raised his paw and scratched the freshly painted surface.

"What is it, boy?"

Again the Doberman scratched the pillar. Ernst knelt down and explored the fresh plaster with his fingers. It was still tacky. Someone had been here recently.

"Herr Teschler, *kommen und sehen!*" Goebbels's nasal voice shouted from the lobby. "The mayor of Munich has arrived. We shall take pictures." Goebbels's smile was framed by his skull-like features as he approached the group.

The mere sight of the man sent a chill down Ernst's spine. "But, mein herr, there is something I want to check out."

"We don't have time. Kommen, schnell!"

Ernst spied Barron sniffing the wood again. He shook his head as the two exited the auditorium.

*　　*　　*

That night, Hitler was to speak at nine, but he arrived unexpectedly an hour early. The band played a triumphant march, and the crowd sang a rousing chorus of the *Horst Wessel* song.

Ernst and Barron were stationed stage left, steeped in pungent cigarette and cigar smoke from the rowdy crowd in the auditorium. At a quarter after eight, the Führer soared into his speech.

The three wooden pillars were flanked by SS honor guard, who stood perpendicular to the Führer as he incited the audience to roaring applause at each paragraph. Just before nine o'clock, Ernst could feel

Barron bristle under his leash. When released, the Doberman trotted directly to the center column and scratched at the very same section of plaster at the base. Ernst remembered the tacky feel of fresh plaster from that afternoon.

He strode behind the SS honor guard, up to the chief of SS security. After an exchange of words, the chief signaled his men seated in the front row. Two uniformed officers stood and clapped as a prearranged signal of eminent danger.

So enraptured by his own rhetoric, Hitler never missed a beat. Five minutes later, he stopped abruptly. Half-drunk, the crowds went wild and stood with thunderous applause. Ernst hurried to the chief of security. "Get the Führer out of here, schnell!"

With the audience oblivious to the danger at hand, the SS honor guard escorted Hitler out of the hall. Inhaling the frigid November air, Hitler and Himmler took their seats in the rear of their Mercedes limousine, and the motor roared to life. The rear door still ajar, the muted sounds of the crowd inside singing another chorus still could be heard as Ernst and Barron jogged to the side of the car.

"Heinrich, I certainly had the crowd in my hand tonight," Hitler said.

"You are the torch of victory for our people, mein Führer." Himmler nervously glanced through the rear window.

"It was glorious! I tell you, simply glorious!" Hitler said. "Who signaled me to leave? I could have roused that crowd to a greater frenzy."

"Sir, Lieutenant Teschler discovered a bomb."

Hitler's mouth gaped. "Did you say . . . ?"

Ernst leaned through the open door. "Pardon the intrusion, mein Führer. Driver, to the Munich train station—schnell!" Ernst slammed the rear door closed just as the sedan's tires screeched away from the building.

Ernst signaled another SS vehicle at the curb. Barron and he jumped into the rear cab. "Follow that sedan, schnell!" In a few minutes, Ernst was able to catch up to the limousine. He could see Himmler's face through the rear window just as the sound of an immense explosion shook the car. Ernst turned to look as the compression wave ripped through Bürger-bräukeller Hall.

Both cars screeched to a halt. Ernst leaped out of his car, ran up to Hitler's limousine, and opened the rear door. "Mein Führer, are you alright?"

In shock, Hitler stood next to the automobile and watched the towering flames a block behind them. His face flushed as he cursed his unknown assailants.

"Mein herr, we barely had time to evacuate you," Ernst said.

Hitler stood aghast at the flames spurting from a massive hole in the partially collapsed roof. "*Gott im Himmel!* To my train, schnell!" The Führer's greyish-blue eyes locked on to Ernst's with a fierce intensity. He clasped Ernst's hand. "You saved my life! This I will never forget, do you understand, Lieutenant?"

Ernst's sedan followed closely behind until Hitler's entourage skidded to a halt beside a special platform at Munich station.

Hitler was hustled aboard the Brandenburg, his personal armored train. The engines were already fired, ready to go. With diesel smoke surging from underneath the massive steel wheels, the majestic locomotive rumbled out of the station.

Ernst led Barron on a leash toward the station house, when out of the shadows a helmeted SS soldier walked up to him.

"Heil Hitler! Mein herr, Reichsführer Himmler wishes to see you—at once."

Ernst and Barron were ushered by two SS security men across a side platform to Himmler's private train. One of the men turned around and held his hand out. "Herr Teschler, I'll watch your dog."

Reluctantly, Ernst released Barron on the platform and entered the third train car alone. The dimly lit carriage boasted green velvet furniture and matching curtains. Toward the front of the car was a sitting area centered around a glass-enclosed hearth, already ablaze for the brisk night. Ernst could see the profile of a rotund man.

"Good evening, Herr Teschler." Without turning around, his gruff, raspy voice was all too familiar.

"Herr Weisthor." Ernst stepped closer to see tarot cards spread across a green marble table.

The occult priest methodically matched selected cards as if some esoteric force was guiding his hand. "Lieutenant, some seek God and the afterlife. I deal in the ancient mysteries and master the supernatural reality that surrounds us. Would you like to know your future, Herr Teschler?"

"A profound question, if I do say so myself." Himmler closed the door and took a seat next to Weisthor. "Congratulations on the Gleiwitz affair. The Führer is very impressed."

Ernst removed his hat and sat across from the two Nazi chieftains.

"At Gleiwitz, thirty-three men died," Ernst snapped.

"Thirty-three subhumans died for a greater cause. We gave Hitler his war! It was a proud day for the Teschler name."

Weisthor looked up at Ernst for the first time, his eyes shimmering in the firelight. "At Gleiwitz, you tasted blood."

Ernst remained silent, ignoring the man's ghoulish expression.

"As the bullets ripped into flesh, it felt as if you were floating above the carnage, watching yourself and your men from a distance. Then you felt a surge of power electrifying your limbs, your mind—your vision. Our Dark Lord enabled you to carry out your mission. You knew at that moment but would never admit it—with your actions that day, history turned upon a hinge, and the beasts of hell were let loose by your hand."

Himmler retrieved a wooden box from a cabinet. "Tonight, that bomb could have killed the Führer, but you saved his life. Hitler will celebrate your promotion at the Eagle's Nest." He placed the long, narrow container upon the coffee table next to the cards and opened it.

Weisthor lifted a card and held it up to the flickering hearth light. It showed a black-armored knight upon a horse riding into battle. "These events will lead to your ultimate challenge, Herr Teschler. High upon Mount Kehlstein, the Führer has secured a sacred spear. To him, it's a mere relic, a museum piece. But to us, the Spear is a precious symbol—a religious icon."

Himmler held up the imitation spearhead. "Without the knowledge of the Führer, you will exchange this replica for the original. This is the final test to prove your worthiness to the SS, Teschler."

Ernst's eyes felt heavy, weighted as if he were sinking into a dark, murky pool.

Weisthor's silvery eyes shimmered in the coach light as he dealt more cards upon the table. "I now show you the chariot card." The rotund mystic tapped the knight's card. "You are the Dark Knight on a mission! Hear me well, Teschler. When you bring the trophy back to us, you will sit in a high-born seat of the most secret society inside the Third Reich, the Order of New Templars."

Weisthor placed the card on the table in front of Ernst. "Bring us the true Spear of Longinus, then you will rule with the master race!"

Ernst shook his head. "The Führer's entourage is well guarded day and night. It won't be easy."

"We have confidence in your ingenuity," Himmler said.

Weisthor stretched out his left hand, palm down. "Teschler, show us your SS Honor ring." Weisthor summoned a devilish smile as Himmler and Ernst slowly placed their hands in the circle. As if energized by one another, the red rubies began to glow. One look at the liquid pools that were Weisthor's eyes, and Ernst felt utterly intoxicated. The memory of the murdered Polish Jews faded into the twilight of light and glory.

*   *   *

Venlo, Holland, November 9, 1939

Walter Schellenberg masqueraded as a German officer ready to surrender a list of German resistance officers to two British MI6 agents, Richard Stevens and Payne Best. Walter had agreed to fly to London with the list, and the Brits were to finalize plans at a meeting in Venlo. Hitler's "near miss" the night before gave even more credence to Walter's credibility.

Dressed in a brown tweed suit, Walter sat at an outdoor café of a Venlo hotel just forty meters from the Dutch-German border. Looking over the waist-high brick wall surrounding the café patio, he noted two Dutch guards at the border gate armed only with pistols. Just beyond them were Neame, Max, and their men in unmarked cars parked in the German zone with engines idling.

The British agents arrived in a dark-colored Renault. After they parked their car, Walter shifted his hat, signaling Max Schumann. Just as Stevens and Best greeted Walter, Max's lead car smashed through the wooden border gate.

From the rear car, Neame's men sprayed the pavement in front of the guards with submachine gunfire, forcing the Dutchmen to duck for cover. Max accelerated the lead vehicle directly at the seated party and screeched to a halt before the shocked British agents. Handcuffed, the Brits were quickly tossed into the rear seat. With the border in sight, Max jammed the gearshift into reverse and floored the gas pedal. Screeching tires gripped the pavement and catapulted the vehicles backward across the line into German territory as the Dutch guards cowered in disarray.

"Keep moving!" Walter shouted at Max as he pointed his Luger at the two Brits.

Both cars turned around and sped away pell-mell back into Germany.

Max shouted, "Did you see those guards? They were dancing a polka on their toes!"

Walter looked out the rear window. "Don't get cocky, Schumann. The border guards may come after us."

Max kept an eagle eye as the border receded in the rearview mirror. Only a plume of dust trailed behind them.

Well into German territory, the SS vehicles stopped. Walter confronted Stevens and Best with a grin. "My name is Walter Schellenberg, counterintelligence—SS. You are under arrest for the attempted assassination of Adolf Hitler." The looks of surprise on the faces of the two Brits were priceless.

*   *   *

Berlin, SS Headquarters

A week later, Reinhard Heydrich sat alone in his office making final notes in the Venlo file. With more than five hundred rounds fired during the raid, there was not one casualty. The capture of Captain Best and Major Stevens as Hitler's British "assassins" would be Germany's excuse for invading Belgium and Holland in a few months.

In Munich, Ernst Teschler became a clandestine hero. Reinhard glanced again at Hitler's most recent memorandum placing the SS in charge of his personal security. "With a few more ingenious moves, my nephew will have direct access to the Führer. Oh what a web we weave," Reinhard smirked.

Pressing a concealed button, the secret wall panel behind his desk slid open. He secured the folder in his garden of nasty secrets. With these perennial blooms, he controlled the elite of Nazi Germany. Then he imagined the smug faces of Himmler and Hitler. "Tell a fool what he wants to hear, and he will follow you anywhere." Opening his violin case, he tuned the strings and immersed himself in Wagner.

*   *   *

Alfred Neame stepped onto the gymnasium floor at SS headquarters. Dressed in his fencing whites, he limbered up and cut diagonal lines in the air with his Höller Solingen saber. He had been confident, if not cocky, earlier that morning when Heydrich challenged him to a duel, but now beads of perspiration dotted his forehead. Pacing, Alfred whipped his sharpened blade in a butterfly pattern.

Heydrich emerged from the locker room. Ever so debonair, he held his sword in one hand and his wire mask in the other. Reinhard Heydrich was a master swordsman, and he let everyone know it. "So, Neame, you think you can best me on my own ground?"

Alfred took a deep breath. More than merely a skirmish of steel, this would be a contest of nerves. "General, I'm here to serve at your pleasure."

Both men donned their wire masks and protective gloves, then mounted the wooden platform.

Heydrich gently rotated his blade around his opponent's, gently tapping metal against metal. "I know about the tapes from Salon Kitty you made of Helga and me. My orders to turn off the recorder in Room 7 were explicit, Major!"

Alfred assessed the reach of Heydrich's saber and stepped forward. "I am not a threat, but it would be gratifying to be recognized for my loyalty and success. Perhaps a well-deserved promotion?"

Heydrich cocked his blade, then unleashed a true "blitzkrieg." As the SS general plunged his blade into Alfred's armpit, the SS assassin lurched backward and dropped his foil.

Heydrich whipped his blade in roundhouse fashion upward between Alfred's legs.

He screamed, swallowing the pain as he slumped to the floor in agony. He looked up into Heydrich's eyes in abject horror, expecting the next stroke to emasculate him.

Heydrich took off his mask. "You were my best, Neame—unprincipled, ruthless. But no one takes advantage of Reinhard Heydrich. No one!"

On his back, Alfred lay trembling, the pain clouding his eyes with tears. Upon the brutal streets of his home in Kiel, he knew pain—but such humiliation!

"You will bring the tape and all copies to my office by tomorrow morning." The master swordsman slapped his blade sideways across Alfred's inner thigh. When his victim flinched, Heydrich leaned over his opponent.

"Major, I'd say I won the point and the match."

Alfred rolled onto his side as Heydrich strode off to the locker room chuckling. *One day, Heydrich, I will stand over your dead body!*

Chapter Twenty-One

Berlin, November 1939

From the time Lina and Reinhard Heydrich moved to the prestigious "lakes section" of Berlin, they socialized with the Canaris family. Since the war began, the two spy chiefs got together even more frequently to keep an eye on each other. As was their custom, Lina and Reinhard arrived one evening at the Canaris villa with his violin case in hand. With so many pressures at work, Heydrich looked forward to the evening together.

Erika Canaris ushered her guests into their living room and offered wine and some hors d'oeuvres. "Wilhelm is in the kitchen preparing one of his favorite dishes."

"A spy by day and a chef by night. Erika, how on earth do you keep up with him?" Lina asked.

Reinhard placed his glass back on the coffee table. "He is like his beloved Arabian horses. They run wild in the meadows by day but always return to the barn for their master's care at night."

Lina gloated. "Ah, now I know who rules this roost, and it's not the admiral."

Erika laughed as she retrieved her violin. "Reinhard, you favor Wagner. Let's begin our duets with the 'Bridal Chorus' from *Lohengrin*." They both stroked their bows with passion and spirit.

Before the music ended, Canaris entered the parlor, brandishing a colorful Spanish apron and a basting syringe in hand. "Good evening, everyone! Tonight, I have prepared saddle of boar in a dough of black bread. It's my favorite dish."

Erika stood. "Willy, you do become so enthusiastic with the marinade."

Canaris beamed as he handed her the syringe. "Here, my dear, please continue basting for twenty more minutes."

The admiral removed his apron and refilled their wine glasses. "A Navarra '34, from the Tierra Estella region."

Lina lifted her glass by the stem and swirled the red wine to release the aromas. "Willy, you are so talented in the kitchen."

"Well, I'm sure Reinhard has many 'hidden talents' outside the home." Canaris's feline paw playfully toyed with Reinhard's mouse.

"Willy, you were going to show me your new collection."

"Splendid idea. Follow me."

Exiting through the French doors, the two men strolled down the hall into the admiral's library. Glasses in hand, they both were drawn to the large picture window that boasted a panoramic view of three connecting finger lakes. Colored lights streamed from palatial homes bordering the shoreline.

Canaris took a sip. "You snatched Major Stevens and Captain Best without informing me first?"

"It was an SS operation. After the bomb attempt in Munich, the Führer demanded retribution. It was quite a catch, you must agree?"

Canaris lifted his glass to his lips and paused. "We have known each other since our ship days together on the *SS Berlin*."

"Seventeen years."

"You owe me, Reinhard. We have worked to keep our two organizations independent. And today, the SS is much stronger than I would have ever imagined when I took over the Abwehr."

"I'm flattered." Reinhard rolled the delicate wine over his tongue.

"You should be." Canaris's aging eyes narrowed. "It is time I shared with you some tactical information vital for your personal security."

Heydrich's smile receded. "Oh?"

"The Abwehr has discovered evidence regarding your father's mother, Eva. Apparently…she was a half Jew."

Without missing a beat, Heydrich donned his poker face.

"There are three documents that I have deposited in safekeeping. We are securing this information away from Himmler and the Führer for your protection."

Reinhard circled the edge of his glass with his forefinger. "Who else knows about these papers?"

With another sip of the Navarra, Canaris drew a thin smile. "As long as I'm alive and in command of the Abwehr, free of the jurisdiction of the SS, then this information is secure. Is that clear?"

Reinhard bristled at Canaris's long, prickly tentacles. He turned back to the majestic view of the lake in an uneasy silence.

"Next time you will inform me of major operations *before*, not *after* they happen."

"You know, Willy. The waves of time can topple the most formidable castles of sand. And in time, the tide will turn against you and the Abwehr."

"My dear Reinhard, we shall see."

*   *   *

Bavaria, near the Austrian Border

A contingent of SS security troops guarded the gates of the Berchtesgaden Cemetery as the sun started to set. In a remote section, the Führer walked alone past a thicket of grave markers to stand before a polished marble headstone. He leaned down on one knee and traced the engraved letters with his fingers: Dietrich Eckart: Born 23 March 1868—Died 26 December 1923.

"I can remember the day we first met, old friend. It was Munich, 1919. You introduced me to the occult traditions of the Thule Society. It took me years to understand what you knew from the first day. That I would become Führer, born to lead the Aryan super race."

Hitler bowed his head beside the gravestone and wept. The tears did not cloud his memory of that fateful night when he lay naked upon a frigid stone altar. Illumined only by a flickering torchlight, he was surrounded by twelve black-robed disciples chanting a satanic mantra. Then Eckart initiated young Adolf with a razor-sharp ceremonial knife.

"Through the agony came my ecstasy. And ever since, Lucifer has smiled!" Hitler stood, kissed the headstone, and looked across the valley at his beloved mountain retreat. A starburst of crimson light penetrated the majestic purple-hued clouds above the sacred site.

*   *   *

The next afternoon, a Nazi-flagged Mercedes motored its way up the mountain road toward Hitler's Berghof retreat. In the rear, Ernst sat next to Captain Schellenberg. The young lawyer's winsome smile and charming, easy manner cloaked a calculating mind.

Barron lay on the rear seat, lightly panting between the two soldiers. Schellenberg eyed the killer beast. "Lina never stops talking about her wonderful nephew. You have made quite an impression on her, Lieutenant."

Peering at Schellenberg through the rearview mirror, Heydrich's tone was guarded. "Much as she never stops talking about you, Walter."

Ernst sensed some "history" in the comment as their car maneuvered around a hairpin curve. Never a dull moment in Berlin.

Tall evergreens towered majestically against a backdrop of sheer rock precipices. The Austrian Alps were crowned by billowy clouds over the Berghof. Fifteen years earlier, Hitler had purchased a cottage known as Haus Wachenfeld. At the cost of millions to the government, the small alpine house had been transformed into an entire resort complex.

Surrounded by two sets of barbed-wire fences, Ernst's excitement grew as their car penetrated the security perimeters of Germany's most powerful leader.

Soon they arrived at the main lodge situated on the lower level of the Berghof. When Barron emerged from the car, Ernst threw a rolled newspaper up into the air.

"Fetch, Barron!" Flexing his powerful hind legs, his Doberman leaped and gracefully caught his prey in midair. "Come on, boy. Schnell!" Barron ran back, dropped his prize at his master's feet, and barked with glee.

Instinctively, Ernst looked up. A sole spectator stood at the balcony rail. Hitler's piercing eyes gazed down upon the playful scene, then he stepped back inside.

Uncle Reinhard's entourage strolled into the two-story foyer and was escorted down a long hall into the great room. The design of the cavernous salon had been drawn from "Jack and the Beanstalk," scaled for giants.

Barron trotted stoutly at Ernst's side. When they passed an alcove, the muscular Doberman found himself looking squarely into the face of a growling Alsatian. Hitler's dog lifted her ears and let out a piercing bark.

Hitler entered the room, pride accompanying his steps. "Blondi. Sit." The Alsatian obeyed and silently panted. "Watch this, gentlemen." Hitler placed his thumb and forefinger in his mouth and emitted a shrill whistle as he extended his right arm upward. Blondi neatly rolled over twice as the group applauded to Hitler's delight.

Heydrich stepped forward. "Bravo, mein Führer. I see Blondi has made great progress."

Hitler leaned down upon his knee next to Barron. He stroked the animal's fine, short hair along his muscular contours.

"His name is Barron," Ernst said.

"He is a marvel of Germanic breeding." Hitler stared deeply into Barron's stark black eyes. When the Doberman extended his paw to "shake" hands, the Führer laughed. Not to be upstaged, Blondi walked over and nudged Barron softly with her moist muzzle.

"Blondi and Barron will be good friends." Hitler stood and extended his hand to Ernst. "Lieutenant Teschler, welcome to the Berghof. As I told you in Munich, I will never forget that you saved my life."

As the Führer moved down the reception line, Schellenberg snapped the heels of his boots together. "Congratulations, Schellenberg. You made a fine catch of these British assassins."

"Mein Führer, it is good to see you alive and well."

"I'm alive thanks to Captain Teschler—and to Barron."

"It's Lieutenant, sir," Ernst blurted out.

Hitler twitched a pencil-thin smile. "Never contradict the Führer! For your cunning and prowess in the line of duty, I have promoted you to the rank of Captain SS. And Herr Schellenberg, you shall now answer to the rank of Major."

"An honor, sir!" Schellenberg bowed his head.

Heinz Linge appeared. "Mein Führer, refreshments are now served in the parlor." They all took their seats and the house staff presented a colorful buffet of greens, fruit, and sweetbreads.

Afterward, Hitler took Ernst and Reinhard aside by the massive window facing the valley below. "Captain, tell me about Barron's bloodline."

"Barron was a gift from my uncle."

Reinhard nodded to take credit. "Keitel has a farm near Hamburg. The litter was limited, and I had first choice."

"And what about your father?" Hitler's voice was intimate.

Ernst glanced down. "His name was Rudolf Teschler. He was a successful trial lawyer in Berlin after the Great War. He, um . . ."

"Mein Führer, Ernst's father recently died—murdered by Jews!" Reinhard scowled.

Ernst swallowed the tears. He could not show his raw feelings in front of Hitler and his uncle.

"Appalling!" Hitler's eyes loomed large. "I am sorry for your loss, Captain. But understand this—your father shall be avenged. No German is safe until every last Jew is cleansed from this land!"

"Sir, my father was a war hero. I do not look behind but forward to lead the new Germany into its glorious future! As a soldier, I now stand committed to discern who are the true enemies inside the Reich."

The Führer's striated grey eyes were a vigorous chorus to his verse. They reminded him of Weisthor's—shimmering in the twilight.

Hitler's words were paced and emphatic. "Captain Teschler, together we shall reestablish the Religion of the Blood, pure to the seventh generation. Once again, Germans shall arise and take our true place in history! In Munich, you saved my life; now you shall save many German lives by hunting down and destroying the enemies of the state."

"Sir, my honor is loyalty." In the moment, a surge of pride overwhelmed Ernst.

Hitler placed his arm around his new protégé. "Tomorrow morning, I shall give you and Barron a tour of the Eagle's Nest."

*　　*　　*

Berlin, December 16, 1939

With Ernst's name on the return address of the letter, Eva Kleist ran up three flights of stairs to her apartment. Catching her breath, she threw her coat over a chair, then ripped open the envelope postmarked "Bavaria." With eager fingers, she unfolded the pages and held them up to the sunlight streaming through the sheer curtain.

> *My dearest Eva,*
>
> *The most extraordinary thing has happened. While on duty in Munich, Barron and I were able to perform a great service for the Führer. I cannot tell you the details now, but the Führer was so impressed that I have been promoted to Captain SS. Isn't it wonderful? I just wish*

my father could be here to share such a great honor bestowed upon the Teschler name.

Uncle Reinhard is ecstatic. He's so proud of my work. Max received a promotion to Lieutenant SS in order to remain my adjutant. We have been assigned to security duties inside Germany. I don't know when I will return to Berlin. I long to see you, to touch and to kiss you passionately.

Loving you madly,
Ernst

Eva imagined Ernst's tender voice as she clutched the letter to her breast, yearning for their next embrace.

She glanced at the clock on the mantel. It was still several hours before she was due for work at the Bismarck, so she curled up into the love seat and fell asleep.

From the twilight of a very pleasant dream, the sound of a door knock interrupted her slumber. In a sleepy haze, Eva answered the door. Saul Avigur held his finger up to his mouth to silence her as he closed the door behind him.

"Sarah, aren't you going to hug your cousin?"

"Saul, you take chances. The Gestapo keeps an eye on this building . . ."

". . . because you are kept by an SS officer?"

Before she knew it, she slapped Saul in the face.

"I deserved that. But never *ever* do that again."

"In Berlin, my name is Eva."

Rubbing his face, Saul walked to the kitchen table. "We have family business to discuss. In six months, there is a boat out of Istanbul for your parents and you. Since your father is imprisoned in Sachsen-hausen, we have to get him out. Tell me more about this Lieutenant Teschler."

"He is now a captain," Eva said with pride. "Besides, where would my parents go?"

"Palestine. They would be safe with our people."

To free her father, Eva would have to tell Ernst the truth about her past. For her betrayal, he might shun or even kill her.

*   *   *

SS Headquarters, Berlin, Spring 1940

Ernst read the weekly SS intelligence report. The Führer had traveled by rail to the Brenner Pass, secluded in the Alps between Italy and Austria. On board Mussolini's private train, the Italian dictator had secretly pledged his armies to Germany against Britain and France. Then there were copies of several coded messages between Hitler's private train and SS headquarters.

Heydrich had reassigned Ernst and Max to SS counterintelligence under Major Schellenberg. They were on their way upstairs to report to his office for their new orders. The corridors were bustling as they made their way to the second floor.

Schellenberg pushed the file across his desk toward Ernst. "We've just received word that Chamberlain has resigned and Winston Churchill is to become prime minister of Britain. Within two days, German forces will invade France, Belgium, and Holland. Soon we will be camping in England's backyard. The Brits will not sit still for long."

"And our orders?" Ernst asked.

"You will gather and interpret intelligence reports from our agents inside England. Their MI6 organization has tried multiple times to penetrate top German officers. We have an agent, a mistress placed close to the British minister of economic warfare. Here is her last report."

```
2 May 1940

TO: Munich Station
FROM: Trolley car

The War Cabinet will soon implement plans for
the SOE, Special Operations Executive. Their
agenda: sabotage and assassination inside
the Fatherland. Sir Hugh Dalton will oversee
operations from headquarters at 64 Baker
Street, London. Potential targets: Göring,
Himmler, Ribbentrop. They have gathered
information regarding the Berghof. Suggest
immediate countermeasures!
```

On May 10, the blitzkrieg into Belgium began. The French and British took the bait and exposed themselves to a lightning tank attack through the Ardennes. Ernst tore the message from the teletype machine. "Max, our troops are moving deeper into France. We're ahead of schedule."

"Soon the Brits will swim back across the Channel. We have them on the run!"

*   *   *

Brussels, Belgium, May 1940

Weeks later, after the German High Command occupied Holland and Belgium, Ernst sent an urgent message to Schellenberg.

```
Urgent—must stop Daisy's participation
in public events when visiting Paris.
Noncontrolled exposure!
```

"Who comes up with these code names for Hitler?" Max asked.
The teletype operator handed Schellenberg's reply to Max.

```
Take what measures you can. Escort Daisy to all
events. Will send reinforcements—Schellenberg.
```

"An assassin most likely would be French," Ernst said.

"I have a very bad feeling about all of this." Max threw a knotted piece of leather to Barron, who chomped on it with vigor.

"For every battle won, the Führer marches closer to a sniper's bullet." Despite the exhilaration of victory, Ernst's thoughts turned to Eva. He retrieved the most recent letter he had penned.

> *My dearest Eva,*
>
> *I'm stationed west of Berlin—far away from you. My heart longs to see your smile, your bright blue eyes, to feel your fingers combing through my hair. . . .*
>
> *Max and I see victory for the Fatherland in sight, but at great cost. Many Germans have died, but then again, the enemy has fallen. Soon, we will cheer over those who have defied the Third Reich. But none of this can replace the joy I experience in your embrace.*
>
> *Ever yours,*
> *Ernst*

He folded the letter carefully but left it unsealed, just in case another endearment came to mind. In the crowded confines of the train's sleeper compartment, Ernst's attention drifted, imagining their next romantic rendezvous.

On a secure line, the next morning Ernst called his uncle. "Sir, when can we be relieved? I want to see you and the family."

"Perhaps after your Paris detail. Schellenberg has given you and Schumann high marks. Now give me a full report on Himmler. He has constantly been meddling in my affairs."

"But, sir, I would like to see . . ."

"Fräulein Kleist? Of course, but duty first, Ernst. The Führer is depending upon you. You have become his good-luck charm."

Ernst slammed the telephone receiver onto its cradle with every one of his uncle's constant delays now in question.

Chapter Twenty-Two

London, MI6 Headquarters, June 1940

Hugh Dalton had just returned from meetings of the War Cabinet at 64 Baker Street. The newly formed office of the Special Operations Executive had just been approved for European espionage activities. Alone in his office, Hugh sat across from Colonel Mason-MacFarlane. He could almost taste the spirits in the colonel's glass. "Go ahead, finish your drink, man. I can only watch, now that I have these blasted ulcers."

"Thank you, sir. I'm knackered. The trip from Berlin was strenuous."

"Well now, tell me more about your plan to deal with our friend Hitler."

"I am quartered at No. 1 Sophienstrasse, just thirty-five meters from Hitler's reviewing stand in Berlin. These Germans stage a parade for almost anything. All I'd need would be a high-velocity rifle, telescopic sight, and a clear shot. Now Ambassador Hendersen has quashed this idea but—"

"Such a feat in the Führer's backyard would get you killed," Hugh said. "No, it would not do for the British military attaché to assassinate the Führer in Berlin."

"But, sir—"

"No, not in Berlin, but Paris would be another matter."

"The French have all but told us to get stuffed! You want me to work with the Frogs? They are about to capitulate."

"Not at all, Colonel. It's time to send in a specialist." Hugh pressed the intercom button. "Send our man in." All eyes trained on the door when a muscular man with short-cropped curly black hair entered wearing a dark-green herringbone suit. "Colonel, may I present Saul Avigur, a major with the Shai unit of the Israeli Haganah. He has been training with the exiled Czechs in Surrey for a very special kill."

*   *   *

Just North of Paris, June 21, 1940

The military train accelerated toward the French capital. In a rear compartment, Ernst stared stoically out the window of the speeding train, thinking about their mission, when Barron stirred beside him. Ernst stroked his flank.

Max slumped down on the opposite seat. "Paris. After all these years since the Great War—we've finally conquered the French!"

Ernst kept his eyes fixed on the passing terrain.

"You seem worried, Ernst."

He looked at his friend. "I was just thinking."

"About French women, perhaps?" Max drew a sly grin.

"French women—me? No. Do you really believe that young mademoiselles would find you handsome and dashing?"

Max slid the window down, then stuck his head out into the rushing wind. "Hello, Paris! Max Schumann is coming!"

Ernst burst into laughter. "You are a fool."

"Oh, but I am a fool for love." Max twitched his eyebrows.

Ernst shook his head. For months, he and Max had jockeyed between train stations and hotels, and they were exhausted. They would be stopping at Compiègne today. SS intelligence reports had identified multiple threats. Perhaps with the final collapse of France, he would be granted leave—and a chance to see Eva.

An adjutant knocked at the door and delivered a file. Max opened the seal and read the cover letter. "It's from Schellenberg."

"Well?"

Max unfolded a map of France on the table disclosing various sites marked in red. He read the accompanying letter. "Our agents in London sent a message yesterday. It referred to 'Foxley.' Probably a code name, but for what, we are not sure."

"Or whom?"

Max continued. "The German brass will soon arrive in Paris, and the Führer will be an open target throughout his stay. Schellenberg tells us to take all precautions."

Approaching Compiègne, their carriage lurched as the engineer applied the brakes. Ernst looked out his window. Waffen-SS engineers had torn down the side wall of a prominent brick building and removed the very railcar in which the humiliating Armistice of 1918 had been signed. A frightening thought struck Ernst. "The French and the British will know the exact date, time, and location of the German surrender ceremony."

*   *   *

Compiègne, France, June 22, 1940

The next morning Ernst, Barron, and Max joined the special SS security police who had cordoned off the perimeter around the "Glade of the Armistice." All wore the special gold-embossed emblem assigned to those who had clearance to be inside the perimeter.

"Ernst, come and see this," Max said as they gathered before an inscribed marble monument. "HERE, 11 NOVEMBER 1918, SUCCUMBED THE CRIMINAL PRIDE OF THE GERMAN EMPIRE, VANQUISHED BY THE FREE PEOPLES IT SOUGHT TO ENSLAVE."

The words were astonishing at first, then hauntingly painful. Ernst had never thought of the Great War from the enemy's perspective. "This would be a good place for an assassination attempt against the Führer."

Max slung his Schmeisser machine gun over his shoulder. "I'll start in the western sector and meet you in the south quadrant."

Ernst inspected the dignitaries' section for "line of sight" vantage points in the forest for potential sniper fire. Beginning with ground zero at the railcar, the two then spiraled out.

The French arrived by train about 2:00 p.m. and were secured by the perimeter guards. About an hour later, a cavalcade of motor vehicles pulled into the glade. The Führer emerged from the third car, followed by General Brauchitsch of the army, Admiral Raeder of the navy, and Reichsmarschall Göring, whose Luftwaffe had made short work of the Allied air force. Then the Führer's special guard detail cordoned off the walkway to the historic monument.

Hitler glared down at the offensive inscription and spat upon it. General Keitel then read a statement. "To erase once and for all by an act of reparative justice a memory which was resented by the German people as the greatest shame of all time!"

*   *   *

Sitting securely in the crevice between the trunk and multiple limbs of a green spruce ten meters in the air, the sniper affixed a modified Haube silencer to a '33 British Enfield "trials rifle." Despite the ten-round .303-caliber magazine, at fifty meters he would have time to release only two or three rounds before Hitler's goons rushed his nest.

Inhaling the mixed scents of nature, he scanned the forested field before him. Mentally, he rehearsed each step of targeting, execution, and retreat as he adjusted the SGT. No. 32 telescopic sight for windage. Only the first shot would be truly steady.

The assailant, dressed in civilian garb, propped the rifle's barrel on a branch and took aim at the German dignitaries gathering outside their vehicles. Hitler was surrounded by his security detail, but the height of his tree nest afforded a potential head shot. With a hint of a smile, the assassin chose a spot midway to the carriage car where a ninety-degree bend in the walkway would spread out the guards shielding the Führer. He chambered the first round and waited.

*   *   *

Away from the carriage, Ernst trained his binoculars into the forest beyond the clearing. Behind him, just as the German delegation approached the railcar, Ernst caught a momentary flash of light in a distant treetop about forty meters out. It became obvious. Hitler would stand on the platform for a brief moment—fully exposed!

It could just be a stray reflection.

He pivoted and again lifted his field glasses into the sunlight.

*   *   *

Perched in the tree, the sniper "led his target" with the barrel as he calmly placed his finger on the trigger. The many voices of his past victims cheered him on. Hitler entered the target zone. In his peripheral vision, the sniper saw an SS soldier walk in front of his mark with field glasses in hand. Now was his chance!

The trigger began its arc to ignite the bullet, when the whole visual field of his scope absorbed a blinding flash. He could feel his rifle barrel sway to the right just as the bullet released in a belching *huff*.

*   *   *

Ernst felt a puff of air as his hat lurched off his head and something plowed into the ground seven meters in front of the Führer. *A bullet!*

Oblivious, Hitler entered the carriage with his entourage.

Ernst bolted into the forest with Barron bounding by his side. Alarmed, the commando guards took Ernst's cue and tightened their human shield around the Führer at the train car.

Max ran from the far side of the clearing, closing in fast. With his legs pumping, Ernst braced himself for more gunfire. With Barron in the lead, two other soldiers were in close pursuit. The Doberman was the first to reach the clearing.

"I saw a flash in the trees near this spot!" Ernst shouted as Max raced up beside him. "Let's spread out!"

Barron nosed around the brush, then followed a scent to a tall spruce tree. Ernst spotted a spent .303-caliber shell wedged in the tall grass near the trunk. Still hot to the touch, he inspected the polished brass as the guards arrived.

"The sniper may still be in the area. The Führer is to know nothing of this until after the ceremony, understood?"

"*Jawohl,* Herr Captain." The guards quickly fanned out.

Max visually gauged the line of fire from the tree to the train carriage and shook his head. "Ernst, you really are Hitler's lucky charm."

Ernst smelled the burnt cordite residue in the shell. "I saw one of these at Bernau. It's British-made."

"Schellenberg was right. The Brits are going after 'Foxley.'"

"That's one possibility, Max."

A corporal handed Ernst his officer's hat with a salute. As Ernst probed the bullet hole just above the silver braid and the polished Death's Head insignia, he shivered.

He and Max crossed knowing glances, then Max said, "But what about tomorrow? Hitler goes to Paris. All of Paris wants him dead."

Ernst snapped his hat onto his head. "This has become a security nightmare!"

*   *   *

Paris, June 23, 1940

In front of their hotel, Max sat behind the wheel of their command car. With the motor idling, he landed on the horn. Ernst rushed out the guest entrance and jumped into the passenger seat with his satchel. "Ja, ja, what's happened?"

"The Führer is gone! He went to the opera house ahead of schedule." Max turned into early morning traffic and accelerated.

"So who needs a security team in occupied France?" Ernst shook his head in disgust. He flipped through the pages in the file, noting the site maps, security systems, and exits. "At least I studied the floor plans last night. The main complex stands on three acres of land. The auditorium seats two thousand people, and a labyrinth of catacombs stretches five stories below it. Anyone could attack the Führer and hide in those caverns for days."

Angry gray clouds hovered over an endless field of red-and-white Nazi banners waving all over Paris. Their automobile sped through the city and arrived at the opera house in record time.

Max slammed a full magazine into his Schmeisser machine gun as he exited the automobile. Upon entry into the lobby, the guards confirmed Hitler's arrival just twenty minutes earlier. Ernst turned to the nearest soldier. "Give me your Schmeisser, schnell!" The soldier surrendered his gun as Ernst perused the cavernous five-story lobby.

Another guard opened a door. "The main auditorium is through here; turn right, then down the center aisle, Captain."

When Ernst entered the theater, he heard muffled voices emanating from the stage. He signaled Max to search the balconies to the right, while he took the left bank of box seats high above the stage. Lifting his Zeiss binoculars, Ernst rotated the focus collar, clearing for distance. Magnified images filled the eyepiece as he scanned the elevated box-seat section. From the seventh box, there was a brief flash of light.

"Herr Teschler!" a commanding voice echoed from the stage. "How good of you to come," Hitler shouted. "Come join us."

Distracted, Ernst lowered his binoculars but for a moment.

A single shot rang out, echoing throughout the hall. Apart from the confused voices of alarm vaulting from the stage, the cavernous hall was empty. Ernst looked in several directions at once with no point of origin to be found.

Trying a different position, Ernst peered through his binoculars again. This time he found himself staring at a man in a dark woolen ski mask holding a high-powered rifle protruding from the third-floor curtain of royal box number seven.

Hitler shouted just as a thunderous volume of shots rang out from above. As he dove to the floor, Ernst fired his Schmeisser from the hip. In a staccato roar, a barrage of bullets climbed the walls, smashed mirrors and tore through the box's red velvet curtains.

A cadre of SS soldiers flooded onto the stage and shielded the Führer, while Max and a few guards fanned out in pursuit. Ernst rushed back into the lobby. Playing his hunch, Ernst bounded up the red-carpeted staircase toward the balcony.

At that moment, the would-be assassin charged down the opposite staircase with his silenced pistol spewing flame. Ernst fired his machine gun, and the chandelier above his target exploded. Through a shower of cascading glass, the assassin disappeared down the opposite stairwell.

Ernst leaped over the railing and landed on the lobby floor. Jamming another magazine into the Schmeisser, he edged down the stairs into the dark bowels of the theater. Hugging the plaster wall, he suspended the Schmeisser on a shoulder strap and took out his silenced Walther pistol.

He stepped onto the first subterranean floor, then lowered himself to his knees. Ernst craned his head slowly around the corner, holding his breath. He could almost taste blood as he imagined himself swallowing a bullet.

*   *   *

The masked assassin scurried down two more staircases and through a dimly lit corridor. With the stealth-like moves of a cat, he entered the caretaker's apartment for the second time that morning. The elderly man lay still upon the floor with a broken neck, his frozen eyes staring into space.

Stepping over the body, the intruder closed the door and listened. He could hear scattered steps and voices above him, scouring the opera house. In the dimly lit quarters, he swiftly disassembled his rifle and secured its components inside the fake shell of his trombone case. Then he moved back through the corridor to the rear stairs, when he heard more German soldiers burst into the stairwell several stories above.

He quietly descended to the next level. A faint noise sounded—just one flight above. He again removed his silenced 9mm pistol from his coat and stood still. Could this be Teschler?

The assassin inched up and peeked over the railing. Catching a glimpse of Teschler's pistol, he jerked his head back into the shadows. Above him, the clatter of the soldiers' rapid footsteps came closer with every step.

He leaned out just as Teschler arched his head over the railing, extending his gun barrel. His heart fluttered as he sprinted down the last set of stairs to escape his pursuer.

Cloaked by the shadows, he waited in the alcove for Teschler to enter his trap.

*   *   *

Ernst stalked down the corridor, his heartbeat sounding louder with each step. His eyes slowly became accustomed to the scant light. He searched every crevice, every doorway, looking for some sign of movement. He stopped to listen. One false step and he would be a dead man.

A floorboard creaked. The sound was ever so slight, but was it in front or behind him? With a deep breath, he prepared to bolt back up the stairs. He discharged a single silenced bullet off the stone wall five meters across from him. He froze.

His decoy shot failed to flush out his prey. With a two-handed grip, he wove his pistol in a cross pattern for cover as he retraced his steps back toward the stairs.

Just as he stepped in front of the darkened nook, he heard the faint sound of a hammer as it cocked. From the elbow Ernst rotated his Walther up and under his left armpit. He spun his body, dipping his head.

With the sound of a pronounced cough, a weapon fired and a bullet scorched the side of his head. His left foot slid out from underneath him, and he slammed into the railing. Ernst landed with a thud as his Walther flew across the floor.

His spectacles lost in the fall, Ernst saw only a dark blur, leaning over him with a flash of steel. He released his special truncheon and armed the firing mechanism with his thumb. Just as the assassin placed the blade across his throat, Ernst discharged the truncheon point-blank.

The small explosive charge plowed its wooden tip into the dark woolen mask, snapping the man's head back. The assassin howled from the pain. Holding his cheek, in a flash the assassin disappeared down yet another staircase.

His hair sopped with fresh blood, Ernst grew faint, and he reclined upon the wood floor. Like the *Phantom of the Opera*, the assassin could hide forever in more than three acres of subterranean lakes below.

In a haze, Ernst recognized Max's voice as a squad of SS soldiers arrived. Nausea was his last memory before he slipped into a veil of darkness.

*   *   *

The masked intruder hustled down an alley behind the opera house and entered an abandoned building. He made his way into a bathroom, holding his throbbing cheekbone with one hand. Gingerly removing his mask, SS Major Alfred Neame examined the huge black-and-blue welt and grazed skin in the mirror. He dabbed the blood with a towel.

He cursed to himself. *Himmler will have a tantrum when he finds out I failed.* His face was red and swollen. His eyes were ripe for revenge. "Teschler—I will make you pay for this!"

Chapter Twenty-Three

Lido di Venezia, Italy, July 7, 1940

Seduced by the subtle drone of lapping waves licking the shore, Ernst closed his eyes. *He imagined Eva's becoming smile when she drew back her white-laced veil. Her azure eyes glistened in the streaming sunlight, filtered by the church's stained-glass windows.*

As the minister pronounced their vows and they gave consent, strangely her glimmering lips moved but no sound emerged. With the minister's nod, Ernst embraced her with a kiss that would last an eternity. . . .

"Ernst, Ernst—wake up, darling." Eva rolled closer to him in the hot sand. She lifted his strands of light-brown hair draping his healing wound. "That gash in your head is coming along, but you'll have a little bald spot right here." She tickled the side of his head with her fingers.

"Stop! You make me out to be an old man?"

"Well, I have always been attracted to older aristocrats."

Ernst leaned back, digging his elbows into the sand. "And how many such beaus have you had?"

"A respectable woman would never reveal such a thing." Eva offered a flirtatious grin.

As the dark-blue waters of the Adriatic Sea embraced the pristine white sands of Lido di Venezia, Ernst drew close and kissed his bride-to-be. Her lush lips bathed his in the allure of her perfumed scent. He could feel the silky oil on her skin as he stroked the inside of her forearm.

"I can imagine a life together with you, Eva. We would have children and grow old gracefully. Tell me your thoughts."

Lifting her hand to shade her eyes, she gazed upon the secluded beach. "Maybe one day we could run away and discover a safe harbor together. Away from the war, away from those who would hurt us."

Ernst could hear the hesitancy in her voice. "Yours is a wonderful dream, darling. But you aren't telling me everything."

"If I were not a mystery, Captain Teschler, then you could not be Germany's top counterespionage agent. Just think of me as your sultry nemesis. Your assignment, if you choose to accept it, is to discover all of my secrets."

Her seductive figure rose from the sand, silhouetted by the setting sun. She lifted her towel and slipped into her sandals. "Come, Ernst. We must get dressed for dinner. I am eager to meet your cryptic Herr Richardt."

*   *   *

The next morning, Ernst met his Swiss banker at the hotel dining room. Having selected a window-side table, Ernst moved his chair to avoid the bright sunlight. "Last night, Fräulein Kleist was enticed by your charming personality, Herr Richardt."

"It comes naturally in the presence of such a beautiful mistress, Herr Löeb."

The word *mistress* caught in Ernst's throat. Eva was so much more than that.

Richardt retrieved a notebook from his coat pocket. "Now to business. I travel to this beautiful coast two or three times a year to negotiate currency transactions."

"Reichsmarks?"

"The Balkan markets are highly profitable. But they want to accumulate anything *but* German currency." Herr Richardt's smile was all business.

"Herr Heydrich told me to give you this." Ernst handed him a sealed envelope under the corner of the table. "Monies due on his private arrangements with you."

With a nod, Herr Richardt slipped the envelope into a brown leather folio at his side. "In three days, I will meet you in Merano, Italy, the German section. I'm inspecting various properties for potential distribution next year. We can move large amounts of product there, but you must come alone."

"That will be no problem."

Richardt stood and shook Ernst's hand. "Auf wiedersehen, Herr Löeb."

As Richardt departed, Ernst turned his thoughts to Eva. They would have only two more precious days together at the beach for their Italian holiday. *If only she would marry me.* Together they would build a life in Shangra-la.

*   *   *

Berlin, Abwehr HQ, September 23, 1940

Admiral Canaris's conference room was darkened. The reel of the 16mm film projector turned, flashing black-and-white images of violence, torture, and death upon the screen. Dietrich cringed at the stark portrayal of SS brutality.

"These scenes were shot in Poland by Abwehr agents," Hans Dohnanyi said. Everyone stared in horror as the film chattered through the projector gate. "The aggression of Waffen-SS troops against the Polish resistance was merciless. After Warsaw finally capitulated, German troops continued farther east to the Soviet treaty line."

Colonel Oster took a drag on his cigarette. "In every major campaign, the SS has sent their Einsatzgruppen troops in after the regular army to 'eliminate' undesirables in captured territories."

"You mean the Jews?" Dietrich asked.

"Not only Jews." Hans stood by the screen. "In the September '39 offensive in Poland, almost seven hundred Catholic priests were arrested. Four hundred and eighty were placed in concentration camps, and the rest were . . ."

"Executed," Dr. Josef Müller said. The stocky Catholic lawyer looked polished in his three-piece pinstriped suit. He had a pleasant pug face with a pronounced nose. "In one diocese alone, two hundred and fourteen Catholic priests were murdered by the SS."

Dietrich clasped his hands together. What kind of evil attacked God's priests?

Dietrich's brother-in-law turned on the lights. "Here is Heydrich's telegram to the Einsatzgruppen."

Our final aim is the concentration of the Jews from the countryside into the larger cities between the areas of Danzig and West Prussia, Posen, eastern Upper Silesia. Only cities that are rail junctions, or at least are located along railroad lines, are to be designated as concentration points. We shall incarcerate all Jews in these containment cities.

And from these sites, final disposition shall be considered. —Heydrich

Colonel Oster stood with lights on. "Our agents inside the SS say that the Warsaw and Lodz ghettos will soon be sealed."

Canaris stepped over to a German-Polish map on the wall. "Three months ago, Himmler opened the camp at Auschwitz. From Berlin, it is about six hundred kilometers by train. Himmler's deal with IG Farben is to provide slave labor for their chemical factories. But what if they are planning something else?"

"Nothing is beyond these butchers!" Müller exclaimed. "I have been negotiating with Father Robert Leiber, an assistant to Pope Pius XII. With papal permission, he and Monsignor Kaas have conveyed our documents to Sir Francis D'Arcy Osborne, the British Minister to the Holy See. Both Rome and the British know that highly placed German officers are willing to revolt against Hitler if the Allies promise us aid."

"Much like my liaison with Bishop Bell," Dietrich said.

"I only hope your efforts meet with a better response than mine," Müller said. "The British may be stringing us along. Every time we talk, they gain information on the German resistance. Then they stall."

"We are all aware of the problem, Herr Müller," Canaris said. "Please update us on Black Chapel."

As Müller revealed the carefully devised scheme to remove Hitler and topple the Nazi government, a thousand questions stormed through Dietrich's mind. *How can I explain my presence in a military plot to execute Adolf Hitler?*

Canaris interrupted his thoughts. "Herr Bonhoeffer, we are assigning you to our Munich office. Along with Dr. Müller, you will provide area intelligence from church leaders."

"We could stay at the Benedictine monastery in Ettal. I know the director well."

Oster handed Dietrich an envelope. "To establish your Abwehr status, you will consort with our agents in full view of the Gestapo. So when you travel, you can pass through border checkpoints with these Abwehr credentials unchallenged. You must be ready to travel at a moment's notice."

Dietrich gazed at the haunting images frozen upon the screen. "Sir, it is certain that the Gestapo has me on their list."

Colonel Oster grinned. "And we have Hitler on ours."

*   *   *

Switzerland, February 26, 1941

Dietrich met his old friend Bishop George Bell at a small inn near the British embassy in Basle. It was an unseasonably cold, rainy night. "George, I brought you a Bavarian umbrella, a belated birthday present."

"Dietrich, you will never have as much rain as we do in England."

During dinner, they reminisced about church and their school days. When dessert was served, Dietrich finally turned to business. "During the initial invasion of Poland, the SS incarcerated or murdered over six hundred priests."

George lowered his fork on his plate.

"The Nazis are targeting the people of God, George."

"The British papers have not reported such stories. I'm sorry. I didn't know."

The whole world appeared to be asleep. "In the last ten years, the Reich Church chose to remain deaf, dumb, and blind when the devil came knocking at the door." Dietrich strained for the last sip in his wine glass.

"You have spoken about the Jews and the dissidents."

"We fear the worst. Himmler's Einsatzgruppen are trained assassins. They follow the regular army, corral Jewish civilians, and kill them by the thousands every week," Dietrich said. "Certain German generals are ready to assume command of a new German government, but we can't fight both Hitler and the British army at the same time. Our people need a clear commitment from Churchill before we start the revolt."

"What do your colleagues have in mind?"

"We need the Allies to suspend military action against Germany during the uprising. We hope that the Allies will allow the new German government to make a gradual, orderly transition to a more democratic regime."

George sighed. "You know Churchill has demanded an unconditional surrender."

"George, *please*. You must realize that those connected with the Abwehr conspiracy are at risk by our very meeting."

"Why would a theologian associate with military agents?"

Dietrich searched for words. "Ja. As a Christian, I must take a stand! The Führer has declared war upon the Jews and Confessing Christians alike. The Germany I once knew and loved no longer exists."

George caressed his chin with his thumb and forefinger. "I will present your case to Sir Anthony Eden, but I cannot make any promises."

A few tables away, someone turned up a radio, and a familiar announcer from the BBC shouted out his report. ". . . Luftwaffe is dropping hundreds of bombs on the city of London! I'm standing on the roof of a hotel near the Thames and I can see . . . Oh, my! An incredible blast from the warehouses down by the docks . . ."

Dumbfounded, both clergymen looked at each other. "George, it would appear that the devil now stands at England's door. God help us all!"

*   *   *

Berlin, Spring 1941

Early that evening a gentle mist descended on the city streets. Alone at the Bismarck Tavern, Ernst nursed his third glass of schnapps. Like Papa, he had begun to develop the ability to cloak its effects. At sunset with car keys in hand, curiosity led Ernst to the entrance of *that alley*. The scene of his father's murder.

A crack of thunder could be heard in the distance, signaling the arrival of something ominous. A chill crept up Ernst's spine as he penetrated the first corridor of the dark alley. As he rounded the corner into the final brick alcove, his breathing became thick and shallow. Though he could not see anyone, Ernst prayed to God for strength. But there was only an unnerving silence.

He reached out into the shadows. "Papa, where are you? I miss your strong hands on my shoulders."

At the end of the alcove where his father's body had been discarded in a crumpled heap, Ernst stopped and tried to remember his father's face. With a clap of thunder nearby, the lightning ignited the screams of his father begging for mercy. He called out again and again for help, but no human soul would answer his frantic pleas.

Ernst reached up to the sky as a light rain splashed his tears of regret down his face.

Then he felt a tap on his shoulder. It was God. Ernst looked Him square in the eyes and asked, "Why did Papa have to die?"

After a moment of silence, familiar voices arose from the cobble-stones and began to chant. Then a luminous cloud appeared, just like the one he saw on Kristallnacht. Arching over him, Ernst bellowed a primeval scream into the vapor that was his father, and he fled the scene of the crime.

By the time he parked his car in front of Pastor Bonhoeffer's house, it was storming hard with sheets of rain pounding the pavement. The walkway from the street to his pastor's front steps seemed endless. Ernst reached for the door chime. Though muffled, he recognized a vigorous melody of Bach on the parlor piano from inside. The music stopped and eventually the front door opened. "Pastor Bonhoeffer."

"Ernst, what brings you out on such a night? You're soaked. Come in out of the rain."

"I could use a strong cup of *Kaffee*."

In the kitchen, Dietrich prepared a pot while Ernst removed his drenched black tunic. "The family is out this evening, so this is a good time to talk."

"It was too loud at the Bismarck. For a long time I sat and watched the patrons. You know, you learn much about people by listening. Those people actually listen to each other's endless banter."

Dietrich turned down the stove. "You were drinking alone?"

"Yes, indeed. When I don't sleep, I drink."

Dietrich poured their coffee and sat down. "Nightmares?"

"Ah, does God know you're a prophet? Ha!" Ernst lowered his head. "I can't sleep because I still remember that dark day at Gleiwitz. It was a secret operation. I trust you not to tell anyone. The Polish army was to attack a German radio station, and our armies would blitzkrieg to Warsaw."

"It was your first battle then. It must have been traumatic."

"The whole operation was an SS deception. We placed empty guns in the hands of all the prisoners, we scattered them on the grass as if there was a great battle, then. . . . Dr. Bonhoeffer, I came this evening to let you know I learned something about God tonight."

Dietrich put his cup down.

"Before I came here, I went back to the alley where my father was murdered. I tried to pray, but I could only hear the tortured screams of my father begging for his life. I called out for help, but no one came to help. Then I felt a tap on my shoulder. . . ."

"And?"

"It was God. I looked Him in the eyes and asked Him, why? Why did Papa have to die? Then there was silence. He bellowed back at me. 'Why did thirty-three innocent Jews have to die?' Then I heard voices. Then a few more—and from the dark shadows of that alley emerged the faces of the dead."

Ernst's eyes swelled with the tale. "Gleiwitz was a staged event. We targeted thirty-three innocent Jews. I was ordered—to give the command. One by one, SS soldiers murdered them with injected poison and bullets fired point-blank. In the victims' eyes, I saw denial of their fate . . . screams for their loved ones and blind resignation to their deaths. Some would call it murder, but I call it the Gleiwitz Massacre. It began with the command at the sound of my voice. My honor is loyalty. Don't you understand? My honor is obedience! And so, we gave Hitler his war—all for the glory of the Reich. Sieg heil!"

"Ernst, you must turn back to God!"

"Ever since that fateful day at Gleiwitz, God has pursued me. I deserve the hell of sleepless nights and the tyranny of the bottle, just like my father." Ernst darted his gaze across the kitchen, and he stood. He glanced over his shoulder. "Now that I have confessed, I must go— before my pursuer arrives."

"My boy, God can forgive you even when you cannot forgive your- self. You must reject the claims that the Nazis have over your life. And do it soon. Life is short, my friend."

"Pastor, did you not hear? The relentless eyes of thirty-three dead Jews glare at me every night. I will never be able to forget, and I will not allow anyone to forgive me." Tears erupted from Ernst's soul.

He stood erect and snapped his black Death's Head hat over his brow. "I have come to warn you. My name is Captain Ernst Teschler, SS. We have come for the Jews. We are coming for the Confessing Church. Given time, Pastor, I will come for you."

*   *   *

Berlin, May 7, 1941

A few weeks later, Eva heard a knock on her apartment door, a light tap- ping at first, then with more conviction. Clad in a rose-colored scooped- neck sweater, she briefly checked her makeup before her mirror, then opened the door. Ernst stood before her bathed in shadow and light. He stood tall in his sleek black SS uniform. "Ernst!"

"Fräulein, Captain Teschler requests the pleasure of your company. I warn you though, my personal interrogations will take days."

Eva's eyes glistened. "Oh, Ernst!" She arched up on the tips of her toes and wrapped her arms around his broad shoulders. He carried her inside and kicked the door closed behind him. Their lips touched again and again, discovering a new language. Minutes passed before either of them spoke.

"Ernst, it has been months! Where have you been?"

"In five different countries and nearly every town in Germany. But now, I am here with you."

She pulled him down onto the sofa, nibbled his ear, and made her way slowly to his lips. Her deep-red lipstick left telltale marks on his cheek.

Eventually, she leaned back, fingering the silver captain's insignia attached to the open collar of his tunic. "So now you are a captain in the SS."

"Are you impressed?"

"I'm impressed that I never see you. You have become a ghost!"

"My current assignment is confidential."

"But how long can you stay?" Eva tilted her head, letting her gaze linger on his handsome face.

"I dream about you every day, my *liebling*. I want to belong to something—to someone."

"And?" Eva so desperately wanted to hear the words.

He placed his fingertips on her lips. "With my promotion, my status and pay allows me to consider marriage." He paused. "Do you understand what I'm saying to you?"

Eva parted her lips. "Have you talked to your uncle recently?"

Ernst sat up. "No, but he is certain to approve. I am confident that I could provide a good life for you. Our children would be raised within one of the most respected families in the Reich. Eva, I want you to be my wife!"

She reached out and held his hands together. "Ernst, you are welcome here anytime. The only commitment I need from you is your love. My heart is yours and always will be."

He did not miss a beat. "Madam, I intend to make an honest woman of you. You won't have to swing your hips about the Bismarck for gratuities."

Eva pulled away. "But you can't marry without permission from the SS. You know the rules."

"Ja, but look." He pulled a sheaf of papers from his tunic pocket. "These are the required forms. They can be completed tomorrow. I'll have Uncle Reinhard sign them and personally submit them to Himmler. We can be married in a matter of weeks!"

"But spouses of SS officers must have 'pure blood' to the third generation." The "royal" wedding of her dreams might never happen—not with SS Captain Ernst Teschler. The truth stuck upon her tongue just like the lies she had told Ernst about her life.

His eyes bore into her. "Please, I am asking you to marry me."

Eva stood counting the costs to her family. During the last year her cousin Saul had failed twice to free her father from Sachsenhausen. And her mother Nina continued to hide with neighbors in Wittenberg. All because Eva refused to tell Ernst the truth about her family.

With the veiled threats of Reinhard Heydrich echoing in her mind, she arose from the couch. "My dear, all of this is so sudden."

"You don't want to be my wife?" Bewilderment drew his brows together.

Eva averted her gaze as she struggled to find the words. "Ernst, more than anything, I want to be with you. It's just that . . . I don't know who my parents are. The SS will find out, and your family will shun me." She buried her head in his shoulder and wept.

"Eva, darling, I want to spend my life with you!"

"Your family is SS royalty, and my ancestors are unknown. I didn't want you to find out."

He stroked her back. "Look, the SS will investigate, and we can help you find out who your parents are. We can make this work."

Eva crossed the room and pulled a handkerchief from her purse. Dabbing her smudged mascara, she glanced over her shoulder.

"Ernst, you are so naive. The Reich demands pristine wives for picture-perfect officers. You are a prince in Germany, but I can guarantee you that I am no Cinderella." Again, she broke into tears, ran into her bedroom, and slammed the door behind her.

He knocked on the door repeatedly. "Eva, let me in!" His muffled voice was full of pain and anger. Then with a crash, the wood-paneled door gave way, and he stood silhouetted by the hall light. Eva was stretched across her bed, still sobbing.

Sadness clouded his features. "Why do you shut me out?"

She lifted her head. "I'm not good enough for you, Ernst. Can't you see that? Just let me go!"

He sat next to her. "I will not let you leave me, Eva. Not in this life—" He stroked her bare neck with the tips of his fingers, and her body went limp. Their lips touched, again and again.

Bathed by the blue moonlight streaming through her bedroom window, they both lost all sense of time. . . .

Chapter Twenty-Four

Sachsenhausen Camp, June 1941

Entering Blockhouse 13, Ernst walked past prisoners working at production tables and printers, to find Bernhard Krüger in his office inspecting English currencies with a magnifying glass.

"Guten Tag, Major. General Heydrich sent me for the latest results."

"Our forgers and artisans have duplicated multiple British denominations. Initial distribution tests in Lisbon, Rome, and Athens are most promising."

"General Heydrich needs to know your plan for England."

"We are now focused upon the Bank of England's five-pound note. With enough forgeries in circulation, we could eventually debase their currency. I want to test distribution in Switzerland by September. Our agents there are making arrangements now." Krüger handed a set of notes and magnifier to Ernst.

Stepping closer to the window, Ernst held up the specimens to the sunlight.

"Well, Captain, can you tell the difference? The color and print quality are almost perfect, but we are still having problems with the paper.

We're close but still there is work to be done." A knock sounded on the open doorway. "Come!"

An SS security guard prodded a short prisoner into the room and pushed him into an empty chair. With wire-framed spectacles, shorn hair, and his ragged striped uniform, the inmate was unmistakably a Jew. His features were gaunt, yet Ernst sensed something familiar about his weary brown eyes.

Krüger handed the prisoner's file to Ernst. "Captain, this is Abraham Kleisfeld."

Kleisfeld looked back at his captors vacantly. The guard nudged his ribs with the butt of his rifle. "Ja! I am Kleisfeld."

Krüger stepped around his desk. "Teschler, you first met our distinguished forger in Wittenberg a few years ago. He set that Jewish trap for you and Neame at his shop—all that gold he promised. It's all in his file."

"Wittenberg, that was the fall of '38." Ernst recalled the disastrous incident. The prisoner before him was easily forty pounds heavier back then.

Kleisfeld stared at the floor.

Ernst studied him. "What were the names of the assassins?"

The prisoner squinted up into the streaming sunlight. "Some Czechs came to the shop. They wanted money. I didn't have it. They threatened my family several times, so we fled."

Ernst's eyes needled his prey. "Tell me the truth!"

"I am a master engraver! My grandfather taught my father, and my father taught me."

Krüger sat behind his desk. "I suppose you taught your Jew son the trade as well?"

Kleisfeld clenched his coffee-stained teeth. "I have no son."

Krüger sneered. "No son? Why, I've been told you Jews propagate like rats."

Ernst glanced at the file. "Your papers say you have one son."

"He was murdered—on Kristallnacht, November 9 . . . 1938."

Ernst walked over to the window. Through the latticed panes of glass, he saw hundreds of Jews penned up like animals. Like a bolt of lightning, he remembered that dark alley, his papa's face frozen in a grotesque death mask, and Uncle Reinhard's high-pitched voice. *"Ernst, the Jews did this! They branded your father like a steer. Butchers, that's what they are!"*

Krüger handed a magnifying glass to Kleisfeld. "I want you to examine each of these documents on the desk and tell me which are genuine and which are fakes."

The engraver picked up each pair of documents in turn, rubbed the papers between his thumb and forefinger, and swiftly sorted them into two piles, almost as if he were dealing cards. He tapped the pile on the left with his finger. "These are all forgeries. Mediocre ones at best."

Krüger leaned back in his chair. "How do you know?"

Kleisfeld shrugged. "The feel of the paper—it's not genuine. And the hue of the blue ink on the British note is off just a shade."

Ernst turned away from the window and stared again at the prisoner's sunken cheeks, scraggly beard, and rugged features. "Herr Kleisfeld, those Czechs back in Wittenberg, would you recognize them if you ever saw them again?"

"Perhaps. But that was some time ago."

"Those men were professional soldiers . . . from the Balkans?"

"No, from Palestine—eh . . ." Kleisfeld's eyes swallowed his own words.

How ironic. Israeli assassins hunting Nazis.

*   *   *

Near Berlin, July 1941

Their apartment was located in the low-rent district of Oberkrämer, a small town about twenty-six kilometers northwest of Berlin. With a mitted hand, Saul Avigur poured hot diluted coffee from a metal carafe into military-issue tin cups. "German coffee is sour, eh Malachi?"

"This country is cold even in July." Malachi was a short man, a half Jew by birth. With his black hair and dark skin, he could pass as a merchant from Turkey. "For ten days I've tried to follow Heydrich, but his security makes it nearly impossible to get close. His schedule varies from day to day. He comes and goes from SS headquarters at different hours of the day. I tell you, the man is expecting a bullet."

"And it will be mine."

Malachi took one more sip and grimaced. "So, why is Heydrich on the top of our list?"

"The SS just signed agreements with IG Farben to build a chemical factory by a concentration camp—Auschwitz."

Malachi shook his head. "Never heard of it."

"New construction. Since the German army conquered the occupied territories in Poland, the SS has herded Jews into ghettos—maybe three hundred to four hundred thousand in Lodz and Warsaw alone. We think there's a connection. Rumor has it that a massive train construction project is soon to begin. It would connect the dots."

"And Heydrich is in charge of the project."

Saul nodded. "The Haganah wants him dead. Maybe, just maybe, we need some bait. Tell me more about Heydrich's nephew."

"In the last two weeks, SS Captain Ernst Teschler and a Major Neame have been to Sachsenhausen three times. Teschler arrives with nothing in hand but leaves with a leather briefcase handcuffed to his wrist."

"They have kept my cousin Abraham in that hellhole for a few years." Saul scowled at the bitter coffee.

"They're trying to duplicate British currency. But word is, they've had problems."

"Malachi, I want you to break into Sachsenhausen and talk to Abraham. It's the only way to confirm details of their currency operation."

"Why take the risk? About twice a week, Neame's men take your cousin and some others to a factory in Spechthausen, just east of Sachsenhausen. It will be difficult to get to him undetected, but it can be done."

Saul picked out the burnt coffee grounds stuck between his teeth. "No one on this continent wants to deal with Jews—but they will deal with our money. What if we embezzled a few million in counterfeit currency? That would buy boats to freedom for thousands of Jews."

"My friend, you're a genius. So tell me why Captain Teschler is so important?"

"Teschler is both Heydrich's nephew and Hitler's guard dog. If we watch him carefully, we'll catch up to Heydrich outside of Berlin unprotected. When the general is dead, we'll see how close we can get to Hitler."

"What about your cousin Sarah?"

Saul stood at the sink and poured the coffee over a week-old stack of dirty dishes. "She must never know that I was the one who killed Ernst Teschler."

*   *   *

Berlin, August 1941

At 9:00 p.m. Eva had already dressed for bed. In her maroon robe with her blonde hair pinned back, she was comfortably curled up in her sofa, trying to think of some romantic words to write.

> *My dearest Ernst, words elude me when I think of how much love I have to give. . . .*

The sound of a light rap at her apartment door interrupted the intimate thought. It sounded again. Annoyed, Eva slowly rose and opened the door, then backed away. She gazed into the piercing dark eyes of General Heydrich.

"Good evening, Fräulein." His expression was coy as he walked into her foyer. His aide reached in to pull the door closed, sealing the two inside.

Eva labored to find breath as her pulse raced. Fight or flight was not an option. She was trapped in her gilded cage.

There was a momentary silence. "Fräulein, I hope I'm not disturbing your evening." His tone was pleasant, but the way his eyes scrutinized her from the top of her head to her feet and slowly back up again said something else altogether. "You were going to offer me a seat?"

"Certainly, mein herr." She gestured toward the living room, and Heydrich eased himself into a worn easy chair and looked around the room. It was sparsely furnished. Her heart pounded as she perched upon the edge of the love seat.

"Surely I can call you Eva. We are friends! We shared that wonderful chat on my train."

She knew what was coming. He had known her secret in the railcar that day—and now was her day of reckoning. Eva let out a slow exhale.

Heydrich brushed a piece of lint from his trousers. "My dear, Eva. When Ernst was promoted to captain, he joined a new class of society. And that, my dear girl, is a problem where you are concerned." Heydrich's eyes narrowed.

Eva had been playing this game too long to give anything away. "A problem, mein herr?"

"Come now, you know that I collect dark secrets professionally." From a breast pocket of his uniform, he produced an index card, flicked it into the air, and it landed on the coffee table in front of her.

Without glancing at its contents, Eva nonchalantly removed a cigarette from a silver box on the coffee table and eased back into the love seat. "You look like a man who enjoys little secrets."

Heydrich tilted his head as he produced a lighter from his pocket. "You are really very good, *meine Liebchen*. And you have such nice legs." Peering through his cold, black reptilian eyes, he ignited a flame.

She was a Jew in the hands of one of the highest-ranking SS officers in the land. This man could do anything he wished to her, and she knew it. Cautiously, she leaned toward the flame.

"So," Heydrich said with a casual wave of his hand, "you are the paramour of my nephew, a high-ranking member of the SS. And you—are a Jewess. What shall we do about this problem, my dear?"

It was as if her life and her lies were projected upon the wall frozen, still framed in a projector. Exhaling the rich unfiltered smoke, her voice faltered. "What do you have in mind, mein herr?"

"Ernst believes that he loves you. He is a young man of limited experience when it comes to women. He fancies himself a knight errant. Chivalry is his weakness. And all of this, you have played to your advantage. Is this not so, Fräulein?"

Eva gazed back stoically as her mind raced toward dark places.

"I have plans for Ernst. And they do *not* include marriage—not yet. Actually, I appreciate this casual relationship you have with Ernst, so hear me well. You will not marry him. If I see you moving him in that direction, you will simply disappear one night. You understand?"

Her throat constricted, and she was transported back to that beach in Italy. She could feel Ernst's fingers stroking away the tears on her cheeks. She could hear the soft timbre of his voice when he spoke of his love, of his desire to spend his life with her. She opened her eyes. "Ja. Only too well, mein herr."

"Do not reveal your parentage to him—ever! Is that understood?" Heydrich's menacing eyes glistened as a smile played across his thin lips.

"Ja, mein herr, I understand perfectly."

Heydrich stood and stepped in front of her, cooing a chuckle. "You know, Eva, in different circumstances, I should very much like to become better acquainted with you, ja?" He took her hand and kissed it. "Until we meet again."

When he closed her door, it shut with such finality. Eva sat for some time on the love seat as she fingered the partially written words of her letter to Ernst. Then with a curse, she tore the paper into tiny pieces. For now, it was nothing but a symbol of her shredded life.

*   *   *

27 September 1941

TO: Obergruppenführer Heydrich
FROM: Adolf Eichmann

Congratulations on your appointment by the Führer as Reichsprotektor of Bohemia and Moravia [stop] The initial results from Zyklon-B gas tests this month were most favorable [stop] Einsatzgruppen reports indicate heightened hostilities by Russian Jews near Kiev [stop] Will transmit statistics from Babi Yar when available [stop] During our meeting in Prague, 10 October, we can discuss deportations from the Protectorate to Lodz, Minsk, and Riga and the establishment of the ghetto in Theresienstadt [stop]

All is well,
Eichmann

*   *   *

Wewelsburg Castle, October 18, 1941

Seated at a table in the conference room, Weisthor calmly placed another tarot card into a new configuration. "Heinrich, tell me what you see in the Russian campaign?"

Tapping his teeth with his thumbnail, Himmler studied a large map of Russia tacked to the wall. "Hitler is greedy and hates Stalin. He wants Russian oil fields, but our soldiers will pay a steep price in a bitter Russian winter." With no response, he turned to his occult master. "Are you listening to me, Weisthor?"

"I'm always listening, Heinrich. You were saying?"

"Concerning Russia, the Führer has acted rashly with little thought."

Weisthor contemplated a card. "Adolf is motivated by a lust for power but is driven by fear. He knows that if he does not kill the bear now, it will eat him for breakfast later."

"What do the cards say about me?"

The middle-aged prophet placed the Magus card at the head of a pyramid formation, then presented the Knight Errant card. "Heinrich, the Spear of Destiny will soon come into our possession. Herr Teschler will soon arrive. I can feel the presence of The Infidel."

A half hour later, a secretary announced their guests. Ernst marched briskly into the map room with Barron at his side. He snapped his heels together and saluted. "Heil Hitler!"

Himmler limply lifted his hand in reply and looked over his spectacles at the Doberman. "Captain, the Führer may be enamored by your dog, but I am not. He is dismissed."

"Jawohl, mein herr! Barron!" Ernst snapped his fingers, and the sleek black animal trotted out into the hall.

"Now, Captain, Operation Bernhard—what is your report?"

"Major Neame's group has been tackling various manufacturing problems, but they have arranged a trial distribution of British five-pound notes in Zurich at the end of the month. He is hopeful—"

"And the gold shipments?" Himmler asked.

"On schedule. The Reichsbank is smelting gold collected in volume from Belgium, France, and Holland, with lesser amounts from the camps. We are making monthly shipments to Zurich and Bern."

Magnified by his lenses, Himmler's eyes grew to the size of bottle caps. "Few countries will sell Germany the necessary raw materials for our armies. Converted to foreign currencies, that gold will allow us to purchase the goods through our agents abroad, even from the Americans. So protect it with your life, Captain."

"Sir, my honor is loyalty!"

"Come with me." Weisthor gestured brusquely as he led Ernst into the library. Himmler followed, switching on a series of spotlights that illuminated a row of portraits, each mounted upon custom cherrywood panels. Ernst recognized about half of the black-uniformed leaders of the SS—thirteen portraits in all.

"Here you see my disciples—the new royalty of Germany!" Weisthor's voice echoed behind Ernst as the occult priest stepped into a pool of light. "These are the leaders of Weltanschauung, our Religion of the Blood! We in the SS rule the masses by our mystical power."

"You said, 'religion'?" Ernst shifted his weight uneasily.

"Our mystical religion! In ancient Egypt, the swastika was a symbol for destruction introduced by the Angel of Light."

Himmler interrupted. "Every one of our early military campaigns has cut across Europe in that formation, like a scythe harnessed for harvest. Our victories confirm our destiny until now!"

"There were others—the Cathari in the eleventh century, the Illuminists during the Spanish Inquisition, and the Illuminati during the French Revolution." Weisthor felt the smooth cherry finish of the picture frame. "Within these walls I am grooming thirteen disciples—and each is preparing a protégé to take his place should he fall. When Heydrich dies, you have been designated to join our coven." He sensed a deep resistance in young Teschler. In the end, would The Infidel come to faith?

Himmler stepped closer. "But now we give you a task to prove your loyalty to the Religion of the Blood, Captain Teschler."

Ernst blinked.

Himmler walked to the library table and pulled a dark cloth away from an exquisite black leather case. Himmler released two separate brass latches on top and unfolded overlapping lids. "This case is totally functional." He pointed to a series of vertical file folders. "But when you press this switch—" A false bottom section extended to the side, revealing a spear-like object. "We have a very special and secret mission for you, Teschler."

"This is a replica of the true Spear of Longinus!" Weisthor's voice boomed.

Himmler placed the spearhead into Ernst's hand. "The Führer has the original heavily guarded in the Eagle's Nest. We have arranged for you to be invited there soon."

Weisthor leaned closer to Ernst. "It has been foretold that you will bear the unholy talisman and bring it to our shrine at Wewelsburg."

"When you have the opportunity, you are to switch the relics and bring the original to us." A smug grin appeared on Himmler's peevish face.

"But that would be treason!"

Himmler lifted his nose like a hawk. "You spoke of your honor—"

"My honor—is loyalty, Herr Reichsführer!" The words tumbled out of Ernst's mouth.

Weisthor stepped between the two SS officers. "Gentlemen, present your Totenkopf rings." Each man in turn extended the fingers of their left hand forming a circle of human flesh. Their priestly SS Death's Head rings—silver, black onyx, and eyes of red rubies encircled their wedding fingers.

Weisthor invoked the unholy spirit upon the Black Knight. The crystal eyes of all three rings simultaneously glowed. Weisthor gazed into Ernst's aura and saw the future of his Teutonic order intact.

Chapter Twenty-Five

Bavaria, the Eagle's Nest,
October 24, 1941

High above Hitler's Berghof complex, Ernst's SS Mercedes maneuvered along a seven-kilometer asphalt road etched into the granite face of Mount Kehlstein. Passing through an electrified fence, they approached two tall bronze doors. As the metal doors groaned open, the vehicle penetrated the bowels of the dark cavern beyond. With Barron panting by Ernst's side, their headlights illumined machine gun nests placed every seven meters.

At the end of the tunnel, Ernst and Barron were escorted onto a very large, elaborate elevator by two SS guards. The frosted glass doors closed behind them, and the cab lifted. "The main shaft was vertically bored through almost seventy meters of solid rock—up to the very top of Mount Kehlstein. The Eagle's Nest took two years and thirty million Reichsmarks to build." The opulent lift boasted polished brass fixtures, richly upholstered chairs, and paneled glass mirrors mounted along three walls. They ascended with such quiet ease as Ernst leaned over and brushed Barron's flank.

The elevator doors opened to a set of towering Roman pillars, flawlessly hewn from Italian marble. A tuxedoed manservant bowed. "Captain

Teschler, welcome back to Eagle's Eerie." Herr Linge glanced down at Barron. "The Führer has ordered special arrangements for Master Barron during your stay." He glanced at the black leather case held by the SS aide. "May we inspect this?"

"Certainly."

An SS guard emerged from a hallway and probed the case's nooks and crannies with his fingers. With a nod, Linge dismissed the guard. "Please follow me, Captain." Barron trotted beside Ernst as they stepped down into a vaulted living room as opulent as the portico. Across the mahogany floor, Herr Linge entered the "tea room." Ernst faced a stunning wall of lattice-framed glass that exposed the starlit sky. The huge grandfather clock by its entrance sounded eight chimes. "The Führer will arrive soon."

"Thank you, Herr Linge."

Hitler's manservant departed. Left on his own, Ernst explored the room, admiring the sparkle of cut-glass objects, the reflections of polished brass, and the artistry of carved stained wood. It all appeared so fantastic.

"Ah, Captain Teschler!"

Startled, Ernst whirled around and gazed into the eyes of Adolf Hitler. "Mein Führer!" He stiffened into a salute. "Heil Hitler!"

Hitler waved his arm as if to say, "That is not necessary here."

The Führer knelt before Barron and vigorously stroked his bluish-grey flank. "Barron is welcome here any time."

"It is an honor to be in your presence, mein Führer."

Hitler glanced at the leather case. "Ever diligent I see, but I want you to enjoy my hospitality this evening."

Ernst calculated a 60 percent chance at best for switching the spearheads. Even then, how could he possibly escape through all the defenses of the Eagle's Nest?

"Sir, I receive and transmit coded messages throughout the day."

"You are a man of honor and duty!" Hitler rose to his feet. "I wish my generals would follow suit. You are a symbol to me, Teschler. You with your fierce beast at your side." The Führer pulled a cord, and Herr Linge returned. "Heinz, I want you to take very good care of Captain . . . no, I mean *Major* Teschler."

"Excuse me, sir. My rank is—"

"Heinz, this man saved my life thrice!" Hitler stepped closer. "Ja, you didn't know that I knew about the Glade of Conquest, and the "phantom" in the opera house in Paris, did you? Your exploits are becoming legend." From Herr Linge's tray, Hitler presented a set of polished insignias highlighted by silver SS runes.

Ernst snapped to attention.

"It's official. Captain Teschler, you are hereby promoted to the rank of Major SS."

"I am greatly honored, mein Führer." *If only my father could be here now.*

Hitler led Ernst into the dining room. "I have a present for you." Hitler opened a long rectangular box revealing seven golden coins seated in green velvet. "Austrian One Ducat gold coins, minted in 1882 and part of the Habsburg Museum collection."

"They are beautiful."

"To the victor go the spoils, Major. Be a wolf like me."

Heinz and his staff served Ernst a sumptuous sautéed veal, while Hitler feasted on a vegetarian medley. After dessert, the servants disappeared. The Führer lifted his glass to the glistening stars. "Major, to the New World Order!"

Ernst lifted his glass. "To the Fatherland!"

Hitler beckoned Ernst and Barron into the crystal observatory. They eased into a set of enormous brown leather chairs that faced the crystal wall. Hitler's features softened. "There, across those mountaintops, you see the lights of Salzburg. Wait until you gaze upon the view in the morning. It will astonish you. I feel at home up here in the clouds—where only eagles dare."

"It is a wonder that you would ever leave such a place."

"When I was a young boy, my parents forced me to take a Catholic education at Lambach Abbey. The symbol of the swastika was chiseled in its stone columns. It symbolizes the destruction of darkness by the Light. It predates the Hebrews in Egypt, and Illuminists have passed down a sacred body of knowledge from one generation to the next—all under the cloak of secrecy. From ancient times, it has been prophesied that one day a leader would rule one mighty world kingdom."

Ernst was mesmerized by the Führer's magnetic eyes. "What is the Light?"

Hitler brushed his mustache with his forefinger. "The question to ask, my boy, is *who* is the Light? The Angel of Light is the immortal enemy of the God of Abraham. The Light is the most intelligent being in the universe. The *Light* shall send his son to rule over a race of super beings." The Führer paused with a glint in his striated grey eyes. "Follow me, and I will show you your future!"

Hitler led Ernst past the elevator, through a doorway, and down a flight of steps. They walked through a dimly lit hallway to a metal door Hitler unlocked.

"Through here." The Führer touched a switch illuminating the chamber. The light issued from a translucent sphere that protruded halfway through the floor. The intense light projected strange symbols onto the ceiling and walls.

Ernst recognized some—runes of the ancient Norse gods, swastikas, and cast upon the ceiling just above the dome was a pentagram. Feeling light-headed, Ernst could hear faint whispers. Something evil was in this place.

Hitler placed his hand on Ernst's shoulder. "Only the elite few know the secrets of the Holy Grail."

"The cup of Christ?"

"No, that was the myth our Templar predecessors spread during the Middle Ages. *Sangrael* was the original term. It refers to 'bloodline.' Our Aryan prophecies hailed the arrival of Lucifer's son, the one and true messiah!"

Ernst listened, but the words were surreal. "But the German church says—"

"Lies!" Hitler roared as he approached a purple velvet curtain and drew it back.

The sphere's low-angled light revealed an inverted cross, a mockery of the cross of Christ shaped from rough-hewn timbers. Where the beams crossed, there was a small mantel that displayed the one thing in this room Ernst had seen before: a bronze spearhead.

Ernst held his breath in awe as he recalled Himmler's order. *"You are to switch the relics and bring the original to us!"*

Hitler picked up the original Spear of Longinus and stroked its tarnished bronze surface with affection. "Here is the proof of the hoax of Christianity, Teschler. This is the Unholy Talisman that was thrust into the side of Jesus as He died upon the cross. Jesus died, Teschler, never to rise again. Our Unholy Order has survived through every generation. Soon you will possess this sacred knowledge—and with it, the power to rule with us."

Suddenly the Führer clutched his breast with his free hand. He stumbled sideways into the wall. Slowly sliding down to the floor, he uttered a guttural hiss as a great sigh burst from his lips. His eyes rolled upward, and he began to sputter words under his breath.

Ernst stepped closer to help when Hitler's face morphed into something alien.

"Nein, don't touch us! This is our abode!" a deep guttural voice consumed the host. "Teschler, your body, mind, and soul will become one with us."

Ernst shook Hitler by the shoulder. "Mein Führer, what's wrong?"

When Hitler opened his eyes, Ernst leaned back, his mouth falling open. Blood trickled from the man's eye sockets. Ernst rushed to the doorway. "Herr Linge, come quickly!"

Ernst turned back to see Hitler's head slumped and his face beaded with perspiration. Herr Linge hurried into the chamber. Together, they lifted Hitler to his feet and helped him to the stairs. "Major, the Führer is having one of his spells. Please help me get him to bed."

Afterward, the butler led Ernst back to the guest bedroom. "The Führer will be all right now. Please, do be discreet about what you say to him at breakfast concerning his . . . *visitation*."

"Certainly," Ernst said as Herr Linge closed the bedroom door behind him. At the foot of his bed, Ernst looked fondly at a pair of adoring eyes. Barron's ears perked up and he uttered a soft squeal. For the next hour, Ernst stroked Barron's flank as he listened for any signs of movement in the Eagle's Nest.

Ernst eased out into the hallway and crept past the observatory. The distant lights of Salzburg brilliantly refracted through the wall of crystal. All was calm and silent. As he recalled the image of Hitler's brazen eyes, he felt another chill. He retrieved his black leather case on the table. *It is now or never!*

With a flash of adrenaline, Ernst eased his way down the hall to the secluded staircase. Below, he discovered the steel door to Hitler's chamber was still ajar. Switching on the luminous sphere, he spotted the spearhead on the floor. He released the secret compartment under his briefcase and exposed the fake spearhead.

Carefully positioning Himmler's copy on the floor, Ernst replaced the original and then inserted the real blade back in the case. His heartbeat drummed in his head as he felt eyes from the dark, watching him.

Moments later, he sat upon the floor of his bedroom as Barron calmly panted by his side. His instincts told him that whatever this artifact was, whatever its story, it was better off with him than in the possession of these madmen. Then it struck him. The Spear of Destiny—the actual weapon that had pierced the side of Christ—was now in his possession.

His lips dry, his eyes opened wide, Ernst whispered, "Our Father, who art in heaven, holy is Your name. . . ."

*   *   *

Southern Bavaria, October 1941

In a distant dreamlike fashion, SS guards marched the prisoners around the stockade naked. In the autumn sun, perspiration dripped onto Dietrich's rounded spectacles as sharp pebbles cut into the soles of his bare feet. Prodded by the guard's rifle, the steel muzzle felt cold against his back.

The order to halt came, and the prisoners were lashed to wooden posts. The rough-hewn splinters lacerated their backs as they squirmed to loosen their hands. Not seven meters in front of them, the firing squad took their positions.

Thirty-five years to create a lifetime, thirty-five seconds to end it all.

Dietrich Bonhoeffer scrutinized the faces of the German soldiers who would take his life. They were all so young.

Then he could hardly believe his own eyes. The squad commander was none other than Ernst Teschler. Ernst had warned him that he would come for him someday, but Dietrich refused to believe it could happen.

"Load weapons!" Ernst bellowed. The sound of iron bolts chambering their deadly payload echoed off the stone wall.

Dietrich conjured a picture of his beautiful Maria—her blonde hair coiffed in a bun . . . her rose-colored cheeks. He smiled as she strolled through the flower garden at Patzig. He could smell a hint of her favorite fragrance as he felt the warmth of her breath upon his—

"Take aim."

The demons had devoured the fertile minds of the young in Nazi Germany. And Satan had consumed his young friend.

Captain Teschler sneered. "Fire!" The explosive discharge was deafening.

Dietrich jerked upright from the pillow. His eyes popped open wide as he was catapulted back into consciousness. Beads of sweat dripped down his puffy cheeks. He struggled to catch his breath, then reality set in.

It was four in the afternoon, and he was alone in his dormitory at the Abbey.

Wide awake, he opened his briefcase and removed an envelope. He rushed downstairs past a bevy of Benedictine monks praying silently in the chapel when he spotted Dr. Josef Müller. The Abwehr agent was seated on the expansive western porch facing the Bavarian mountains.

The stocky Catholic lawyer looked polished, dressed in a brown tweed sport coat that complimented his dark-brown hair. A generous smile on the man's pleasant pug face greeted Dietrich as he sipped a glass of wine. "Herr Bonhoeffer, do join me in a glass of this fine Riesling. The monks here have an excellent reputation."

"Of course," Dietrich said as he opened the envelope. "Josef, before I send this letter to Bishop Bell in England, I would like your opinion. Let me read it to you."

Since Hitler's euthanasia law was passed in '39, almost two hundred thousand mentally ill and disabled "Aryan" Germans have been executed at legally approved "care facilities."

On 3 August, the Bishop of Münster, Clemens von Galen, openly criticized the Nazi government in a sermon that was printed and distributed throughout Germany. Within days, three of the bishop's priests were found dead in their churches, beheaded, with a copy of the sermon stuffed into their mouths.

George, I was sickened by the Reich Bishop's formal rebuttal of the Galen sermon: "The Party stands on the basis of Positive Christianity, and Positive Christianity is National Socialism. Bishop von Galen believes that Christianity consists of faith in Christ as the Son of God. Nonsense. Christianity has been co-opted by the Party. The Führer is the herald of a new revelation."

A pained expression dawned on Josef's face. "The Gestapo brags about their acts of treachery against priests and ministers. You know, the Nazis could have been stopped ten years ago, before Hitler was elected chancellor. But churches remained silent."

Dietrich remembered the scowl upon Ernst Teschler's face when he said, "They now come for us."

Josef nodded. "Send your letter. Stand tall in your pulpit wherever God sends you—and proclaim the truth!"

Dietrich looked out across the valley blanketed by myriad vibrant fall colors. The sun was beginning to set across the Bavarian Alps. In the conviction of God's Spirit, he knew he would soon be on the move.

*　　*　　*

Bern, Switzerland, November 1941

Dressed in a gray herringbone suit and fedora, Ernst emerged from the polished-steel vault, carrying his empty document case. The original Spear of Longinus was now secure in deposit box 777 of the International Bank of Switzerland.

Herr Richardt met Ernst in the lobby and escorted him to his private office. "Herr Löeb, here are your keys. The box numbers have been removed as you requested. Did you bring the signature card?"

Seated across from the banker, Ernst gave him a photograph and a card. "Here is a copy of my associate's signature. Please arrange access to my box for him."

Herr Richardt perused the photo.

"His name is Max Schumann."

"But, mein herr, bank policy requires an original witnessed signature on file."

Ernst pushed a thick envelope of Swiss francs across the desk. "I'm sure you can make the necessary arrangements." He lifted his left hand. "You see this ring? Two red rubies make it unique. If this man appears with this ring and the key, he is authorized for access."

Herr Richardt smiled as he thumbed through the currency. "It is always a pleasure doing business with you, Herr Löeb."

"I believe you have a summary statement for the Heydrich accounts?"

Richardt retrieved a folder from his lap drawer. When he opened it, his eyes widened. "As you will see, the 5 percent contribution from each gold shipment received is considerable." He handed the file to Ernst.

It took everything he had to remain stoic at the sight. The vast sums were already in the millions. The numbers were printed in black ink, but the possibilities were golden.

"Only General Heydrich and you are authorized on these accounts. Herr Löeb, if General Heydrich became indisposed, who would be successor?"

The weight of that decision was staggering. In whom would he bestow such wealth and power? *In whom would I trust?*

Outside the Dressler Building on Viktoriastrasse, Ernst hailed a taxi. On the way back to the airport Ernst became apprehensive, for the "game" was about to begin. One false move and everyone close to him would certainly die!

*   *   *

Prague, November 1941

Ernst arrived in Prague a week later and was driven to the chateau in Panenské Březany. The Heydrichs had been in residence since October, when Hitler had given his uncle the prize and promotion to Reichsprotektor of Bohemia and Moravia.

Ernst joined Aunt Lina in the parlor of the Heydrich estate. When the maid poured coffee from a sterling silver carafe, Lina signaled for privacy. "Ernst, darling, it's so good to see you again. Being a lady of state is quite lonely in this mansion. Reinhard spends more and more time away from me and the children. Frankly, this new title of his has gone quite to his head. He claims he is now only one seat away from becoming Führer."

"I look forward to seeing Uncle Reinhard when he arrives tonight."

"It will be grand to spend a few days together! Now, tell me more about Fräulein Kleist."

"She is so beautiful. She makes me feel special, like I'm the only man in the room."

"You are almost thirty years old. You should marry."

"I came here to ask for your help. I submitted my marriage application twice this year to Uncle Reinhard. He says he will consider it, but so far he hasn't signed the document. I am at my wit's end!"

"I'm sorry, I didn't know. I certainly will find out the mystery. I will use all of my feminine charms to persuade him."

"Thank you. I knew I could depend on you." Ernst gave her a boyish grin as he placed a small box on the table.

Lina's eyes widened. "A gift. Why, Ernst, it's not even my birthday."

"No, no. It's a secret that I want you to keep safe for me."

Lina cooed as she opened the lid and discovered a stout gold-chain necklace threaded through the eyelet of a bronze key.

"I want you to secure this key with your finest jewelry. One day, either Max or I will come to collect it."

"Reinhard and I love secrets." She clapped. "What is this all about?"

"Aunt Lina, please, only you must know of its existence. My life may depend upon it."

"Oh my. Then this will be *our* little secret."

Chapter Twenty-Six

Wewelsburg Castle, November 1941

High atop the north tower, Weisthor stood in the Seeker's Portal. With the stars covered by thick clouds, he looked out the window into the blackness of night. With his hands clasped, he paced across the stone floor.

Down the hall, the distinctive stride of Reichsführer Himmler could be heard. The little man burst through the doorway, holding up a crumpled telegram. "Teschler did not obtain the original Spear! Claims that Hitler's guards blocked his access."

Weisthor flexed his upper lip, exposing his incisors, and let out a subtle hiss. "Please tell me something I don't already know." He sat at the black onyx table. With three cards dealt facedown, he paused, then flipped the center card. He lifted the tarot card and pressed it to his lips.

"Weisthor, I must possess the Spear!"

"The operative word is 'we,' Heinrich. *We* must possess the Spear. Have you read today's dispatches from the Russian front?"

"Yes, after a victorious summer campaign, we have suffered a recent series of . . . defeats."

"Coincidence, I think not! Teschler was at the Eagle's Nest in late October, then all hell breaks loose in Russia. Don't be so gullible, Heinrich. Teschler has the authentic Spear."

"But his report says—"

Weisthor held up the Magus tarot card to Himmler's face. "As we have deceived Teschler, he has deceived us."

Himmler's face flushed. "Then where is the Spear?"

"Well hidden, I should imagine. We have underestimated our young knight."

"And I have underestimated Heydrich. Hitler has chosen him over me as Reichsprotektor."

"You are destined by the black powers to ascend the throne as Führer one day. That is why I am your link to the dark realm. That is why we shall implement the master plan together."

*   *   *

East Prussia, November 12, 1941

With immense pride, Reinhard Heydrich piloted his Junker JU-52 airplane toward a meeting with the Führer at the "Wolf's Lair." Having braved British Spitfires to the west, Reinhard boldly danced on the clouds as the sun glistened upon his wings. Eventually, he touched down at the military airfield near Rastenburg.

As a small SS contingent escorted Reinhard through the dense forest, his thoughts turned to Himmler's intercepted telegrams to his nephew. The "Little Imp" desired to seduce Ernst into his entourage right under his nose.

The column of SS vehicles braked to a halt in front of the guardhouse. Behind the barbed-wire fence, three German shepherds snarled and pummeled the gate furiously until the entourage passed through the barriers.

Arriving at the main complex, Reinhard entered the Führerbunker with great anticipation. As Reichsprotektor, he would have no problem trumping both Himmler and Martin Bormann. His quest was to become the Führer's "heir apparent."

Passing more guards, Reinhard entered the conference room with a stiff salute. "Heil Hitler!"

"Reinhard, you're just in time." Dwarfed by detailed wall maps behind him, the Führer pointed at Prague. "Czechoslovakia is critical to our campaign in Russia. The new weapons plants, what's our status?"

"On schedule, mein herr. The new production lines will commence at the end of this month. The Slavs will forge new armaments for our troops in the east."

"Very efficient, Reinhard."

Reinhard used his charm to play the dictator as he might a fine violin. "The Czech citizens under your command will obey your will—or they will suffer the consequences. Mein Führer, you are invincible!"

"Pride and fearless courage are the reasons why I have promoted you to Reichsprotektor. I trust this will not interfere with your implementation of the Final Solution."

"My honor is loyalty! The Final Solution will commence according to plan. The new expansion at Auschwitz is ready. I will convene a meeting in Berlin in the new year to coordinate the activities of all Reich ministries."

Hitler turned back to the towering map mounted upon the wall, perforated by countless color-flagged pins.

"Concerning Russia, General Brauchitsch has guaranteed me victory, but progress is slow. These Slavs are stupid creatures. They simply fall down before our war machines and gum up the gears of our Panzers with their bodies. Heydrich, muster the Slavs, produce our munitions, and you shall reap the spoils of German victory!"

"Without fail, mein Führer!"

With a nod, Hitler managed a gentle smile. "By the way, I enjoyed the company of your nephew at the Eagle's Nest."

"The family was honored by his promotion."

"A singular honor, don't you think, for one so young?"

"But certainly not undeserved, mein herr." Reinhard's eyes savored his prey like a carnivorous spider. Hitler was a mere fly caught in his silken web.

*   *   *

Two Days Later

Late in the morning, Ernst, Barron, and Max arrived at Görlitz, the Wolf's Lair private train station deep inside Poland. Traffic to and from this secret track junction was just thinning out. Hitler's Brandenburg was powered by two massive diesel engines in tandem. They pulled fifteen cars, including two special flak wagons, one forward and one aft, armed with antiaircraft guns.

Hitler's entourage began boarding at noon. Various Wehrmacht and SS officers were followed by the waitstaff. An SS colonel rushed onto the platform obviously late. The mustached officer with flowing gray hair and wire-rimmed spectacles produced his identity papers and boarded.

Ernst made sure the porter sealed the door, then Barron and he moved along the rail bed to join Max for final security inspections. "Max, you're not bored, are you?"

"Only a fool would attack this train, but I'm here to protect your rear end when the shooting starts."

Ernst patted his own rump. "Ja, just like you covered my flank in '38—139 stitches worth!"

Max raised both hands. "I swear, I never meant to blow you through that window."

When they reached the first passenger car in front, the porter held the door open for the trio to board. "The trip to Munich will be thirteen hundred kilometers through extremely rugged terrain. No one has ever attacked this train, and for good reason. It is a moving steel fortress."

Continuing their inspection, Ernst and Barron walked toward the rear of the train through the Führer's car when a compartment door slid open. Ernst blinked and saluted. "Heil Hitler!"

Hitler saluted. "You see, gentlemen, Major Teschler is ever vigilant, performing his duties with determination. Hello, Barron." The Doberman barked as Hitler drew his hand down Barron's head to his muscular flank. "A magnificent creature, Major. Do carry on."

Soon the train pulled out of the station and, in the first several hours, made good speed southwest toward Prague. After a casual dinner of sauerbraten and cabbage, most of the passengers retired before ten. Around eleven, Ernst and Barron patrolled through the main passenger cars. As the two approached the end of a corridor, Barron tensed. His growl erupted into a cheerful bark when Blondi rounded the corner.

At the other end of the leash was Adolf Hitler dressed in his English country squire suit. The two dogs playfully nuzzled each other. "Blondi, you remember Barron?"

"You're up late, sir."

"I sleep only three or four hours at night, but Blondi has had a long day. Good night, Major."

Ernst decided to check in with the engineers up front, so he stepped outside into the cold November wind in between cars.

*   *   *

Having casually walked between four passenger cars, the mysterious SS colonel approached the forward flak car. As the car swayed in rhythm of the spinning wheels, he drew his Walther PP pistol with silencer from its holster. He eased open the door and confirmed the position of the three SS soldiers on duty. Two were up in the ceiling turret, while a corporal slouched in an easy chair dozing.

No one saw him enter as the colonel eased the door closed behind him. He held the weapon underneath his overcoat and leaned back against the wall next to the rear door. Just as he targeted the corporal, the door popped open and cloaked him behind the door panel. Looking through the hinged crevice, he recognized Ernst Teschler.

Ernst shouted, "*Wach auf!* Schnell! Corporal, don't you *dare* sleep on my watch."

The SS soldier launched to his feet in a salute. The other men up in the turret tried to scramble down the ladder but blocked each other. "Schmidt, who are you talking to?"

"Well, Corporal Schmidt, tell your friends there will be security inspections throughout the trip. Carry on." In a huff, Ernst swung the door closed.

The two other SS men climbed down from the turret and looked at each other with a deep sigh of relief. The third man's expression widened in horror as the Walther's extended barrel flashed. The 9mm bullet torqued his head into a plate-glass window. The Walther coughed again three more times to drop the other two men as they scrambled toward the door.

The assassin forced crowbars through the door handles of both fore and aft compartment doors. He then climbed into the ceiling turret and skillfully armed the 20mm cannon, pivoting its barrel toward the rear of the train.

Himmler's voice droned again in his mind. *"Into the Lion's den you go. But remember, the Führer must not survive. Leave no evidence, no witnesses—including yourself."*

A sour taste permeated his mouth as he fingered the cyanide capsule pinned underneath his tunic lapel.

Expecting a series of sharp curves in the tracks ahead, he practiced his aim at the three cars in the rear. He sighted his target during the first curve, waited during the opposite turn, then squeezed the trigger, launching a shell into the third car. The explosion obliterated the car, the coupling, and the rear end of Hitler's sleeper car.

With a grinding clash of metal upon metal, the derailed cars snaked off the tracks onto an embankment. The mangled steel yielded to earth and stone as the detached cars screeched to a halt on the embankment.

*   *   *

The remaining twelve forward cars lurched back and forth, pitching Ernst to the floor in the dining car. Looking out the window into darkness, he heard the shouts of men pouring out into the corridor. Half-dressed, Max appeared clutching his submachine gun. "Max, call the engineer, schnell!"

Ernst led Barron back to Hitler's sleeper car. Pushing through some disheveled SS soldiers, they maneuvered through three train cars. Ernst charged through the secure door into the Führer's quarters. "Mein Führer! Mein Führer!"

"He's gone!" an SS soldier shouted.

A rush of cold air enveloped him when Max arrived. The last third of the car's back wall had been blown away. He could see the burning wreck of the derailed cars disappear into the distance as the train surged ahead.

Amidst the chaos of soldiers pushing their way against him, Max turned to Ernst. "They've killed Hitler!"

Ernst assessed the gaping hole in the back wall and shouted, "Follow me, Max!" They shimmied through the crowded corridors of the full length of the train. When they arrived at the forward flak car, Ernst tried to open the door. "The door's jammed from inside. Help me, Max." He grabbed a fire ax and battered the lock. The blade striking metal spit sparks into the air.

Two other SS guards with heavy iron crowbars appeared. Wedging the rods into the hinge-side of the door, they plied it using their full body weight. The top hinge snapped, blocking their way. When Ernst saw the dead soldiers through the crevice, he rushed out onto the service apron between cars and looked up at the antiaircraft gun turret.

Still emitting traces of smoke, the barrel retracted, which signaled a new payload. Ernst could see the profile of a man in the glass cockpit. When the enemy closed the breech, another 20mm shell would be ready to fire.

Barron was raging rabid. "Max, secure Barron in the other car." Max grasped Barron's leash, forcing him into the next car to the rear.

The barrel of the cannon appeared to be jammed on its rotational gears. The man in the cockpit kept trying to rotate the motorized turret.

With the Schmeisser slung over his shoulder, Ernst climbed up the outside ladder on the moving train. When he peeked over the ledge of the roof, Ernst could see the soldier still trying to rotate the lethal cannon barrel. With a thunderous roar, Ernst launched a volley of bullets that snaked across the carriage roof and smashed through the turret.

He shimmied across the flak car top toward the shattered turret, but it was now empty. With a curse, Ernst rolled sideways to the ledge of the carriage roof and stared down in horror. The train was barreling across a bridge suspended above a series of trestles twenty meters in the air. The base of the bridge was brightly lit for repair crews.

The intruder stood upon the metal apron between the flak car and the forward engine as the train came out of the series of curves and moved across a bridge above the Vistula River. The assassin leaped off the train, flailing his arms wildly as he struck the water feet first.

Ernst craned his neck but lost sight of the soldier as the train car arced into the next bend in the track. Suddenly, his feet lost traction, and he reached out to catch himself, launching his weapon out into space.

Hanging on to a rail guard with only one hand, Ernst dangled helplessly in the air. Pain shot through his arm into his chest as he struggled to clasp the rail with his free hand.

Max reached out and pulled Ernst to safety. Once down the ladder, they both heaved for breath. "Ernst, the Führer is dead! Shall I stop the train?"

Ernst stared into the distance. "Nein. There may be other assailants by the tracks."

"Who was that man?"

Ernst shook his head. "I don't know." The other SS men finally broke into the flak car. Ernst and Max followed, inspecting the corpses. "Probably a 9mm—"

"Major, again, you have saved my life."

Max turned and lurched back on his heels at the man standing at the entrance. "Mein Führer!"

To Hitler's chagrin, Barron playfully nipped at Blondi's snout. "Teschler, my instinct to leave my sleeping car for a stroll and your gallant efforts have brought us through yet another crisis."

Ernst dropped his jaw. "But, sir, your car was demolished."

"The Spirit of Odin prevailed. This episode is another sign, a divine affirmation. I now know our army will be victorious over Russia! I told you my vision. It is my destiny to conquer." Hitler held up his fist as he disappeared into the next car.

Stunned, Ernst and Max just stared at each other. The trio returned to their compartment. "Max, someone inside the SS just tried to assassinate Hitler."

Chapter Twenty-Seven

Munich, November 1941

Ernst, Barron, and Max marched down the station platform to Himmler's private train. They had been summoned two days after the Brandenburg incident. An attractive secretary stoically greeted the trio. "The Reichsführer will see you alone, Major Teschler."

"Max, take Barron for a walk."

Max took Barron's leash. His expression said, "Good luck!"

The secretary ushered Ernst up the steps and through a guarded corridor into the next carriage. Himmler sat behind his massive mahogany desk, signing a sheath of papers. Ernst stepped forward, snapped his heels together, and saluted. "Heil Hitler!"

"Sit down, Teschler." Himmler did not look up.

"Jawohl, mein herr."

"Now, tell me exactly what happened on the Führer's train."

"The intruder was a professional. He knew armaments, train schedules, and had access to authentic SS uniforms and identity papers."

"Whom do you suspect?"

"The Führer assumes it was the British or perhaps the Poles."

Himmler glared at Ernst with his piercing bespectacled eyes. "I asked for your opinion, Teschler."

"I believe it was someone inside the SS, sir."

"You are to thoroughly investigate this incident. Every resource shall be at your disposal. Report your findings to no one but me. Now, as to the Spear, you were not successful in obtaining it. Why?"

"I gave you my full report—"

"Weisthor believes the Führer no longer has the real Spear. Where is it?"

Ernst paused. "The Führer took me to the shrine room."

Himmler's eyes widened as he leaned forward. "Tell me everything."

"There was only one light, a luminous dome at the center of the floor. On the wall was an inverted cross with a wooden mantel at its center."

"Where the Spear of Destiny had been placed?"

Ernst nodded. "I stayed up half the night waiting for an opportunity, but too many guards were stationed throughout the building."

"So you say. You are playing in a high-stakes game, my boy. If you are lying to me, my black wraiths will hunt you down without mercy. Your orders stand. Bring me the original Spear of Longinus. Next time, do not fail!"

Ernst snapped to his feet. "Jawohl, Herr Reichsführer!"

*   *   *

Berlin

From her bedroom window, Eva stared down at the street corner. A middle-aged woman with a large yellow star sewn upon her coat stepped up on the curb. A Jew! The yellow badge of shame had been decreed by the SS since September.

She pushed the sight from her mind as she stepped in front of her floor-length mirror. *I look like an Aryan!* None of her coworkers would suspect that she was Jewish. No one knew in Berlin but Heydrich. She had kept her word to him and kept Ernst at a distance.

She wanted to claw the pathetic creature in the mirror. "This situation is impossible."

Eva dabbed a lavish French perfume inside her wrists, unleashing its subtle intoxicating fragrance. She wandered into the living room brushing her blonde hair when a muffled knock sounded at her door. She paused. Then the knock came again. *Ernst?*

Eva put on her "pretty face" as she excitedly unlocked the door. Her mouth gaped as she stared into the haggard face of Nina Kleisfeld. "Mama?"

"Sarah, my darling child, it's really you!"

There, sewn upon her mother's breast, was a bright yellow Jewish star. "Sssh!" Eva craned her head out into the hallway to check for neighbors, then pulled her mother into the apartment and closed the door.

Eva stared at her mother, then squeezed her eyes shut. The apartment was watched by the Gestapo for her security. They would report the Jewess standing before her, and suspicious questions would follow.

"Why are you here?"

Mama's expectant eyes sank at Eva's expression. "We haven't seen each other for two years. I needed to know that you were safe. To see what kind of life you've made for yourself. Sarah, I love you. I've missed my only daughter."

"Cousin Saul checks on me from time to time."

"He told me about your working *arrangement* here in Berlin and your *friends*. I wanted to see my little girl, before I—"

"Before what, Mama?"

Her haggard eyes narrowed. "My health is failing, and I still have nightmares about Aaron. Did Papa or Saul tell you what the Nazis did the night your brother died? The nightmare began back in '38—November 9. Your father and I watched from our bedroom window across the alley." In an instant Mama relived the moment as her tears flowed. "All we could do was watch. The soldiers had trashed the house and shoved a piano off the balcony. Someone ignited the wreckage on the sidewalk. Your brother was thrown off the balcony into the flames."

Eva embraced her mother as she trembled and sobbed in her arms.

"Your father and I could not save our boy. I had to come to see for myself that you were alive and safe!"

Aaron's memory seemed so distant. They always had a sibling rivalry. Eva still could hear neighbors whispering about the Jewish family next door when she was a little girl. In school the popular boys would pull her curls and push her out of line. She'd realized being a Jewess was the problem. As she grew older, she experimented with makeup, cultural dresses, and hair color to create a new person. And so Eva was born and she was embraced.

"Oh, Mama, I'm so sorry for your pain." The two women sank onto the couch, and Eva rocked her mother gently. "When I came back to Wittenberg, the neighbors said you and Papa had fled the neighborhood."

Her mother collected her thoughts. "We went into hiding at a friend's farm for weeks. Your father fretted about you so. Then he left me there to find you in Berlin. I begged him not to go, but then he never returned. I was left all alone. Several months went by before Cousin Saul first told me that Abraham was in a concentration camp near Berlin."

The haggard woman gazed into her daughter's eyes. "Saul says you know people in the SS. Perhaps they could do something to free your father? It has been over two years!"

"But if I were to ask them for help, they will ask questions—all the wrong kinds of questions, Mama."

Her mother gave her a knowing look. "Your Nazi friends don't know you are a Jewess?"

Eva avoided her mother's eyes. "I might be able to get an exit visa. The two of you could flee the country and be safe."

"And what about you?" Mama's knowing eyes lanced right through Eva. "You are in love with someone. Who is this man?"

"Mama, I will survive this war. I will get married and have a family."

She leaned back. "Aryan babies, Sarah? These Nazis have deceived many people, but you, my dear, have deceived yourself."

Eva stepped away from her mother, picked up her hairbrush, and stared at the fantasy in the mirror. She continued to avoid her mother's pleading eyes. "It would be better for us both if you left now. The Gestapo is always watching—for my security."

In the mirror, Eva saw her despondent mother shake her head. "There is a basement door—leave that way."

"Sarah, remember: Your Father and I—we love you."

"Yes, Mama. I love you too.

Her mother lowered her head, picked up her bag, and walked out the door.

Eva continued to brush her blonde hair. Too many secrets. Too many lies told. Eva reached out to the mirror and cried out for the man she loved. Only Ernst could take her away from the nightmare that was her life.

*   *   *

Berlin, Abwehr HQ, November 1941

A week later, Admiral Canaris's office was bustling with urgent activity. As officers and staff delivered a continual flow of military updates, Dietrich stood looking out the tall windows. The streets below were teeming with Germans on the way to work. A woman with two young children turned to enter a store when she was stopped by a shopkeeper. Some heated conversation ensued, and the man pushed the woman away. Then her yellow star came into view. Such altercations characterized German "hospitality" to Jews everywhere in the city. Such blind cruelty was also extended to the young and innocent.

Colonel Oster slapped a file onto the conference table. "The SS is deporting Jews by the thousands."

Stroking his dachshund Seppel, Canaris sat behind his desk lost in thought.

Hans Dohnanyi exhaled a waft of cigarette smoke. "They have broken seventeen national laws that I've been able to identify so far."

Across the cobblestone street below, SS soldiers marched in goose step. For Dietrich, the sight was chilling.

"Hitler and the SS believe they are above the law of human decency," Canaris said.

Oster turned. "Admiral, we cannot help the Jews escape en masse, but we are planning the exodus of six or seven Jewish families to develop our methods. Perhaps the Conzen and Rennefeld families?"

Hans frowned. "Only seven families?"

"With the SS watching us, it will be dangerous."

Dietrich retrieved an envelope from his coat pocket. "I have already contacted my colleagues in Switzerland for help." He read aloud:

> TO: Herr Superintendent Albertz, President
>
> Federation of Swiss Churches—Zurich
>
> We are contemplating the arrival of non-Aryans in Basle early next spring. They will travel under official work permits and will have minimal funds upon departure from Germany.
>
> We need your help. We humbly request that the Swiss churches make provisions for thirteen to fifteen individuals once they arrive. We ask God, the Father of the forsaken, to provide an exodus out of their dire distress.
>
> Dr. Dietrich Bonhoeffer

Canaris stood with Seppel in his arms. "Dr. Bonhoeffer, you're already a step ahead of us."

Hans removed his spectacles and rubbed his tired eyes. "A few Jewish families are one thing, but will the Swiss eventually accommodate twenty-five to thirty thousand?"

Canaris carefully placed Seppel on the rug. "In any event, we shall soon see what our Swiss friends think of the Jews."

*   *   *

Eberswalde, Germany, December 1941

Saul Avigur's colleague, Malachi, had hidden himself in the warehouse section of the Spechthausen printing works, fifty kilometers northeast of Berlin. If he was right, the counterfeiters from Sachsenhausen would arrive in the morning.

Hours later, Malachi awoke to the chatter of voices emanating from the main offices in front. He inched his way to the door and peered through a crevice. He recognized Abraham Kleisfeld.

The Jewish engraver held a five-pound British note up to his ear and crinkled it. "This almost sounds right. Here, Dr. Langer, listen to the sound it makes when we compress it."

"Almost? Kleisfeld, we have been at this for months. Berlin wants results!"

Abraham stroked his straggly salt-and-pepper beard. "Look, we know that British paper is made of linen and ramie spun from Asian nettle. In Germany, we can get flax in quantity, but we must go to Hungary for the ramie plant. I have found glue made from calves' hoofs will provide the correct consistency. Yet, the ultraviolet light test still yields a pink instead of the correct lilac hue."

Dr. Langer glanced at his watch. "We're wasting time. Try the new dyes. We have the best engravers, chemists, and forgers on this. We must succeed!"

Abraham made his way to the rear and through the warehouse door. Halfway down the aisle, he riffled through labeled bottles.

"Mazel tov, Abraham," Malachi whispered.

Abraham froze. He looked back toward the front, searching for any stray guards. "You must get word back to Saul. I have already duplicated the paper texture for the British notes, but the Nazis do not know."

"Abraham, then soon you will help our cause!"

"Soon, yes, but these Nazis are not fools. They will keep us alive only as long as we are needed."

"You are a wise man, Abraham. With counterfeit notes, we will buy ships to smuggle many Jews to Palestine." Malachi donned a greedy smile. "And after the war, we could make a lot of money together on the streets."

Abraham scoffed. "If we survive the war, that will be our reward."

Malachi gripped Abraham's shoulders. "Get back to the laboratory. You must delay these cretins as long as you can, my friend."

Abraham returned to the front with chemicals in hand.

Malachi quietly waited for hours until sunset to escape. His mind raced. The Haganah could fund an underground railroad out of the Balkans to Istanbul and then on to Palestine with an endless supply of near-perfect counterfeit five-pound notes.

He stepped outside. The bitter December frost penetrated the woven fabric of his brown double-breasted coat. He cursed the wind and Hitler all in one breath.

Chapter Twenty-Eight

Abwehr HQ, Berlin, December 19, 1941

Dietrich entered Admiral Canaris's office, where he joined his brother-in-law Hans and Colonel Oster at the conference table. Chilled, he sat with his overcoat still buttoned. A somber mood permeated the air.

Canaris arrived thereafter, bundled heavily for the snow outside. In his woolen topcoat, the admiral gravitated toward the blazing fire in the hearth. Shivering, he stood holding his gloved hands near the flames. "All right, Colonel, why was I called back ahead of schedule?"

"General von Falkenhausen urgently requested this meeting," Oster said.

Hans nursed a cigarette burned almost to the nub. "It could be news about the Russian campaign. Our armies faltered weeks ago. They are too far behind schedule to be redeemed this winter."

Canaris removed his gloves meticulously. "General Brauchitsch had better stand by his word or all could be lost." The aging spy chief pursed his bluish lips. "Any progress on Operation U-7?"

Hans drew the last of his cigarette. "I've been working with Reich Security-Head Office. We can transport our Jewish friends out of

Germany as Abwehr employees, but timing will be everything. As soon as we get their names off the general deportation lists, the Gestapo adds them back on."

"I've had problems in Switzerland." Dietrich opened his satchel. "Albertz sent this response."

Dear Dr. Bonhoeffer,

On behalf of the Federation of Swiss Churches, I have forwarded your request for economic assistance for your Non-Aryan associates. Their reception inside our country appears near impossible. Our police refuse entrance ·across the border in many cases. Obtaining work permits for these people will be difficult. While I do not carry much hope, I will keep trying.

Sincerely,
Superintendent Albertz

Still shivering, Canaris moved closer to the fire. "Herr Bonhoeffer, how is it that we can get SS authorization to transport Jews out of Germany, but the Swiss will not accept them into a neutral country?"

"Prejudice and fear, sir. The kind that breeds contempt." Embarrassed, Dietrich had had such high hopes.

Oster offered Hans a fresh cigarette. "The longer we wait, the more dangerous this all becomes. I want our Jewish friends out of the country by Easter."

Canaris's secretary entered the room. "Admiral, General von Falkenhausen is here."

With concern etched on his chiseled face, von Falkenhausen brushed past the woman as she closed the door behind him.

"Have a seat, General. You look like you have something on your mind," Canaris said.

"The Eastern Front is an abysmal failure, but the Führer refuses to face reality. We cannot succeed!" The general fumed hotter than the tip of his Havana cigar. "And it gets worse. Brauchitsch will soon be relieved of command."

A stunned silence choked the room.

"Hitler is firing him?" Oster asked.

The general nodded. "Few people in Germany know what has taken place in Russia. I was there in June when Hitler gave our field marshals the Commissar Order to shoot unarmed Soviet officers as political criminals. It's unthinkable!"

"Go on," Canaris said.

"In mid-October we were storming toward Moscow, town after town—Odessa on the 16th, Kharkov on the 24th."

"Get to the point, General," Canaris said.

"Since the 24th of October, it's been as if the gods have turned against us. On the 27th of November, the Soviets reclaimed Rostov. On December 5th, we abandoned the attack on Moscow, and the next day the Soviets launched a powerful counteroffensive. Then the Japanese bombed the Americans, and Hitler declared war on the United States. It's as if an unseen force has turned against Germany!"

"General Brauchitsch is essential to our plan," Hans said.

Von Falkenhausen stood and snapped his hat over his head. "Well, I've got to report to Keitel. Let me know what you want to do by our usual contact."

Oster escorted the general to the door. "Sir, thank you for coming." They both saluted in traditional Weimar fashion. After the rotund officer departed, Oster poured a few glasses of schnapps.

Hans took a glass. "If the army will not support a revolt—then we must eliminate the Führer." With a grimace, he took a stiff drink.

Dietrich furrowed his eyebrows above the wire frames of his spectacles. "Indeed, there is a madman at the wheel of the automobile."

Oster swirled his drink. "Herr Bonhoeffer, according to George Bell, exactly what do the English want in order to proceed?"

"Evidence, gentlemen. They want to know who's behind our conspiracy."

The Confessing Church pastor never thought his role would go this far. How did one determine God's will in such circumstances?

Canaris leaned back in his chair. "If we reveal the names, we will be exposed for SS reprisals or extortion by the Allies."

"We could provide a few names and only part of the plan," Oster said.

Canaris looked intently at Dietrich. "Then the evidence you shall carry must be enough to convince the Brits to either help us or bury us."

Canaris's secretary stepped into the room and handed the admiral a dispatch and departed without a word.

"Gott im Himmel!" Canaris gasped. "Hitler has just fired Brauchitsch—and has declared himself commander in chief of the entire German army!"

*   *   *

Berlin, January 9, 1942

Reinhard Heydrich had returned to his villa in the capital city for high-level meetings. The next morning after breakfast the telephone rang. His housekeeper stepped into the parlor. "Sir, it is Major Teschler."

Reinhard picked up the receiver. "Hello, Ernst, how is my favorite nephew this morning?"

"Your *only* nephew is just fine. The meeting is still at 11:00 a.m., but the Führer has changed the location."

Reinhard frowned. "The man is obsessed with security. Where then?"

"The Chancellery."

"Very well. Pick me up at the villa at ten."

"Uncle, have you reviewed my marriage application yet?"

Eva Kleist was a direct threat to his political plans. "With the war escalating, perhaps you should postpone your personal plans for a year. Schellenberg is talking about expanding your duties in Switzerland and Italy next year."

"But, sir, you promised you would personally submit my application to Himmler."

Reinhard scowled. "We'll discuss your future this weekend." There was an uneasy silence at the other end of the line. "I'll be ready by ten sharp." He hung up the phone. *If Ernst presses me, he will sign her death warrant.*

*   *   *

When Hitler's meeting adjourned, Himmler, Heydrich, and Ernst departed the Chancellery by automobile. In the front passenger seat, Ernst pulled Eva's edge-worn picture from his wallet and touched her face. With the world at war, the only certainty was the woman he loved.

His uncle raised his high-pitched voice to Himmler. "Just promoted to colonel, Schellenberg will transfer to AMT VI, Political Intelligence, next week. He will reorganize the whole unit splendidly. But sir, Theodor Eicke has done a mediocre job supervising the camps. There have been reports of poor management and budget overages for the past six months, and still he is in command. Now that the Führer has approved my plan for the Final Solution—"

Himmler glared. "Why not replace Eicke with you?"

"Of course, you know I'm superior in every way."

"With your responsibilities in Prague, how can you run the camps from Berlin? No, Reinhard, you must work with Eicke to resolve the Jewish problem."

Reinhard's look soured into silence. He removed an envelope from his satchel and handed it to Ernst. "After the Wannsee Conference, you will deliver these orders personally to Franz Stangl at the new Sobibor

Camp—no later than the first of February. It will be my little Sabbath present to the Jews in Poland."

Ernst caught his breath as he read the orders silently:

TO: Oberstumführer Franz Stangl

FROM: Obergruppenführer Reinhard Heydrich

From the city of Chełm, you have reported approximately seven thousand Jews in detention. At your discretion after February 1, confiscate all valuables and eliminate the "goods" with due haste. All authority over military personnel in the area is at your command.

Auf Wiedersehen,
Reinhard Heydrich

The word "eliminate" leaped from the page. Looking above the dashboard, the rearview mirror captured his uncle's cavalier eyes and charming "public smile." Then reality struck home. Uncle Reinhard had delegated the bloody deed to him.

Ernst held his left hand up to the sunlight. The ruby eyes of his SS Death's Head ring glowed. *When I deliver this letter to Stangl, seven thousand Jews will die!*

*   *   *

Berlin, Wannsee Lakes, January 20, 1942

Heydrich had invited the upper echelon of the Nazi government to orchestrate the detailed plans for the Final Solution. The conference was to take place at a posh lakeside villa in the swank suburb of Wannsee.

Days prior, SS personnel had invaded the property in due force to set up security. When Ernst, Barron, and Max arrived, it was an icy-cold sunny morning.

During their initial tour of the grounds, Ernst was haunted by the execution order in his briefcase. Within ten days, he would travel to Bucharest and send seven thousand human beings to oblivion. The Gleiwitz incident was still fresh in his mind, and the taste in his mouth was indeed sour.

An hour later, Ernst stood along the rear wall as General Heydrich arrogantly approached the conference podium. "In 1939 there were over 250,000 Jews inside Germany. Now, three years later, only an estimated 132,000 Jews remain. There are over 5 million in Russia, 3 million in the Ukraine, and almost 2.2 million Jews in Poland."

Ernst did the math. With the Jews in England, there must be 11 million Jewish people living within planned areas of conquest.

Heydrich's tone was matter of fact. "Their presence is not acceptable to the Reich. We propose to exploit the Jews in the east as forced laborers for the military. Those who have strength will build roads and man our factories. Now too little food, sleep, and medications will rid us of a great number, but those who survive—eventually will be put to death."

Dr. Josef Bühler, state secretary from Poland, stood. "Finally, Berlin is going to do something! Over two million Jews in the Polish ghettos are disease infected. They are black-market operatives and unfit for work. When will you begin, General?"

"Our Einsatzgruppen units have already removed over 750,000 from your lists."

Hermann Göring stood. "The Führer promised the Economic Ministry that he would provide Jewish labor for my military factories." The rotund Göring shook his fist at Goebbels. "Joseph, you've tried to deport my workers ever since!"

Goebbels sneered. "When I walk down the streets of Berlin, our Aryan children are exposed to their germs everywhere. And you want to keep them in Germany for labor!"

"To build airplanes, Joseph."

Heydrich held up his hand. "Now, now, gentlemen. New camps will be built near designated production facilities to provide labor, Hermann. As for the details, Adolf Eichmann will brief us on the new furnace technologies."

The short, unimpressive Eichmann stood behind the podium and hoisted his horn-rimmed glasses upon his beaked nose. "The 'Final Solution' will use modern methods to transport, exploit, and finally eliminate nonproductive Jewish laborers. In our efforts to be more efficient with mass disposals, a recent experiment was conducted using over six hundred Russian prisoners at Auschwitz. The test results of Zyklon-B gas have been successful."

As the SS chieftains and government bureaucrats applauded enthusiastically, the pit of Ernst's stomach tightened into a fist.

Eichmann flashed an arrogant smile. "Reichsführer Himmler has negotiated multiple labor contracts with key German companies that will build factories near the camps and cofinance the operation."

Hermann Göring finally smiled.

Ernst signaled Max to follow him out of the room. They walked down the hall, past a guard, out of earshot.

"Just think of it, Germany will be *Judenfrei*!"

Ernst glared at his friend.

"What's wrong? What did I say?"

Ernst stopped and grabbed Max's lapels. "What's wrong? Max, they are going to kill eleven million people!"

"Not people—they are just Jews."

Ernst let go of Max's jacket and clenched his teeth. For the first time in his life, he wanted to pulverize his best friend.

Max held up both hands in surrender. "Look, everyone is just obeying orders. You're upset. So settle down. We have a job to do here."

"I need some fresh air." Ernst turned on his heel and stomped off toward the lake. After a walk along the shore, he rejoined the conference.

At noon the elite gathering broke for an elaborate buffet. Heydrich and Ernst mingled with the crowd.

"Dr. Goebbels, you remember my nephew, Major Ernst Teschler."

"Major, the Führer has spoken highly of your prowess in security."

Ernst paused. "My honor is loyalty, mein herr."

"Tell me, Major, if we remove all of the Jews, does this not enhance security in Germany?" Goebbels's skin stretched across his face with the appearance of parchment vacuum-sealed around a skull. Goebbels's cruel, sunken eyes unnerved Ernst.

"Sir, my orders are to provide counterespionage services for the SS. I have little time to devote to the Jewish issue."

Goebbels's grin widened. "My, aren't you the politician? Heydrich, I see you have trained this man well."

Heydrich beamed. "Of course!"

"If you'll excuse me, I must check in with my men." Ernst disappeared into the crowd. The image of Goebbels's stretched face lingered. He snatched a glass of wine from a waiter and strutted outside onto the patio. His gaze was again drawn to the lake. In minutes, the winter cold anesthetized his limbs. *How can I do this? How can I participate in this madness?*

Bundled up, Max walked down the stone steps and handed Ernst his black topcoat. "You must be drunk. It's freezing out here."

Ernst shivered as he donned the coat.

"You're welcome, Ernst."

Ernst fired a warning glance. "Goebbels wants to kill Jews as if they were bugs. Did you see the look in his eyes? Max, these are the most educated, powerful men in the Reich, and they are planning mass murder."

"Goebbels is a very powerful man."

"And that face! Max, his face is a skull with stretched skin and fanged teeth."

"Be very careful what you say."

The memory of his last conversation with Papa arose. "I said those very words to Papa before they killed him."

"The Jews. They murdered your father."

"Did they? I wonder. We never saw evidence or a trial."

"We don't want to end up in a concentration camp for the sake of a few Jews." In a huff, Max sighed. His warm breath vented from his iced lips. "I'm going back inside."

The truth tasted bitter. Ernst cocked his arm and pitched his wine glass as far as he could. Barron barked playfully and sprinted toward the shore as the long-stemmed glass arced upward, then gracefully plummeted into the lake. Barron romped close to the water's edge.

Through his visible breath, Ernst took solace in the placid water flanked by snow-covered trees. Then mysteriously through the flecks of light shimmering upon the surface of the water, Ernst saw the "face" of a Polish prisoner at Gleiwitz—then another, and another. Soon the silent screams from nameless Jewish faces thundered through his conscience. Nearby, Barron growled and barked. When Ernst looked again at the water, the haunting faces began to recede into the lapping waves.

At the side entrance to the mansion, Ernst commandeered a car. Through the rearview mirror, the driver asked, "Sir, what address?"

"Just drive." The wave of Ernst's gloved hand set the Mercedes in motion.

*   *   *

Ernst felt compelled to see Canaris, but he had to be careful. He sensed that the admiral was a man of honor—a true soldier of the old Germany. Surely he had to know about the Final Solution. It would be a betrayal, but Ernst had already betrayed Hitler—for Himmler! Every time Himmler asked about the Spear, he had lied. For Ernst, deceit was now a way of life, a necessity for survival.

Ernst exited the car in the middle of Berlin. He walked a few blocks to make sure he had not been followed, then he flagged a taxi to Abwehr Headquarters. Arriving unannounced, he had to wait an hour to see Admiral Canaris.

"He will see you now, Major," the secretary said.

Canaris stood by the tall stone hearth, warming his hands near the log fire. Despite his heavy woolen tunic, the small, thin man shivered. Without facing his guest, Canaris spoke.

"Major Teschler. The winter is particularly bitter this year, don't you agree?"

"Thank you for seeing me without an appointment." Ernst circled the sofa and saw Seppel and Sabine curled up on the rug.

"In the last several months, you have been promoted twice by the Führer. Congratulations."

Ernst tipped his hat. There was no fear in the older man's eyes, only the wisdom from too many years of politics.

"Do sit down." Canaris squatted near his dachsunds and brushed their backsides.

Ernst took a seat. In profile he saw the flicker of the flames' light dance upon Canaris's worn, wrinkled features. "Sir, I am not here on SS business. In fact, General Heydrich would be furious to learn I had come, but I—I am facing a dilemma, a crisis."

Canaris raised an eyebrow and stood, his deep-blue eyes glistening.

Despite his uncle's stories of the decade-old rivalry between the Abwehr and the SS, Ernst was strangely at ease. "I've come to seek your counsel, because you struck me as a forthright man in our last meeting."

Canaris took a deep breath. "I know your uncle well, Major. We were in the navy together when he made some . . . foolish choices. So you will forgive me if I exercise some caution in our conversation."

Ernst compressed his parched lips. "I have just come from a meeting at Wannsee Haus. Perhaps you know of—"

"The Final Solution?"

Ernst widened his eyes.

Canaris's weary eyes hardened. "An estimated eleven million Jews within German-controlled territories, Russia, the Slavic countries, even England." With some hesitation, he stepped over to his oversized oak desk and picked up a copper-colored figurine. "Eleven million human beings." He leaned back on the front of his desk as he stroked the heads of three bronze monkeys. "See no evil—hear no evil—speak no evil."

"The Reich government does not consider the Jews to be human, Admiral."

Canaris chuckled. "You sound like one of my pet monkeys, Major. Take some advice—don't parrot the voice of fools."

Ernst swallowed hard. "I need advice. I have been dispatched by my uncle—to Bucharest." He removed the folded document from his inside coat pocket. "He has ordered me to deliver this."

Canaris picked up a pair of reading spectacles and scrutinized the typed print. "So you have been ordered to murder seven thousand 'sub-human beings.' Well, Teschler, it seems the monkey population in Nazi Germany has expanded by at least one." The elder spy chief handed the document back. "How does it feel?"

"Sir, I can't do this."

"A decorated SS officer, a favorite of Adolf Hitler, and now you tell me you have a conscience? Well, son, you are an enigma. However, orders are orders. 'My honor is loyalty' is the slogan you people profess?"

"Exactly."

Canaris walked back to the hearth, stooped down, and doted on his dachshunds. He rubbed the smooth short-haired flank of Sabine as she licked his fingers. "You are a Reich officer under orders. If you fail to deliver these orders, Himmler or Heydrich will send someone else in black uniform. Surely, you know that."

Ernst frowned. "But then their blood would not be on my hands."

"Ah. That is the way of the Third Reich but not of the Germany I know. It is always someone else's order, their responsibility—and never ours! Can't you see, Herr Teschler? At this very hour, blood is dripping from all of our hands." He stood across from Ernst, eye to eye. "I appreciate your confidence in me, Major. And do not question for a moment that I will keep our talk a secret. But I'm not the advisor you need right now. You need a priest or a minister. Perhaps you should see Dr. Bonhoeffer?"

"You know him?"

Canaris smiled. "With all the resources at your command, I am sure you can find him."

Again Ernst looked into the admiral's languid blue eyes. They felt warm as he stood. "Thank you for seeing me." He extended his hand to Canaris. "I apologize for the interruption."

"At heart, you are an honorable man, Major. But now you need a higher power."

At the street, Ernst flagged a taxi, rode three long blocks, then took another taxi to his command car. On his way back to Wannsee Haus, Ernst became convinced that the Sobibor order had to be stopped.

The conference center was encircled by an iron fence. He braked several meters before the main gate and looked in between the vertical bars at the mansion. Within those walls he saw the lethal menagerie that was the Third Reich. He could not shake the incantation of the three monkeys from his mind. *See no evil, hear no evil, speak no evil.*

The sound of Canaris's soft voice rang true. *"You sound like one of my pet monkeys, Major. Take some advice—don't parrot the voice of fools!"*

Chapter Twenty-Nine

SS Headquarters, Berlin, January 22, 1942

Ernst descended the stairs into the Security Office's communications division at 8 Prinz-Albrechtstrasse. It was the hub of all intelligence for the SS. Two of his confidants on staff produced the operations file on Dietrich Bonhoeffer. After the minister's employment by the Abwehr, the Gestapo monitored his whereabouts, and current entries indicated Ettal, Germany.

The next day, a Junker JU-52 transport plane landed at the military airfield in Munich. There was only one passenger. Dressed in a three-piece wool suit and overcoat, Ernst disembarked carrying an overnight case to an awaiting automobile. During the eighty-five-kilometer journey into the Alps, he recounted events at the Wannsee Conference.

With seven thousand innocent lives at Sobibor in jeopardy, Ernst had a monumental problem. The road curved up and down as the Mercedes traversed the foothills reaching up into the Alps. Rounding a hairpin curve, the Ettal Monastery loomed into view. Majestic in scale, the ancient building and grounds were founded in 1330. Having arrived unannounced, Ernst created quite a stir with the monks. Eventually, they escorted him to one of two massive libraries.

A solitary man sat reading before a fire burning in the hearth. Ernst walked up from behind. "Dr. Dietrich Bonhoeffer, I presume."

Startled, Dietrich turned in dismay. "Ernst, am I under . . . ?"

"Arrest? No, I am not here on Reich business. I'm alone." Ernst lowered his voice. "Pastor, I am in trouble. I need your help."

"Is it Eva?"

The young soldier retrieved Heydrich's orders. "Nein, the problem is this."

Dietrich grasped the parchment with hesitance. "My boy, Germany is already a spider's nest of secrets." He angled the paper toward the table lamp. Reading, the pastor stared at Ernst. "This is beyond belief!"

Ernst sat across from Dietrich. "Sobibor is a new camp built but for one solitary purpose. This order is part of the camp's inauguration." He blinked. "Seven thousand human beings! When all is said and done, I will have been directly involved in mass murder."

Dietrich sat back in the chair. "Ordinary citizens of Berlin hear rumors, stories of the camps, but most have no idea how far it's gone. Well, son, how does it feel to dance with the devil?"

"For me, it began when the Jews killed Papa."

Dietrich leaned forward lowering his voice. "Are you sure? Did they ever catch the criminal?"

"My uncle told me—"

"But was there any proof? Ernst, General Heydrich hates Jews. Here is the evidence. He did not deliver these orders; he's making you do it. Ernst, in your heart, you know that you are not one of them." He placed the letter back into Ernst's hands. "You know the Word of God, young man. You do this, and you will personally answer to God. Make no mistake about that."

"Herr Bonhoeffer, my time is running out!"

"I would say time is running out for those prisoners."

"Even Himmler must know about this mission. I have no choice."

"But you *do* have a choice. God is convicting you of your guilt. Ask for His forgiveness now before it's too late. The Lord Jesus—He is God!

You must make a decision. Follow the God of Abraham, Isaac, and Jacob, or follow the master race as a mass murderer!"

Ernst stared into Dietrich's penetrating eyes in a cold silence.

After a long pause, Dietrich stood. "Tonight, you have confessed your secret burden, so now you will discover mine."

Dietrich opened his Bible and retrieved the photograph. "The young woman in this picture—her name is Sarah Kleisfeld."

Ernst laughed. "Preposterous! Why, this is Eva."

"I asked her to tell you, Ernst. Many times. . . ." Dietrich pressed the worn photograph into Ernst's palm.

In stone-cold silence, the black-and-white glossy seared into his heart. "You don't understand." Ernst raised his voice. "If this were true, my uncle would know."

"Your uncle does know. How many times has he delayed your wedding? You can imagine the scandal if you were to marry a Jewess."

Now everything became crystal clear. Ernst understood it all—why Eva would not commit to marry him, why Heydrich had urged him to merely "play with" but not get serious with her.

"Ernst, Reinhard will never give you permission to marry this woman. If you ever ask him, I would fear for her life."

Ernst restrained his tears. "My uncle will send someone to kill her."

"Someone had to tell you the truth."

"This is a train wreck in the making. People will die!"

"People closest to you who truly love you are a clear and present danger to the Third Reich."

"I cannot control this domino when it falls."

"You are precisely where God wants you."

"How so?"

"God is in control of the universe. Ernst, a man cannot serve two masters. You must choose whom you will follow."

"That is a mighty high price to pay."

"And Jesus already paid it the day He died for you and your sins. Son, it's time for you to pick up your cross and follow Christ."

Ernst's silence probed his mind as he replayed scenes from the Gleiwitz Massacre. With restrained tears of sadness, anger, and remorse, Ernst looked into the blazing hearth. In its flames, his wicked heart beat in rhythm with the goose steps of Hitler's legions. He was appalled by his face that was chiseled in stone.

"Ernst, remember God loves you—but only He can pay your debts. Only He can truly forgive you for what you have done."

Overwhelmed, Ernst stepped back. "Sir, I need more time."

"The clock is ticking for the seven thousand, for Eva, and for you. Make your peace with God soon or it will be too late."

Ernst donned his fedora and walked to the door. Once outside, the frigid air smacked him back to reality. When Eva's secret surfaced, the SS would hunt down and kill the only woman he had ever loved.

*   *   *

Sachsenhausen Camp, January 24, 1942

Blockhouse 13 was busy as skilled inmates initiated a production run of English five-pound notes on state-of-the-art presses. Major Teschler inspected the rank and file, then returned to the shop offices. A guard prodded Abraham Kleisfeld through the main door wearing a tattered wool coat, the snow fresh on the prisoner's worn shoes. Past the front desk, the guard shoved the middle-aged prisoner into the shop office.

Ernst followed them and eased himself down behind a desk. With a wave of his hand, he dismissed the guard. "Herr Kleisfeld, please have a seat."

Abraham eased onto a wood chair and nervously stroked his gray-streaked beard.

For some time, Ernst stared at the prisoner.

"Sir, did I do something wrong?"

"Yes, you were born a Jew in Germany." Ernst placed a black-and-white photograph on the desk in front of the prisoner. "Identify everyone in this photograph."

Abraham peered through his dusty spectacles, and his cheeks flushed. "Sir, where did you get this?"

"Just identify everyone in this picture!"

"Why, this is my family—my wife, Nina, and my daughter, Sarah, and Aaron, my son. Sir, where did you get this?"

Ernst lit a cigarette and took a slow drag. "What is your daughter's full name?"

"Sarah Annia Kleisfeld."

"Where does she live?"

Abraham raised his voice. "What do you want with my Sarah?"

Ernst stepped around the desk and presented a more recent color photograph taken of Eva at the SS cotillion. "This woman lives in Berlin. Do you know her?"

Abraham adjusted his spectacles and fingered the photo's glossy texture.

"Do you know this woman?" Ernst shouted.

Abraham's hands began to shake. "The Gestapo has taken my business, stolen most of our valuables, but I have managed to hide some gold. I will pay you to protect my Sarah."

Ernst tapped the woman's photo with his finger. "This woman calls herself Eva Kleist."

"I know in my heart one day God will bring my family back together again." Abraham embraced himself with his arms.

"This woman waits tables at the Bismarck Tavern in Berlin. She dances with Nazi soldiers six nights a week. She tells Gentile escorts that her parents are dead. That Aryan blood flows through her veins."

"How dare you! She is flesh of my flesh. She is my lovely daughter!"

Ernst leaned back against the edge of the desk. The room closed in on him. If only he could breathe. *So all of it was a sordid lie. I have been deceived!* As the words churned in his mind, he wiped tears from his flushed cheek. He had allowed the woman's charms and romantic words to completely blind him to the truth.

Still dazed, Ernst signaled the guard. "Take this man back to his cell block."

Abraham pulled away from the guard. "Major, Sarah is my only child left. I will do whatever you ask. Just please do not harm her. She is my life's blood!"

The guard raised the butt of his rifle.

"Nein. This man's skills are valuable to the Reich." Ernst watched as the Jewish engraver departed. Through the office window, he perused the forgers restocking the printers with fresh paper.

A few minutes passed when one of the prisoners walked into the office and handed him a brown envelope, unsealed. "It did not take much time, Herr Teschler."

Ernst unfolded a perfectly forged document. It was a replica of his uncle's orders to Sobibor. The changes made would alter the fate of seven thousand human souls.

```
1 February 1942

TO: Obersturmführer Franz Stangl

FROM: Obergruppenführer Reinhard Heydrich

When new facilities are completed, from
the first group of detainees, you are to
divert seven thousand Jews under Eichmann
Order #113 from Sobibor to the Majdanek
Camp for the purpose of forced labor.
```

"Sir, no one knows of my work for you. You are a very brave man." The Jewish prisoner smiled with his front tooth missing.

"Brave? No, I'm a fool. But perhaps some of these Jews on the list will survive the war."

Just then, muffled screams erupted outside the blockhouse and shots rang out. No doubt, another Jew would be dead. In a rush, he picked up the telephone receiver. If only he could speak to Eva.

"Delay that call, Major," said a familiar voice at the doorway. "It's time we had a talk."

Ernst's eyes widened. "Colonel Schellenberg?"

Walter Schellenberg placed his briefcase upon the desk. "So then, Teschler, give me a full report on Operation Bernhard."

"Sir?"

"Let us not be coy, my friend. Soon Major Neame will be replaced and my office will be in charge."

Ernst's mind raced. "The Jewish prisoners have finally duplicated the fabric and dyes of the paper. We now have a perfectly forged British five-pound note."

A devilish glint sparked in Schellenberg's green eyes. "Excellent! We shall build a distribution network throughout Europe. I want you to divert 15 percent of the finished notes to my department on an ongoing basis."

"By whose authority?"

"Mine, of course. Your uncle will not know about our arrangement, will he, Teschler?" Schellenberg started toward the door and pivoted. "The Jew, Kleisfeld, has more to do with you than forged banknotes. I have read Heydrich's file on Fräulein Kleist. I'm sure you will protect 'our' economic interests as I shall surely protect your secret in Berlin. I will be in touch with you soon."

Ernst leaned back into his chair. As he ran his finger across Heydrich's forged signature on the altered order, Weisthor and his tarot cards came to mind. What if Ernst forged alternative orders on a regular basis? How many Jews could he save? What if . . . ?

*   *   *

Berlin, February 1942

Inside, Eva stood facing her balcony window, dressed elegantly in a blue satin nightgown. The brilliant shafts of moonlight streamed through glass and pooled around her like liquid silk. The sleeves caressed her skin like a cool autumn breeze. Her living room behind her was dark. All was silent until keys rustled in the door lock.

The door opened and there Ernst stood. The hall light outlined his silhouette, his uniform reflecting the black, red, and white symbols of the Third Reich. In the dark, his heavy breathing signaled what was to come.

Eva stepped closer. "Ernst!" She reached out to him—but stopped. As her eyes grew accustomed to the dark, she could see that Ernst was trembling. "Ernst?" One look into his hazel eyes, and her heart told her the truth. Ernst knew her secret. She leaned back against the balcony door.

"Why, Eva?" His voice stammered.

Her ruse was over, but like an actress walking back onstage, she resumed her character. "Why what, darling?"

He closed the door and turned the lock. "I met your father this morning."

She could hear the tumblers of the lock fall into place as her heart thumped, dreading his next words. "Ernst, I could not tell you about—"

"Your father! He is rotting away in a concentration camp."

She froze, her toes gripping the coarse carpet.

"Tell me your father's name!" His tongue lashed out like a rapier's blade.

"Kleisfeld. Abraham Kleisfeld."

Ernst gripped both of her clenched fists and shook them as tears streamed down his cheeks. "You look quite different in his family picture. Dark hair—no makeup, your Semitic features are barely traceable." Ernst sniffled. "Herr Kleisfeld did not think much of my picture of you. Blonde hair, blue eyes, and your makeup. Tell me who is real—Eva or Sarah?"

Eva sobbed helplessly as she turned away from the man she loved. "I am a survivor, Ernst. You have no idea what it's like to walk down a street and have people leer at you just because you are a Jew!"

Ernst's hazel eyes were vacant.

"When I was young, my 'friends' and their parents would make snide comments about Jews all the time."

"Eva, I know what it's like to be different, to be an outsider. But time and time again, *you* publicly derided Jews to deceive me and everyone else."

"I worked day and night to shape the Eva you know. Over time, I buried Sarah along with my brother, Aaron." Without warning, a rogue wave of emotion struck Eva as she fell to her knees in tears. "On Kristallnacht, the Nazis came and threw my little brother over a balcony three stories high into a bonfire. All to the glory of the Reich! My father could not save him, and he cannot save me."

Ernst pulled Eva to her feet. The moonlight revealed his forlorn eyes.

She shook her head. "How did you find out?"

"Pastor Bonhoeffer showed me your picture. Eva, who else knows about you?"

"Your uncle. He told me that I could be your lover but I could never marry you! He could not have his precious protégé marry a common gutter *Jüdin*, could he?"

"But how long has he known?"

"From the beginning, Ernst. Don't you know who your uncle is? Don't you know *what* he is? I have watched him turn you from a proud German into a—"

"Into what, Eva?"

"Into a ghost! You're a phantom of the night, with the Death's Head on your cap. You have become a monster, like all the other ghouls in black!"

"We are SS. My honor is—" Ernst lowered his head.

"People on the street are terrified of the SS—their black uniforms, the parades, the guns. All of you think you are so dashing, so irresistible. In the beginning, I created Eva Kleist simply to survive. But then you came into my life. You treated me like a lady—the flowers, the restaurants, the moonlight walks in the park. I wanted to be the woman you could love, so I gave you Eva Kleist."

"I thought you loved me, Eva."

"I do love you, Ernst. I have been the envy of the girls at the tavern because even they could tell—you know how to love a woman with your soul and not just your body. I have always wanted you."

In a plea, he unfolded his hands toward her. "But you already have me!"

"No, Ernst. I can never have you. Your uncle said so in this very apartment."

He raised an eyebrow. "Reinhard was here?"

"Your precious uncle instructed me to 'play' with you—to keep you satisfied, to string you along. But if I valued my life, I was to stifle any talk of marriage."

Ernst walked to the foyer. "I should have left you a long time ago."

"My heavens, Ernst, take my life if you must, but do not leave me— not in this world!"

Grasping the door handle, Ernst wiped his cheek with a coat sleeve. "I do love you, Eva. I always have, and I always will."

She ran across the foyer, only to have the apartment door slammed in her face. She leaned back against the door. Eva had never felt more ter-rified or alone in her life. All of her dreams for a life with Ernst Teschler lay shattered upon the floor.

Chapter Thirty

Oberkrämer, Germany

S aul Avigur's hidden lair was a dilapidated apartment building twenty-six kilometers northwest of Berlin. He sat at the kitchen table in a sweaty undershirt, inspecting the bolt action on his 1933 British Enfield trials rifle.

As keys rattled in the front door, he laid the rifle down and removed the safety on his Walther PP pistol. His fellow Haganah agent entered, then locked the door. Saul reengaged the weapon's safety. "Malachi, why are you back so soon?"

The thin man with dark curly hair looked at his watch. "I followed Teschler to the Bismarck and waited. He never came back out."

"You fool. You lost him through the back door." Saul loosed a string of Yiddish curses. "Next time, I'll do it myself."

Malachi bristled. "Suppose you succeed in killing him. The Nazis will send more goons to hunt us down and put ten thousand more Jews into camps."

"We kill SS men one at a time. Jewish revenge is sweet." Saul finished disassembling the rifle on the table. Delicately cleaning the firing mechanism, he imagined his next victim.

"But why is Teschler so important?"

Saul speared Malachi with a devilish smile. "Because Teschler is the Führer's 'guardian angel.' No one has been able to get a clean shot at Hitler whenever Teschler's around."

Malachi snorted with laughter. "He already sounds like a legend. You actually think you're going to assassinate Hitler?"

"If I follow Teschler, he will lead me to Heydrich. Killing the architect of the Final Solution has merit." Saul placed the rifle barrel and shoulder stock into a wooden case and snapped the lid shut. "Teschler is in love with dear Sarah Kleisfeld. He'll return to her nest sooner or later. And I will be waiting for him."

*   *   *

Two hours later, Ernst stood again outside Eva's apartment. Fueled by rage and fear, he had driven the streets of Berlin utterly alone. He turned the doorknob—still unlocked—and cautiously entered the living room. A cold breeze brushed his face. In the light of a solitary lamp, he noticed the balcony doors were open with the curtains gently stirring. Without a sound, Ernst moved closer.

Through the sheer curtains, Eva stood silhouetted by the moonlight. Dressed in a sheer nightgown, the tawny blonde drew down on her cigarette and released a column of smoke.

Ernst stepped behind the curtain. When she leaned back on the railing, the moonlight outlined her voluptuous figure. He imagined the ebb and flow of her every breath.

"Darling, I would feel those eyes anywhere," Eva purred.

He held the curtain back, his heart simmering with desire. "When I look, I see only you, Eva."

She moved into his embrace, their lips longing for each other. Eyes closed, he held her close, craving the warmth of their bodies.

A crisp updraft stung Ernst's ears. "Aren't you cold?"

"I thought I had lost you, Ernst. The wine dulls the senses."

"You will never lose me, Eva." He lifted her into his arms and carried her inside, then nudged the door closed with his shoulder.

She slid out of his arms onto her bare feet. "You can take me away from all of this, Ernst. We could escape and make a life together."

They slumped onto the couch and caressed one another. Ernst's very soul simmered in the heat emanating from the fire in the hearth. He yearned for her but could sense Eva holding back. "Tell me what it was like back in Wittenberg."

"My father and mother were hardworking, always honest, but our Gentile neighbors all knew. We were Jews. On the street, most people were polite to your face, but you could hear cruel words at a distance."

Ernst stroked her forehead, brushing her bangs to the side.

"So I came to Berlin to start a new life. In a matter of days, Eva Kleist was born. You have every right to be angry. In the beginning, I didn't know about your family. You were just a young SS officer at the Bismarck who was handsome and kind. I was a lonely woman who met a young man at a tavern. You invited me to dinner and treated me like a lady, like someone special. What I really wanted was someone to love, someone who would really love me."

Ernst kissed her cheek. "From the first moment I saw you, I wanted you in my life. You could have been a housemaid or a teacher. It wouldn't have mattered."

"With a name like Kleisfeld, I doubt if you would have noticed me."

"Well, Eva, as it stands, you are a threat to the whole Heydrich dynasty. A man who can kill thousands of Jews with the stroke of the pen will not hesitate to kill one troublesome Jewess."

"No one is safe in Nazi Germany, not even you, Ernst."

"Then I'll have to get you out of Germany."

She wrinkled her brow. "But I have no papers."

"You forget, your father is a master forger at my command. Eva Kleist will soon disappear without a trace. And someday soon, I will join you."

"Oh, Ernst!" Eva buried her face into his shoulder and wept.

Minutes passed, he lifted her head back and kissed her passionately. "Now, Eva, I must go. I have to make arrangements."

She clung to Ernst. "You can't leave me here. Your uncle will be the first to know that my secret has been discovered."

"He doesn't know about the Kleisfeld connections."

"But the Gestapo has been watching my apartment." Eva pouted.

"Stay here while I make arrangements with a friend. I will come back for you tomorrow. I promise!" That promise had no guarantees. Ernst could not even promise that he would be alive. Once more, their lips melded, then Ernst disappeared into the night.

*   *   *

Saul was right. He knew Major Teschler would return to Fräulein Kleist's apartment. After Ernst appeared at the window of Eva's apartment, Saul sought the high ground to get a good shot. From an adjoining roof four stories up, the Haganah agent trained his rifle's scope upon Eva's apartment window and waited. "Teschler, I will trap you in your own love nest."

Still, it was a surprise when Teschler left early, not even twelve thirty by his watch. The stairwell had small windows at each landing. Saul raised his rifle and adjusted the focus collar on his scope. As Teschler walked down the steps, he moved in and out of a window frame at each stair landing. When Teschler reached the first-floor landing, Saul fingered the trigger and was ready to fire.

Then through the scope . . . a bizarre, blinding light filled the glass. Saul pulled away from the scope and blinked. A swirl of white light, like the glory of the Shekinah, appeared to weave itself around Teschler as he walked down the sidewalk!

With his adrenaline pumping, Saul again pressed his eye to his scope and took aim. But there it was again, blinding his view through the lens. When he jerked his head up again, Teschler was gone.

Enraged, Saul looked up and down the sidewalk but to no avail. He cursed to himself as he darted across the rooftop. Down some stairs, then he leapt into the car and started the engine. His hands were shaking.

Though not a religious man, Saul had seen the Shekinah Glory of God before—twice in Palestine. Rabbis claimed it was the power of God. He clasped his hands together to stop the shaking. How was he going to explain what happened to Malachi?

*   *   *

Abwehr HQ, Berlin, March 1942

Wilhelm Canaris scowled from behind his desk. "I don't like it. The Brits' demand for a list of conspirators is dangerous. All of us would be at the mercy of Sir Anthony Eden." Oster, Dohnanyi, and Bonhoeffer exchanged nervous glances seated around the hearth.

"Nothing would surprise me since the SS kidnapped those MI6 agents in Venlo," Oster said.

Wilhelm massaged his lower lip with his pipe stem. "They are very polite people, the Brits, but they can be prickly when roused."

Hans von Dohnanyi lit a cigarette and sat back on the arm of the sofa. "We are in the game now. We must respond soon."

Wilhelm puffed on his pipe. "Herr Bonhoeffer, suppose you are stopped on the way to Stockholm to see Bishop Bell? With that list, the Blackshirts would hang us all with piano wire!"

Dietrich stroked his neck. "Piano wire—really?"

"That's Hitler's favorite." Oster retrieved a book from his briefcase. "Admiral, this is Dr. Bonhoeffer's Bible." It boasted a worn black leather cover and dog-eared pages. Oster removed an ornate bookmark with a woven tassel and held it up. "It appears to be an ordinary bookmark. Under the heading, *Those for whom we pray*, in Bonhoeffer's own hand is the list."

"It looks like my handwriting—" Bonhoeffer said.

"The SS is not the only intelligence service in Germany with expert forgers."

The admiral looked intently at the strip, then forged a grin.

"What is it?" Bonhoeffer asked.

Wilhelm leaned over to present the small banner. "Look closely, Herr Bonhoeffer. Right here. At a certain angle in the light, you can see three watermarks—one the official seal of the Reich, one of the Wehrmacht, and the third of Abwehr intelligence."

Dietrich's eyes bloomed. "Followed by the list of conspirators."

Oster nodded. "Yes, these watermarks will convince the Brits that we authored the list."

Bonhoeffer gave the bookmark to Oster. "I will see Bishop Bell in Stockholm in a few weeks."

Wilhelm pondered the fate of those gathered in that room as he puffed his pipe. "Oster, keep the Bible locked in a safe until the very day Dr. Bonhoeffer leaves."

He placed his hand upon Dietrich's shoulder. "Herr Bonhoeffer, we are entrusting our very lives in your hands."

"Well, Admiral, you are a man of faith after all."

*   *   *

Berlin, SS Headquarters, April 1942

A knock sounded at Heinrich Himmler's door. "Kommen."

His secretary delivered a large brown envelope marked *Confidential.* "This Enigma message was just intercepted. You asked me to keep you informed about Teschler's activities."

"Danke, Ingrid. Hold my calls." The names Reinhard Heydrich and Eva Kleist commanded his immediate attention.

14 April 1942

TO: Sturmbannführer Alfred Neame

FROM: Obergruppenführer Reinhard Heydrich

SUBJECT: Eva Kleist

-While Kleist's family connections remain confidential, her usefulness has passed.

-Her departure must be permanent.

-No knowledge of this must ever come to Teschler.

-Signal me when the task is completed.

Heinrich contemplated the teletype message for a moment, then buzzed his secretary. "Cancel all my appointments for today. Find Major Neame and have him report to me. Then get Wewelsburg on the line. I need to speak to Weisthor." Nursing a cup of hot tea, he began to think of the possibilities. Fräulein Kleist was the key to controlling Teschler. Only then could he obtain the Spear of Destiny.

A few days later, Alfred Neame entered Heinrich's office and saluted.

"Neame, I have a collection you might have interest in seeing." On the table was a series of intercepted teletype messages.

17 April 1942

TO: Sturmbannführer Alfred Neame

FROM: Obergruppenführer Reinhard Heydrich

SUBJECT: Eva Kleist

It has been three days! Report your status immediately.

18 April 1942

TO: Obergruppenführer Reinhard Heydrich

FROM: Sturmbannführer Alfred Neame

SUBJECT: Eva Kleist

I have just arrived back in Berlin. Kleist's apartment is deserted. Request further instructions.

"Herr Reichsführer, I can explain."

"Nein. I called to offer you an opportunity you can't refuse. I have a certain stone in my shoe that requires removal."

"Sir?"

"Your man in Prague."

Neame raised an eyebrow. "You mean—Heydrich?"

"Let's just say it would benefit me if the Führer would have to replace the Reichsprotektor of Bohemia and Moravia. You are uniquely skilled for such a mission."

"That would be daring and difficult. And to avoid retribution, I'll need to deal with Teschler afterward."

"Under no circumstances will you touch Teschler. Your priority will be to arrest the Kleist woman as soon as possible. She will bait my trap for young Teschler. I will force him to give me a very unique relic."

Neame brandished a wide grin. "Do tell me the details."

*   *   *

The Bonhoeffer Home, April 1942

Dietrich was savoring a piece of Bavarian chocolate cake when someone tapped on the kitchen door. He switched on the porch light and peered through the window. Ernst and Eva stood huddled in a corner. He turned off the light and ushered the two inside.

Ernst was dressed in a gray business suit and a fedora. "Thank you for helping us, Pastor."

"You are welcome, my friends!" Dietrich led the couple into the library where they sat down. "Ernst, I must confess I have grave doubts. Not for my own safety, but for Eva's. The Gestapo has been watching this house for some time."

"Of course they're watching it. I placed a surveillance team on this house weeks ago. In the morning, they will file a report that two strangers came in the middle of the night. I will be duly impressed with their competence, then tell them to continue watching for any unusual visitors."

"Good Lord, Ernst, you're playing a dangerous game."

"No more dangerous than the one you are playing with Canaris."

Dietrich leaned back. "What do you know?"

"You are a spy for Abwehr intelligence. Beyond that I know little, and I'm doing my best to prevent others from finding out. I have a man stationed inside the SS communications department who relays to me all correspondence concerning you, then he 'misfiles' the documents."

"But how—?"

"By direct orders of the Führer, I have unlimited access to the Gestapo for counterintelligence. Until my uncle learns that Eva has disappeared, he will have no suspicions. He is very busy in Prague these days."

Dietrich looked at Ernst with some pride. "We have a room set aside for you, Fräulein Kleist. Within a few days, we can arrange the next step of your journey."

Eva's eyes were full of doubt. "All of this is happening so quickly. I had little time to pack."

Dietrich smiled. "Not to worry. I have several sisters who have spare clothes in the house. Besides, a change of appearance might be wise."

Ernst clasped Eva's hand. "It was important to leave your apartment as if you just left for a momentary appointment. That will keep the Gestapo waiting for a few days."

With a nod, Eva squeezed Ernst's hand. He glanced at Dietrich. "Perhaps you could give us a moment, then I will go."

"Certainly." Dietrich closed the door behind him and walked into the dark foyer. Through the sheer curtains, he looked out the window. Up the street, a familiar black sedan was parked with two men inside. The glow of their cigarettes confirmed their presence.

*   *   *

Berlin, May 3, 1942

A few days later, Dietrich and Eva met his colleague Friedrich Perels at the Berlin train station. Eva wore one of his sister's flowered dresses, much more fitting for a middle-aged mother than a barmaid. Her sultry blonde hair had been pulled tightly into a bun, and she wore reading glasses to add some years to her appearance. With Eva at his side and the Abwehr list in his Bible, Dietrich led the trio through the busy concourse.

When Eva went to the ladies' room, Friedrich pulled Dietrich over to the side. "Patzig may not be a safe place to hide. Does Countess Ruth know you're bringing Teschler's woman right into their living room?"

"No one is to know Eva's real identity."

"My friend, you are placing everyone at risk!"

"The countess is a courageous woman, Friedrich. On the train, the two of you will sit together as father and daughter. I'll be a few rows behind you, just in case."

Eva returned. "My ticket is a general pass to Pomerania, but where is our final destination?"

Dietrich paused. "You will know soon enough, my dear." Shortly, the train pulled into the station. "Well, goodbye for now, Friedrich."

Dietrich shook his hand and walked down the platform toward the concourse, pretending to leave. At the last minute, he circled back and boarded the rear of the train. Dietrich walked forward through several cars and sat six rows behind Eva and Friedrich. The train had already pulled out of the station before he noticed two suspicious men seated across the aisle and two seats ahead of Eva and Friedrich. *Of course, the Gestapo.*

Then a short, muscular man in a grey tweed suit sat across from Dietrich. "Good afternoon, Herr Bonhoeffer. Would you like a cigarette?" His pleasant smile was crowned with sinister eyes as he moved Dietrich's briefcase by the window.

"No, thank you." Dietrich's heart raced as he nervously eyed his briefcase and the Abwehr list inside. "Do I know you?"

"My name is Alfred Neame. Let's just say I'm an associate of Ernst Teschler. Here is my card. In a few minutes, the train will make an unscheduled stop. Fräulein Kleist will leave the train, but you will travel on north. You will tell Teschler that you have delivered her safely into my care. Tell him our superior expects his 'package' to be delivered soon—very soon."

"But, am I under arrest?" Dietrich stammered.

"To the contrary, Herr Bonhoeffer. Go wherever you wish. Our business is with Ernst Teschler."

Just thirteen kilometers northeast of Berlin, the train stopped at the Bernau station. To Dr. Perels's dismay, Neame and his associates quietly forced Eva off the train.

Dietrich's stomach twisted into a knot as he watched the SS men escort Eva across the vacant platform. She glared back frantically at Dietrich with the smoldering eyes of a woman deceived.

Oh my Lord, what have I done?

As the train surged into motion, Dietrich sank back into his seat. Dietrich and Friedrich avoided each other for the duration of the trip.

An hour later, the train pulled into the Stettin station. With his briefcase and the list in hand, Dietrich rushed to a pay phone to chance a call to Ernst—but then stopped. The Gestapo could be on the line.

Dietrich joined Friedrich at a prearranged restaurant. "What if I can't reach Teschler? We cannot go on to Patzig. The Gestapo will follow us for sure."

Friedrich shook his head. "This cannot end well for Fräulein Kleist."

Dietrich shuddered at the thought of the Abwehr list hidden within his Bible. That woman was not the only secret on board their train.

Friedrich gathered his things. "I'm going on to meet our contact at the Stettin Harbor to discuss alternate sailing schedules. Afterward, I'll return to Berlin by train from the closest town. That will give us some time to sort out this mess."

"But I've got to tell Ernst about Eva."

Friedrich paused. "That man who kidnapped Fräulein Kleist knows everything about you. You can't save others from a prison cell. My advice—get out of Germany!"

After his colleague departed, Dietrich tried to focus. He walked to the local post office. The Abwehr list must be protected at all costs. In a box with a scribbled note, he mailed his Bible to Berlin addressed to his mother, Paula Bonhoeffer.

On the street again, he walked a few blocks. Then a voice spoke from behind him. "Doctor Bonhoeffer."

Dietrich froze. His worst fears seized him. He slowly turned to see the brash handlebar mustache of Colonel Hans von Wedemeyer, Maria's father.

"I waited at the train station for you. The countess and the family are eager to see you. By the way, where are our guests?"

Nonplussed, Dietrich took a deep breath. "I'm afraid there has been a change in plans."

Chapter Thirty-One

Berlin, May 1942

Ernst arrived at the small café across the street from Zion Lutheran Church wearing a business suit. The manager handed him an address, and Ernst departed casually, zigzagging through a few streets. Keeping an eye out for anyone who might follow, he entered an old apartment building and rang the buzzer for Apartment 102.

"Come, come in quickly, Ernst. I have been trying to reach you for days." Dietrich looked bleary-eyed from lack of sleep.

Ernst entered the living room and peered through the closed curtain. "I just came from Eva's apartment. It's been ransacked. The Gestapo was thorough, but they did not find my personal letters." He patted his coat pocket. "How's Eva?"

Dietrich's face turned ashen. "Ernst, something dreadful has happened."

Ernst stepped closer. "Where's Eva?"

Dietrich presented Neame's business card. "This man Neame and his men took Eva off the train at Bernau. I am so sorry."

"What did he say? Tell me precisely!"

"He said that your superior is expecting 'his package,' a relic of some kind. It didn't make any sense at all."

"It makes perfect sense to me. Were your friends up north discovered?"

"No, but Dr. Perels remained in Stettin to make arrangements to smuggle you and Eva out of the country."

Ernst started to pace. "How naive could I have been?" There were no happy endings in Nazi Germany.

"What does Neame want from you?"

"Neame works for Himmler, and Himmler wants an ancient artifact that I have."

Dietrich furrowed his brow. "I don't understand."

"Did Neame leave a telephone number, an address perhaps? Please, try to remember everything the man said."

"He gave me nothing but that business card and instructions to contact you."

"Then Alfred Neame will certainly find me."

*   *   *

Berlin, SS Headquarters, May 1942

Ernst took a discreet route back to 8 Prinz-Albrechtstrasse. Half an hour later, he stood in the SS communication center talking to one of his confidants.

"Any trace on line 435-256?"

The SS clerk quickly thumbed through the evening log. "That would be the residence of Dr. Karl Bonhoeffer. Just local calls except one to the Stettin area, but it was not long enough for a complete trace." The clerk stood and retrieved an opened package from a shelf. Its brown wrapper revealed the name of Frau Paula Bonhoeffer and the Bonhoeffer home address. "This was mailed from Stettin, sir."

Ernst unwrapped the Bible with Dietrich Bonhoeffer's name imprinted in gold leaf. But why would he mail a Bible to his home? Ernst scrutinized the wrapper in more detail until he noticed the post date. It was the day Eva was kidnapped! In his hand, the pages naturally opened to the tasseled bookmark inside.

"Sir, shall we send the book on to their home?"

"No, I'll take care of it. Monitor that telephone line closely. Call me when you have an address in Stettin, and keep this confidential, understood?" Ernst ripped the notes on the top page off the clerk's clipboard and left the room. He mounted two flights of stairs and entered his office. It was 6:00 p.m. He opened the Bible to no particular page, when his eyes were drawn to Matthew, the sixteenth chapter.

> *Then Jesus said to His disciples, "If anyone wishes to come after Me, he must deny himself, and take up his cross and follow Me. For whoever wishes to save his life will lose it; but whoever loses his life for My sake will find it. For what will it profit a man if he gains the whole world and forfeits his soul? Or what will a man give in exchange for his soul?"*

"*For what will it profit a man if he gains the whole world and forfeits his soul?*" Ernst repeated to himself when his telephone rang. He picked up the receiver. "Major Teschler here. Ja, Herr Reichsführer. Right away." Up one flight of stairs, and within minutes Ernst stood before Himmler's desk.

"Teschler, what is the status of the Spear of Destiny?"

"The original Spear is not in my possession."

"Then where is the replica?"

"I—"

"Speechless, eh Teschler? You are very cunning. Just as Weisthor's prophecies predicted, you have become our Knight Errant. But, you have lied to me."

Though trapped in his deceit, Ernst was no longer afraid of the Reichsführer.

"We have Fräulein Kleist safely tucked away, my boy. I am told Major Neame is a most congenial and tender host. Bring me the Spear of Destiny within ten days—and Eva Kleist lives. Fail me again, and Major Neame will have his way with her. Permanently."

"Sir, where is Fräulein Kleist?"

"Show me the true Spear of Destiny, and I will give you the girl, Major." Himmler pursed his lips in his resolve.

Ernst departed and returned to his office. He imagined Eva's tender smile, her radiant blue eyes, and her warm lips. He shuddered at the thought of his beautiful Eva in the cold, cruel hands of Alfred Neame.

*   *   *

Near the Czech Border, May 27, 1942

Ernst and Max's flight toward Prague had been turbulent. With Eva in Neame's hands and her location unknown, only the Spear of Destiny could save her. As storms stirred across the horizon, their plane was forced to land in Dresden for a fuel line repair.

Ernst had to first reclaim the key from Aunt Lina and then make the subsequent trip to Switzerland. With only seven days left on Himmler's deadline, was there enough time?

Eva could be hidden anywhere in Germany. If not in Berlin, then it could it be in his castle fortress: Wewelsburg. The thought of Neame's hands on his precious Eva was too much to bear. More questions swirled in his mind as their Junker plane cut through the darkening clouds before them.

"We'll be on the ground in thirty minutes," the pilot announced.

Max looked at Ernst. "You realize we are taking on Himmler and the whole SS Corps?"

"I give us a one-in-three chance of survival."

Max brandished his boyish grin. "Well, that's a relief." He placed his hand upon Ernst's shoulder. "Don't worry, I'll help you find Eva. Then we'll deal with Neame together."

Ernst's lips lifted in a subtle smile as he stroked Barron's muscular shoulder.

As the airplane's engine droned onward, Ernst remembered the first time he saw the Spear of Destiny. Was it a mere ancient relic, or an actual talisman of demonic power?

*   *   *

Prague, May 27, 1942

Reinhard Heydrich delayed his departure to town that morning to enjoy his children in the gardens of his impressive estate. The night before, he and Lina had attended a gala at the music hall, where Nazi officials had paid homage to the new royal couple. Despite her pregnancy, Lina looked radiant.

"Lina, Hitler will eventually send us to Paris, and then I will be in position to succeed the Führer when he dies."

Lina raised a cautious eyebrow. "Reinhard, do not talk too loudly about the Führer's death."

"We are a long way from Berlin, my dear. We are both doing our duty for the Fatherland." He patted her swollen belly.

Lina scoffed as she turned to their three children, all dressed in color-ful Hitler Youth uniforms.. "Klaus! Heider! Silke! Come and kiss your father goodbye."

Reinhard gazed down into their bright blue eyes. "You boys will be princes someday, but first I have to conquer the world." He kissed each boy and then his daughter. Reinhard and Lina walked from the garden to his waiting automobile. Reinhard took his usual seat in the rear of the open command car and breathed in an air of invincibility as he departed through the main gate.

*   *   *

Not a half hour later, Ernst arrived at the Heydrich mansion in Panenské Břežany—fourteen kilometers north of central Prague. Their Czech maid escorted him up a massive marble staircase to Frau Heydrich's sitting room.

"Aunt Lina!" Ernst swept into the room to find her adorned in a casual dress.

"Ernst, my boy, what a pleasant surprise. You just missed your uncle."

Ernst managed a winsome smile. "Actually, I came to see you."

Lina led her nephew to the long couch. "Well, sit down. Your mother just wrote to me about the special woman in your life. In time, she is hopeful that you will fill her home with grandchildren. So tell me the latest about Fräulein Kleist."

"I gave my marriage application to Uncle Reinhard weeks ago, and he still hasn't given it to Himmler. I have discovered the woman I want to marry. Aunt Lina, I hope both of you will welcome her into our family."

"If Reinhard has interfered with your happiness, my dear, I shall certainly turn the tide."

"Months ago, I gave you a necklace for safekeeping. I need it back."

"The one with the cute bronze key. Why of course." Lina disappeared into the next room. Minutes later, she emerged with the necklace in hand.

Relieved, Ernst pocketed the key. "Aunt Lina, you are such a dear."

"Anything to help, my boy. If you have a moment, let me offer you some tea. Your uncle is rarely home, and I rarely have opportunity for decent conversation."

"Of course, that would be a pleasure." After a time, Ernst looked at his watch. He hoped to catch up with Max and Barron at SS headquarters in Prague, then they would drive back to the military airport for their flight to Switzerland.

*   *   *

Reinhard's open-air Mercedes maneuvered over the country roads toward Hradčany Castle. Near the outskirts of Prague, there was a sharp curve in the road that led down to the Troja Bridge. With little traffic in the vicinity, he could see a tram grinding up the hill.

As his car approached the curve in the road, a man loitered on the sidewalk. He flashed a mirror. As the Mercedes slowed down for the turn, another man across the street threw back his poncho revealing a British Sten gun. At point-blank range, the submachine gun stuttered, popped, and misfired.

Incredulous, Reinhard stared down at its menacing barrel not five meters away. Momentary fear morphed into anger, then exploded into rage. "Klein, stop the car!" He stood in the rear of the car waving his pistol.

The man with the mirror pulled the pin of a grenade and tossed it toward the open touring car. The bomb glanced off the rear door and landed beside the right rear wheel. Reinhard shielded his face with his arms just before a thunderous explosion rocked the Mercedes's undercarriage.

The blast lurched the car sideways and bounced it into a ditch, throwing Reinhard over the front seat. Through the haze and the smell of acrid smoke, he could see one assassin reel backward, clawing at his bleeding face. Passengers on the tram screamed as shards of metal had torn through the side of their carriage.

Both Reinhard and Klein were dazed. Reinhard still managed to climb out of the wrecked car, waving his pistol and cursing. The two assassins disappeared into the gathering crowd. Suddenly, his head began to spin. Reinhard collapsed against a railing, staggering like a drunk. He managed to hold himself up with one hand as Klein came running.

Reinhard waved him back. "No, Klein, go and shoot them all!"

While Sergeant Klein pursued the fugitives on foot, Reinhard stumbled back and fell against the hood of the wrecked Mercedes. He grabbed his lower back and felt wetness, then lifted his bloody hand. *It's like paint. Like red paint.*

Then a bolt of excruciating pain plunged him into darkness.

*   *   *

The maid interrupted Lina and Ernst in the Heydrich's upstairs parlor.

"Madame, two SS officers just arrived. They say it is an urgent matter."

"Excuse me, Ernst. They probably want to speak with Reinhard."

The servant shook her head. "No, Madame, they want to speak with you."

"Oh my—" Uneasiness filled her voice.

"I will accompany you." Ernst stood and offered her his arm.

"Thank you, Ernst." Lina hesitated a moment but then followed.

At the bottom of the ornate staircase, two SS officers stood there with grim expressions. The senior officer in charge stepped forward. "Frau Heydrich, I regret to inform you that there has been an assassination attempt—"

Before he finished his sentence, Lina gasped and stumbled back upon the steps.

Ernst caught her in time. "Gentlemen, help her into the library." It was imperative to discover the identities of the assailants. Other SS leaders or the Führer might be next!

Once in a chair, Lina began to sob.

There was a stir and voices rang out at the front door, then Max and Barron joined them. "Ernst, we came as soon as I received word."

One of the officers spoke. "Major, General Heydrich received multiple shrapnel wounds. I know Dr. Deckart at the Bulkova Hospital. He's a good German surgeon, but General Heydrich won't let him operate. He wants to wait for the surgeon general to arrive from Berlin."

Ernst's face flushed. "Lieutenant, make sure your men secure this house. Aunt Lina, you stay here with the children while Max and I go to the hospital."

Lina looked desperate. "Don't let my Reinhard die, please!"

With Eva at Neame's mercy, the Spear in Switzerland, and his uncle critically injured in Prague, the clock kept ticking. "Lieutenant, take us to the hospital, schnell!"

*   *   *

Wewelsburg Castle, May 1942

High atop the south tower, Eva sat before a smoldering fire set in the stone hearth. As the days wore on, her tears had long since dwindled. From her window, she could tell that the castle was secluded in the countryside but not much else. She was mesmerized by the burnt-orange glow of the setting sun.

Somewhere far beyond its beveled strands of light, she knew Ernst was looking for her. But in his absence the shadows grew tall at night, and eerie sounds would bellow with the wind. In desperate straits, somehow the words of the Shema came to her lips.

"Sh'ma Yis'ra'eil, Adonai Eloheinu, Adonai echad."

Hear, Israel, the Lord is our God, the Lord is One.

"Barukh sheim k'vod malkhuto l'olam va'ed."

Blessed be the Name of His glorious kingdom forever and ever.

"V'ahav'ta eit Adonai Elohekha b'khol l'vav'kha uv'khol naf'sh'kha uv'khol m'odekha."

And you shall love the Lord your God with all your heart and with all your soul and with all your might.

"How quaint are those pious words, my dear. I should imagine your father taught them to you." The deep, gravelly voice interrupted her prayer.

Eva sat up and spied a short grey-haired man in uniform entering the room. The man's beet-colored jowls quivered ever so slightly with each step. His silverish eyes shimmered in the firelight.

"Who are you? What do you want?"

"My name is Weisthor." A wry smile dawned upon his features. "Fräulein Kleist, your time in this life grows short. You should know that it was Ernst Teschler who arranged your visit with us."

"Liar! Ernst would never—"

"How do you think we knew exactly where you and Dr. Perels would be? Did you really think a mongrel Jewess could marry an SS officer of Teschler's breeding?"

"Stop it!" Eva lunged at the short, rotund creature.

Weisthor grasped both her arms and slowly drove Eva back into her chair. "You see, my dear, your Hebrew god is impotent. He cannot save you, and your precious Ernst . . . well, let's just say he now finds you an embarrassment." Weisthor released her arms, and Eva slumped to her side, sobbing.

"Why are you tormenting me?" Eva screamed through her tears.

"My, I was so enjoying our little chat." With a look of self-satisfaction, Weisthor departed.

The door closed with a thud. Cautiously, Eva made her way to the desk. Earlier that day, she had discovered stationery and had already begun a letter.

> *Dearest Ernst,*
>
> *I know you did not send these horrible men to take me captive. I know in my heart that you care for my well-being. I yearn for your lips and your caresses. You hold me as no other can.*
>
> *As to my family and heritage, it has caused so much pain and rejection. When I arrived in Berlin, I wanted a new life. I wanted someone like you to take care of me. To be a new family. But now, I realize I deceived you to survive. I did not honor our relationship in the deceit. Forgive me, Ernst. For no one else can.*
>
> *Ever yours,*
> *Eva*

A few tears sealed the letter. She hid the missive on a bookshelf, not knowing if her dearest Ernst would ever see it.

Chapter Thirty-Two

Prague

D riven by a junior officer, the SS staff car tore through the streets of Prague. Ernst sat in front with Barron and Max in the rear. "What happened to General Heydrich, Lieutenant?"

The officer steered around slow-moving traffic. "A grenade. General Heydrich received multiple shrapnel wounds in his back. Witnesses reported two assailants. We think they may be Czech resistance. They escaped on foot, but we have dispatched fifty to sixty soldiers to hunt them down."

Ernst glanced at his watch again. "Capture them alive. We need to find out who sent them."

Max tapped Ernst's shoulder. "Should I alert Berlin? Other party leaders may be in danger." Barron pressed his head between the two front seats to nuzzle his master.

The outline of Bulkova Hospital appeared against the skyline. The endgame for Eva and his uncle was unknown. What could happen next? Ernst felt inside his tunic for the Swiss deposit-box key draped around his neck on a thin steel necklace. *Perhaps the Spear of Destiny can save the people most precious to me.*

Once at the hospital, the doors to the emergency room burst open. An SS contingent and Dr. Deckart escorted Ernst, Barron, and Max through a maze of hallways.

Deckart was emphatic. "X-rays reveal a broken rib, a ruptured diaphragm, and splinters of metal imbedded within his spleen. If we don't operate now, he's at risk for major abdominal infection." The attendants opened the examination room door, and Ernst approached the bed.

Stripped to the waist, perspiration bathed Reinhard's hairless chest. He was packed in ice, and bandages were wrapped around his partially shaven head and torso. At his uncle's side, Ernst's eyes were glued to the bloody sheets.

Reinhard opened his eyes and flinched in pain. He faintly smiled. "Ernst, I knew you would come."

Ernst squeezed his uncle's hand. "You must listen to the doctors."

"Did you get them?" Reinhard raised his incoherent voice. "Did you kill the scum . . . who did this to me?"

Ernst was taken aback by his uncle's ashen face and the restraints laced around his arms and legs. The sight made him think of Eva lying in a cell, helpless. *The Great Ernst Teschler. I couldn't protect my father or Eva, and now this!*

He shook his head in disgust. "I promise you we will find the assassins, but you can't wait. They must operate."

"Tell the doctors to patch me up quickly. I am flying to Berlin tomorrow to meet the Führer." Reinhard's voice faded. His eyelids fluttered as he slipped into unconsciousness. Exhausted, Ernst eased back into his chair. With little he could do, he was forced to sit and wait.

*   *   *

Berlin, SS Headquarters

Heinrich's secretary buzzed. "Herr Reichsführer, I have Major Neame on the line."

Heinrich picked up the telephone. "I understand your men paid their respects to the gentleman in Prague."

"Nein, Herr Reichsführer. It was discussed, but you never gave the final order."

"Two agents just bombed General Heydrich's car a few hours ago."

Neame paused on the line. "Sir, I know nothing of this."

Good Lord, then could it be a British or French plot? "We must increase security for all top officials—and the Führer!" Perspiration beaded upon Heinrich's brow.

"Sir, shall I go to Prague to investigate?"

"No, stay at Wewelsburg with Teschler's woman. Keep her alive and well until Teschler brings me the goods." Heinrich replaced the receiver on its cradle and pressed the intercom. "Get me Major Teschler, Bulkova Hospital, Prague—immediately!"

An hour later, Heinrich's intercom buzzed. "Sir, Major Teschler is on the line."

Heinrich softened his voice. "Teschler, my sympathies to you and the family. What is Reinhard's condition?"

"Multiple wounds from shrapnel. Infection is the doctor's main concern. Sir, we have to tighten security in Berlin and Paris."

"I have already sent out the alert. Major, you are at risk of losing two people very close to you. What is the status of your personal mission?"

"But, mein herr, where is Fräulein Kleist? Is she alive?"

"I told you that Major Neame is entertaining her. Now, when shall I receive my package?"

"I need more time. Security here in Prague has been breached."

"Fräulein Kleist has little time left. Need I say more?"

"Please, I . . . Where do I deliver the item when I get it?"

"When you have the package, call my secretary in Berlin, day or night. I will give you further instructions then. Auf Wiedersehen."

*   *   *

Down the hall at SS headquarters, Colonel Schellenberg clicked off the reel-to-reel tape recorder and drew down heavily upon his cigarette.

What could be in Teschler's package for Himmler? The thought dangled in his mind as he dialed the operator. "Get me the Bulkova Hospital, Prague. Yes, I want to speak to Major Ernst Teschler."

The line was silent for a few minutes. Walter waited.

"Major Teschler here."

"Teschler, this is Schellenberg. Tell me, is Heydrich going to live?"

"Grenade shrapnel penetrated his chest cavity from the rear. They must operate right away, but Himmler insists that we wait for a specialist from Berlin."

"Major, I'm considering the possibility that Himmler ordered your uncle's death."

Ernst paused. "What makes you think so?"

"Furthermore, I know Major Neame is holding Eva Kleist captive in an undisclosed location. Would you like some assistance?"

"In return for what, Schellenberg?"

"To confirm our financial arrangement. It will be in my interest to help a partner. Himmler will never suspect me of helping you find the Kleist woman, and he would never suspect you of siphoning off part of the Reichsbank gold reserves and counterfeit British pounds to my department at RSHA. I can't help Heydrich, but we can mount a well-financed counterespionage offensive inside the SS."

"You are asking me to commit treason!"

"The clock is ticking for the Kleist woman. And when she is dead, Neame is coming after you. You don't have the luxury of time, my friend. So . . . do we have an agreement?"

Silence hung between them, then the telephone line to Prague went dead.

Walter replaced the receiver upon its cradle. Time was running out. In order to reach Eva Kleist in time, young Teschler would have to abandon his uncle on his deathbed.

*   *   *

Bulkova Hospital, Prague

Ernst, Barron, and Max scurried down the hospital corridor into a large conference room commandeered by the SS as a command center for the emergency. Three SS officers stood and saluted. "Sir, a five-block square around the bomb site has been cordoned off for the search. We have over fifty soldiers scouring the area for the assassins."

"Increase the search party to one hundred soldiers. We can't let these assassins escape!" Ernst picked up the telephone receiver. Schellenberg's words echoed in his mind: *the possibility that Himmler ordered your uncle's death.* He started to dial.

The duty nurse approached. "Herr Teschler, Dr. Gebhardt has arrived. The doctors want to speak with you."

Ernst slammed his palm down on the desk, startling the nurse. "Tell both surgeons to operate immediately. Start the operation now or there will be hell to pay."

"Ja, ja," the young Czech woman stammered, shrinking away from Ernst's viselike gaze. She opened the door on the way out as three men entered.

SS officers entered with a Catholic priest in tow. "Sir, this is the senior priest from Saints Cyril and Methodius Cathedral. The assassins were seen near the church. We are questioning the locals about the fugitives."

The bald cleric had his dander up. "Who's in charge here?"

Ernst turned. "Excuse me, Father—"

"Father Petrek is my name. Officer, your Gestapo men barged into God's church. They made wild accusations and disturbed services."

An SS lieutenant said, "Major, we have witnesses who claim they saw the assassins run into an alley to the rear of the church and enter."

Ernst glanced at Max. "Father, has anyone claimed sanctuary in your church today?"

"All who enter His church are sinners before God. Officer, do you wish to claim sanctuary?"

Ernst calmly placed his hand upon the cleric's shoulder. "Do you really think there is any place in the Reich where one might be safe?"

The cleric stood nonplussed as Ernst pivoted toward Max. "Max, this search could take days. Get on the radio for more men. We must find them as soon as possible."

Max frowned. "Alive?"

Ernst pulled Max to the side and whispered, "We must speak to the Czechs *before* the Gestapo has them. Schellenberg thinks that Himmler may have planned it all. As long as my uncle is alive, these killers may try again."

Later that afternoon, Ernst and Max stood vigil in the surgical ward. Dr. Gebhardt and his team performed the surgery. SS guards were posted at all entrances and hallways of the hospital complex. Security was tight. When Himmler arrived, all hell would break loose. Many innocent people in Prague would soon die or be thrown into concentration camps.

Eventually, Dr. Gebhardt emerged, still wearing his surgical gown. "I've repaired the diaphragm, the punctured lung. Then I removed most of the bomb fragments. Despite the infection, I left his spleen intact. Heavy doses of sulfonamide will help, but I am concerned about peritonitis."

Chapter Thirty-Three

Bulkova Hospital, May 22, 1942

No one noticed an old musician struggle out of a taxi at the hospital entrance. He carried a trombone case. The Gestapo agents checked his expertly forged German papers and searched the case. Finding nothing suspicious, they waved him through the gate. Secured beneath old brass tubing under a false bottom was another lethal instrument. Disguised in a gray beard and dyed hair, Saul Avigur was cool, calm, and collected as he strolled into a hornet's nest of SS soldiers.

His mission was the backup plan. He would act only in the event his fellow assassins Gabčík and Kubiš failed at the Troja Bridge strike point. For months, the Israeli assassin had trained with a squad of Czech agents in Surrey, England, under the command of the British Special Operations Executive. Now he was committed. Reinhard Heydrich must die!

Saul faked a limp toward the emergency room doors. At seven o'clock that night, the hospital was nearly vacant. He sat next to a woman and her ill daughter. He played the doting grandfather for a few hours before the change of shifts. Then Saul overheard a guard.

"They are moving General Heydrich to Room 122 early in the morning, south wing."

Still disguised as an aging musician, Saul shuffled through the halls of the hospital toward the south wing. When he saw multiple guards in the corridor, he stopped short and ducked into the men's room. Perpendicular to the south wing, Saul cracked a window open. He spied a series of large lattice-paned windows bordering Heydrich's room. Across the alley, he spotted an apartment building, four stories tall. One of the apartment windows was wedged open for the spring breeze. The line of sight was perfect.

He limped back to the ER and spoke to a guard in broken German. "My daughter sick—are you doctor?" The guard shook his head and pushed Saul toward the waiting room. He retrieved his trombone case and walked out of the building. No guards checked persons leaving the premises. Once outside, he inspected the surrounding buildings and confirmed his strike point.

*   *   *

Early the next morning General Heydrich was moved to a private room, and a team of nurses again applied ice packs to relieve his raging fever. Ernst sat next to the bed barely noticing the doctors and nurses coming and going.

Dr. Gebhardt arrived. "I am afraid the infection is spreading. I've ordered morphine for the pain, Major."

"What are his chances?"

Dr. Gebhardt's expression was grim. "At best, two out of five. I am very sorry."

Looking down at Reinhard, Ernst thought back to 1938—his uncle's speech at the Bismarck Tavern. He remembered the glassy-eyed fervor of the crowd, the shouts of adoration and applause.

Max stepped in. "Ernst, your aunt is bringing the children here in about an hour. I'll be close by when you tell her the news."

At that moment, Ernst felt an overwhelming affection for his friend. "First, my father dies and now Uncle Reinhard. You're the only ones left, you and Barron." Ernst hugged Max.

The sound of troop carriers rumbling through the street outside drew Ernst's attention to the large lattice-paned window. Across the alley there was a brick building. A few stories up, he noticed a row of open windows. Then a sinking feeling twisted his stomach. *A perfect line of fire into this room!*

Adrenaline pumped as Ernst rushed back to the door. "Guards! Guards! I want a detail in here to move the general to another room. Schnell!"

As the SS guards leapt into action, Ernst commandeered some binoculars and manned his post at the windowsill. Panning the telephoto lenses, magnified images of dirt-streaked apartment windows filled the eyepiece. A flash of sunlight reflected something metallic. *Déjà vu!*

Ernst found himself staring into the front end of a telescopic sight perhaps thirty meters away, protruding from a third-floor window at a thirty-degree angle. In a blink, he identified an automatic rifle modified with a silencer.

"Take cover!" Ernst shouted, just as a shower of bullets shattered the windows, plowing into the plaster wall inches above Ernst's head. A web of glass fragments swept his face as he dove toward the foot of his uncle's bed. The collision propelled Reinhard's bed off to the side.

A squad of SS soldiers rushed to the window to shield Heydrich. A few soldiers fired out of the shattered window while others evacuated everyone from the room. A burning sensation stung his face and hand, and Ernst looked in a mirror. Small glass splinters were embedded in his face. Droplets of blood speckled his left cheek and neck as if he had been stung by a swarm of hornets.

"Max. Get some men and follow me. Schnell!"

*   *   *

Across the street, Saul squinted again through his scope. He could see blurred figures rushing Heydrich out of the hospital room. With a scowl, he lowered his weapon and rushed back to the kitchen. He quickly disassembled the rifle and placed its components inside the trombone case, next to the sprawled body of an elderly Czech woman.

Her gaping eyes confirmed the expression of horror, frozen at the moment he had entered her home and neatly snapped her neck. With no remorse, he retrieved an armband from his coat and draped it around her neck on his way out the door.

Just as the Haganah agent reached the rear exit of the apartment building, he heard muffled shouts and commands of the SS entering the front doors. He mounted a bicycle stashed in the alley. Still posing as the old man with gray shocks of hair and beard, Saul Avigur calmly pedaled his way through a back alley toward a busy marketplace. Confident that Heydrich was dead or dying, Saul contemplated his next target.

*   *   *

Armed with Schmeisser submachine guns and pistols, Ernst, Max, and their soldiers rushed up the front stairs of the apartment building. Deploying guards at each level, the squad finally reached the third-floor landing. Only two apartments faced the hospital. The front door to one was ajar. The other soldiers provided cover from across the hall while they entered the open room.

Guns primed, they rushed into the apartment and found the sniper's nest intact by the front window. Ernst and Max slowly moved into the kitchen and stopped. They stood over the dead woman on the floor.

"Ernst, now what?"

Ernst scrutinized the corpse and discovered the armband with a yellow star draped like a necklace over her neck. He shouted through the door, "Sergeant, secure all exits, then search every apartment from the top floor down. Schnell!"

As their men were deployed, Ernst inspected the woman more closely. "Her neck was broken between the third and fourth vertebrae."

He removed the yellow star. "Max, we are dealing with a professional here."

Max lowered his pistol. "We're wasting time. That's two attempts on General Heydrich's life in two days."

Ernst dabbed his bloody face with a handkerchief. "There is a team of assassins in Prague. And they are not finished." And the yellow star was their signature.

Max stared at Ernst as if he were a ghost. "Our plane is due to leave this afternoon. What about Eva?"

*   *   *

SS Headquarters, Berlin

Just before noon, an Enigma code operator handed Heinrich Himmler a telegram in his private office.

29 May 1942

TO: Reichsführer Himmler
FROM: Untersturmführer Max Schumann

Second   assassination   attempt   on Heydrich   was   not   successful.   General Heydrich's   condition   remains   extremely grave. Sturmbannführer Ernst Teschler received minor wounds while protecting Reichsprotektor   Heydrich.   Awaiting further orders.

Heinrich read the words twice, his stomach twisting into a knot. If Neame did not attack Heydrich, then who did? If Heydrich was first, who would be next?

These questions swirled in his mind as he issued a full security alert through all SS networks. "Reichmann, take a message."

```
TO: Sturmbannführer Teschler
FROM: Reichsführer Himmler

Will   arrive   Prague   AM—May   30.   Will
discuss  Reich  security  measures  and  the
"package"  you  promised.  Confirm  receipt
of this transmittal.
```

A few hours later, Heinrich's train departed Berlin station. He placed a telephone call to the Führer. Hitler ranted at the top of his lungs. "If Heydrich dies, one hundred thousand Reichsmarks will be offered for the arrest of his assassins! In reprisal, I want a thousand Czechs arrested. No, make that ten thousand Czechs!"

Heinrich's shadow shrunk as Hitler's voice of scorn boomed over the telephone. "Mein Führer, Heydrich is still alive, but there is infection. Bomb fragments, they tell me."

"This is a plot hatched by the Jews. Somehow they must have learned of Heydrich's role in the Final Solution. We shall make the vermin pay for this!" Hitler launched into another tirade.

Exhausted, Heinrich finally interrupted. "Mein Führer, I have an inspiration. Let us raze a small Czech town to the ground—along with every adult male. Every Czech citizen shall come to know the penalty for resisting the iron will of the Reich."

"Annihilate a whole village? Hmm, now that has real possibilities."

Hours later, with his private train en route to Prague, Heinrich telephoned his agents at the Bulkova Hospital. He authorized "appropriate treatment" for Heydrich at first opportunity. Code for a stealth termination.

One false move and he could be hung for high treason. Killing enough Czech "traitors" would cloak his participation.

When his train arrived in Prague, his entourage rushed to the hospital. "Reichmann, call Berlin. Divert more Waffen-SS troops here immediately. The Czechs will regret their part in this plot against the Reich."

"Jawohl, mein herr."

Outside Heydrich's room, Heinrich spoke to Dr. Gebhardt. "What is his condition?"

"The infection has already begun to spread—"

"Not Heydrich, I mean Teschler."

"Oh, he was treated for minor flesh wounds, then released."

A junior SS officer interrupted. "My men took the major and Lieutenant Schumann to the airport."

Heinrich narrowed his eyes. "Lieutenant, fetch his flight plan for me, immediately."

Reichmann whispered, "But, sir, Teschler knew you were coming to see him."

"Don't worry, Reichmann. Major Teschler is operating under sealed orders."

Chapter Thirty-Four

Zurich, May 30, 1942

D ressed in business suits, Ernst and Max climbed the marble stairway up to the second floor of the Zurich branch of the International Bank of Switzerland. Ernst approached the reception desk of the private banking department. "Guten Tag. My name is Herr Löeb. I called earlier about opening a new safe-deposit box and a gold bullion account."

"Certainly, sir." The attendant showed them to a small private office. "You may complete the necessary forms here, then bring them back to me." The banker returned to her duties.

Ernst lit a cigarette. "Schellenberg's men have discovered Eva's location—Wewelsburg Castle. He's trading Eva for a percentage of the gold."

"What are we going to put in the safe-deposit box?"

"Nothing. The Zurich bank is a decoy."

Max stared at Ernst. "I know you have a plan in all this, but what is it?"

"We can't trust Himmler. If I give him his precious Spear, then Eva and I become expendable."

"So . . . you're going to give Himmler a key to an empty box?"

"It will buy us one maybe two extra days while he sends his people on a wild-goose chase to Switzerland." He slid a form across the desk. "Here, sign."

"Ernst, how will we escape? Himmler will set loose the whole SS Corps after us once he finds out he's been duped."

"That's where Schellenberg comes into the picture. He's agreed to provide safe passage for Eva in return for access to one of our gold accounts in Zurich."

"What about the Melmer accounts in Bern?"

"I'm transferring just enough gold to Zurich to whet his appetite."

The lady banker returned and placed an envelope in Ernst's hand. "Two keys for Box 3333 as you requested, Herr Löeb."

He handed her the signed forms. "Danke." On the way out of the bank, Ernst placed one of the deposit-box keys in Max's hand.

"Wealth, power, and glory. That's why I joined the SS. We're not going to come out of this alive, are we?"

Ernst felt the warm bond of their friendship. "You've been a good friend all my life. Thank you for helping me rescue Eva."

They gave each other a long bear hug. Then the two childhood friends stepped through the revolving glass doors into the night lights of Zurich.

*   *   *

Prague, June 1942

A few days later, Reinhard was wheeled on a gurney into the X-ray room. Since no one was allowed inside except the patient and the technician, the soldiers stood guard outside in the hallway. Although medicated, Reinhard would not lie still, so the technician restrained his arms and legs. With the room cleared and the drugs taking effect, the technician took the X-rays, then exited the room to develop the films.

He began to hallucinate. Through a hazy fog, Reinhard stared at the numbered tattoo branded on his arm. He looked into a broken mirror mounted on a concrete wall. His perfectly coiffed blond hair had been shaved. He felt his head swirl, and he found himself in the concrete shower block pushing against the door.

Through the small, round glass window, he saw his Nazi guards. "You filthy Juden swine! You smell of horse dung. Be good little Jews and take a shower. . . ."

The sound of Zyklon-B tablets being dropped from above into the disbursement domes was thunderous. Inhaling the foul stench, Reinhard's eyes began to burn and mucus filled his lungs. Heaving for breath, he realized that he stood among hundreds of naked bodies screaming and heaving for death. He must be dreaming. All that he had to do was wake up and all would be well.

A dark stranger appeared among the dead and dying. In the reflection of the creature's black eyes, Reinhard could see his own emaciated body, bone on bone rippled through ninety pounds of flesh. "Herr Heydrich, I do this in the name of all the murdered Jews of Europe. There will be no mercy for your soul."

Reinhard panicked and his eyes bulged as he lifted his head off the gurney. With each gasp, he sucked what felt like sheaths of plastic into his nostrils. The stench of human decay was hauntingly sterile.

Within seconds, he felt as if a sheet of iron had compressed his chest. To and fro, he twisted against his restraints but to no avail. His lungs heaved. Screaming for breath, he wrenched his head side to side, trying desperately to suck in life.

With one last burst of energy, Reinhard raised his chest up off the metal slab. For a moment, his body froze in the grip of the icy tongs of death, then slumped down on the cold metal frame—lifeless.

In a flash, there was the Light. From midair, Reinhard looked down at the corpse upon the X-ray table. His physical pain intensified as the Light passed over him. Then in the mouth of a great, dark chasm, he saw the gaunt, hollow faces of countless Jewish souls sent to their deaths by his order.

And from below, the dark minions of hell arose, their red eyes ablaze with anticipation. They began to chomp upon his feet, shredding bone from sinew and flesh. His screams crescendoed as their razor-sharp teeth slashed upward and severed his twisted torso like a great white shark in a feeding frenzy. In life, he had never experienced or imagined such agony. Then shredded pieces of Reinhard's soul drifted down into the depths of hell.

*   *   *

The SS security officer on duty immediately sealed the hospital corridor and suppressed the news—a total blackout. Word of Heydrich's death reached Reichsführer Himmler en route to Berlin on his private train.

Himmler calmly placed a call to the SS chief in Prague. "Secure Heydrich's body with all evidence of foul play. Apprehend the two Czech assassins. Then after the state funeral for General Heydrich in Berlin, prepare our SS troops for action. You are familiar with the Czech village of Lidice?"

"Yes, Herr Reichsführer. It is about seventeen kilometers from Prague."

"In retribution for the murder of Reinhard Heydrich, the Czech people will witness the utter destruction of all buildings contained within the city limits and the execution of all men over the age of sixteen. All women and children will be sent to concentration camps. I want pictures of every gruesome detail published nationally in Czech newspapers."

"Sir, you want evidence of a massacre published?"

"It will teach the Czech people that Germans are the master race. These creatures are *untermenschen*—subhuman. Like animals, they need to be disciplined. Carry out your orders!"

*   *   *

Westphalia, Germany, June 4, 1942

The Junker JU-52 cut through a pillow of clouds, heading north just over Frankfurt toward Paderborn. As the late afternoon sun penetrated the dense haze in scattered shafts of light, Ernst viewed a radiant rainbow of colors cascade across the horizon. Above the engine noise, the copilot stepped out of the cockpit and shouted, "Paderborn will be another thirty to forty-five minutes."

Barron lay panting by Ernst's feet. When the plane hit an air pocket and dropped abruptly, the dog yelped and buried his muzzle in Ernst's lap.

Schellenberg laughed from the seat across the aisle. "Your Doberman does not like heights, eh, Teschler?"

"Appearances can be deceiving, Colonel." Ernst snapped his fingers. Barron arched up face-to-face with Schellenberg and bared his fangs with a guttural growl.

Schellenberg's complexion turned ashen. "I'll keep that in mind."

With Ernst's whistle, Barron retreated and sat by his master, lightly panting.

"Our people in London have confirmed, British intelligence ordered your uncle's assassination. Operation Anthropoid. They used a Czech assassination team."

"What about Himmler?"

"My man on Himmler's Berlin staff said Fräulein Kleist is being held in the south tower on the third floor of Wewelsburg Castle. I will keep Himmler busy while you and Schumann tend to Neame."

"Schellenberg, you seem to have few loyalties."

"This venture is a simple business proposition. You get the woman, and I get the gold."

"Himmler would be furious if he finds out you now have access to one of his Melmer accounts in Zurich."

"But he won't find out, will he, Teschler?"

At that moment Schellenberg's aide, Lieutenant Steiner, emerged from the cockpit and handed Ernst an Enigma cipher sheet, decoded. Ernst read the words aloud.

TO: SS Major Teschler

FROM: Dr. Gebhardt, Bulkova Hospital-Prague.

Regret to inform you, General Heydrich died this AM from complications due to septicemia & infection of the spleen.

Office of the Reichsführer will handle transport of the body to Berlin.

Our condolences to your family.

Ernst felt the air rush out of his lungs.

"My sympathies for your loss," Schellenberg said.

Uncle Reinhard was both his mentor and his enemy. To Heydrich, people were mere pawns in a chess game. Betrayed, Ernst looked fondly upon Barron. They shared a mutual trust.

Max placed his hand on Ernst's shoulder. "Himmler will make the Czechs pay dearly for his death."

"With innocent blood to be sure, Max." Ernst nursed the anger swelling inside him. Ernst's war was about to begin, and his first target: Major Alfred Neame.

Chapter Thirty-Five

Wewelsburg Castle

The full moon illuminated the cloudless night sky as Schellenberg's SS command car approached the castle complex. Its cold light washed the stark ramparts above, silhouetting the black-uniformed SS sentries. Their faces glowed, like ghosts floating above the walls. They stood rigid as their watchful eyes followed the intense beams of roving searchlights, strategically perched atop three corner towers.

Crossing a stone bridge, Ernst and his entourage arrived in the main courtyard just before 8:00 p.m. After Lieutenant Steiner backed the Mercedes into one of three open garages and subtly unlatched the trunk lid, he followed Schellenberg to the main entrance of the castle. Meanwhile, Ernst and Max crept out of the trunk compartment and made their way to a side entrance through the servants' quarters.

Knowing that Schellenberg and Steiner would be escorted through the library, Ernst and Max quietly made their way to the second floor. They dodged a few guards, then wove their way through a long vacant hallway to the south tower. Ernst whispered, "Max, stay here."

Alone, Ernst walked farther down the hall and heard two SS guards talking. He doubled back into an open parlor and pushed a standing bronze lamp over. Its glass globe smashed into crystal splinters across the floor. When the two guards rushed through the open arch, Ernst ducked around them, through the main corridor, and up the stone steps undetected.

At the top of the stairs, Ernst tried the large wooden door. It squeaked open, revealing a large sitting room, illuminated only by a fire blazing in the stone hearth. Near the hearth were three tall-back easy chairs. Ernst quietly drew his pistol from his holster.

"So nice of you to join me, Major Teschler." The familiar raspy voice echoed through the room as fire-lit shadows danced upon the walls. Ernst circled around the high-back chairs and discovered Weisthor manipulating tarot cards on a coffee table. "Through the Seeker's Portal, I knew you would come. Don't worry, we are alone."

"Those silver rings of yours—the secrets they must tell. Where do they say I can find Fräulein Kleist?"

Weisthor smiled as he presented a card, a picture of a medieval buffoon. "You abandoned your uncle upon his deathbed, just to travel here for the woman? Love will be your downfall, Teschler. But no matter. You have the Spear of Longinus. Give it to me and I will tell you where to find the woman."

"Where is she?"

"Major Neame has her safe and sound nearby. First, show me the Spear!"

Ernst removed the metal necklace with the bank deposit-box key and held it up. Weisthor leaned forward, his eyes magnified by his spectacles. With an open palm, the occult priest cooed, "Show me what you have, Herr Teschler."

Ernst dropped the bronze key into his nemesis's flabby hand. Weisthor perused both sides of the key with growing irritation. "The box number has been filed off!"

"No one sees the Spear of Destiny until I see Fräulein Kleist alive!"

The occult priest picked up a tarot card. "The cards say you tell the truth, my boy." Weisthor's puffy red eyes shimmered in the firelight. "The Spear that pierced the side of Christ so long ago. It must have been a glorious sight."

"And you shall be given the Spear's location and box number when I have Fräulein Kleist."

"You will find the woman and Major Neame quartered in the castle stables about one kilometer from here, off the main road to Paderborn. Himmler has men stationed above in the hayloft at all times. If you succeed in obtaining the woman, leave no witnesses."

Suddenly, it all became so obvious to Ernst. "You plan to keep the Spear for yourself?"

"Quid pro quo. If you win the contest, then I will ensure your seat within the inner circle. Time is of the essence, Major. Go quickly and claim your prize."

*   *   *

Max quietly drove Ernst in Schellenberg's command car to the Wewelsburg stables. In the passenger seat, Ernst could see that the renovated two-story structure was at least thirty meters long with an ornate Tudor façade.

"Max, expect two or three men in the loft, maybe more."

"How come I never get the woman?" Max flashed a roguish grin as he slipped a loaded magazine into the heel of his silenced Walther. "I'll use the Schmeisser only if things get out of hand." Max retrieved a metal clicker. "Two clicks—danger. Three clicks—clear." He climbed the wooden ladder secured to the exterior wall.

When Max entered near the second-floor hay-load pulley, Ernst made his way through the side entrance. A solitary lamp lit up the center of the interior corral. He lowered his head and hugged the latticed horse stalls. Two horses nearby whinnied at his arrival.

Ernst looked up in the loft and could see the silhouettes of two guards, perhaps five meters apart. The muffled sound of Max's pistol silenced one guard as he slumped to the floor. Stirred, the second guard moved into the shadows of the loft to investigate. Moments later, a second *cough* silenced him. Max's three clicks signaled to him.

With his Walther primed, Ernst moved toward the horsemen's quarters. A sliver of light invaded the darkness from beneath the closed door. He edged closer and slowly unlocked the bolt. The door squeaked open. A lit kerosene lamp revealed Eva dozing on the lower mattress of a bunk bed. With growing excitement, he stepped across the wood floor and touched her tousled blonde hair. "Eva."

She roused slowly. "Ernst?" Then she bolted out of the bed into his arms. "Oh, Ernst!" As their lips found each other, he imagined themselves somewhere far away, safe from the madness of this place.

"Good evening, Teschler." Alfred Neame's insidious voice penetrated his momentary fantasy. "I knew you would come for the woman." Ernst could see the ebb and glow of Neame's cigarette as he entered the room. He held a Luger pointed at Ernst. "Tell Schumann to come down from the loft or Fräulein Kleist dies."

"Max! Come on down. Neame has a pistol trained on Eva."

Max's pistol landed on the packed clay just outside the bunk room. With his pistol Neame waved both Ernst and Eva out into the cavernous barn. "Now, Teschler, you will show Fräulein Kleist your skill and courage."

As Max descended the loft steps, Ernst gauged the distance from the ladder to Neame. "I'm glad you could join the party."

"It seems like I'm always bailing you out of trouble, Ernst."

"Not this time, Schumann." Neame pointed his pistol at Max. In a flash, Ernst drove a sweeping roundhouse kick into the back of Neame's right calf, launching him off his feet. Tumbling backward, Neame landed on his butt, discharging his pistol into the ceiling two stories above.

When Neame moved, Ernst smashed the heel of his palm into the gunman's elbow. In two quick Savate moves, Ernst disarmed Neame. Breathing hard, Neame leaned back on his elbows, looking up at his protégé.

"So, the mighty Ernst Teschler tries to save his Jew hussy."

In a rage, Ernst threw a roundhouse punch, but his teacher artfully blocked the blow.

"Neame, you were always quick with your fists and your lies." Ernst's voice echoed across the wooden floor as he stepped around for position. "The pupil will now teach the teacher a lesson—permanently."

"Teschler, do you have any idea how many men this hussy has seduced? I should know."

Eva's cheeks flushed.

"Silence!" Ernst thundered. He slowly drew his truncheon from his leather belt.

"We are the master race, and you chose a Jewess?" Neame slowly rose to his feet. "Your uncle knew of her deceit from the beginning and played her just like his beloved violin."

With a guttural scream, Ernst smashed his lead-filled shaft through a kerosene lamp slung from a nearby post, glass shards exploding in all directions.

Neame's eyes narrowed. "Both your uncle and Himmler have played you like a puppet from the very beginning. It was Heydrich who condemned your sweet Eva to death. Twice now I almost killed you—in the Glade of Armistice and the opera house last year. Only luck has kept you alive until tonight." Neame unsheathed his SS knife with his left hand.

Ernst set his jaw. Slowly circling his opponent, he taunted Neame with the tip of his truncheon.

"So, Teschler, did I tell you how your father died? At your uncle's orders, I brutalized him in the alley behind the Bismarck." Neame retrieved a pocket watch from his coat, popped open its lid, and lobbed it on the ground.

Ernst saw his picture in his father's gold watch.

"A trophy I took for the first Teschler I tortured and killed. Your father was a coward, but you are SS. So I will make your death quick and easy!" Neame circled sideways until he and Ernst were within striking distance. "As the inevitable victor, I'll take pleasure with your woman, then torture her slowly."

The SS assassin moved his free hand in rapid decoy movements, then whipped the blade in two fast swipes. The blade nicked Ernst's arm, the pain searing into flesh.

"Perhaps you'll still be alive when I slit Eva's throat."

Ernst narrowed his stance. As Neame jabbed the blade toward his throat, Ernst rotated and arched his foot into the air, clipping his opponent on the elbow. Neame's knife flew into an open horse stall.

Eyeing his pistol on the dirt floor, Neame lunged. Ernst countered, stomping on the back of Neame's calf. His nemesis cried out in agony.

"Tell me, Neame. What did my father say when you gutted him like a pig?"

Neame's eyes scoured the room for a weapon.

"Did he plead for his life?"

As Neame struggled to stand on his good leg, Ernst cocked his truncheon and swung it full force through the air. The sound of Neame's kneecap splintering could be heard by all. With a guttural scream, Neame slammed back into the wall and shuddered.

"You know, I could have killed you in Paris, but you were lucky." Pain drove tears from Neame's eyes.

Ernst shook his head. "Not luck, Neame. I had my guardian angel."

At that moment, Max stepped forward and produced his Schmeisser submachine gun. "Don't take any chances, Ernst. Just finish this!"

Neame winced as he gingerly stroked his mangled leg. "Well, Teschler, if you believe in God, then I'll see you in hell." Ernst's nemesis grinned as he drew a small-caliber pistol from inside his jackboot.

Ernst's eyes flared as he thrust his truncheon upward to deflect the gun barrel. With his right hand, he drew his dagger and rammed the blade up underneath Neame's jaw and through his tongue imbedding the tip into Neame's palate. Crimson red spurted over the hilt of the blade onto Ernst's hand.

The assassin flexed onto the balls of his feet in an attempt to release the blade. In shock, Neame gagged, gasping for breath to the very last. The man who taught Ernst the art of killing drowned in his own blood.

Ernst relaxed his grip on the knife, and Neame's body fell to the floor in a mangled heap.

Eva leaned against a stall, trembling, her eyes wide open. Ernst slumped against the stall next to her, utterly exhausted. Eva stared at the skewered head of Alfred Neame, his face contorted by death. She closed her eyes, then collapsed into Ernst's arms. "Thank God you are alive!"

"Max, you could have helped me," Ernst quipped.

"What, and miss the excitement? You just killed Alfred Neame. What's Schellenberg going to say?"

"That's what I would like to know."

In unison, Ernst and Max turned around and faced Schellenberg standing at the entrance to the stable. Beside him, Lieutenant Steiner leveled a MP40 Schmeisser at the group.

Schellenberg's eyes perused the scene, then he stooped to inspect the corpse. He winced at the mangled flesh that once was Neame's face. "A bit melodramatic aren't we, Teschler?" He searched through Neame's pockets. He retrieved some folded papers, thrust them unread into his pocket, and then whispered something to Steiner. The officer secured his weapon and walked out of the barn, down the stone path toward a cluster of automobiles.

Ernst was utterly confused. "Sir?"

"My report will show that Eva Kleist was murdered by Major Neame and that you killed Neame in a duel of honor. Major, do you have anything to add to my report?"

"Sir, why are you so . . . generous?"

Schellenberg laughed. "Generous? Think of it this way, Teschler. You are now further in my debt."

Lieutenant Steiner crossed the threshold of the barn with a half-naked corpse of a soldier draped over his shoulder. Steiner tottered slightly as he abruptly dropped it next to Neame. Schellenberg retrieved trousers and a shirt from his satchel, then offered them to Eva. "Fräulein, I will need your dress—quickly. We must make your death look convincing."

While Eva changed clothes in a stall, Ernst wrapped up Neame's bloody knife in a towel.

Schellenberg glanced at his watch. "We have little time. Steiner, release all the horses, then torch this place to the ground."

Steiner carefully positioned the two corpses and doused them with gasoline as everyone else evacuated the building. Outside, Schellenberg pulled Teschler aside. "And now, Teschler, for your part of the bargain."

Ernst handed his superior an envelope. "Here are the account number and pass code for the gold account at the International Bank of Switzerland-Zurich. It is unknown to both the Reichsbank and Himmler. The bank has your photograph and is expecting you to provide your signature. You will not want to be late."

"You know, Himmler will try to kill you."

Ernst raised an eyebrow. "In the SS, that's an occupational hazard."

Schellenberg and Steiner slipped into the front seat of the lead sedan. "If you survive, in three days I'll meet you and Fräulein Kleist on the northern coast near Stettin."

Ernst walked back to the second automobile. He stole a moment alone with Eva as he stroked her silken blonde hair. "Eva, I almost lost you. I could not live with that."

She lowered her head. "All of my lies, my deceit. How can you tolerate the sight of me?"

Ernst embraced her, drawing in the fragrance of his life. "Perhaps we can escape this nightmare and find a life together."

"You proved something to me today. You do love me."

Ernst took her hand. "Max will take you to Dr. Bonhoeffer. I will meet all of you soon—up north. Together, we'll go to England."

She shook her head. "Tell me the truth, Ernst. Will I ever see you again?"

From a distance the stable was rocked by a loud explosion. They held one another close. Ernst and Eva watched fire spew out of the windows—their lives as they had known them went up in flames. The two lovers melded their lips together, then parted.

Max cleared his throat. "Ah, Ernst. What do we do about Himmler?"

"I'm going back to face him and Weisthor alone. It will buy time for you and Eva to escape."

"But that's suicide!"

"Not if you hold the trump card."

Steiner's car engine roared to life. Ernst passionately kissed Eva once more, then released her to his best friend. Schellenberg would escort Max and Eva in the lead vehicle on the way to the airfield while Ernst faced his darkest enemy.

He turned the key to the Mercedes and revved the engine as his mind raced ahead. Imagining the peevish scowl of Heinrich Himmler, each stroke of the powerful engine stoked his anger all the more.

The two sedans passed through the stable gates. As Steiner turned toward the airfield, Eva waved at Ernst through the rear window. Tears threatened to overwhelm him, and with an endearing smile he waved goodbye.

In the opposite direction, the solid hum of his Mercedes's engine grew louder as Ernst approached the daunting ramparts of Wewelsburg Castle. The three gothic stone towers were silhouetted in the moonlight.

Only a fool would dare go back into the lion's den twice in one night.

Chapter Thirty-Six

Wewelsburg Castle, the SS Occult Center

T he full moon gleamed brilliantly in the night sky. Ernst drove the Mercedes across the stone bridge and through the main gate of the castle. Following protocol, the guards at the entrance challenged the unannounced caller.

"Tell the Reichsführer that Major Teschler is here to see him again on urgent business."

Escorted high up the east tower to Himmler's personal quarters, Ernst found the head of the SS seated at his desk. Himmler lowered his pen. "Well, well, Major Teschler. Have you brought me the authentic Spear of Destiny?"

"No, sir, I have brought you something else for your collection— Neame's SS dagger." Ernst set the blood-splattered blade on Himmler's sheaf of papers. "He will not have need of it."

Himmler's eyes were glued to the fresh blood soaking into the letter he had just signed. "I would have liked to have witnessed such a duel. And what was the fate of Fräulein Kleist?"

"There was an explosion and fire in the stables. You will find the charred remains of both inside. Your horses were loosed in the fields."

"How thoughtful of you." Himmler stood at his window and gazed at the distant flames.

"Fräulein Kleist was a necessary sacrifice for the Reich. If I am to rise in your ranks, she would have been a liability."

Himmler turned and stared at Ernst. "Quite so."

Ernst sensed the gears of this madman's mind turning, weighing his choices.

"Teschler, I have been a patient man. Show me the true Spear of Longinus."

Ernst stared at the blood pooled by the dagger. The bitter taste of deceit swelled in his mouth. Clenching his teeth, he so wanted to impale the coward who stood before him. "Sir, you have never told me why the Spear is so important to you. Just what is its value?"

"I demand that you escort me to the Spear immediately!"

"Sir, I'm afraid that won't be possible. The spearhead and Neame's private diary will remain in my safekeeping."

Astonishment swept over the Reichsführer's face. "Neame kept a diary?" He wiped his brow with a handkerchief.

"Think of it as my new lease on life. If I thrive under your command, then Hitler will never know you plotted the Spear's theft and his death."

Himmler's eyes burned with anger. "All of my problems evaporate if you disappear, Major."

"An uncontrolled chain reaction occurs at my death. Agents inside Germany and outside our borders have instructions. If I do not check in on schedule, they transmit criminal evidence about you to the highest authority. They also will transfer over twenty million in gold in your name as enemy of the state. The evidence will be sufficient to convict you of high treason."

Color draining from his face, Himmler stepped over to his credenza. "And if you live and serve the SS in your current role?"

"We both shall live to see a German victory."

With a slight tremor, Himmler poured two glasses of Rhine wine and offered one to Ernst. "In honor of your initiation into the German Order of New Templars, Herr Teschler."

Ernst clicked his heels. "I am greatly honored, Herr Reichsführer!"

"As you should be. King Heinrich the First is mounting the German forces for a new initiative to the east." Himmler walked across the room to the massive portrait of the historic monarch. "We shall be victorious, and I shall reign alone at last."

Ernst raised a skeptical eyebrow as he placed the glass untouched upon the desk.

"You know, Teschler. Weisthor revealed your destiny to me. Your rise to glory is your destiny—a gift confirmed by the Odic forces. With all due respect to your uncle, Heydrich never exhibited the kind of belief I demand from those in the inner circle. I hope to see much more 'spirit' in you."

"My honor is loyalty." Ernst had learned to loathe that pledge.

Himmler lifted his glass. "To our destinies, Teschler. The Spear of Longinus shall be *our* true power and glory!"

*   *   *

The next day the Order of New Templars was convened at Wewelsburg Castle. The SS chieftains sat casually around the massive oak table in the great hall. Engraved in silver upon Heydrich's former chair was a new moniker: The Infidel. Ernst Teschler shifted uncomfortably in his uncle's chair.

Himmler picked up his goblet. "Let us toast our departed comrade, Obergruppenführer Reinhard Heydrich!" Everyone at the table stood and lifted their glasses toward the cremains in the sculpted pewter urn at the center of the table. "To the grandmaster of espionage, to the architect of the Final Solution, to a most noble example of the Aryan race, we salute you!" Everyone raised their glasses in unison. "The Fatherland shall prevail! Sieg heil!"

Weisthor stepped forward. "We shall now commit the soul of our departed colleague."

With anticipation in their eyes, the column of Templar Knights walked through the concealed passageway behind the hearth and down the stone steps into the Well of Souls.

Ernst felt the arched stone walls hover over him. Below, firelight emanated from the ceremonial pit at the center, highlighting the twelve pedestals evenly spaced around the chamber's perimeter. The bright rays of blue moonlight streamed through three large windows cut high in the dome. Embossed at the pinnacle of the arched ceiling, the huge stone swastika appeared to pulsate. Ernst felt like he had entered a twilight dimension, another world.

As the Templar Knights circled the ceremonial pit, their shadows danced upon the walls behind them. The last knight to enter carried the urn to the center of the chamber. Himmler recited, "Now we commit our departed colleague to the eternal light."

Then the knight carried the urn out of the circle and carefully placed it upon one of the twelve stone pedestals.

"And now, we shall celebrate the Unholy Eucharist," Himmler said.

Weisthor emerged from the shadows and presented an ornate silver tray. Ernst's eyes were glued to the black shroud that cloaked an object beneath. Weisthor's voice deepened. "The Order of Templar Knights gathers tonight to celebrate the life of Reinhard Heydrich, his mystical name to our illumined order was Thor. His life began and ended in the realm of our master, the Dark Lord of the Golden Light." With a flourish, Weisthor removed the black shroud.

Ernst gasped—for staring back at him, wide-eyed and stoic, was the severed head of Uncle Reinhard. As Weisthor stroked the blond hair of the "Aryan specimen," Ernst could sense something evil invade their presence.

Himmler lifted his right hand. "Who now commits our brother to the eternal flame?"

Weisthor held both palms together as if to pray. "The Knights of the Order of New Templars commit the flesh and blood of our brother to the flame so we of pure blood may live unto eternal glory."

The pit beneath them exploded into a column of red and orange flames, engulfing the skull and its platform. Ernst and the knights recoiled, totally mesmerized by the column of dazzling colors. The flame melted the flesh, leaving only the skull intact. Ernst's heart pounded in abject terror.

Beads of perspiration glistened upon Himmler's brow. "And who has been chosen to replace our brother Thor?"

Stepping behind Ernst, Weisthor placed his hand on Ernst's right shoulder. "His name is Ernst Teschler. His blood is Nordic-pure from the seventh generation."

Himmler stepped behind Ernst's left shoulder. "Then what shall be his princely name?"

"He shall be called The Infidel, 'the unbeliever'!"

Despite the hot smoke that permeated the room, Ernst's whole body was goosefleshed with chills. *It's all a lie! I do believe but not in your god!*

He heard the voice of the Holy. It was the God of Abraham, Isaac, and Jacob. In an instant the Holy Spirit intervened, and Ernst's whole life flashed before him. Then he saw the face of the true Messiah, Yeshua. In His hands was the power to heal. And He touched the bowed head of Ernst Teschler.

At that moment something went horribly wrong in the Well of Souls. A hissing sound erupted from the pit as if water suddenly poured upon the fire. Startled, Himmler darted his gaze wildly about. The hellish pit now bellowed forth steam—angry, hissing steam as if the fires of death collided with the waters of life.

The knights staggered away from the fire and smoke as Himmler shouted, "Weisthor, tell me what is happening!"

Weisthor lifted his hands, mumbling a strange language.

Something inside Ernst compelled him to break out of the circle. He vaulted the spiral steps, two at a time, until he emerged into the dining hall.

*   *   *

While Weisthor ranted in a demonic tongue, from beneath the pit a groaning shudder emerged, then rock shifted. As the stone floor and walls began to rumble, this once brave and noble band of knights clawed at one another to be first up the stairs. Weisthor and Himmler rushed to the landing above and watched the fire pit below erupt, spewing out undulating shards of reddish light.

Himmler's terror transformed into utter fury. "Weisthor!"

Halfway up the steps, Weisthor wheezed out of breath. "It is young Teschler. The spirits have rejected him! We must expel him from the castle immediately or these stone walls might collapse upon us."

Himmler raced up the stairs and through the castle corridors, shouting at the guards, "Where is Teschler? Find *The Infidel*!"

An SS officer bellowed down the hall, "Teschler's gone, mein herr!"

"Gone." Himmler's voice was drowned out by the supernatural rumblings from below. Then there was a haunting silence. As if the living stones of Wewelsburg had finally been appeased.

Weisthor peered out the large latticed window. "I have never seen such a clash of celestial forces in my life. It was magnificent."

"Magnificent? *Igitt!* We could have been killed!" Himmler paced back and forth before his mystical portrait of King Heinrich.

A momentary silence separated the two as the SS chieftains panted to catch their breath. Weisthor secretly fingered the Swiss box key in his pocket Teschler had given him.

"The Well of Souls and the chambers on the first floor sustained no damage. Though you and I would swear that this ancient fortress was being shaken to the core. It is as if the cataclysm never happened. But who or what protected Teschler?" Then a knowing look dawned upon Himmler's face. "Of course, the Spear of Longinus."

Weisthor stared nonplussed at his protégé.

A righteous anger etched into Himmler's features. "I swear to you, I will retrieve the Spear and then hunt Teschler down and kill him!"

Chapter Thirty-Seven

Near the Northern Coast of Germany, June 1942

D ietrich Bonhoeffer and Friedrich Perels sat on the back porch of the main house on the Patzig estate as they discussed affairs of the Confessing Church. Dietrich admired the gardens that flourished around a large pond. "We have beaten the odds, my friend. We both should be in a Nazi camp by now. The Nazis may run the German government, but God is in control."

Friedrich nodded. "You are a man on mission under sealed orders. God seems to show up just in time."

Dietrich smelled the fragrance of the flowers in full bloom. His heart was at peace despite the perils of the day. "The providence of God has spared us for a reason. I made the right choice to return to Germany. I am at peace knowing I am in God's will."

"Let's go over Major Teschler's plan." Friedrich opened a map of Stettin and pointed to the harbor. "The *SS Hansa* is a forty-year-old passenger ship of Swedish registry. It has been moored in Stettin Harbor a few days for repairs and will soon sail for Copenhagen. It is an old ship with dilapidated staterooms, but it's an ideal vessel to transport Eva Kleist to a neutral port, then on to England."

"So we embark tomorrow night?" Dietrich asked.

"I will pick up the tickets later today, then drop them off at the front desk of the Gruenwald Inn. Rooms have been reserved at the rear of the property in my name."

Dietrich pointed to the road from the harbor to the Gruenwald Inn. "Fräulein Kleist and I will drive to the inn and go to Room 28 after dark this evening. Ernst will rendezvous at the inn tomorrow after 6:00 p.m. Then we will drive to the docks."

"The captain assures me this ship sails at 10:00 p.m. sharp. Have you heard any more from Teschler?"

"He is to arrive in Stettin late tomorrow." Dietrich frowned. "Stettin is a small town. His rendezvous with Eva will be dangerous."

Friedrich stroked his chin. "Are you sure you want to risk your life for these people?"

"Everyone in Nazi Germany is at risk. Just telephone my room at the inn when you're ready to take on passengers."

*   *   *

Upon entering the house, Dietrich ran into Countess Ruth in the grand hall across from the parlor. "Good morning, Countess. The gardens are magnificent today." From the corner of his eye, he noticed Maria in the alcove checking her makeup.

Having just pinched her cheeks, the young woman turned from the mirror. "Hello, Dietrich. I thought you had left for the city."

"I was enjoying a chat with Friedrich."

The countess cast a winning smile at him. "I hope you and your friend can spend a few weeks with the family. We so enjoy your company, don't we, Maria?"

"Thank you for your hospitality. We will be leaving shortly, but I look forward to our next visit. Have either of you seen Fräulein Kleist?"

Maria's expression sank, and her cheeks flushed at the sound of Eva's name.

The countess led the trio into the parlor. "You have made the arrangements for Eva then?"

Dietrich walked on eggshells. Any slip of the tongue could endanger his friends. "There has been some progress."

Maria compressed her lips. "Dietrich Bonhoeffer, where are you going with Fräulein Kleist?"

The countess winced. "Show some manners, my dear. Our pastor has official business with her."

"Well, I have things to do." With a pout, Maria scurried out of the room.

In the parlor, the countess and Dietrich eased into two cherrywood rocking chairs. "I am sorry for endangering you, Countess."

"The Nazis wouldn't dare touch me. They would have a hard time dealing with an elderly aristocrat like me."

He nodded. "To be sure."

"About Fräulein Kleist, how long will our guest be staying?"

"We leave Patzig late this afternoon."

"Oh my, today! Maria will be . . . quite upset."

"Once we get Fräulein Kleist out of Germany, we will stay with . . . well, the fewer details you and the family know, the better."

"I understand. Will you come back to Patzig, Dietrich? It's a safe haven, and let's be honest. You know Maria has feelings for you. She is so very young and fragile."

"The feelings are mutual. I just wish her mother thought better of me."

"She is just an old woman who is dreadfully afraid of the Nazis invading our peaceful world."

Dietrich lifted an eyebrow. "If your daughter is old, then that makes you . . ."

The countess laughed. "The ancient of days."

Dietrich chuckled as he grasped her hand. "Grafi's right, but I have deep feelings for Maria. You know that."

"If God wants you and Maria together, then all the Nazis in Germany cannot stop you. Our Lord believes in marriage."

"Thank you for being such a faithful friend." Dietrich gently kissed the elderly lady upon the cheek. He made his way back out to the veranda when he saw Eva on a wooden bench near the pond. He descended the rear steps and quietly approached. Dietrich's image reflected clearly on the water's glass-like surface before her.

Eva looked up. "It's so peaceful here among the flowers."

Dietrich pondered his response as he sat beside her. "Our plans have changed."

"When will I see Ernst?"

"Tomorrow evening."

Eva sprang to her feet, then hugged Dietrich. "It has been so long—"

He held up his hands. "For everyone's safety, you must not know any more."

Lifting her head from his shoulder, her eyes glistened. "Tell me we have a chance—for Ernst and me to be together again."

"Eva, all things are possible with God and . . . Ernst is in love with you."

She leaned her head back down on Dietrich's shoulder. "Oh, if only I could believe."

*   *   *

At her bedroom window, utterly crushed, Maria looked down on Dietrich and Eva. She rushed down the back stairs and waited impatiently in the kitchen until Eva entered the house and made her way upstairs. Then Maria marched across the veranda and down to the pond. With one look, she unleashed her wrath.

Dietrich widened his brilliant blue eyes. "Maria, what's wrong?"

"Herr Bonhoeffer, I . . . I've misplaced my feelings for you. You obviously have someone else in your life."

Dietrich stepped closer. "What? What are you saying?"

"That Kleist woman! I saw you with her by the lake. You have *never* taken me for a romantic walk by the lake."

"Why, Maria von Wedemeyer, you are jealous. Soon Fräulein Kleist will marry a good friend of mine. They've asked me to conduct the ceremony."

"You mean, she has someone?" With a surge of relief, her anger evaporated.

"Yes. Maria, you are the woman in my life. You are the only woman in my heart." Dietrich lifted her hand to his lips. Maria buried her head against his barrel chest and wept.

Dietrich embraced her tenderly. "Now, now, don't cry. I will be leaving soon, but when I return, we will spend some serious time with each other."

"Leaving, when?"

"Very soon. I need you to be brave. Your family wants you safe. Sometimes it takes courage to wait. The Lord will give you strength."

"I will pray for you, Dietrich Bonhoeffer."

"When you pray to God, I will hear your prayers. And Christ will send my love to you wherever I am."

Looking over his shoulder at the glass-like water, Maria saw their two images merge into one. Feeling his warm breath, ecstatic tears bathed her brimming smile.

Chapter Thirty-Eight

Gestapo HQ, Stettin, Germany

The telephone rang in the office of the local Gestapo chief, Horst Schulgar. Still nursing a hangover from the night before, he slowly picked up the receiver. "Ja, Schulgar here. Berlin?" With a shock he sat straight up. "Jawohl, Herr Reichsführer!"

"Several weeks ago you worked with Major Neame on the surveillance of Eva Kleist, Friedrich Perels, and Dietrich Bonhoeffer."

"Yes, mein herr. I still have their photographs in our files."

"Gut," Himmler said. "I am sending the photograph of Major Ernst Teschler this morning by courier. Teschler's train is scheduled to arrive at Stettin late this afternoon. Follow him at a distance. Wait until Teschler and Kleist are found together, then arrest them both. They are wanted for questioning. They are not to be harmed under any circumstances."

"Sir, thereafter, what are my orders?"

"The SS will take over from there. I dispatched a special team on an earlier train. My men will arrive this afternoon. Whatever happens, keep Teschler under surveillance." Himmler abruptly hung up.

Horst blinked. He had just spoken with Heinrich Himmler. This would be a story to tell his grandchildren. When the courier arrived, Horst collected all of the photographs in his leather messenger bag. He gave thought to escape routes out of the area—by train, plane, or boat. He turned to his part-time secretary. "I'm heading down to Stettin Harbor."

*   *   *

Two hours later Horst was just about to leave the docks when he spotted Friedrich Perels at the pier. Like a hound catching the scent, he tracked him. At the harbor's main entrance, Perels flagged a taxi. Horst tailed him in his unmarked automobile to the Gruenwald Inn.

At three o'clock that afternoon, Perels entered the lobby of the inn, a quaint country establishment seven kilometers from the harbor. Horst walked into the lobby and found an empty chair, then kept an eye on his mark.

Perels stopped at the front desk and presented a sealed envelope to the clerk. "Please give this to Herr Karl Schmidt when he arrives this afternoon."

What was in the envelope? Who was Karl Schmidt? Horst wrote the details on his notepad.

"Yes, sir. Shall I give him your name?" the clerk said.

"I'm his cousin." Perels placed some Reichsmarks on the counter, then hurried out of the lobby.

Tension held Horst in its thorny grip. The trail had split. Follow Perels or the package? He snapped on his fedora, stepped up to the front desk clerk, and flashed his Gestapo credentials. "My name is Schulgar. The item you took from that man—let me see it."

The clerk hesitated for a moment but then surrendered the envelope. "Where is the kitchen?"

Perplexed, the clerk directed Horst toward a hallway. In the kitchen, he stood over a stove and proceeded to steam open the envelope to reveal three tickets to Copenhagen on the *SS Hansa* for tonight. Even the Reichsführer would be impressed by his detective work. He resealed the envelope with the tickets intact.

Horst returned to the front-desk clerk. "Give me your home address." The clerk turned pale. Very slowly he wrote it down.

Horst returned the resealed envelope. "Give this to Herr Schmidt when he arrives as planned. For your family's safety, my men will be watching your home. I trust you will not mention my presence here today."

"Whatever you say, Herr Schulgar!"

*   *   *

The City of Stettin

At 4:00 p.m., Maria's father dropped Dietrich off at Stettin's main square. While browsing through some local shops, he noticed a peculiar man. He forced himself to remain calm. The "fellow shopper" had glanced his way a little too frequently. Coincidence was a possibility, but Dietrich dare not take a chance.

He walked toward the taxi line. He hesitated until two of the three waiting taxis were occupied, then he abruptly hailed the last car. Hopping in, Dietrich directed the driver north. "I'm in a hurry, schnell!"

Looking back through the rear window, he could see the waylaid shopper frantically try to flag down another taxi. *How could I have been so stupid?* The Gestapo still had him on their watch list.

On schedule, Dietrich arrived at the Gruenwald Inn. Friedrich had chosen the property because it had several detached chalets—very private rooms secluded from the lobby. The forest backed up to the chalets, providing a handy escape route if needed.

Dietrich entered the lobby and rang the bell at the front desk. "Excuse me, my name is Herr Schmidt."

"Ah yes, your cousin left this for you, sir." The clerk presented the envelope.

Dietrich sauntered out the rear door leading to the gardens, then looked to see if he had been followed. Satisfied, he made his way over the path to the forested perimeter of the property. Eventually, he arrived at a quaint chalet. He took a deep breath and knocked at the door.

"Ja, who is it?" a soft feminine voice responded from within.

Dietrich knocked again. "Herr Schmidt."

The door opened, revealing Eva wearing a conservative dress, wire-framed glasses, with dyed-brown hair spun tightly into a bun. "Is everything alright?"

He shut the door and glanced around the room. "We will meet Ernst soon. We must be careful. The Gestapo is in town." Dietrich tore open the envelope and held up the ship tickets.

"I want to see Ernst." Eva had just started pacing when there was another soft knock at the door. Both Eva and Dietrich froze.

He slipped the tickets into his inside suit coat pocket, then opened the door. His muscles stiffened at the black SS uniform in front of him, then he relaxed. "Ah, Lieutenant Schumann, you are early."

"Hello, Dr. Bonhoeffer." Max presented Eva with a solitary red rose and a smile. "Ernst sends his love, my dear. Is everyone ready for this little masquerade?"

"You seem awfully confident. The Gestapo has been on my heels all day," Dietrich said.

"Ernst and I always enjoy a challenge, sir."

"Max, where's Ernst?" Eva's eyes demanded an answer.

"My car is just beyond the clearing. We'll wait until dark, then leave. Don't worry, you will see him very soon."

*   *   *

Stettin Train Station

Friedrich Perels ordered a beer in the station restaurant and took a seat by an open window across from the arrival gate. The only thing he could do was wait for Ernst Teschler and relay the change in plans. The soft summer breeze offered little solace for their wavering plans for Ernst and Eva's escape. The schedule and the logistics were too tight. Too many things could go wrong. He envisioned a cold, damp jail cell reserved for him at Gestapo headquarters. After a few sips,

Friedrich looked outside at a little man standing in a brown three-piece suit and fedora.

The gentleman paced slowly, glancing down the railroad track. He kept looking at his watch and growing more fidgety. The little man sat on a bench and retrieved what appeared to be photographs—pictures of a man in an SS uniform. Friedrich could not see the details, but his intuition told him Gestapo.

With the piercing cry of a train whistle, the five o'clock train pulled up to the gate. The little man eyed the disembarking passengers when a squad of eight stone-faced SS soldiers emerged. Five carried automatic weapons. The nervous little man stepped forward and flashed his credentials. "Captain, I'm Horst Schulgar, Gestapo. We were expecting Major Teschler on this train."

The captain's expression was all business. "The train must have been a ruse. Your telegram mentioned the Kleist woman?"

Schulgar removed a card from his pocket. "They have three tickets for the *SS Hansa* in Stettin Harbor. It sets sail for Copenhagen late tonight. The Reichsführer believes that Fräulein Kleist is in the vicinity. I have three cars waiting to take your men to the docks."

"Where's Teschler?"

"Eventually, he has to go to Stettin Harbor." The Nazi entourage departed heavily armed for Teschler and his woman.

Friedrich leaned back into the sunlight streaming through the window. Having heard every word, he panicked. The very boat tickets he delivered would send his friends to their deaths. He stood. *I have to stop Dietrich and Eva. They are walking into a trap!* He rushed to a telephone booth.

The hotel telephone rang and the front desk clerk answered. "Guten Tag, the Gruenwald Inn."

"Chalet 12, please hurry!" The telephone rang in the room ten times before Friedrich slammed the receiver on its hook. "This cannot be happening. What have I done?"

Chapter Thirty-Nine

Somewhere East of Stettin

The summer heat permeated the metal-sheathed warehouse as Ernst paced in the dispatcher's office. A foghorn sounded in the distance. "I understand this little town is attracting some attention these days."

Ernst pivoted, his hand gripping the Walther in his belt. "You're late, Schellenberg."

"I wouldn't miss this party for the world. Besides, word has it that eight of Himmler's men arrived at the Stettin train station a half hour ago. They should be on their way to the docks as we speak."

Ernst checked his watch. "We're cutting this very close."

"We will soon see if we hold the trump cards." Schellenberg turned back toward the door. "I'll check with my men. This may turn out to be quite a firefight before it's over."

Ernst picked up his Schmeisser submachine gun and slapped a long magazine into the housing. The shuddering sound of two large metal doors sliding open could be heard from the far end of the warehouse. In the flood-lights, Ernst strained his eyes, then he saw Eva. Max and Dietrich followed.

Ernst ran across the concrete floor, swept her off her feet, and gave her a passionate kiss on the lips. "Oh, darling, you made it."

Her silken lips caressed his. "Ernst, what took you so long? You should never keep a lady waiting."

He eased her down with a long breath. "I have been waiting for you all my life."

Max cleared his throat. "We really don't have time for this, people."

Dietrich shook Ernst's hand. "When do we leave?"

"Soon enough." Ernst's tone was all business. "Max, let's get their luggage onboard now."

*   *   *

Three Gestapo vehicles passed through the harbor's main gate and slowly approached the central pier. A dense fog draped across the three ships moored in the harbor as darkness descended. Parked behind one of the warehouses, Horst Schulgar showed a map of the Stettin docks to the SS captain. "The *SS Hansa* is at the far end of Pier 3."

The SS captain gauged the distance to the ship and gathered his men around the map. "If we take positions here at these three places, we should be able to contain them."

As the soldiers in black primed their weapons, Horst retreated. "I will stay back here with the automobiles and keep watch."

The SS captain scowled. "Herr Schulgar, you will stay with me. That's an order. All right, men. Team one takes the port side, team two, starboard. Search every cabin. Teschler is armed and dangerous. Himmler's orders— take them alive. If they cooperate, fine. But if they fight, shoot to kill!" With that, he dispatched his soldiers aboard the ship with weapons drawn.

Horst lit a cigarette and noticed the buildings to his left. For a moment, the fog clouded his vision, but at the entrance of the metal warehouse, the profile of an SS soldier came into view. He could not be sure, but the man looked like—

"Teschler? Captain, I think that's Teschler!"

The SS officer snapped back the firing bolt of his Schmeisser. "Come on, men, he's over there." The SS soldiers quietly released the safety locks on their weapons and circled their target. "Halt—in the name of the Third Reich!"

*   *   *

Across the bay some five kilometers away from the Stettin docks, Ernst emerged from the hangar onto the tarmac of a small military airfield. Through the fog, he could see Max secure the last of the luggage in the cargo hold of a Junker JU-52 aircraft. His gaze traced the scattered lights that dotted the fenced perimeter, looking for unusual movements.

Ernst led Eva by the arm out to the waiting aircraft. "We'll fly to Stockholm, change planes, then we should arrive in England sometime tomorrow morning."

She leaned into his shoulder. "You seem to have a guardian angel."

Ernst looked up at the stars appearing on the horizon. "Yes, indeed."

A mild breeze displaced Eva's dyed-brown bangs. "Darling, can we finally be together again, away from this nightmare?"

"I have to get you out of Germany—well beyond Himmler's reach. We can trust Pastor Bonhoeffer. He has friends in England. They will keep you safe." Their lips touched one last time. Tenderly, they embraced. Her brilliant blue eyes dazzled and her winsome smile ensnared Ernst as no other woman. "Sarah Kleisfeld, remember I love you for who you really are."

Eva wept as they embraced one more time, then Ernst led her up the stairway into the plane. "I'll join you in a few minutes."

From the bottom of the gangway, Ernst and Max crossed back over the tarmac. "Max, I'm leaving you in the middle of a hornet's nest."

"With Schellenberg and his men, I give the enemy a one out of three chance of survival." Max flashed his boyish grin.

Ernst opened his shirt collar, removed the chain from around his neck, and pressed the Swiss bank deposit-box key into Max's palm. "Himmler will not rest until he gets his hands on the Spear of Destiny. This relic may be the only bargaining chip we have for the rest of the war. So, guard this secret with your life. If anything happens to me, you have your instructions."

Max secured the necklace and key in a leather pouch and tucked it inside his black tunic. He glanced at his watch. "Himmler's men will soon discover they've been duped. I'll go check the crew for their fueling status."

When Ernst reached the edge of the tarmac, Colonel Schellenberg waited by the aging tin-plated hangar with two armed SS guards stationed nearby. At some distance from the plane, they walked side by side toward a row of automobiles.

"I knew you were a shrewd man, Teschler, but I'm surprised how ruthless you can be."

"Neame taught me well. Kill or be killed," Ernst said deadpan.

Schellenberg nodded. "Himmler's men will wait only a short while at the ship before they discover their mistake. Can you imagine the Reichsführer's reaction when he finds out that everyone escaped?"

"Sir, what if Himmler holds you accountable?"

"Multiple witnesses will testify that I was in Berlin all day. Major, the plane is at your disposal. I'll be returning to Berlin by car. Barring evidence to the contrary, I was never here."

Ernst stopped short and faced his superior. "You seem very confident, Schellenberg."

"I consider your recent transfer of funds to my Swiss account a mere down payment. And with the counterfeit British pound notes, I envision building a new railroad, a golden railroad. You and I shall build it together."

"I'll be in England for a matter of weeks. Then I shall return."

"Don't worry, Teschler. It's in our mutual financial interests for me to protect you and your friends. I will send you your new assignment after your honeymoon."

"Do I have a choice?"

"None!" A broad smile spread across Schellenberg's face. "Major, this could be the beginning of a very profitable friendship." With that, Colonel Schellenberg tipped his officer's hat and walked to his waiting car.

"Ernst!" Max called out from the tarmac. "The pilot says they're refueled and can take off in fifteen minutes."

"Be careful in Berlin, my friend. Remember, avoid the pretty barmaids. They are a danger to your health."

Max slapped Ernst affectionately on the back. "I'll see you at the Bismarck Tavern!" His silhouette faded into the dark mist.

Through the fog, Ernst looked at the plane's row of windows. Eva's beautiful face pressed on the glass pane. He could feel his heart ache for the woman his uncle said he could never have.

*   *   *

Inside the aircraft, Dietrich sat across the aisle from Eva. His brown leather briefcase lay open on the window seat next to him. The fear and tension had eased, but he still did not know if his Bible and the Abwehr list had arrived safely at his parents' home.

If Himmler doesn't execute me, Admiral Canaris should! With eyes open, Dietrich silently prayed for those brave souls on the list of Abwehr conspirators.

As the copilot secured the plane's entrance hatch, Ernst edged his way down the aisle and sat next to Eva across from Dietrich. Her gaze reflected the intensity of her love as she wrapped her fingers through his.

Ernst looked over at Dietrich with a gentle smile as the fueling crew detached their gear from the aircraft. "Herr Bonhoeffer, tell me—do you believe God still exists in Nazi Germany?"

Dietrich searched his young friend's hazel eyes for some hint of his meaning. "He certainly does—despite men like me who fall short, who fail to be faithful."

Ernst reached across the narrow aisle and placed his hand on Dietrich's arm. "Fail, did you say? You taught me God's Word every week for over ten years when I was a child. You touched me in God's name on the night of my father's murder. You cared about me faithfully even while I pursued evil in the name of the Third Reich. And now you risk your life to rescue the woman I love. How can you speak of failure?"

Dietrich sighed. "If you only knew what I have done."

"Oh, I know what you've done, Herr Bonhoeffer." Ernst nonchalantly removed a book from his satchel. "You read to me from this Bible." He fingered through the pages to the bookmark inserted near the end of the text. "For instance, I thought there were twelve disciples, not twenty-four." Ernst gave the bookmark to Dietrich.

It was his "prayer list" of Abwehr conspirators. Dietrich held up the bookmark to the light. His heart sank. "Then you have known all along?"

Ernst shook his head. "Only for a few days. Now, it is imperative that you take this list to England and make sure George Bell delivers the package to Sir Anthony Eden."

"Ernst, if the SS were ever to obtain this list . . ."

Just then the airplane's engines sputtered to life. "Pastor, this war will be over eventually. Of this I am certain—God will have the last word in Nazi Germany. Consider that which you hold in your hand as some measure of proof."

The thrust of the plane's propellers pressed the passengers back into their seats. Ernst put his arm around Eva as the plane lifted off the ground. Dietrich was looking out his window at the receding runway lights below when he felt a sudden urge to check the "list" one more time.

He flipped the bookmark over. As he scanned down the list of familiar names, he saw a change had been rendered to the page—quite professionally. A name had been added below "Dietrich Bonhoeffer."

The last name now read: "SS Major Ernst Teschler."

Tears overwhelmed Dietrich as he again gazed out the passenger window. Through the evening fog, he envisioned Ernst as a little boy standing alone at the church door. As the plane slowly banked into a turn, the image of the young lad lifted his arm and waved. He was like a little boy saying goodbye to his father.

Dietrich leaned back into his seat to face his future. Whatever else happened, he knew that he had not failed, but that God had ultimately succeeded.

As their plane lofted into the night sky over Stettin, the sound of Ernst's voice echoed in Dietrich's mind. *God still exists in Nazi Germany. And of this I am certain—God will have the last word!*

THE END

A Brief Bibliography

Historical Insights "behind the scenes" of *THE INFIDEL*

The Nazi Regime, the Reich Church, and German Resistance

Barnett, Victoria J. *For the Soul of the People: Protestant Protest Against Hitler*. New York: Oxford University Press, 1992.

Bergen, Doris L. *Twisted Cross: The German Christian Movement in the Third Reich*. Chapel Hill: University of North Carolina, 1996.

Bethge, Eberhard. *Dietrich Bonhoeffer: A Biography*, Revised and edited by Victoria J. Barnett. Minneapolis: Fortress Press, 2000.

Bonhoeffer, Dietrich. *The Cost of Discipleship*. New York: 1st Touchstone Edition (Simon & Schuster).

Hockenos, Matthew D. *Then They Came for Me: Martin Niemöller, the Pastor Who Defied the Nazis*. New York: Basic Books, 2018.

Stroud, Dean G. *Preaching in Hitler's Shadow: Sermons of Resistance in the Third Reich*. Grand Rapids: Wm B. Eerdmans Publishing Co., 2013.

Tietz, Christiane. *The Life & Thought of Dietrich Bonhoeffer*, Translated by Victoria J. Barnett. Minneapolis: Fortress Press, 2016.

Jewish Perspectives on the Holocaust

Berenbaum, Michael. *The World Must Know: The History of the Holocaust as Told in the United States Holocaust Memorial Museum—2nd Edition*. Baltimore: John Hopkins University Press, 2006.

Friedländer, Saul. *Nazi Germany & the Jews 1933–1945 (Abridged Edition)*. New York: Harper Perennial, 2009.

Hayes, Peter. *Why? Explaining the Holocaust*. New York. W.W. Norton & Company, 2017.

Levi, Primo. *Survival in Auschwitz*. New York: 1st Touchstone Edition (Simon & Schuster), 1996.

Rittner, Carol & John K. Roth, editors. *Different Voices: Women and the Holocaust*. New York: Paragon House, 1993.

Snyder, Timothy. *Black Earth: The Holocaust as History and Warning*. New York: Tim Duggan Books (Penguin Random House, LLC), 2015.

Wiesel, Elie. *Night*. (New Translation) New York: Hill & Wang, 2006.

The Holocaust: Himmler's SS Corps and German Military Intelligence

Burger, Adolf. *The Devil's Workshop: A Memoir of the Nazi Counterfeiting Operation*. London: Frontline Books, 2009.

Cook, Stephen & Stuart Russell. *Heinrich Himmler's Camelot: The Wewelsburg Ideological Center of the SS 1934–1945*. Andrews, NC: Kressmann-Backmeyer Publishing LLC, 1999.

Gerwarth, Robert. *Hitler's Hangman: The Life of Heydrich*. New Haven: Yale University Press, 2011.

Goodrick-Clarke, Nicholas. *Occult Roots of Nazism: Secret Aryan Cults and Their Influence on Nazi Ideology*. New York: New York University Press, 1993.

Kahn, David. *Hitler's Spies: German Military Intelligence in World War II*. New York: Hachette Books, 2000.

Manvell, Roger & Heinrich Fraenkel. *Heinrich Himmler: The SS, Gestapo, His Life and Career*. London: Greenhill Books, 2007.

Mueller, Michael. *Canaris: The Life and Death of Hitler's Spymaster*. London: Frontline Books, 2017.

Paehler, Katrin. *The Third Reich's Intelligence Services: The Career of Walter Schellenberg*. Cambridge UK: Cambridge University Press, 2017.

Shirer, William L. *The Nightmare Years 1930–1940*. New York: Rosetta Books, 2014.

Taber, George M. *Chasing Gold: How the Nazis Stole Europe's Bullion*. New York: Pegasus Books, 2014.